EVERYTHING WILL BURN

THE QUILL POINT CHRONICLES 2

EVERYTHING WILL BURN

4 Horsemen
Publications, Inc.

OCTOBER KANE

Published By: 4 Horsemen Publications, Inc.

4 Horsemen Publications, Inc.
PO Box 417
Sylva, NC 28779
4horsemenpublications.com
info@4horsemenpublications.com

Cover and Typesetting by Niki Tantillo
Edited by Laura Mita

Library of Congress Control Number: 2023941331

Paperback ISBN-13: 979-8-8232-0272-5
Hardcover ISBN-13: 979-8-8232-0273-2
Audiobook ISBN-13: 979-8-8232-0271-8
Ebook ISBN-13: 979-8-8232-0274-9

For everyone who's read the first book.
Thanks so much for being here.

Acknowledgments

This book was perhaps the most ambitious and complex piece of fiction I've ever written. The fact it's a book that you'll be reading, that you're holding in one form or another right now, is even more amazing than the first time. And I need to thank everyone who made it possible. My friends, family, and everyone who's been supportive since I embarked on this author journey. Seriously, thank you *so* much. I don't know how I'll ever express how grateful I am.

TABLE OF CONTENTS

PART 3   KNOWING TOO MUCH

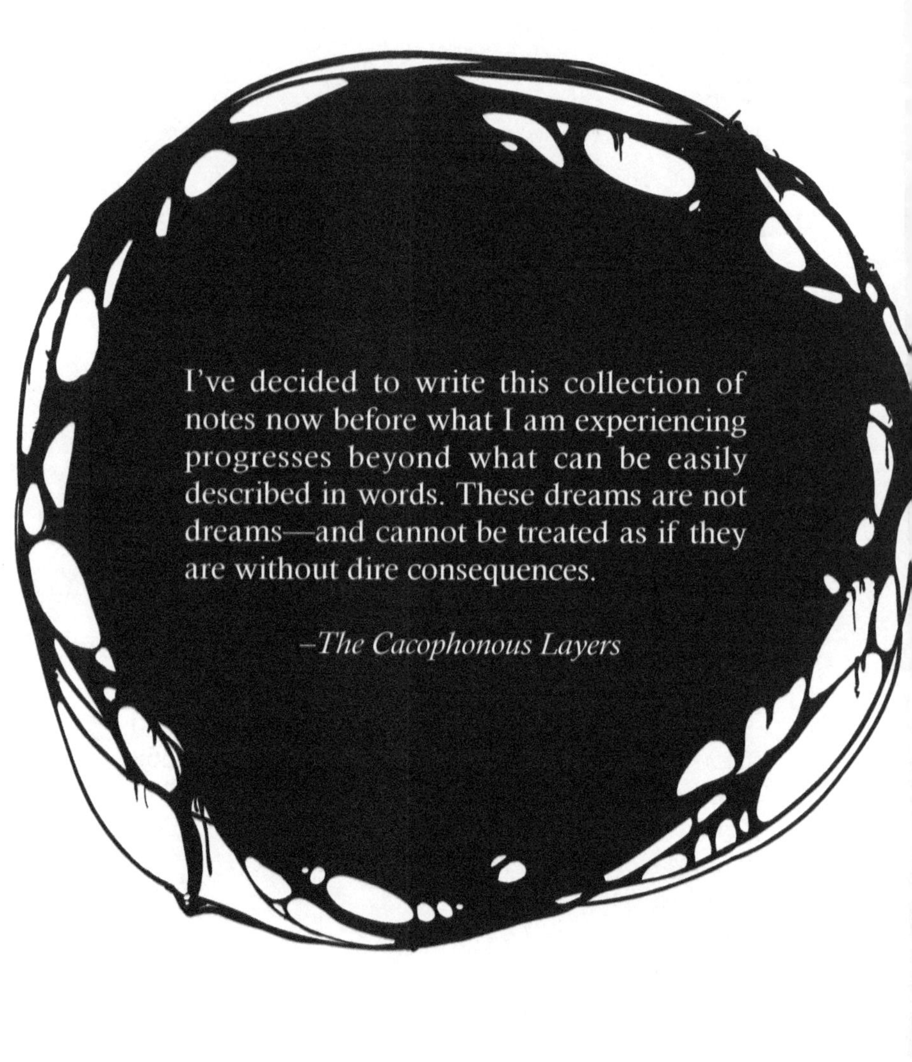
I've decided to write this collection of notes now before what I am experiencing progresses beyond what can be easily described in words. These dreams are not dreams—and cannot be treated as if they are without dire consequences.

–The Cacophonous Layers

Part 1

NowheretoGo

Chapter 1

ECLAN KNEW HIS ENTIRE WORLD would fall apart. He just thought it would happen a little slower. That it would happen alongside everyone else. The storms would come, the coasts would flood, and the heat would become unbearable. A global tragedy as climate change ended the world.

It never occurred to Declan he could lose it all long before that happened.

The field of ash was darker than even the surrounding night. The piles of burned wood, plaster, and linoleum were a vast sea. He dropped to his knees but didn't dare touch. There was no way to know which parts consisted of charred human flesh and which were the hospital's constituent parts.

Declan pursed his lips against tears, but there was no reason to hold them back. He put down what he was carrying, sat in the dirt, and tucked his knees to his chest. The pain needed no prompting. The pain was always there. It rushed to the forefront the second he let it.

Sobs buffet him, one horrible salvo at a time. Going on until he felt numb. It was the only routine that worked anymore. Let the sadness hit, let it pass, and expect it again. Whoever said time heals all wounds has never lost someone.

Declan wiped his nose with his hand. He looked at the back of his hand then wiped blood and snot on his olive-colored hemp pants and adjusted his lime green beanie.

"Okay," he said. "I guess I…"

He turned to the small plastic terrarium sitting beside him in the dirt. Inside it, a corn snake peeked out its head from a pile of wood chips. His head was mostly orange with a few red spots that reminded Declan of tiger stripes. His forked tongue darted out for a moment.

Declan wanted to smile at him, but he couldn't muster the expression. Despite knowing Susurrus for the snake's entire life, he'd never gotten a connection with him. Never felt the same adoration that people have for a dog or a cat. To him, Susurrus was like a houseplant that needed more than water and sunlight.

But his father had been *beaming* when Declan got him for his fifth birthday. Had seemed so certain that he would love reptiles, snakes, and spiders like his dad, and Declan had faked it long enough that his dad seemed pleased with his great gift.

It was only fitting that Susurrus was the last thing to go.

"I think you might do better than us," Declan said, taking the terrarium to his chest. "Whatever this is…"

He looked at the night sky. Only on the first day had it taken people, but there wasn't a single person in Quill Point who wasn't always eyeing it. Always expecting another Murder Sky.

"Whatever this is … I don't think it attacks animals. Maybe it's trying to save you guys. Make a planet that'll be better than the one we've made."

Declan popped off the top and gently shifted the contents over a patch of grass. Susurrus dropped with the rest of his home. Susurrus's head rose, and his tongue darted out again.

Declan frowned, watching. Susurrus had never been in the outside world before. His dad had hatched him for Declan. He'd only ever known what he'd given him.

After a second, Declan gently nudged Susurrus's head with his finger. The snake moved then, slithering into a patch of taller plants. The tip of his tail darted away. He was probably looking for food—Declan hadn't been able to feed Susurrus much lately.

After a moment, Declan let another sob wrack his chest.

"I'm sorry," Declan said to the air. "I hope you do okay."

His shoulders dropped, and he clutched at his forehead so hard it left little white crescents from his nails. Declan wasn't even sure he'd be able to catch a mouse or a rat. He wasn't sure his pet would find water in time.

But he didn't move.

Didn't go find him.

Didn't *let* himself move.

The task was done.

After twenty minutes of sitting in numbness, Declan stood up and brushed himself off. He wiped his nose again with the back of his hand, leaving a thin streak of red across his tanned white skin. He grimaced slightly.

His stomach growled, the background radiation of hunger leaking into his perceptions. Time, it seemed, for the next stop.

A few blocks away, a sign sputtered against the night. A sign older than him. Most of the letters didn't work anymore. The letter *I* looked like it wouldn't last more than a week—but that had been the case for as far back as Declan could recall. The only thing on it that still shined properly, still fought the night with enthusiasm, was the feather part of the logo. It dipped itself into a gray, sputtering approximation of an inkwell.

Declan's stomach rumbled again, harder. Lightheadedness danced in him. He sighed hard. This part of the plan felt the most difficult—and *could* have been avoided. His backpack *was* full of soy crackers, peanut butter, and all the vegan protein bars he'd stashed before Quill Point started hard-enforcing rations. He could last days on it if he paced himself.

There wasn't a reason to go, not really.

But he still wanted what might be a last meal.

Chapter 2

The Ink Well Diner was perhaps the most successful, non-government building in Quill Point. Despite the sign, despite it passing through a few owners, despite everything. It had hosted *so* many birthday parties that balloons were often left in the back corner, ready to go. The Ink Well Diner had been the site of uncountable holiday celebrations, meetups, and awkward first dates. Every age bracket. Every occupation. Rich. Poor.

Everyone had eaten at the Ink Well Diner at some point. And Declan walked toward it slowly, his feet dragging.

Off to one side, the looming forest sat like a black curtain waiting to part. On the other, empty buildings and dead cars. The corpse of vehicles dotted all of Quill Point. They were stuck where they'd been before Murder Sky. It had somehow rendered all cell phones unable to get a signal and all motor vehicles inert metal blocks. Declan had never even learned to drive, unhappy with what cars did to the environment, but seeing them there bothered him. It made him regret never at least taking one for a cruise, even if just once.

He walked around the sleeping giant of a massive truck and traced his finger along a smaller car's hood. As he approached Ink Well, a faint light came from the windows.

The outside looked old. White paint on the walls was just maintained well enough to not earn any ire from anyone. Now, though, several pieces of graffiti dotted it. One read, in big letters, *Property of the Mayor's Men.* Declan rolled his eyes.

The door had the remains of some logo or another, and the paper was water damaged. He vaguely recalled one owner attempting to get some mascot going for the place.

The door wasn't locked when he pushed his way in. A speaker weakly pretended that he'd moved a bell. The tinny sound was too quiet to be useful and too sharp to be pleasant and lacked any proper echo.

Declan almost walked back out. He'd often eaten at the Ink Well Diner but didn't *like* the restaurant. It always smelled like grease, burned coffee, and aggressive amounts of sugar. Those smells were already hitting him as he stood in the mini foyer among the décor. The foyer was filled with gumball machines and rigged skill cranes awaiting quarters. A large poster board had advertisements for basically every local business.

He tried *not* to glance at the one for his dad's reptile shop. That would not help. But the snake Declan had drawn in crayon when he was ten—a green and yellow squiggle with large eyes—peaked out from beneath an advertisement for a catering service.

A sharp intake of breath—the tears would come if invited.

Always, always, always.

Declan closed his eyes and entered the restaurant through the archway entrance.

He could hear the faint and far-off tune of some pop song. It was a female signer talking about love. And, hitting every beat, was someone else humming. Declan knew who would be here at the diner this late, but it still got the faintest smile—before smiling made him feel guilty.

Declan got his face neutral and pushed his emotions back. His next mission was to find Grace.

But despite her humming, it wasn't the easiest task.

The Ink Well Diner had several layers to its seating. It was almost a miniature labyrinth, built mostly of cheap plastic. Stairs with only three steps lead to elevated areas with cramped round tables, then descended around high-tops, then hitched right back up to a section of booths. It made somewhat of an island, a horseshoe, and a hallway around the building's perimeter. The upper layer's walls were high. Between all of that and the random load-bearing pillars, there was no feasible way to see every spot in the diner at the same time.

Declan got lucky. Her head bopped up for a moment. A flash of black hair in a pixie cut. She was in the middle island section.

He could wind the snaky path or cross a section with a wet floor sign to get there. The mop and bucket were still there.

Declan waited a few moments to see if she'd notice him organically. Maybe stand up and glance in his direction. He didn't want to startle her. Especially not this late at night. Not in Quill Point.

But Grace kept humming and doing her thing.

Eventually, Declan walked over to the cash register and gently tapped the bell. It didn't quite make the right sound. So, he slammed his hand down again.

"Holy shit!" Grace yelled.

Grace popped up from behind the tall plastic wall. "Who is it?"

"Hi…" Declan said. "It's, uh, it's just me."

"God, Dec! You almost gave me a heart attack."

"Sorry—I didn't want to trip."

Declan halfheartedly gestured at the wet floor sign and grimaced.

Grace shook her head slowly, but then chuckled. The sound made Declan relax a little.

Grace took a roundabout path to the front of the restaurant, going all the way to the back, then, finally, descending steps to the lower floor. She kept humming the whole way. As she got closer, she took out her cell phone, stopped the song she'd been playing, and then shoved the phone into her jean pocket.

Declan watched her silently the whole time. He didn't have the energy to say anything to her.

That was fine; Grace filled the silence anyway.

"You really scared the living daylights out of me. I thought I was going to be alone all night."

"Sorry," Declan repeated.

Grace took a sharp turn through a door, then emerged behind the register seconds later.

Grace was taller than Declan by a few inches, being almost six feet. She had a pinkish complexion, black hair, and brown eyes with deep bags underneath them—though those were *almost* hidden by expertly applied makeup. She was still wearing her Ink Well Diner uniform: a light gray shirt with a slightly darker gray quill and inkpot logo. It was a running joke of a uniform, always needing replacing because of food stains.

Grace put on her best customer service smile. "It's all good, Dec. What can I do for you today? Can I get a pie started for you?"

"Do you even have stuff for a pie?"

"I have bread and tinned apples—I can surely manage something. Put enough sugar on it, and we can call it a pie."

Despite himself, that got a small laugh out of Declan. And then he felt guilty again.

"Uh, no pie, but I need some food." As if on cue, Declan's stomach rumbled again. "Really soon, I think."

"I know that sound. Sure, let's see what we can do. I've got a lot of time on my hands to help you."

"Did that rhyme?"

"Did not mean to," Grace responded.

"Well, okay," Declan said.

Grace chuckled a little more, putting her face back into a smile. But, for a second, she glanced at the foyer. A flash of something in her eyes.

Declan quickly followed her gaze. She'd looked out the windows.

At the shadowy—but empty—parking lot.

Declan said nothing about it.

"The food around the bonfire isn't good lately?" Grace asked brightly.

"The Mayor's Men only gave me hotdogs and fucking pork gravy and biscuits. At least one of them has laughed about it."

"Oof. I see why you came here. Is any of that even remotely vegan?"

"No," Declan said bitterly.

"Well, then." She stepped out from behind the register and gestured to the door to the kitchen. "Come on in, and food you can eat shall await you."

"Even the biscuits aren't vegan," Declan mumbled, walking toward the kitchen.

Grace apparently could still hear him. "They're doing what they can, I'm sure. But I know what we've got in this town—they could've accommodated your dietary stuff. Maybe they're just busy with other stuff. There is a lot to do."

"Yeah … there is…" Declan said.

"Yeah…"

They both stopped walking for a moment.

It was amazing what went unsaid nowadays. Around the bonfire, among people. Quill Point was on its *third* mass funeral. The Prayer Spire. The Kraken Hotel.

Irena Ink Memorial Hospital.

The food was running out. The water was limited, and people rarely got a chance to take showers. Tampons, deodorant, toothpaste—all of it was used sparingly. But mentioning any of that stuff usually hurt the speaker *and* the listener. So, it passed like a ghost haunting every quiet moment.

"Thank you for this," Declan said, breaking the silence as his thoughts moved to a specific ghost. "I know it's against the rules and all."

"Yeah. Of course. Can't turn a customer … away." She turned around to look at him, her lips pursed. "I haven't seen you in a bit. I really missed the visits."

"I didn't want to see anyone," Declan said. "It was too hard to be around anyone else."

Grace nodded. And the silence reclaimed.

For Declan, it felt like the huge emptiness of the restaurant invaded then. The air conditioning echoed.

"Okay," Grace said. "Would you like to talk about it?"

"I'd rather we didn't right now," Declan said. It sounded more forceful than he intended.

But Grace only smiled again. After one final moment of silence, she walked through the kitchen doors and held them open for Declan.

The coffee and grease smell worsened, rolling alongside a mixture of cleaning supplies and myriad food residue. Every item on the menu was burned a little into this space. Never truly leaving. Soaking into every linoleum tile and red and blue plastic cup.

Declan glanced at a large stack of bags on the counter as he walked into the narrow room. They were probably for the people at the bonfire. Every few days, they dropped off a selection of food supplies for the people who couldn't make the trek to the diner.

Inside that bag, if it was anything like the others, was stuff like canned beans, canned corn, canned meat. There'd be broth in their paper cartons, dried fruits, and beef jerky. Almost everything fresh in Quill Point had long since spoiled, been eaten, or gone into the hidden and probably doomed farming efforts.

Grace opened up the storage closet and stepped inside. "Uh … vegan, vegan, vegan. What's vegan… Oh! I'm seeing some potatoes that could honestly use cooking. Any longer in there, they'll grow legs."

"That'll work," Declan said. "I like potatoes…"

But he wasn't paying attention anymore.

Because as he stood idly, he noticed the thing in the room that didn't belong in a diner's kitchen. He'd noticed the air mattress stuffed in the corner. Lying on it was a shirt, a pair of pajama bottoms, a cell phone charger, and a small pile of makeup, shampoo, conditioner, and skin cream.

Grace returned from storage with a bag of partially sprouted potatoes, then stopped in her tracks. Looking at where Declan was looking with furtive glances. Her mouth made a tight line.

"Just been getting some extra work done," she said stiffly.

"That so?"

An oily feeling was spreading through Declan's chest. A sinking sensation.

"Yeah, they ran out of my sleeping pills a long time ago. It's not like I can sleep much anymore, so I figured I could get more done for the town."

Declan debated how he wanted to respond. Debated if he wanted to push on that line of logic. Grace hadn't pushed him too hard to talk about his thoughts—about what had happened recently.

Maybe it was only fair he did the same for her.

He took two quick, deep breaths, then nodded at the potato bag. "Could you make the potatoes into fried slices?"

It was subtle, but Grace's shoulders relaxed. She nodded a little too quickly, then got out a handheld potato peeler from a drawer. The clatter was far, far too loud.

"Sure. That's going to take a minute, though."

"That's fine," Declan said. "Mind if I put my backpack on your bed?"

Grace's voice went a little distant. "Yeah ... that's no problem."

Declan walked over, placed his backpack by the pile of makeup, and then hovered nearby, unsure of what he wanted to say. Any causal talk was a minefield in Quill Point.

Turns out, Grace was in somewhat agreement with that. She stopped talking. Heated the grill. Skinned the potatoes with a practiced hand.

Each thud of the knife cutting through the potato sounded too loud in that space.

And there's only so long an uncomfortable silence can hold, really.

"So…" Grace began. "I take it you've not been sleeping much, either. Not many people come here this late."

"I've been sleeping during the day, mostly," Declan said.

"Why is that?"

"Just not been enjoying being around people. It's an easy way to avoid them."

"I guess it would be, yeah," Grace said.

Grace put some vegetable oil onto the stovetop and then the potato slices. They sizzled with fury; an almost startling hiss rose from them. All other smells were blasted away for a second. After cracking pepper and sprinkling salt, she took out a spatula and started gently flipping them over and over. A little too often than needed, really. She was staring down at them. Looking at nothing else. Her hand tightened just slightly around the spatula.

And the potatoes kept sizzling away, steaming and—

The words rushed out of Grace's mouth.

"*Okay*, I think we should just talk about it. I think we need to talk about it *now*. Is that okay with you? Please?"

Her mouth was in a thin line.

Declan nodded slowly. "Okay, fine, I'll start. Why is your bed in here, really? I thought you were sharing that place with a friend?"

Grace grimaced and sighed. "The Mayor's been seizing properties. Even the ones that didn't get destroyed. I even don't know anyone who's living in houses anymore—except some of the Mayor's Men. But there's not even enough of them for *all* the houses. He said something about needing the rest for something special. Who needs them besides *us*? I don't know. It was in that thick political speak he does, so I'm not sure what he's doing with them."

Declan nodded again. "Uh huh?"

"And … well, someone's got to feed everyone. It's easier to move the bulk of the rations through this place. We have the refrigeration; we have the right kind of storage. I've been helping handle it. I volunteered."

"You mean he ordered you to?"

"Yeah … he ordered me to." Grace's shoulders dipped. "Look, it's the apocalypse, and people are hungry. I really don't mind helping."

"That doesn't quite explain the bed."

Grace looked away for a second. And Declan knew whatever she said next would be a lie.

"It's easier if I sleep here. I can have the coffee ready for everyone who comes over here in the morning."

Declan pursed his lips. "Is someone at least helping you?"

"We're a little short-staffed," Grace said, her voice cracking. "I'm sure Caleb would have helped…"

Declan winced. Sometimes he forgot that other people had lost someone when the hospital burned. It wasn't the same, of course. A coworker compared to a father. But loss *is* loss. People died. God, so many people had died. That hospital had been so full of people…

"Hey, uh, Declan…?"

Declan snapped out of his thoughts and looked at her. Grace looked close to tears. She swallowed and spoke like it was hard to get the words out.

"Please tell me you're not doing… please tell me you're not thinking what I think you are. Please tell me that backpack is just to carry extra food."

The potatoes started to burn, adding a smokey smell to the room. Grace turned off the stove without looking. Even the sizzling sound was fading now, leaving the room to be slowly eaten by silence.

Declan considered lying.

Considered trying to spare her feelings.

Convince her somehow that she hadn't put the pieces together.

But would that be the kindest option?

Back before everything, when things were okay enough, she was the *best* part of the diner. The salad might've sucked, and the soda was always flat, but Grace had some joke when she delivered it. "The leaves are just tired—they need dressing to perk them up," she might say. When Declan went through his last breakup, Grace said she had some "extra" sorbet in the back she could bring him. Sorbet wasn't usually on the menu; it was for birthdays only.

He wanted to keep a person like that happy. There was so much unhappiness already. But he couldn't lie to Grace's face.

Not now, not when there was a chance, a small chance, but a *chance* that she was the last human he'd ever talk to. The shape of the lie couldn't even form in his mouth.

"I'm going. There's nothing for me here."

Grace's entire body tensed. "You can't, Declan! Please! I know it's been really hard. I know that with what happened to your father…"

Declan couldn't remember a time recently when he *wasn't* already thinking about his father, yet the mention of him felt like a slap.

"I *have* to get away from this town," Declan said. "I have to escape it. It's got to be better in that forest than it is here. There's got to be a chance we can get out of this town."

Grace was silent.

The smell of burned potatoes filled the room even more. Declan wasn't so hungry now.

When Grace finally spoke, her voice was tight. "I don't think he would want you to do that."

Declan's face burned. He knew that too. Knew that his father would insist they stayed in Quill Point to help all they could. That it was their community. But Grace didn't *understand*. All she knew was that he was in the hospital when it burned, like all those doomed patients. She hadn't been close by. No one knew what caused the fire, but it had burned so fast and so hot. Hadn't seen Declan's father as the building burned, looking out the window with a blank expression. Not reacting to his son screaming out for him, unable to get close as the flames climbed higher and higher.

To be in the same place, the same town where that happened, was *poisoning* Declan's *soul*. The sky had killed people. Snatched them up with shadow claws as it screamed its death toll. Everyone in that old hotel had been *pulped*. Monsters were real in this town. Every horror story was plausible in Quill Point now, and he didn't want to be anywhere near it.

"I don't think I care" was how Declan communicated that.

Grace quickly looked away from him. Her shoulders rose. She said nothing. Didn't need to. She moved robotically, placing the potatoes on a clean plate, and walked with it out of the kitchen. Declan scooped up his backpack and took one more look at the bed.

"I'm *leaving* Quill Point," he said to himself.

And then he followed her out. She'd sat down at one of the nearby elevated booths, staring over the faint smoke of his potatoes.

Declan debated leaving. Maybe that would be better—but he was getting lightheaded with hunger. And wasting food, even simple, burnt potatoes, felt wrong.

So he sat down.

Grace looked right at him, her eyes pleading.

Declan wondered what it said about him that he still wanted to go.

CHAPTER 3

DECLAN SCOOPED THE CHARRED POTATO slices into his mouth and chewed. It wasn't eating so much as mechanically taking in calories. The salt dried his tongue, and the pulpy starch mash slid into a yawning stomach with an almost thud.

Grace moved her mouth in gentle twitches, clearly thinking about what she wanted to say.

Declan expected her to chastise him. Get angry with him. Yell maybe. Instead, her eyes simply had a deepening sadness. It made him wish he'd just lied to her.

"I really don't want you to go," Grace said simply. "If you go into the forest, I'm going to be all alone."

Declan didn't expect the stab that went into his heart. How had she found the one way to evoke emotion out of all the things he'd expected to hear? He'd only seen her once or twice a week since the apocalypse started, usually to get rations from the diner with groups of people. They barely knew each other beyond customer and server. They'd never hung out in any other context—never went to school together. As far as he knew, she'd never been to the pet store.

But it still hurt.

The restaurant felt somehow even *more* empty. Like the space was widening out. Becoming a huge, sprawling warehouse. And just them still inside. Just her soon.

"I'm sorry," Declan said.

He meant it, but it changed nothing.

"Do you think anyone actually got out?" Grace asked. "Like, they're in the next town over or something?"

That was the big question. People went into the forest all the time. Families fled as groups. A camping club made a pilgrimage, prepared in every way possible.

And no one ever came out of that forest again.

"Maybe it's a quarantine situation," Declan said, not believing his words. "Maybe no one is allowed to go back in. Maybe the government is just outside the forest, trying to find a way to help us."

Grace nodded, and her mouth relaxed a little. Declan hoped that meant she was on board with what he was doing. Or at least wouldn't stop him once he finished eating.

But her next words had the crack of someone fighting off tears.

"*Please* don't."

"I really can't stay here anymore. I mean it."

Grace's jaw tightened. She glanced at the clock, the parking lot, and then back at him. Tears ran down her face.

"Can you at least stay for a little longer?"

Declan stopped chewing. That didn't sound like worry. Or anger. Or sadness. That sounded like *pleading*. Desperation. Fear. Was she trying to use guilt to stop him?

No. Not unless Grace was a better liar than he knew.

Declan stopped chewing. Stopped even breathing. His mind was trying to catch onto something he'd missed. Some other aspect of what was going on that he hadn't seen.

"Grace, what are you expecting to be here?"

Grace's eyes went wide, and she looked away.

The lack of an answer was the loudest answer.

"Grace, what the hell is happening? You're stuck cooking here; you look exhausted and…"

His stomach dropped. The lump of carbs in his stomach felt like a solid brick, tugging down at him, making him nauseous.

"…why are you really awake?"

Grace tightened her hands into fists slowly, digging her nails into her palm. "I didn't want to worry you. You seemed like you had enough going on, and you can't help—"

"What the fuck is going on?" Declan said again, amazed at how angry his voice had become in such little time.

"People are getting desperate," Grace said. "Or greedy."

"Did you fight someone?

"Not much of a fight when you kick them in the balls."

Now that Declan was noticing things, he kept noticing. Grace wasn't tired; she was ragged. There was a bruise on her knuckles. The skin there looked like it had split.

"Who?" Declan asked quietly.

Grace looked at the clock again and let out a nervous chuckle. "The Mayor's Men like to take the little alcohol we still have. The Mayor said it was okay, but then they tried to take all our bread. *All* of it."

Declan's jaw tightened. He'd been lucky not to get harassed by the Mayor's Men *much*, but he'd seen them pick on plenty of people. They'd kick people's tents over. Cut people's rations randomly. They were another reason he wanted to leave this hell-bound town.

"I can stay for a little longer," he found himself saying, relief attached to the words, even if he didn't want to acknowledge them.

"Thanks."

"But I'm still leaving, Grace," he forced himself to say. "Tonight, before sunup, I'm leaving for the forest. I'm leaving Quill Point. I'm sorry, but I have to. I really need to get out of here."

She didn't say anything about that. Just looked at the clock again.

Declan picked up the ketchup, hoped it didn't have honey in it, and squirted it on the worst of the burned potatoes. Eating them was giving him a headache.

But he ate them slowly, looking across at her. A nearly silent half hour passed of more unspoken words hanging in the air. Declan started committing her face to memory.

He ran his fork along the ketchup residue, uncomfortable with how much it looked like blood. Declan stopped when a sound drifted closer. Something not of the usual Quill Point night. Gradually arriving. Gently flowing, then louder.

Grace tensed up before Declan could even discern the noise was mostly yelling.

A shiver went down Declan's spine.

The Mayor's Men.

They sounded angry.

CHAPTER 4

GLASS SHATTERED NEARBY. GRACE AND Declan both looked for which window it had been, where the damage was.

But it was too small a sound.

Too tiny and sharp and specific.

Someone had thrown a bottle.

Another crash came near the door. Then the twinkling wind chimes of glass shards falling across the ground. The angry yells turned into jeering, joyous shouts.

Grace's eyes went wide. "Oh fuck. Usually, there are only three."

Before Declan could say anything, a new faint sound drifted over to them. Declan's pulse spiked, and he could feel his muscles freezing up on him. It was the chime of someone having opened the door. And next, they would step right through the archway—

Grace and Declan turned to see three guys step into the store, two flanking the third in the middle.

Declan recognized the guy at the front.

Brook Chambers. He was tall and handsome, with broad shoulders, bright blond hair, defined muscles, and a golden tan on his white skin. He'd gotten a tattoo since Declan last saw him: a line of fire down the length of his left arm. He was wearing a blue dress shirt and gray slacks.

Grace darted out of her chair and stood in front of Declan. She balled both her hands into fists. The voice that erupted out of her didn't sound like anything he'd ever heard from her before.

"You get out of this place. *Right. The fuck. Now.*"

Brook smiled, taking another step closer. "Whatever happened to the customer always being right? We just came by to get some food. We don't get to take food whenever we want."

His eyes locked on Declan, and he smiled.

"Not like some people, it seems."

Declan looked around for an escape option. There was a door through the kitchen and a fire exit by the bathrooms.

"I said leave." Grace stood even taller. "Get the fuck out of this restaurant. Now."

Brook didn't react at all to her words. He took leisurely, almost theatrical, steps forward. His two friends fanned out, one inching toward the kitchen.

Declan immediately felt cornered.

"I heard you cut one of my men," Brook said. "You attacked someone with a knife, Grace. What the hell were you thinking?"

"I didn't fucking use a knife. I found Arthur trying to smuggle all the bread out of storage," Grace replied. "That food is for everyone. There are kids in this town, asshole."

Brook's smile dropped for a second, and his jaw twitched. He took a deep breath and then smiled again. "That's your excuse?"

"My *excuse*?"

Declan inched toward the edge of the raised platform. He wasn't sure how to help Grace, but if he dropped, he could run around a cluster of dining tables and be right at the kitchen door. Maybe faster than they could catch him. Maybe it would be a good enough distraction to give Grace time to do something.

Brook chuckled. "The Mayor put *you* here. And we are the Mayor's Men. Do you understand that? He put you *here*, Grace, so someone was always watching the food. So, someone was ready to serve the food, yeah? That's a *big* thing. Respectable. But you work for him— we're coworkers, don't you think? If we ask for food, you should give it to us. We shouldn't just get booze; we're working, hungry people. You get that, right? What I'm saying, right? You're here to help us."

"I'm here to help the town," Grace said simply. "And I said to get the fuck out. *Understand* that? *Get* that?"

Brook gave a dramatic sigh and chuckled again. "So are we, Grace. So are we."

Brook was wearing a chain around his neck, and he pulled it up to reveal a silver, polished whistle. He blew into it hard. It was a long, clear note. Probably audible for miles.

But the rest of the Mayor's Men were just outside. And several let out whoops in response. A symphony of bottles exploding sounded off.

Brook shrugged his shoulders. "You're making me do this, Grace. We can't have someone cutting up the people trying to help the town. I was going to let you off the hook, Grace. I like you. I like what you've been doing for the community. But, eh. That's the way it is, I guess. The Mayor made it very clear. If someone was making trouble, we brought them to him."

His gaze fell on Declan, and his face broke into an ugly grin.

"And you are even worse. Stealing food."

"Fuck you," Grace spat.

Declan kept eyeing the closer of the two other Mayor's Men. He'd stopped to hear his boss talk, but that wouldn't last. If Declan didn't move soon, didn't go for it, he would have no time. He glanced at Grace and then at her hand. If he grabbed it and pulled her along, would she react fast enough for it to matter?

Because he didn't want to know what would happen if the mob now streaming in caught them. There were at least five other Mayor's Men. All were wearing button-ups, polo shirts, or suits. They looked like they were here for an office meeting, except for that look in their eyes.

One of them stalked forward, stopping abreast of Brook. Besides blue eyes and auburn hair, he looked like a carbon copy.

Arthur was here.

"She looks like she's not going to listen," Arthur said. He licked his lips in a way that made Declan deeply uncomfortable. "I don't think we can talk this out with her."

Grace tensed. Declan grabbed her hand but didn't pull her yet. Grace glanced back at him, and the fear in her eyes made his heart skip a beat.

Arthur continued, his voice getting louder. "I say we need to ensure she doesn't try anything!"

Arthur reached behind him and pulled a gun from his waistband. A shiny black thing that looked almost too large in his hand. He held it up like a toy, waving it with a loose wrist.

Brook glanced at it and took a slight step back.

"We really should get you a holster there, Arthur."

Arthur just shrugged.

"Well, you heard my second!" Brook said. "Grace, we're taking you to The Mayor, and I strongly suggest you don't do anything we don't like. Same to you, Declan."

For a moment, no one moved. Grace's pulse was racing through her palm, down Declan's arm. His own heartbeat was surging in his ears. Crashing at his mind and making it hard to think. All he could focus on was the gun—the small but lethal barrel that kept sweeping over him.

"Grace…" he whispered.

Grace squeezed his hand twice and then picked up the plate off the table and flung it in a straight line. It cracked Arthur in the head, sending him stumbling back. His hand dropped, pointing the gun at the floor for a moment.

Only for a moment.

Swears and insults rang out in a chorus as Mayor's Men surged forward.

"Run!" Declan shouted.

He tugged Grace's hand, and she was immediately running with him. They reached the edge closest to the kitchen door and went over without pausing. It was less than a two-foot drop, but Declan's stomach still lurched—and his knees and feet hurt from the impact. It was jarring enough that he almost collapsed into a heap, but kept his footing.

The loudest sound Declan had ever heard went off behind them. It pin-pricked his ears and bounced off every wall. He involuntarily clutched at his ears. Plastic shrapnel surged over his head.

Adrenaline spiked in Declan, flowing liquid fire into his limbs. A voice in his mind, insistent and frantic, started and then kept screaming, "*Move, move, move!*"

He listened. Grace apparently had a similar internal command because she easily pulled ahead of him, her long legs pumping fast.

Declan's gaze locked onto the kitchen door. He didn't know how close any of the Mayor's Men were; they could be directly behind him. He had no way of knowing if the gun was aimed at him.

If he died as he ran, he had no say in it. So, he ran.

A partially muffled yell broke his concentration; his ears were still ringing from that gunshot. He looked over at Grace. Most of the Mayor's Men were still navigating their way over through the chaotic diner layout. But one of the Mayor's Men had caught up before they could go out the door. He was a medium-height guy with pale white skin, bright blue eyes, and brown hair. He looked pissed, and his fists were up.

Grace was clutching her shoulder.

But her other hand was swinging through the air in a wide arc. Declan had never seen anyone punch someone in real life, but Grace seemed to know what she was doing.

The sound was meatier than Declan expected. Grace's hand caught the Mayor's Man on the chin, and his head jolted in that direction.

The guy she punched didn't go down like in the movies. He stumbled, clutching at the spot, spit dribbling down his chin. His eyes flared into something hateful, aimed, and barbed. He reached out for Grace.

Only for her to punch him again.

Grace put her whole body into that punch.

The thud of that hit seemed more *significant* somehow. Grace pulled her hand back afterward, wincing.

The person she'd hit, though, looked stunned, almost shocked. He kept blinking, his hand going up to his eye. Thick red blood clouded over the blue. A strong stream of it flowed out of his nose.

The Mayor's Man coughed once. A wet, painful cough. Then collapsed.

Grace screamed in alarm. Declan's eyes went wide.

The gun went off again. Another shot. This one seemed somehow *louder* than the first. A horrible ring went through Declan's ear. Next to him was a hole in the wall that hadn't been there before, bristling with jagged wood.

It was Grace's turn to grab his hand. She seemed to yell something, but he couldn't hear it over that fucking *ringing*.

Grace slammed her shoulder into the door to open it and entered the kitchen. She tugged Declan along with her, then shoved him to the side. Spinning around, she waited for the door to open again before she kicked out hard.

Declan could only partially hear the grunt and whack of the door crashing into whoever was trying to get in. It must have been a hard hit because the door stayed closed for the moment.

"Too many," Grace gasped, shaking. "Holy shit."

Declan darted for the mattress, shoved what he could of Grace's clothes into his backpack, and scrambled for the door.

"Come on," he could barely hear himself yelling.

The now-perpetual cold of Quill Point drifted in as he opened the door to the outside. His eyes landed on the forest. The dark trees waved in that breeze. Each individual tree was lost in the horde of itself. A mass of brush and trunks and shadows. A shushing and swaying that promised never to let anyone out.

He shivered, but pushed out into the night.

Grace followed him, her eyes wide and her breathing fast.

"What are we fucking going to *do*?"

Another surge of adrenaline went through Declan. "I don't know. I don't know. I…"

Shouts came from behind the kitchen door. And around the side of the building. Several swears rang out into the night. Yellow flashlight beams flashed on, aimed at them. More swearing. Then threats. Horrible, violent threats.

A surge of electrical panic hit Declan, making it feel like he had to move… but couldn't move… but *needed to move.*

There was no way the Mayor's Men would take them to The Mayor now. Not in one piece. Not alive.

Grace looked at him, and he looked back, and a horrible, awful understanding flowed between them.

There was nowhere to go.

Well, *almost* nowhere to go.

Grace let out a sob. It erupted suddenly from her mouth. She clutched at her hair.

"*Fuck,*" Declan said.

They ran straight into the forest. While the groups narrowed in on them—one through the kitchen, one from around the building—Grace and Declan bolted in the straightest possible line toward the closest possible escape.

Time felt like it slowed. The moment stretched out.

The dark curtain of trees grew large as they approached, the trees stretched so tall it was like vertigo, and then those trees formed the sky. Those trees ate at the world and engulfed them. The brush slid around their feet, branches clutched at them like demonic claws, and the air took on a quality that could be described only as full of death.

And like that, they were in the forest.

The sound of the chase, of the pursuing Mayor's Men, dropped away so fast it was like the whole thing had been a dream.

CHAPTER 5

Grace and Declan waited in the dark for what felt like a long, long time. They shivered in it. Even this close to the edge, only a few steps in, the world that had been was gone. The only sounds were faint scrambling. A bird or a squirrel. Or something else with tiny, sharp claws.

The Mayor's Men didn't come in after them. If Arthur was shooting at them, it wasn't audible. And the bullets didn't reach them.

Declan gasped against his thudding chest, trying to get his breath even. He'd never had to run that hard before, and now it felt like his stomach and side were trying to stab him. The ringing in his ears had faded somewhat, but the constant, oppressive, wax-deep discomfort made it hard to concentrate. He wanted to puke but kept trying not to, clutching his stomach muscles harder and harder. The potatoes needed to stay in his stomach. He'd need it now. He'd need everything.

He glanced at Grace.

Okay. So he didn't have everything. His rations were now halved. How long could they both survive on it? Even if the forest wasn't somehow haunted, cursed, or something else, how long could two people survive on snacks alone?

Grace winced, looking at her hand. It occurred to Declan then that he'd been so focused on food he hadn't thought about medical supplies. He didn't have bandages, alcohol, or anything.

"What should we do?" he eventually whispered.

Grace looked at him, but it was too dark to tell what expression she had on her face. Her breath had a faint wheeze.

"I don't know."

"Do you think they're gone?"

"I don't know."

"Do you think we can just walk back out if they're far enough away?"

"I—" Grace breathed a little harder. "Probably not."

Declan knew she was right. They were looking *directly* at where they had walked in. It was an impenetrable, hyper-dense wall of foliage. Impossible to walk through, despite them having done so. The wall of it stretched off in both directions.

"Give me your hand," Declan said.

Grace reached out. Her palm felt slick with sweat.

"I guess we can go the other way," Grace said.

"Yeah, okay."

They took a few steps deeper. Then a few more. Going further in wasn't impossible. It felt worryingly inviting. The forest showed increasingly less bramble and dense sections. They passed between dark trunks with wide leaves. The ground underneath was springy. It rustled with each step they took.

When his eyes adjusted enough that Declan could see somewhat through the gloom, Declan noticed a pattern. The path they walked was just that: a path. A formal, standard path. The trees folded around to either side gradually—never obvious in its herding of them—but it *was* herding them. If they strayed a little in any other direction, it was almost impossible to go forward. If it seemed like a new branching path, it was actually gently drifting them back to the same tunnel of foliage.

Occasionally, Grace would make a noncommittal sound like she wanted to say something, then would pause again. When Declan could see her, she frowned to herself, her expression that of someone lost in thought.

Declan didn't know for sure, but assumed she must also be trying to map where they were. That was what he was attempting. He kept looking for landmarks, some sense of direction besides the path laid out for them. Even a firm understanding of their cardinal direction would've been useful.

He glanced past the dense branches above for some celestial body he could use as a reference, but the sky wasn't offering anything. It was the same starless night as it had been since Murder Sky. Even the moon was gone.

And then, as if to frustrate him, a turn came in the path. It was a sharp angle—a clean angle. A solid left turn that threw off his whole internal map. The whole place felt a little like a corn maze.

After they turned, he tried again—but eventually abandoned the idea. There was, apparently, nothing to do about the way it was. It had a way it wanted them to go and hadn't yet revealed any other rules. It simply demanded they walk.

And walk.

And walk.

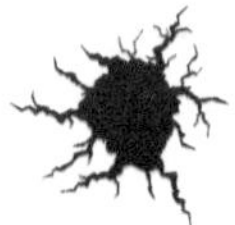

When Declan's feet ached too badly, he tugged on Grace's arm. Grace almost fell from how hard she stumbled in surprise.

"Jesus," Grace said, letting out a deep breath. "You could've said something."

"Shh!"

"What?" Grace said more quietly.

"I didn't… I didn't want to make much sound. We don't know what's out here."

"Oh… good point."

"I don't think I can walk much more right now. My feet are aching. And I don't think we have to worry about the Mayor's Men following us here, anyway."

"Okay," Grace said. "I think you're right. We would've seen them by now. We *should* probably stop for a bit. I'm actually really tired too."

Declan muttered in agreement. He was used to staying up late—had been doing so for quite a while now—but the energy and adrenaline that had surged during the attack were fading out, leaving nothing much in its wake. There was a sense of almost a metal, liquid lead, dripping through his arms, tugging him down.

"Okay, where do we make camp, do you think?"

"Uh, do you know how to make a fire?" Grace asked.

Declan pursed his lips. His dad had known. But Declan had never quite gotten the hang of camping. Never listened too closely to the instructions when they took trips over long holiday weekends.

"Not really."

"Neither do I. At least it's not too cold in here."

As if mocking her, a breeze drifted toward them, letting out a shrill little cry as it spun down the forest path. It swirled leaves in messy twirls, knocked a loose twig off a tree, then passed them by as quickly as it arrived. It left a smell, though. A vaguely unpleasant aroma, sharp and pungent. But it faded so fast that Declan couldn't quite place it.

He shivered.

"We can rest over there," Grace said, pointing.

Her hand was draped in shadows, but Declan could tell what she meant. Underneath a tree was a collection of leaves and moss clustered together, sitting in a mound. It didn't look comfortable—but it was better than just dirt.

"Okay. That should work," Declan agreed.

Grace walked over and leaned against the tree. Her head dipped, and she slid down the side. As she did, chunks of bark fell, raining shavings around her. Once on the ground, Grace brushed her hair with her fingers, knocking away a small piece of wood.

"I think this thing is dead," Grace whispered. "Or at least kind of dead. That was a lot of bark."

Declan walked over to her and looked at the line she'd made from sliding down. She'd stripped a fair bit of the bark, but a few clusters remained, reminding him of scabs.

"Yeah—there might be something wrong with this tree."

Grace pushed herself to stand. "Looking at it, I think a lot of these trees are dead, actually."

"That's … great," Declan said. He almost touched one cluster of bark, but pulled his hand back. "I don't like it. Maybe we should keep walking."

"Maybe," Grace said, gently running her palm over a section.

Even that was too much force. Another chunk of bark sloughed off to the ground, popping with a dusty burst. Where it had covered, now revealed a hole probably only an inch or two deep in the trunk. But in the semi-dark, it looked like a small void. A sideways pit on the surface of a sick, dying tree.

Then, from inside that pit, three halogen yellow eyes blinked on. Two at the bottom, one at the top. Until the triangle of it swiveled like clockwork gears. The halogen lights narrowed like angry eyes.

Grace and Declan screamed. They threw themselves back away from the tree. Bolted down the path. All tiredness was lost for the moment. Only panic. From behind them, the clicking sound continued, growing louder and angrier.

The path took several sudden turns as they ran. The dead, warped trees flew by as they kept going. Left. Right. Right again. Each one was lined with those impossible barriers of shadowy trees.

They'd easily run a mile before slowing to look back. Whatever it was, they'd lost it for now.

CHAPTER 6

GRACE'S VOICE CAME OUT IN DESPERATE gasps. "What the *fuck*. What the *fuck*! What the ever-loving fuck was *that*?"

"I don't know..." Declan breathed, clutching his stomach.

Declan rattled his brain for anything with eyes like that. Anything in the animal kingdom that could glow like mini headlights. Anything, anything at fucking all, with three eyes that looked mechanical but *couldn't* be mechanical.

There wasn't anything except everything he didn't want to imagine. Nothing except creatures that belonged to Murder Sky.

Grace started to speak, but her voice cracked, and she stopped again. She rhythmically breathed through her nose for several seconds. Eventually, she let out a ragged breath that maybe was supposed to be calmer—but it sounded like she was still on the verge of tears when she spoke.

"I don't want to be here."

An explosion of guilt hit Declan. He wasn't quite the reason she was trapped here. That was the Mayor's Men. That was because of Murder Sky. But. But … was the *reason* he had defaulted to running straight into the forest because he was already planning on doing so? They could've maybe gone around the building. Gone for the bonfire. Anything else. Anywhere else.

Did Declan's own stubbornness, his own plan, doom another person?

Declan spoke his next words almost without thinking about them—but, even if he'd had the time to consider, they were all he had.

"We'll just keep going… in case it follows us…"

But even as he said it, the energy sapped out of his legs, making him teeter and wobble.

"Or … we could … check the trees … stay on the path … maybe we won't have to worry about more of those…"

Declan stumbled once, twice, before Grace caught him. She could barely hold him up, her own arms shaking.

"I … uh…"

"Oh fuck," Grace muttered and pulled him along.

Despite what had happened before, Grace moved him to one of the trees. Declan had enough energy to not totally collapse, and they sat down with their backs against it. It was also dead and had strange patches. But, if another monster was hiding inside, it gave no sign.

Declan drifted in and out of his own mind for a moment. Then he took off his backpack. The zipper sounded weird in that forest environment as he opened it.

Just how poorly Declan had packed became obvious almost immediately. It looked like such a small lump of items. So little food. So little clothing.

At least he'd thought to pack a decent coat. He handed it to Grace. She billowed it out in front of them, then pulled it close like a blanket. The edges of it were scratchy, and it didn't cover properly. But, when another of that chilly breeze with odds smells came by, it kept them warmer.

The real warmth was having Grace next to him. Declan had never slept next to anyone. Never had a cozy dog or cat to add to a bed's warmth. It felt like false comfort, but it still felt like comfort. His ears were still ringing slightly from the gunshot, but it was easy enough to ignore. His eyes drifted closed slowly, only for him to force them open once, twice, to make sure nothing was about to attack them.

Next to him, Grace seemed to go through a similar process. Her head dropped; her breath got a little slower. Declan's shoulder was pressed into the side of her arm, and he could feel her relaxing.

Then, a slight tense.

"Declan…?

"Yeah?" Declan shifted his head to look at her better. "What is it?"

"I don't blame you, okay?"

"Oh…" he said quietly. "Okay."

"I don't. It wasn't… it wasn't your fault."

"I… I didn't think it would be like this."

Grace didn't respond for a long time. Declan assumed she'd fallen asleep. Her head hung even lower, and her frame got looser. Grace's breaths flowed out almost too quietly to hear.

But then she spoke again.

"Declan … can you please hold me?"

Declan paused for a second. Then shifted closer. Turned his body. His arms were shaky, burning from exhaustion. But he wrapped them around her. Held her as tight as he could manage.

Grace's body shook, and she curled up against the embrace.

She was crying now—not a deep sob or wailing scream. A slow, almost silent, pouring out of fear. Even in the shadows, in the low light of that forest, Declan could see her forehead tighten and her shoulders rise and fall.

"I'm so sorry," Declan whispered. "I'm *so* sorry."

Grace didn't respond at all that time.

She'd fallen asleep.

Declan lay there, holding her as best he could. Trying not to move. Trying to maintain the same pressure. Even as more and more of his muscles burned and his own tears arrived, spilling down his cheek and along his nose.

Declan's own tiredness couldn't be ignored though. It slammed into his head and forced him to listen to its commands. As he fell deeply, quickly asleep, he hoped for a morning. For sunlight to break some of the darkness.

Assuming that sunlight ever arrived in this place.

CHAPTER 7

ECLAN OPENED TIRED, BURNING EYES to that cursed, hazy forest. The sun had arrived; the light muted. Its beams were cold rays trickling through the trees. A bird chirped. Some leaves shifted. Declan couldn't tell where either was coming from. The sound slipped and echoed through the tree line—losing its sense of place.

Declan shifted too much as he woke up. Grace shuddered to consciousness. Her eyes snapped open. They were red-tinged from crying. Unfocused from dead-tired rest. Then they slowly widened.

Declan could tell the exact moment she realized where they still were.

"Oh fuck," she said. "Fucking no—"

Grace coughed. A wet, harsh sound with the faintest crackle.

"My mouth is so dry," she managed to say.

Declan pulled the backpack to him. He took one of the three reusable water bottles. He'd filled them with as much clean water as he could get back in town. He pushed it into her view.

"Here. Drink it all. You sound like you need it. We can filter a stream or something later."

Declan didn't mention their lack of any filtration methods.

Grace took it. Her arms shook slightly as she hefted it to her mouth. As soon as she took a gulp, some small amount of strength flowed into her. She chugged most of it in moments, taking a singular, gasping break to breathe. She tilted the bottle back and tapped on the bottom a few times before returning it to Declan.

"Oh god, I was *so* thirsty. It's hard to remember when you're on the clock to get water."

"I hope it helps."

"It did, thank you." She glanced at him. "How many more do we have?"

"Two more," Declan said.

"Great."

"Here, you should eat too," he said.

Declan pulled out one of his vegan bars and handed it to Grace. Then pulled one out for himself. He gathered up the coat and stuffed it back in.

"Huh, chocolate flavored," Grace observed.

She bit into it, paused for a second, then shook her head and took another bite.

Declan knew how bad that brand tasted. Before even considering packing for the forest, he'd burned through all his good options. This was the cheap stuff.

His was vanilla flavored. He mustered enough spit to swallow the clump that formed as he chewed.

"Thank you," Grace said. "For… for last night."

Declan glanced at her. "I'm glad I could help."

"Yeah…"

Grace took another bite, chewing slowly.

"Are you okay to keep moving?" Declan asked after a few more moments of their breakfast. "I think we should keep moving."

Grace nodded slowly. She rubbed her eyes and then stood up, offering Declan her hand. As he stood, his legs protested. Muscle pain pinched in several places. He leaned down and massaged the worst spot, trying to alleviate the pain.

"So, just continue this way, I guess," Grace said.

"Yeah—"

Another birdsong chimed through the trees.

The two froze.

It hadn't sounded exactly like a bird. More like something doing a decent job of imitating one. Like someone was watching and had used their hands to make a bird call.

A shiver passed through Declan, his heart rate ratcheting up quickly.

They waited in silence. Declan expected another call. Maybe closer. Maybe *more* artificial sounding.

But nothing happened.

The pale sunlight flowed down over them.

The forest was still.

If it was even a *real* forest. At one point, it had been. That much Declan could be *reasonably* sure of. But as Declan took stock, he doubted what he saw was organic, grown, or even the same location as before Murder Sky. It was even more obvious they were in a tunnel in the daylight. The overhead was a branch latticework so precise it looked artisanal. Crafted. It was interlocking fingers tightly bunched perfectly in rows and lines.

Looking forward, looking down the way, had the same strangeness.

"Where do you think it goes?" Grace asked.

"Maybe wherever everyone else went," Declan replied.

The tunnel didn't have a visible end. There wasn't a wall, smoke, or anything to obscure: it stretched further than the eye could see, like how the horizon fell away by the Earth's curve. The forests around Quill Point were maybe a few miles away from the next town at its biggest. It took a few minutes by car. It was a common enough hiking trip. They should've already walked out with how much they'd traveled.

"Do you think walking faster would help?" Grace asked.

Declan shook his head. "Maybe. Possibly. But I don't want us to burn too many calories. We're going to have trouble replacing them. We should keep to a good, steady pace."

"Okay," she said.

And off they went.

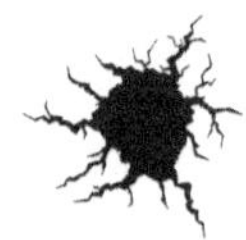

"Maybe the town passed into another dimension," Grace mused aloud after ten minutes of silence. "Maybe this is a portal, and we'll end up back on Earth, eventually. Or maybe the portal is one-way, and the government *has* been trying to get in and help us, but they couldn't. Maybe everyone who went in here is just *there*."

"Maybe," Declan said.

"Or maybe we went back in time—and these were all monsters and stuff that used to exist. Maybe this stuff did in the dinosaurs? It would explain why our phones stopped working. And the cars, right? That stuff didn't exist back then. That stuff wasn't made for hundreds of thousands of years."

"But lights still work," Declan said.

Grace's shoulders drooped, and her expression shifted. "Yeah, that's true. I guess that makes it have to be something else. But it could be some kind of magic, right? Maybe it doesn't have to follow the rules like that. Maybe it's more of a vibe thing. A wizard didn't like cars and cell phones and cursed the whole world."

"Sure," Declan said.

"Just … Dec, I just hope it was only Quill Point. And that stuff isn't anywhere else. I don't want this to be the *whole* world."

"I hope so too," Declan said quietly.

Whatever enthusiasm Grace has mustered faded practically step by step. She went silent after that, keeping a slightly springy pace but not talking anymore. Her eyes focused forward.

They walked for several more minutes before the wind hit again. It didn't feel as cold in the morning sun, but now it smelled much worse. It instantly coated Declan's tongue.

Grace stopped in her tracks and covered her mouth. Declan gagged and then tucked his shirt up over his mouth and nose. The smell was industrial and sharp. A thick smog of scorched metal, burned hair, and rancid gasoline. And underneath it all, a sickly, meaty smell—something he still couldn't quite place.

"What the fuck is that?" Grace pinched her nose. "That smells like my dad's old car before we scrapped it."

Declan swallowed back a surge of bile. The smell wasn't getting any better—it was growing *more* pungent as they stood there.

But the path was as it was. Nothing looked out of place. "Do we keep going?" Declan asked.

He didn't want to think about how bad the smell might get once they were close enough to see the source.

"I'm not sure turning around would help," Grace responded. "I get the feeling … if we tried, we'd just end up going that way, anyway. I think we'd get turned around without noticing."

Declan nodded. As soon as she'd said it, it felt right. Accurate. This forest had their destination in mind.

"Yeah … okay."

"Maybe we could—we'll just inch our way over. Be cautious. See it before anything happens."

"Okay," Declan repeated.

"Can I hold your hand again?"

Declan didn't bother answering—he reached out and took her fingers into his. Whatever they were about to find, he didn't want to be alone when they did.

"I guess, uh, I guess we're going…" Declan said to himself.

Every few feet felt like walking against a force field; Declan tried to block out the smell and blink past his watering eyes. Declan was almost glad he had so little in his stomach—he would've lost it several times over by now.

The landscape subtly changed as they struggled forward. Declan noticed it first and silently pointed at the trees. Grace glanced at it, but then sharply stopped looking.

The burned tree's bark was gradually turning a different color—or perhaps had something on them. It wasn't uniform. It wasn't every tree. But it was increasingly prevalent. Sometimes it looked like paint flecks; sometimes, it was like buckets of it were tossed around. It was a pale, rusty sheen. It went to the branches of some trees.

Declan desperately tried to not make any associations with any red liquids he knew. Eventually, every tree had sections of it. Some of it was less dry than before.

And then Declan noticed the slime.

Between layers of bark were these buildups of light pinkish-red globules. They didn't pulse or push out like they were part of the trees' interior but looked stuck on. They looked like they had the same consistency as hand lotion or soft-serve ice cream.

The back of Declan's mind kept firing off warning bells—which he tried so hard to ignore. Acknowledging what he was seeing was a surefire way to panic. His pulse rose higher and higher. He could feel the same from Grace's hand.

This is bad. This is bad. This is bad.

But there was only one direction to go.

He gritted his teeth and held his breath against another rolling wind of that horrible smell. More trudging forward. More walking into something.

The forest changed again. It was thinning out. The trees stood further apart, having to reach their branches further and further to form their latticework. It was slowly becoming seemingly endless glades. Some were empty, and some were filled with mushrooms and fairy rings. And some had sizable chunks of that pinkish-red slime splayed across the ground. Some chunks of it were so large that Declan expected them to move under their own power.

Then some were even bigger.

Declan refused to think about how they were roughly people-sized.

But with nothing else to think about. And a horrible smell. And it being there. And there. And flung about, and piled—

Hadn't Declan seen something like this a few years ago? Something online, maybe? He remembered it being deeply unsettling. It resembled *something*.

What was it again…?

Declan remembered.

"Oh, holy *fuck*."

CHAPTER 8

GRACE SCREAMED LIKE NOTHING HE'D ever heard. A noise Declan wasn't aware a human body could produce. It was a chest-deep, unrestrained scream.

Declan looked at what she was looking at.

The sensation that went through him didn't feel like part of his body. Or perhaps knocked him right out of his body. A storm surge, electrical meltdown, atomic fission of adrenaline, an emotion that couldn't fit inside him. It scrambled the signals, slashed cohesion—

Declan had watched his dad *burn*. There shouldn't be a world, a lifetime, where he could feel terror like this *twice*.

There was only one glade now. A massive expanse of trees with each spaced several feet apart. The trees were massive, imposing, and burned. Cindery towers, surrounded by dying, rotting, dry brown grass.

And from them hung hundreds of upside-down bodies.

Declan clutched at his mouth, screaming into his palm. Vomit sputtered out, pushed its way through his fingers, and dripped down the back of his hands. He couldn't look away—his body frozen in disgust and terror.

He finally forced his eyes shut, but the image was seared deep.

Desecrated bodies. Suspended by hooks through their stomachs, through their shirts. Arms, legs, faces were stripped to the bone. Exposed nerves, skulls, and connective tissues.

Bruised skin, rotting skin. Sticky strands of human flesh stuck to skeletons.

The mostly intact ones had distinct rings of open, puckered skin around their necks—like a jagged second mouth. And from those cuts dripped trickles—sometimes more—of blood into silver, blood-crusted trays.

And all of them, *all of them*, had a circle punctured right in the center of their foreheads. Those that were reduced to mere skulls had visible trauma cracks. Those with flesh revealed slurry remains of once-active brains, now gray mush.

Declan fell to his knees, buffeted by the smell. The smell of meat. The smell of people. The smell of people meat.

Grace's screams turned sharper, then broke apart into a desperate gasp. A new type of panicked fear.

Along with a whining, clicking, whirring sound getting closer.

"Declan!"

His eyes snapped open, and instinct took over faster than he could process what he saw.

A rush of metal.

Something like a knife, but much bigger. Sharp edges, shiny parts, ragged angles, and a yellow glow.

He threw himself to the side, slamming into the ground, then rolled away.

It kept swinging something at him so fast it whistled through the air. Adrenaline surged into him so hard it almost made him feel numb. He leaped to his feet, feeling the wind of that blade barely missing the back of his head.

Declan broke into the most desperate run of his life, even more so than the night before. He darted for one of the trees, hoping to get something between him and it. Now that he'd gotten a little distance, it wasn't as fast as he'd thought. He'd be dead if it was. But it was big—and had a long reach. Even as he curved sharply around the trunk, the edge of some part of it slammed into his shoulder.

The pain of just that one contact was much worse than anything he'd ever felt. Once, as a young child, he'd put his hand on the stove before someone could stop him, and it had hurt in a wave across his palm and felt like it had pressed deeper than skin.

This was that but across his entire shoulder.

And so hot it had burned immediately through that part of his shirt, semi-fusing the scorched fabric into the skin there.

His mind could barely contain the sensation. He screamed and flung himself away, wanting to clutch at the spot with his hands. But even the faint wind hurt.

The tree he'd hidden behind was massive and imposing.

It did not matter. It didn't slow it down. Whatever it was, it didn't bother to go around the tree.

Splinters flew out like the tree had been hit by a cannonball.

And one piece smacked Declan in the back of the head. Knocking him off his feet with a burst of white light behind his eyes. He blinked away spots for a moment, tears streaming down his cheeks. Every sense felt overstimulated. The sharp tang of burning wood filled Declan's tastebuds. The remains of the tree catching fire choked his nose with a smoky blast.

The metallic monster let out a clanking, whirring sound. Then a pneumatic hiss with the same energy as an angry rattlesnake.

The whole thing took maybe three seconds, but Declan felt like the moment was dragging into eternity. Death was incoming—but it was arriving slowly. Declan rolled onto his back as fast as he could, ignoring the contents of the backpack digging into his spine.

He finally saw the full monster bearing down on him.

It wasn't one creature; its body was partially made of hundreds of what they'd seen crawling inside the dead tree. They interlocked like the gears of a giant, sharp clock. Each tiny, insectile creature had three glowing halogen eyes and spiderlike metallic limbs ending in sharp, tapering points.

But what was singular about it, what made it *more*, was even worse. At its center was a grinding, whirring meat processor. A spinning wheel of sharp edges that could easily reduce a human—bones, organs, skin, everything—into a thick, pinkish paste.

Jutting from both of its sides were mechanical arms bristling with haphazardly arranged knives and skewers. It unfolded more tools and scuttled toward him on five swiveling spider legs.

From within its chest came something that Declan recognized—and froze him to the spot. His limbs stopped working.

A cattle gun. A bolt gun. A stunner.

It was caked in fluids, tiny compared to the normal type, and would go through his head with the utmost ease. Like a cow at a slaughterhouse, it would knock him unconscious—destroy a part of his brain—so he could have his neck cut and bleed out "peacefully." An efficient method. Then he'd be hung up on a tree and drained of any inconvenient blood left in his body.

Or maybe he'd be ground into a pinkish-red slurry of once-living tissue like a chicken before becoming a nugget.

Declan's eyes darted for *any* option. Something he could do to save himself. But he expected nothing. He wouldn't be able to crawl away fast enough. *This* was the long-speculated truth of Quill Point. Like everyone else who wandered into the forest, he would become lost, missed, meat.

The rattlesnake's hiss grew louder as it pushed the bolt gun forward. This close, Declan could smell the burning metal that was the entire monster's being. It washed over him, drying his eyes, mouth, and throat. The multitude of yellow, glowing eyes looked into him eagerly. The entire structure of this connected-piece monster rattled and shifted.

Then most eyes went off him, and its whir sputtered, churned, and caught against something.

Declan blinked in confusion.

"Declan!" Grace called out.

A plank of wood was jutting through the monster's internal configurations. It was, at least for a moment, disrupting whatever tentative connection it had to its own composite form. Pieces of it failed to reconnect, knocking other pieces into disarray. The wood burst into flames in several spots, and Declan could hear Grace scream again.

Declan pushed himself back across the dead grass, not bothering to flip over.

The monster spun in both directions, flinging out some of its bladed arms for both targets. Declan ducked as a serrated knife screamed overhead.

A few clusters of eyes gave him a dispassionate look. Then it clicked all of itself toward Grace.

Grace yelped and leaped to the side as the bolt shot out for her stomach. She dropped the remains of the piece of wood, still burning, and ran around the creature to get to Declan.

After several failed tries, Declan got back up to standing. Grace caught up to him.

The monster chugged and whirred and reassembled itself with a harsh click. It rotated its upper body in a strange clockwork stretch, then fire roared out from various seams, bathing it in red. It sprinted forward at them with alarming speed.

Declan nearly cried out from the sudden heat waves hitting him but still spun and ran. His feet flew out in front of him, uncoordinated and off-balance but moving. Grace pulled alongside him with loping strides.

Declan sucked in gulps of air as he pushed himself forward, pulling from some well of energy he didn't even know existed. His body was desperate to survive.

They bolted past several lines of trees; the long, outwardly stretching lines felt like an optical illusion. It was death and pain organized so efficiently that it seemed almost natural for it to be this way.

That was until the house showed up.

CHAPTER 9

THE HOUSE CREPT UP TO THE HORIZON AS they ran, sitting in the dead center of four corpse-holding trees. Declan nearly stopped running at the sight of it, but when an angry air hiss of a scream came from behind him, he pushed himself even harder.

It was a two-story, midwestern building with an elevated wraparound porch, a closed garage, and twin windows that looked like eyes at the top. It was painted a disgustingly happy blue color and had some white siding. In an almost perfect circle, the surrounding grass was healthy, green, and clearly manicured.

Grace and Declan said nothing; they ran for it, weaving as best they could to put trees between them and their pursuer. Behind them, it whirred angrily, and multiple trees exploded in a whoosh of blazing heat and the ear-splitting pops of bark becoming shrapnel.

Declan reached the porch first. He dropped to his hands and knees to go up the five steps faster. And when he got to the top, he finally looked behind him.

The monster was going at an alarming pace, waving its bladed arms in slashing motions in time with its crab-like scuttering. It whipped out a blade at an angle—

The yell almost burst out of Declan's throat.

"DUCK!"

Grace snapped her head forward, leaning down while still running. The huge saw blade would've beheaded her. She kept her head low as she made it to the first porch step.

The monster was doggedly right fucking behind her.

Declan turned to the door, and for a horrible second, it occurred to him it had every chance of being locked—that there was no reason in a hell like this that they would be *lucky*. He grabbed the handle and spun.

But it moved. The metal was cool to the touch—almost too cold—but it wasn't locked. He flung the door open. And on the other end was a normal foyer, all things considered. A weak light glowed above. A small hat stand stood off to the side with a black bowler hat. Next to the stand was a little bench with three sets of very nice dress shoes sitting beneath. The only thing obviously wrong with it was being in a murder forest.

Declan didn't question that, though. Whatever this house was, it had to be better than what was behind them.

He stepped inside as Grace made it to the top.

The monster barreled up the steps, revving its grinding blades and pushing forward its bolt gun. Its crab legs scuttled up the steps with horrible clicks.

Grace made it through. Declan slammed the door shut. They turned to run. If a tree couldn't stop it…

But, instead, there was a thud of it hitting the door and bouncing off. Then an almost sad scrambling sound. It sounded like a pet scratching at the door, like a cat wanting in or out. It made them both pause for a split second.

The door didn't fall.

Declan froze.

"It can't get in," he muttered. "Oh my god… it can't get in."

"We shouldn't take that chance," Grace said, but stayed still, looking at the door. "We should keep going."

The door wasn't burning. No blades or saw or bolt went through it.

"Okay, that's probably a good idea," Declan said, his voice sounding weak. The adrenaline was wearing off. "But … I need to walk slower."

"Okay. I think I do too."

Declan reached out and clicked the lock, then stepped away. Then another. They backed up as far as they could, eventually passing through the foyer.

The scrambling came for another few moments, occasionally broken by a mechanical scream that sounded too human. But eventually, it stopped. It even sounded like it was clambering down the steps.

"I really don't think it can get through that door," Declan whispered.

"Should we risk it?" Grace replied quietly.

"I think we're as safe as we can be right now."

"Hold on…"

Grace tilted her head. Then pointed at something. Held a finger to her mouth. Crept up to the door.

Declan spotted the tiny golden circle. A peephole. Grace leaned forward, looked through it briefly, and stepped back.

"It's really going away," she said breathlessly. "It's going away. We… we're not dead."

She looked back at Declan and smiled through tears. "We're *not* dead."

Even Declan couldn't help but smile. He couldn't believe it. This house had saved them. He wasn't going to have a bolt gun go right through his skull.

"We're not dead," he echoed.

Declan suddenly stumbled. The relief of those words unlocked the exhaustion sitting, waiting, ready. He leaned against the wall and almost fell to the floor. Light tears crept down his face, using up his water, but feeling fantastic against his heat-dried skin. He let himself have a moment to breathe.

His eyes tried to shut on him; it was getting harder and harder to stand. He had to remember that this house *could* still be dangerous. It could somehow be even worse.

His backpack was smooshed and dirty on the outside but still sealed. He pulled it off, set it to the side, and slid down. The cool floorboard was hard, uncomfortable, and *amazing*. He lay there and let himself breathe.

Grace joined him a moment longer, laying the top of her head near his. She let out little gasps of air and little whimpers of relief.

Now that Declan had time to think again, his guilt welled up. He'd gotten her into this mess. He'd put her here. She could've easily died just then. Would he have been brave enough, fast enough, to stick a plank of wood into a metallic monster?

He doubted it.

CHAPTER 10

THEY COULD EITHER STAY IN THIS SPOT, BY the miracle door, or they could look around.
And neither felt safe.

Whatever was keeping it back could fail. It could spring in with a fury. And literally anything could be in the rest of this inexplicable house. From where he was lying, all Declan could see was a tan couch without seat cushions and a tiny coffee table in what he presumed was a living room.

Declan's stomach growled. He couldn't imagine how many calories he'd burned running for his life.

"Want food?" he asked Grace. "I think we earned it."

Grace rolled onto her side. She'd been staring up at the ceiling for a while.

"Yes, please." Her voice cracked with dehydration again. "And maybe some water again? I'm sorry."

"No, no, it's okay." Declan sat up and tugged the backpack over to him.

Several protein bars were bent out of shape when he opened it. None of the water bottles had broken, at least.

He gave Grace two of the most intact bars and an entire water bottle. She nodded in thanks. Declan pulled out a green tea-flavored one, then counted the remaining. Five bars. Some crackers. Some peanut butter. One water bottle.

Fucking hell. How had he planned so poorly? Didn't his dad teach him better than this? Even if the bag was small and the resources around town were sparse, he could've cut up some edible plants or something.

He had to fight back sudden tears. Had to quell the horrible feeling that stuck in his throat and threatened to tear at him.

As if she could tell what he was thinking, Grace asked, "How are we doing on the stuff?"

"Not much left," he said.

"Okay."

They ate in silence for a moment. Declan's stomach rejoiced as he bit into the bar. It was amazing how the near-death experience improved the general flavor. Declan tried to ignore how thirsty he was. How the taste of vomit still lingered a little in his mouth. Grace deserved the water more. He owed it to her.

"We could check if this place has a kitchen?" she said.

Declan thought for a moment. They were in a house. As inexplicable as it was, that didn't mean it didn't have the usual things in it.

"Yeah … not many other options, really."

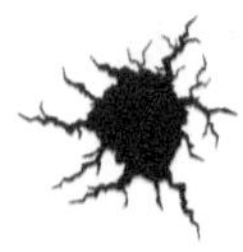

The house was typical in some ways, but fucking *off-putting* in others. The general layout of the space had a logic: the living room and connecting dining room were both visible, with a doorway off to the side of the dining room that likely went to a kitchen. A staircase to the side of them seemed to go up to a second story with several imposing doors.

But it was also a house with *eccentric* décor.

For one, there was taxidermy. Declan's skin crawled at the sight of it. He'd always hated how it looked both alive and dead. A corpse that wanted to move again—was posed like it *could* move again—but with no blood, no life, no nothing.

The biggest taxidermied animal was a polar bear standing between the dining room table and the living room. Its fur was so clean and shiny that it looked brushed and bleached. Its mouth was open in a furious roar, full of some black muck that slowly dripped down its jaw like sap oozing from a tree. A black and white penguin stood directly beneath it. The gunk slid over its eyes and down its beak. It looked like it was crying.

Grace crossed the living room with gentle steps. Declan followed her, catching up in the dining room, where they both navigated past the small-but-tall table with four empty seats.

The hard turn was a kitchen entrance. A narrow kitchen that was more like a tunnel. On one side, a fridge that gave off a worrying smell and a countertop with lots, way too many, closed cabinet doors. Each was about the size of a tin can, with little golden handles. On the other side was a small window with closed curtains and a sink. Above the window was a row of yet more cabinets.

The curtain was covered in little pink T-bone steaks and chicken legs with grill marks.

And that was weird enough, but what was past that made them both stop.

Past the kitchen and over a large granite countertop was an office space on a lower half-story. But that wasn't what stopped them in their tracks. No, that was the taxidermied fish display on the countertop. It was structured around coral. Large, dark yellow coral with branches like an underwater tree. Fish of various species and sizes were on small plastic stands, "swimming" around each other.

The fish weren't in great condition. The same black muck was coating their sides, drawn in weird, half-finished symbols that Declan found hard to look at for too long. And *all* the fish had bite marks somewhere on them. Ragged ovals with strange teeth patterns. From them dripped loose organs, preserved with a shiny, waxy resin so they never actually fell.

It was ghoulish, sure. It made Declan nauseous to look at. But something else about them made him feel *deeply* sad. It bubbled up inside quickly, inexorably. A bone-deep ache of loss only matched by feelings he'd had for his father.

"Gone," he muttered. "All gone."

"What the fuck…" Grace said, shaking her head slowly. "Okay, we'll deal with that after we check the fridge."

Declan frowned. "It smelled weird."

"Doesn't mean what's in there isn't edible," she replied. "It can't hurt to check… probably."

Declan frowned at the same time she did. It *could* hurt, actually. The monster had been made of tinier ones. One of them could be in that fridge. But starvation would also kill them.

"Fuck, yeah, that's probably worth the risk too," Declan agreed.

They both stood in front of it, but neither actually reached out. Declan quickly noticed something weird. The fridge's smell didn't obey normal rules. Only when he was looking at it could he smell that odd, thankfully not meaty, smell. And when he turned his head to glance back at the bear—making sure it hadn't moved—the smell stopped. Then the smell rose again when he looked back.

It was only on eye contact. That tangy chemical smell was seen, not smelled. And it was like formaldehyde and wine.

"…okay, maybe this isn't the best idea," Grace said, laying a single finger on the fridge. "I'm not sure I would want to eat whatever is there."

Declan nodded, thinking.

"There's something about all this…"

It wasn't the weird smell. The act of being around the fridge made his stomach drop. Not nausea—but sadness. The drop in his stomach when he'd discovered his mom wouldn't return after going to her grandmother's place for a few days. The drop he had when he'd discovered on social media that a cousin he'd played with at family gatherings had died.

Declan glanced at the fish diorama and then at the bear. The objects in this place didn't feel like objects alone. They had resonance; they were almost symbolic. He didn't *want* to touch any of it, but it felt like it wouldn't feel real if he did.

"Do you feel…?"

He looked at Grace. She'd been staring at the fridge. Her eyes were wide, and her shoulders were tense. She stepped back and bumped into the edge of the sink.

"Grace! Are you okay?" Declan asked.

"Yeah, I feel something, Dec. There's something wrong with this fridge. Like, you can tell too, right? When I got my student debt bill for the first time… when I found out that my ex-boyfriend had been cheating… it's like getting sucker punched … by fucking *life*. Like things you expected to be one way, but they just *aren't*. God, it's like the floor fell out from under me."

"Yeah…" Declan pursed his lips. "I'm good with not opening it unless we really have to. Maybe we can find something else in here."

"Okay." Grace sounded shaken. "Okay, yeah."

Declan turned away from the fridge, trying not to look at anything but the wooden cabinets. "I really don't like this place."

"Same," Grace said.

"Better than the monster, though."

"Yeah," Grace replied, then made a soft sound. "Hey, uh, Dec?"

The number of times recently that Declan had heard that fear in Grace's voice, that stiffness to it, like she was holding back tears: he hated how familiar it had become.

Declan turned back to her. "Yeah?"

"I think we should, uh…"

Now Declan's guilt and sadness turned to a different type of concern. Her voice wasn't shaken; it was bordering on panic. On screaming out.

"I think we should tell each other … when we feel stuff in here. Any new or random emotion. Like with the fish. You felt depressed looking at the fish, right? Like watching a beautiful painting being ripped apart?"

"I didn't think of those words, but yeah," Declan admitted. He glanced over at it. "It's tragic, and I don't understand why it's so tragic. But it is, and it hurts."

"Yeah … so, what I mean is … if things here can do that. If things in here can make us feel things we don't intend to feel—that don't make sense—we should tell each other immediately. Because, uh, what if it affects our thoughts or something? What if it can mind control us somehow?"

Declan's already dry mouth felt even drier. "Like open the door."

Grace nodded.

"Okay, I'll let you know. If anything else here causes anything like that to … I'll, um, I'll let you know."

"Thanks," Grace said.

"We should… we should look around in here. These cabinets. Find something if we can."

"Okay."

Grace turned to open one of the cabinet doors, not looking back at Declan.

And Declan stood still momentarily, wishing she hadn't pointed that out. Mind control. Emotional control. Wished she hadn't put that possibility in his head. Could he be made to let the monster inside? Was he already, having looked once, *altered?* How does one tell when their own perceptions are being altered?

He stuffed the worries in a box. There was no winning that line of inquiry.

The cabinets, then. The cabinets. Declan picked one at random to start.

The first he opened was empty, as was the second one. The third one had dust. Which meant the skin cells of some living thing. Another thing for the don't-think-too-hard-about-it box.

Behind him, Grace opened a few in quick succession and then let out a disappointed sigh.

The fourth and fifth cabinets he tried were also empty. Six, seven, eight, nine, ten. Empty, empty, empty. Perhaps they all would be. The house *looked* lived in, but there wasn't even a guarantee it had existed five minutes before they'd entered it. The sky in Quill Point had changed so fast. This could've been generated right before they ran up to it.

Or maybe, maybe someone had been here for a long, long time. Taken everything, eventually starving. They could find a starved-out corpse somewhere. What were the odds they were the first and only to survive the slaughterhouse monster?

Grace slammed her hand against the wood. "Come on. Give me *something* here."

Declan went back to opening cabinets. He was now sure he would find nothing. But, on the seventeenth try, things finally changed.

He found an old, very worn, cardboard box. It seemed like the sort that held cereal or maybe a lot of crackers. There wasn't any way to tell. The brand was worn away. The words were a smattering of faded letters. Even the nutritional facts left were mostly squiggly lines. He picked it up, and dust, perhaps crumbs, fell out the bottom.

Declan looked at it closer. He recognized the teeth pattern: rodent. One time, the mice they used to feed the snakes and some other lizards got out, and they'd lost multiple breakfast cereals the same way before getting them all.

He put it back and frowned.

Ever since this house saved them, Declan had been thinking about it being some trap. But that was more abstract. A vague notion of things being too easy. Magic and demons and aliens. But what about mundane traps? Simple traps. The kind humans use on smaller creatures.

What do you do when something smaller, weaker, gets away, and can't be chased down?

"You bait them," he whispered.

The sound of running water came from behind him.

"At least this works!" Grace said.

Declan spun, watching as Grace smiled over the running sink. The water going through was fast, clear, and clean, and Grace reached forward to touch it.

"Wait!"

His voice was too loud, dangerous to be that loud, but he had to make sure—

"Don't do that."

Grace froze. "What?"

"It could be poison. *That* could be the trap." Declan put up his hands. "We *have* literally no idea if it's even water."

Grace looked at it for a moment. It flowed perfectly. The sound was almost comforting. Above it, through that curtain, Declan could partially see the field of dead bodies.

Grace's face fell into another frown, the joy slipping away. "Okay, how much of the bottled stuff do we have?"

Declan's jaw tightened. "Just one."

A long pause then. Grace was standing there, thinking hard. The water was still running. The house was otherwise a quiet, strange place. An AC unit somewhere clicked on. They both jolted slightly. An uncomfortably cold breeze shot out of an air vent above the sink.

Grace took a deep breath. "I think we might need to risk this, Dec. The human body can go a long time without food. But if we run out of water and are stuck here for too long, we will just die."

Declan gritted his teeth. His pulse was jolting, the back of his head fuzzy with electricity. He'd felt *certain* of the danger a moment ago, but despite the oddities of everything, they were just standing in a kitchen. A normal enough room. It looked almost identical to a house he'd been to as a kid. And she was right about the dehydration. Even if *this* water wasn't safe and they searched for other faucets, maybe a bathroom, it wouldn't be any better. The house presumably had the same pipes throughout. The risks were the same the entire way, and it didn't matter when they took them.

"Okay … let me try something, then."

Declan grabbed the cardboard box again and held it underneath the water for a few seconds. Then he put it on the counter and stepped back. The cardboard wouldn't stand a chance if the water was secretly some industrial acid or something supernatural. The already old cardboard crumbled a little, but it otherwise was fine.

They both stared at it for a long time, breathing hard, waiting for something to happen.

Of course, the cardboard could be made of something else. It was of this house—maybe it was there to reinforce the trap.

Was this luck?

Or a quick way to die?

As the water ran, Declan kept noticing how dry his mouth was. How sticky and raw it felt. He could still taste the protein bar. Coating his tongue.

What was the right thing to do? And how the fucking hell had Declan gone from living in a dying, cursed town to somehow being in even more immediate, personal, moment-to-moment danger? Why the fuck had he thought risking the forest was a good idea?

Grace was here, alongside him in this horror, and surely, it *was* his fault.

His fault. *His* responsibility. *His* damning choices. This wouldn't even be a discussion or concern if it wasn't for him.

A snap decision passed through him, then was rejected, then reconsidered, then accepted, all in a blink, a second of introspection.

Then Declan tried to keep his voice level.

"Are you okay with what you had from the bottle?"

"Yeah?" Grace asked, frowning. "Why?"

Before she could say anything, he darted forward, splashed his hand in the water, and licked some of it off. Even that tiny amount was heavenly. Crisp and filtered. Almost pure water and minerals.

"Because if it *is* poison, only one of us will die."

CHAPTER 11

EVEN AS THOSE WORDS LEFT HIS MOUTH, his heart rate sped up. He'd taken the drink with death in mind, knowing that his heart might seize at any moment was another matter. That his throat might close on him. The process of painfully dying was potentially already started and impossible to stop. His entire story—happy moments, sad moments, angry moments, learning, growing, being—might be right at its end.

"Declan, what the *fuck*!"

Declan looked at her, holding back tears. He gave out a little chuckle he couldn't quite explain. It wasn't funny—it was *so* not funny. He touched his dry lips and swallowed a buildup of saliva. Was he already choking on his own insides? Was it actually foam from melting organs he couldn't yet feel dying?

"This way, you'll know," he said, his voice quavering. "You'll be safe. You can have the last water. And if I don't die in the next hour, we've just found a solution to our water problem."

Grace looked at him with wide eyes. He didn't know what emotion she had on her face, but after a second, she cried and rushed forward to hug him.

"Why the hell would you do that, Declan!? We just… we just…"

Her words garbled together, increasingly more difficult to hear properly.

"We just got out of that last thing alive… *we made it*… what the *fuck* are you doing?"

Declan couldn't contain his own tears anymore. And there was no point in holding them back; they flowed down his cheeks and worsened his already dry skin. He leaned into her, hoping that, if he was about to die, it could be peaceful; it could be in the arms of someone who cared about him.

"It's my fault we're in here," Declan said. "You wanted me to stay at the diner with you—and I *should've* stayed! You told me people were coming by and you had to fight them, and all I could think about was how I needed to get away from everything."

Grace held him even tighter. "I… I'm not *mad* at you, Dec. How could I be mad at you? I'm not. I can't *imagine* what you're going through. I never lost someone like that. And it's not your fault. They chased us. They would have shot us, or worse. But Declan, you didn't need to be … a … Declan … I…"

Her voice was gone, and she was simply crying while holding him.

Declan felt nothing new—no rumblings of pain. No sharp internal failure. But it had only been a few moments. How was he supposed to know how long the poison took to activate? How long did normal Earth poison take to go into effect? He dry-swallowed again, forcing down saliva, waiting for any sign.

"I don't want to watch you die," Grace sputtered out. "I don't want to be all alone here."

Shame suddenly burned in Declan. He hadn't thought of that, either. He'd just wanted her safe.

"I'm sorry," he whispered.

They held each other for a little while longer. Nothing happened. Nothing changed. Declan gently pushed Grace away. He touched his chest and felt for his heartbeat. He ran his hands over his stomach, expecting it to gurgle or hurt.

"I guess it's okay." He let out a nervous chuckle. "I guess that it's not going to kill me. It might *actually* just *be* water."

Grace looked at him for a moment, her eyes red from crying and her usual smile forcing itself out. "I'm glad. I'm really glad. Thank fucking god. But Declan, please don't do something like that ever fucking again. I don't know what I would do. We're a team, okay? We survived this far. I need you here."

Declan forced himself to hold her gaze. He could see something in her eyes he hadn't seen since the hospital burned. For most of his life, it had been him and his dad. He'd had more short-term boyfriends than he'd had long-term friends. He hadn't seen such unmitigated affection in a long time.

"Okay," Declan said automatically. "Okay, we're a team."

"Good."

Declan couldn't look at her anymore. He dropped his head slightly, looking at her chin instead.

Declan cleared his throat. "I still don't think you should drink any of that water for at least a little longer—just to be as safe as possible."

"Okay. That makes sense," Grace said. "Then, in the meantime, we should keep looking for food or … maybe a way out?"

"I agree," Declan said. "But these cabinets aren't going to have anything, definitely not anything we can trust."

He glanced toward the fish diorama. Then quickly looked at what was beyond it. The weird emotions the fish caused still hit at the edges of his thoughts.

"I guess we can check out the office, then," he said.

"Okay," Grace said. "Okay, sounds good to me."

Declan took a step, then paused.

He spun back toward her.

Declan couldn't think of a time he'd been the one to initiate a hug. Touching other people had never been something he enjoyed much. But he lurched forward and wrapped Grace in as big of one as he could manage.

"I'm so sorry" was all he said.

"Please … please care about yourself, Declan." She hugged him back. "I care about you."

A shudder wracked through Declan. He didn't want to think too much about the emotions behind it. He had no more tears to cry. He nodded and hoped she could feel how much he appreciated her.

"Okay. I'll try."

CHAPTER 12

THE TWO PASSED THE FISH DIORAMA AND quietly took the steps down to the office area. It was a much smaller area, maybe only a few feet in any direction. There was a narrow and badly lit hallway that curved off somewhere. It didn't look appealing as the next destination—it looked, in fact, like a *great* way for something to be hiding.

Declan shivered and went back to looking at the office. One horrifying problem at a time.

Though there really was so little. No obvious ways out or food. Besides the desks and chairs, its defining feature was a bay window looking out at the horror field beyond. There wasn't even a curtain covering this one—so Declan did his best not to look in that direction.

And, as soon as they stood among the chairs, Declan could tell something new was wrong. It wasn't at the same level as the unnerving taxidermied bear, but it had enough strange features. For one, the seats had some odd smooth surface over them. It was aquatic somehow, like dolphin or whale skin.

But the *screens* really got Declan's attention. They were all turned on and either blurry or dim. He glanced at a computer mouse, debating if jostling it would help with the resolution—but didn't. He'd already taken too many chances today with this house.

Instead, he leaned in close to one of the dim screens. He had to squint, but it was a chart. Lots of them, actually. Charts layered over charts over charts. Line graphs, readouts, pie graphs: the works.

"What is this?" he asked. "I can't tell what it's displaying."

He glanced at Grace. She was also looking at one of the blurry ones. It was *so* blurry. He assumed it was a similar graph, but it could even be a drawing. Or a photo. Or some abstract art. The longer he looked at it, the more variety he saw. The more possible things it could be. It was curious and transfixing and—

A fire.

Smoke.

Melting.

Boiling.

How could one thing be so many horrible things?

How could one thing be a threat to everything?

The scope of it!

The scale of the loss, and the destruction, both in potential and in the immediate.

It was inconceivable, yet there … and yet happening … and yet…

Declan heard himself letting out a high-pitched, droning mutter and shook his head quickly. He forced himself to look out at the field of bodies, at the cut-up corpses. They were horrible. Those bodies suspended with hooks and bleeding. But the thoughts of endless fire stopped increasing, stopped crashing at his perceptions. They receded but didn't fully fade. He was still seeing bits of it in his mind's eye. It left him shaky.

Declan chided himself. He should've guessed that the computers could be another mental danger. That looking at anything out of place was possibly dangerous. At least he'd been fast enough to snap out of it. That he'd been able to get his mind out—

Grace was still looking. She was leaning forward, neck stretched out, enraptured by the sight.

Declan gently pushed Grace's shoulder.

"Grace … Grace … come back. It's another magic thing. You can look away—"

Grace muttered much faster than what Declan had heard from himself. That high-pitched whine flowed from her throat like she was trying to breathe around choking.

"Grace!"

He grabbed her shoulder and spun her around. And Declan almost fell over at the sight.

Grace's face was caught in a scream. Her jaw pulled down hard, even as those sounds still left her throat. Her eyes were focused on something he couldn't see, but Declan knew what it was.

Her eyes widened—her head tilted back slightly.

"It's all…" Grace wheezed. "It's all."

Declan grabbed her shoulders, looking at her, panic flaring faster and faster in his chest.

"Fuck," Declan swore. "Grace—Grace, no, no, no!"

At the corner of Grace's eyes, something welled up. It seemed at first to be tears, but then the first one dripped down her cheeks. It wasn't blood. Too many hues to be blood. It could be ink, could be slime. It was red, blue, and cyan, and it was building up in force, trickling now.

"Grace! Grace, please! I need you to come back here. I … I don't want … want to be alone, either. Please, don't…"

Grace's voice sounded like she was reading aloud from a college essay she wasn't excited about doing.

"But it's all going to burn. We aren't stopping it, and it's all going to burn, Declan. The whole world. The plants are going to die. No more bees or butterflies. The air choking us over and over, even when we're inside. People are going to starve, you know. They're going to hurt each other for food—for their kid's food. So much of what we build is going to end up underwater. We knew for so long that it would happen … and we didn't do anything that mattered enough. We waited too long."

Declan blinked. "I don't understand what you're…"

But he *was* starting to understand. Her words were hopeless. Her words echoed so many others crying out in existential terror. The words of videos and articles and scientists and activists, talking about the damage, about what had been done in the name of profit…

"Are… are you talking about the *environment*?"

"We cannot imagine the magnitude of a loss like this, Declan. We aren't equipped for it. Poverty is going to hit everywhere, and then the resources are going to become scarcer and scarcer. The people like us, the people without resources, we're going to burn for it—"

The slime tears sped up more; they ran streams down her cheeks.

"I used to think about what I wanted out of life. But I'm never going to find a girl who loves me for me, Declan. I'm never going to meet someone who… and my family is never going to…"

The slime was pouring out faster and faster, sliding down her cheeks with such force. It smelled like burned sugar and vinegar. And her voice was reaching this crackle, this horrible snap.

And if it did, Declan didn't know what would happen, but he was sure he *would* be alone.

Grace's shoulders arched, her back straightened—

Declan wrapped her in a hug. Probably wouldn't help. Probably was the wrong thing to do, but it was all he had.

"It's not all over yet, Grace. We haven't lost yet."

An energy, a horrible pulse, pushed off her body. She tried to stop him from holding on, but he kept being there.

Declan wasn't good at words of comfort.

He wasn't good at comforting.

But at this moment, he had a voice in his chest—a voice of simple words, but good, true words—and if that was all he had, he would give them all to her.

"There's still time for all that, Grace. For love and good things and people. You can have a life. You-you can. We'll … get out of this. Fuck, we *have* to. It should've been better … uh … different. This shouldn't be what happened. It's not what I… I'm so sorry about all of it—I'm so sorry that it all is … fuck, you know. You *know*. I'm sorry. I'm so sorry. But there's still time, Grace. It's still possible to fix some things. Please … be angry at me if nothing else. You're a good friend, and I'll go down swinging with you, okay? Grace… Grace … okay?"

A sniffle from her. Sad. Also, a little like Grace.

"Declan?" she said.

Declan pulled back and looked at her—and despite everything, couldn't help but smile. Grace's eyes stopped leaking; the remaining slime fell off her with little splats.

"Yeah, I'm here."

"…thank you."

Grace's head dipped. She reached up and winced as she rubbed her eyes. When she looked back up, she looked more tired than Declan had ever seen her. Even with her bouts of insomnia. Even when he was sure she'd been up all night. This was worse.

Grace nearly fell over, and Declan moved to catch her. Making sure not to look at the screens, he walked her to the bay windows, and they sat on the ledge.

"What happened?" Declan asked. "I looked away fast enough… but I guess those screens are … dangerous."

"It was fire and the environment … and ice caps … and then … fuck. I could see everything I'd ever wanted. Everything I ever, ever wanted for my future. I had a tabby cat and this little orange kitten, a girlfriend who was also ace, and I was getting my degree. And it was all melting … burning away. Like a painting getting all runny."

Grace touched the corners of her eyes and wiped away a little slime residue. She looked at her finger and winced slightly.

"I think … if I hadn't heard you, Declan, I was about to cry away my soul."

Declan's pulse shot back up for a moment. Had he also been looking too closely—if they had both been affected—there would have been nothing to stop it. They would've both cried until … until whatever happened next.

"I'm … really glad that didn't happen," Declan said.

Grace looked at him and nodded. She ducked her head down, away from any possibility of looking at a screen again and stood. Immediately, she almost fell over, but steadied herself.

"Turns out almost losing your soul is exhausting," she said, letting out a very forced chuckle.

"Just tell me if you need to lean on me," Declan said. "I want out of this fucking room."

"I want out of this fucking house," Grace muttered quietly.

CHAPTER 13

HOLDING HIS ARM UP TO BLOCK MOST OF his view, Declan looked around the office. Looked at the sharp hallway again. The monster-could-be-right-there hallway. He hadn't noticed the door, however. Flush to a wall, opposite wherever that angular hallway went, was a door.

"Come on," Declan said.

He reached out his hand.

Grace's hand was there, holding his instantly. She squeezed, and Declan let out a breath he'd not noticed he'd been holding.

Declan inched forward, leaned barely out into the hallway, ready to bolt.

Thankfully, no monster. But down that angular hallway was a weirder door than the one close to them. It was cream white with an overly large brass handle. It had pastel flower molding, but the flowers were clearly moldy and dying.

"Jesus," he muttered.

"What?"

"There's an old-looking door," he said, "and it's making me really uneasy. But … uh … I don't think this one is a magical thing. I think it's just because I'm worried."

"Can I take a look?" Grace asked.

Declan nodded and stepped to the side. As soon as Grace peered around the corner, her shoulders jolted up—and Declan's pulse skyrocketed again.

"*What*," he whispered. "*Are you okay?*"

Grace turned to look at him. "Just a creepy door."

"Oh. Okay."

"I don't think it's any more dangerous than anything else, but it gives me ghostly vibes. Like there's a skeleton or something behind it."

"That almost sounds easy now," Declan said.

But then he imagined it and realized they could really be attacked by some horror movie monster. There wasn't any reason to believe anything was off the table.

"But let's try the other one," he said.

This door, flush to the wall, was mahogany and glossy with varnish. Normal enough—but the location worried him. Assuming the building was laid out like a normal house—a massive assumption—it had to lead to a sub-level. A basement. The staircase they'd seen before would be on the other side of it—there wouldn't be room for anything but a small cupboard.

And, well, he couldn't imagine how horrible the basement would be in a house like this.

"Okay … maybe not."

"Why?"

"It's probably a basement."

Grace swore. "Oh, yep, that seems like the worst possible idea."

Silently, they turned to go to the weird flower door. After a few moments of feeling increasingly tense, Declan threw it open. It was … a bathroom. Normal enough. Toilet. Sink. A shower. No horror movie skeleton, at least.

And as he stood there, it occurred to him he'd not used the bathroom, washed his hands, or anything of that nature since all this started.

"Do you think it's been long enough that we can trust the water?"

"I don't know…"

"I think I need to. Can you stand on the other side of the door?"

Grace nodded. "Yeah, that's probably a good idea. Me afterward."

"Okay."

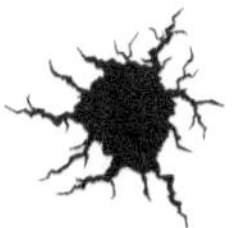

A few minutes later, Declan and Grace stood in front of the probable basement door. Declan's hair was wet from running it under the thankfully working shower. He didn't feel better, but a stream of dirt had come out of his hair. Grace's face was still wet, and any slime residue was gone. They'd filled—and placed apart from the original one in the backpack—the other two refillable bottles with sink water.

"Ready?" he asked.

"Not really," Grace replied.

"Well, here we go."

Declan reached for the door handle, his hand shaking. The handle was smooth and could lead anywhere. How many times already had they faced something like this?

He was about to open the door when a noise came from somewhere in the house.

Grace stifled back a scream, and Declan's entire body jolted. His gaze locked onto the ceiling. It had been above them. It had been old wood creaking. Someone walking around. Declan stood as still as he could.

And there was another and then another. Feet on wood panels. It could be the same thing, one creature, one person. Or it could be multiple—he wasn't sure. It didn't sound aggressive, but he knew where it was headed as it got further away.

They hadn't gone up the staircase in the living room, but something was now going down it. No, there were two pairs of creaks. No, three. Three monsters.

They would be in the living room in a moment. No way back now. And, even if they did go back, all that was outside was a bolt gun for their skulls.

"Shit," Declan said. "Guess we go down."

Grace gave a small noise of agreement.

Declan turned the handle, slowly opening the door. And he was right. It was the door to a basement.

But not any basement in a normal house; not the kind of thing someone would go down to hang out with friends. It was more like the entrance to a dungeon, with darkness that practically oozed up the wooden steps. Only a flickering lightbulb hung overhead; its light was weak and barely able to pierce the gloom. The light was so bad that it was only possible to see a bit of the way down.

A faint breeze came up to meet them, sweeping over Declan and making him shiver.

He moved down to the first step, tensing his muscles. Staring into that inky darkness. If something was going to run up the stairs at them, now was the time. If a smiling face was going to lean out, now was the time.

After a moment of nothing, Declan took another step down.

Whatever else was in the house with them was getting closer. The voices all had deep pitches, didn't quite sound monstrous, but also not human, and they kept speaking over one another, interjecting and teasing. Declan could almost make out some words as it grew a little louder.

"They tried to tell me they had to keep their promises."

"Did they really? Like that would even work."

"Don't they realize how much money they could make if they just listened to us?"

Declan couldn't help but try to imagine, for a second, what things could live in a house like this. Because it was a house with amenities that seemed to actually work. It had a standard layout for a house.

It would be things that enjoyed all that, but also could just look out a window and see a field of corpses— and didn't bother to block that out. Things that had the remains of endangered species dripping black ooze. Who lived around computers that showed one of the most awful possible futures.

What horrible things would live in a house devoted to the end of the known world?

"I think they might try to stick it out."

"That just means they want more cash."

"Well, perhaps we can back an opposition, and they won't have much choice."

Too close. Whatever was talking, they were too close. And they sounded even less human the closer they got. Their voices were almost digitally distorted.

Declan took a few more steps down into that dark.

"Close the door behind us," he whispered.

Grace nodded and stepped down, then gently, so gently that it was almost shocking when it latched shut, she sealed the door behind them. And they stood there in mostly inky blackness.

The voices were muffled but even closer now.

"But what if the objector's vote against it?"

Sweat was pouring down Declan's back. The cold air coming up from below made his teeth chatter.

"What was that thing you were proposing? Wouldn't that leave them too scrambling to vote against it?"

Grace put her hand over her mouth and seemed to stop breathing.

"I like the idea—make 'em suffer."

"Let me get my phone."

The other voices let out a cheer that sounded unlike any human sound Declan had ever heard and like an entire stadium of people all calling out in victory.

It sounded so close it made his shoulders tense up. But then the chatter went silent, which was arguably worse.

Were they on the other side of the door, whatever they were? Declan turned and stared at the space underneath the door, wondering if they cast a shadow.

But nothing happened for a few long, horrible, heart-pounding moments.

And then they heard more talking, but blissfully, it was further away. Drifting away. Declan could hear the distinct sound of a fridge being opened; he barely held back a sob of relief.

"O-okay," Declan said as quietly as possible, "let's get as far away from the door as possible."

Grace nodded in agreement. Her face was pale. Her eyes were wide.

CHAPTER 14

THE PATH WAS DOWN. ONE STEP. ANOTHER. Each step was slow. Each time Declan flinched as he put his whole weight on the next normal-looking step. The anxious idea that the monsters hadn't bothered to come down because they knew they were already dead kept hitting him.

He'd started off bracing his arm against the wall but quickly learned to keep them by his side. The walls *looked* like a normal, coarse material, but they were much sharper. The walls were also vaguely wet.

The air was like standing by an indoor pool. Only it smelled much worse than chlorine. It reminded Declan of when some forgotten salad mix went bad in the back of his dad's fridge.

And, as they got farther down, there was a liquid.

The steps ended abruptly with a small platform and a pool of something dark and sloshing. It moved like an ocean's tide, going away, then returning. This close, the smell was even worse.

"What is this…?" Grace muttered.

Declan kneeled down and debated dipping something in it, like a ripped-off part of his shirt sleeve—maybe see if it was something they could swim in or across. But he paused after a moment. He wasn't willing to press his luck.

"Okay—this seems like a bad idea," Grace said.

Declan turned around, and she was looking at a spot on the wall. He couldn't quite tell what it was in the gloom and the shadows.

"What? What is it?"

Grace didn't so much whisper as gently breathe out her words.

"A switch. Think I should hit it?"

Declan looked around at the strange pool. It felt like the intersection between an indoor pool and some over-flowed basement. He looked up at the low ceiling. In various spots, he could barely see little bumps. Maybe they were lights in some plastic or glass casing.

"I guess so."

A click—and for a moment, nothing happened. Then a soft orange light came across each pod, stretching back and back until it met a white, painted wall—with a single half-submerged door in the center. And between them and it was a small lake's worth of water.

With the light on, Declan could see how disgusting the water was. It wasn't just oil or muck. In some places, the fetid water *had* oil. Dull yellow and purple oil slick. But it was more just *filthy* water, so thick with various things that it was impossible to see down to the bottom.

The tide moved the water closer, splashing the platform's edge. When it slunk back, it left a condom wrapper and the remains of a burger wrapper.

Declan squirmed. "Okay, yeah, what is *this* place? This … is pollution … or something."

"I don't know, but someone else has been here," Grace said quietly.

Declan looked where she was pointing. Floating off to the side of the platform was, basically, a raft. A very barebones raft, but the pile of wood floated well enough. It even had a pair of roughly carved oars on top.

"That's … huh," Declan said.

"Do you think the door over there leads to a hideout?"

"What do you mean?"

"Well, why else would this be here? Who would need to go back and forth between that door and here?"

"You think people?" Declan said. "Or … other things?"

Grace frowned, then shrugged. "If I'm really thinking about it, everything upstairs was nice, clean, and expensive. I don't know if they … would use something like this."

Declan glanced up the staircase, then at the door. Then sharply back down. Even remembering those voices sent shivers up his spine.

"Guess there's only one way to find out."

Grace made a small, disgusted noise as she did it, but she stuck out her foot and dragged the raft closer. It glided across the water without an issue, the horrible gunk splashing at the sides of it. The oars barely moved on top, but Grace still carefully pulled it.

Once he could grab it, Declan pulled the oars off. They were rather heavy and almost made him buckle forward into the water. Holding them, he thought they might be repurposed table legs.

"Think the raft can take two of us at a time?" Grace asked.

"I hope so," Declan said. "I don't want one of us to go alone."

"Yeah, same." Grace pressed down slightly on the raft with an outstretched toe. It didn't rock much. The water sloshed up a little, briefly revealing a rusted soda can.

She tugged it closer and held it there with her foot. Declan dropped to his knees and put his hand on it. He wasn't sure how easily he'd get his weight on it without tipping.

"Try to hold it there," Declan said.

Grace muttered a sound of agreement.

It was a desperate shuffle forward. Fear pulsed in his chest. But Declan got his hands and knees onto it in one shaky scramble. The raft rocking immediately made him feel nauseous—at least he was having an easier time ignoring the smell.

Grace miraculously got onto the raft with little incident. It wobbled hard once, and she screamed, but the door above didn't fly open in the resulting silence. No monsters found them. They didn't fall off into that horrible water.

Then Declan and Grace shifted as a team, slowly moving their weight until they sat on opposite ends. Declan faced the stairs; Grace looked at where they were going. The raft was remarkably sturdy—it could easily hold more people. They both let out sighs of relief at roughly the same time.

Declan handed Grace an oar.

"Okay, ready?" Declan asked.

"...sure.

"No, but are you? Are you okay enough? No emotion-warped magic? Nothing with what was happening upstairs?"

Grace gave a small smile. "No, that's okay for now—I don't feel the same, but I'm okay enough to do this."

Declan nodded. "Okay. Teammates, right?"

"Right."

The room's acoustics were strange now that they were over the water. As soon as they stopped talking, it ate the sound of them. The faint splash, hiss, splash pattern of the water hitting the walls then dropping back was rhythmic, dominating, allowing no contest. It was a breathing pattern, like the inside of a lung. Declan couldn't help but match his own breathing to the pulse.

It almost felt like he was breaking some spell, some stalemate, when he put one oar underwater. The soft splash was too loud. Detritus swirled around the oar. Vague shadows that might've been a sock, a small lantern, or a pill bottle moved in its wake.

Declan wondered how deep the pool went.

"I'll keep count," Grace said, adjusting her oar. "It's been a long time, but we did a little kayaking when I was a kid."

"Okay," Declan said.

"Okay…" Grace let out a breath, her arms tensing. "One."

Declan moved the oar through the water, feeling the resistance. He'd never done this before, but he had to imagine it was thicker than clean water. Harder to move through it.

"Two," Grace said.

He pushed again, slightly slower than she did. They almost went off course, but he kept them from drifting.

"Three."

Another push: about a foot of distance traveled.

Declan's arms were already exhausted. They started to spasm a little. He gritted his teeth and tried not to think about it.

"Four."

This time, they had enough momentum to go a little farther. The door was still so far away.

Grace looped them through the count twice, gradually pushing them across the lake. Declan would breathe hard, then try to match that breathing rhythm again.

Grace moved out her oar when they were closer to the wall, stopping their forward momentum. It sent a solid wobble through the raft, and for a split second, Declan almost thought he would fall off. He quickly leaned forward into his stomach, adjusting his weight on the raft. It took a second, but they steadied again.

The door sat in front of them now, mostly ordinary except for long stain lines where the water had splashed high and then slowly went down again. It was a gray stain, almost like how strong tea could mar the edge of a saucer. Except the wood was also slightly rotting, caving into itself.

Declan's stomach roiled with hot acid.

"I'm feeling some really strong disgust," he said. "I think that's normal, considering where we are, but the feeling is really strong."

"Yeah, I am too. This is worse than a grease trap."

Declan nodded. "You don't feel like doing anything except what we said we would do?"

"You should ask me specifically what that is."

"You're right. Do you intend to open this door to find out what is beyond it?"

"Yep. I think we're okay. This is all sorts of fucked up and weird, and I don't understand how any of this is happening—and I'm kind of fucking freaking out about it—but I want to get through that door. That is what we agreed to do, yes?"

"Yes. And okay. Same. And *same*. Here we go."

The handle was only slightly sticky with who knows what; Declan managed to not let go of it in disgust. The knob spun like it had been perfectly cared for—greased and repaired, despite the horrible environment.

Opening it was another matter.

For a moment, Declan wasn't even sure the door *could* move. He pulled so hard his finger joints ached. When it still didn't budge, he gritted his teeth, leaned his whole body backward, and tugged so hard it felt like his arm would pop out of its socket. The sudden jerk of the door opening barely, slightly, a minuscule bit, made him almost cry out. Fluid rushed in to fill the gap between the door and its jamb, making a mini whirlpool for a few seconds. A battery and a piece of very rotten gum were visible momentarily before submerging again.

Declan immediately gave it another tug, which was a little easier. But he was already breathing hard. His arms were already sore from rowing.

It had barely opened a foot.

"Can you … tag in?" Declan asked, leaning away from it.

"Yep, spinning it around."

"Okay."

Grace used the oar to turn the raft to get closer to it, then stared at the handle for a few moments. She wrapped her fingers around the knob one at a time, her arms already flexing from anticipation.

"Three, two, one," she said to herself, then pulled.

Instead of one long yank, she did it in little pulses. It pushed the water around as she did. Making it slosh. She opened it about halfway before letting her arms drop to her sides.

"Wow, that sucked," she said.

Even with the door only partially opened, they could see into whatever was beyond. It was mostly dark, with fewer orange lights, but something flickered. Not an electric light, either. Something more organic.

Declan could swear he heard a crackle. But now he was on the wrong end of the raft to investigate.

"Can you see anything?" he asked.

Grace leaned as far as she could. The water was still choppy. It kept almost splashing high enough to touch her.

"Uh, it looks like a little campsite … *holy shit…*"

"*What?*"

"People," she said. "There's people over there."

Chapter 15

DECLAN LAID HIS BODY ACROSS THE RAFT to keep balance and grabbed the side of the door. Grace moved to take the handle again.

She looked at him expectantly.

Declan took a second to breathe, pushing past all the soreness. The adrenaline was slowly trickling back in. The willpower rising. One more time! *One more time.* Then they might get some help.

Grace pulled with him. The water made a bigger wave as they got it further open. A collection of plastic forks and knives swam like tiny fish, darting up and flashing against the murky water.

Declan let out an involuntary grunt as they gave one last pull. It was almost like the door had finally given up. In one final surge of water, it opened far enough that the raft could feasibly be angled through.

Silently, but better coordinated than before, they adjusted on the raft and angled it dead center. With a hard push, they floated through the opening. It was a tight fit, only barely going through.

On the other side was a coastline of sorts. Between a further white wall and the water was a raised area of worn, but somehow not rotting, wooden floorboards. It and the wall stretched for miles in both directions, so far out that it was impossible to see the end.

But Declan barely registered that as he stared at the people—and they stared right back. Declan couldn't help it, his mouth hung open.

There were four people huddled around a small fire. They'd torn up wood from the coastline, exposing more water below, and arranged the planks to make a firepit. At the center of the firepit, they were burning paper. The wood, for some reason, wasn't catching fire.

One person stood up from the fire and gestured to them. He was on the taller side, bigger too, and had dark brown skin. He was wearing some tee shirt for a pop culture thing Declan didn't recognize. It was primarily red once, but the pulpy logo was faded between sweat stains and dried muck.

After glancing at each other, Declan and Grace started slowly rowing closer. The distance was only three long strokes. They reached the wooden shore and gently bumped into it.

A woman got up from the fire and stood next to the bigger guy. She had a pinkish complexion, and her hair was thin, wispy, and matted to her scalp in certain areas— with gray streaks drying them in place. What looked like a rash covered her wrist to her elbow.

Grace disembarked first. The raft scraped a little on the coast as she did, and Declan clenched his teeth, hoping it wouldn't shoot back off into the water. It slid a little but was still stabilized enough that Declan could scramble off after her.

As soon as Declan stood, the woman walked around him and grabbed the raft. She tugged it onto the wooden shore.

Declan hadn't realized how tired his feet had also gotten. The planks of wood were slick, almost glossy, and he almost couldn't get his footing stable. His whole body felt both too tense and far, far too loose.

The man gestured toward the fire, standing next to the woman. She gave them a quizzical look.

Grace and Declan glanced at each other, then Grace walked over to the two standing. Declan went for the fire. They were only a few feet apart if something went wrong—a worthwhile risk.

The fire didn't smell great, but nothing did, and the warmth was nice in this weird, cold place underneath the horrible house.

As he approached, Declan looked over the two who hadn't gotten up. They weren't doing too well.

One was violently shivering despite the fire. He was middle-aged and quite thin. When he looked up at Declan, his eyes were desperate and tired. Bags deeper than Declan had ever seen stretched down his pale white skin, and sweat beaded on his forehead. Rather than say anything, he coughed lightly into his clutched hand. His hand came away with flecks of yellow and green phlegm. He quickly wiped it on his filthy pant leg.

The other person, a young woman, moved to help him, wrapping a ragged beach towel closer around his shoulders. She glanced up at Declan, and he was shocked by how blue her eyes were.

But they weren't actually all that blue. The contrast made them seem that way. It had been a long time since Declan had seen pink eye, but this was a *very* bad case of it. It was like a blue marble in a sea of agitated veins. The tanned white skin around it had signs of fever, and she kept using her free hand to brush away messy brown curls that hadn't seen a comb in a long time.

"He's sick," she whispered to Declan. "I wouldn't get too close."

Declan stepped back.

"What's wrong?" he asked. "What happened?"

But it was *obvious* what was wrong. This wasn't an environment fit for people. Down here in this polluted soup, any number of things could make him sick. Any number of bacteria could be in that water, in the air. There was enough garbage and rot around to feed every fungus, bacteria, and parasite Declan could imagine.

The girl didn't answer him, only looking off to the side.

The man coughed harder, leaving a faint trace of blood he had to wipe off his hand, and then he looked up at Declan.

"Got thirsty" was all he said.

Declan recoiled. He felt sick. The worst nausea he'd ever experienced sprung up on him.

"Oh … ah … *oh* … that's *horrible*."

"It was before we ran into Chuck and Cassandra," the girl muttered. "We were trapped at the staircase for a long time, with nowhere to go."

The man's voice cracked. "Got desperate."

Declan held his hand over his mouth, then his nose. He stopped breathing for a moment—knowing he would puke if he let the smell in. If he let that *thought* in.

After a second, he lowered his hand.

"Well, um … I guess I'll introduce myself. My name's Declan."

"Peter," the man replied.

"Aoife," the girl said. "It's Irish."

Declan nodded. He glanced back over at Grace. She was talking to the two others animatedly, all of them going back and forth in a hushed whisper. So far, no one had attacked—so it wasn't *likely* some trap.

"Mind if I sit?" Declan asked, pointing at the other side of the little fire.

"I told you. It really wouldn't be the best idea. We could get you sick," Aoife said.

"Yeah, I'm not sure that's going to matter," Declan said. "I drank water from the tap up above—and I've been down here for what feels like an hour. Whatever there is to catch, I've got it."

Aoife gave him a smile that felt instantly fake.

"I suppose it's fine, then."

Declan returned his own fake smile and sat down around the awful-smelling fire. A silence quickly rushed in, backed by awkwardness. Declan couldn't think of something else to say. The exhaustion settled in as he looked back and forth from the flames to Grace. How long of a nightmare had this newest one been? Two days so far? Declan wondered if it was safe to sleep here.

It didn't feel like it yet. He didn't feel like he should relax even with his arms burning from rowing, his legs sore from all the running, and everything tired from panicking.

"How long have you been here?" he asked bluntly.

Peter said nothing at first. He shivered. Tucked the beach towel over himself tighter.

"Too long," he eventually said.

Aoife gave a small groan. "Yeah, it was a long time ago now. We left right when the hotel thing happened. It seemed like the last straw."

Declan nodded. A lot of people had, he remembered. Each supernatural event sent a large portion out into the woods, unwilling to risk staying.

God, if only they knew where they had been going.

"It's been weeks since then," he said.

"Yeah," Aoife said. "Feels like it."

Declan leaned a little forward. "So, what *is* this place? Do you know?"

Aoife didn't answer. Instead, she took a small sliver of wood and poked at the paper like a fine mesquite log, lifting the charred mass up in one place, then letting it fall.

"It's … not like a normal place," he pressed. "I mean, obviously, it's not, but it kept messing with our heads. There were these screens that if you looked at them too long… did you run into them too?"

Aoife sucked in her lower lip and glanced at him. The anger in her eyes caught Declan off guard for a moment.

"You know, with more people," she said, "we'll have even less food around here."

"I'm … sorry…"

"Yeah … well, it's been fucking hard enough as it is."

"But we've managed so far," Peter chimed in. But whatever cheeriness he had intended in that statement faded almost instantly, and a rattle crept into his voice. "That's something, at least. Something to be hopeful about."

Declan stopped to think for a moment. "Are we the only survivors here…?"

"The others are dead," Aoife said flatly.

Peter shivered again and tucked his legs up as close as he could.

"But, yeah, we had people here," Aoife said. "They got in the house and made it all the way through. We were together for a bit. Then they fucking died."

"Don't swear, Aoife. I promised her you wouldn't … get your dad's foul language."

Aoife glanced at him, and her voice went quieter, gentler. "Sorry, Peter."

"I forgive you."

Aoife gave him a nod—and then that warmth was gone again when she looked over at Declan.

"Can you please stop asking questions?" she said.

"I'm-m sorry…? I just don't understand what's going on."

"Yeah, well, asking questions, being curious, doesn't help much here, okay? It gets you *dead*."

Aoife huffed and stood up. She shook her head. She quietly muttered something. Then wandered a little way down the coast.

Declan sat there, stunned.

"Sorry about that," Peter said. "She's a nice person, I promise. I've known that girl all her life; she's too nice for all of this. Too nice for everything that happened to her, even before this…"

"This hell?" Declan offered.

"Wouldn't be surprised if that was similar, yeah," Peter said. "It would probably have a better fire, though."

"…do you know what this place is?

"I can't help you there." Peter glanced over at the other three, then nodded. "Chuck and Cassandra are the ones to talk to."

Declan turned to look, and Grace, Chuck, and Cassandra walked over to the fire. Chuck picked up the stick as he sat down and poked it as Aoife had. Cassandra sat next to him without a word.

Declan shifted so Grace could sit next to him more easily.

Declan looked at Grace, and how well he could read her face surprised him. She had this look in her eyes, like she wasn't pleased with what she'd discussed with them.

But before he could somehow silently communicate with her, Cassandra cleared her throat.

"I hear you have some food."

Declan's gaze snapped to her. He pulled his backpack around and held it tight to his body. He scooted back.

"*We* have food, yes."

"It's okay," Grace said. "We should trust them."

Declan glanced at her and raised an eyebrow. She nodded.

Declan let out a slow sigh, waiting for his pulse to lower. Then he set the backpack down and unzipped it.

"Okay, yeah. Yes. We have some food. It's not very much. Some water, some vegan protein bars. I didn't expect to … you know…"

"Fall into a metaphysical reality based on the general understanding of climate change?" Chuck rattled off. "Yeah, welcome to the thick of it. Cassie and I have been here for a *long* time now. We actually need that water much more than your food. Can you maybe give some of that to Peter here?"

Declan tensed. His conscience told him he should help, but the part of him getting more and more used to being afraid, more used to expecting death, wanted to refuse. If he didn't have water, he might be forced to drink…

But when Peter coughed again, that ragged, horrible cough that signaled something was probably wrong in his lungs, Declan knew he didn't have a choice. Shame burned him for not thinking of helping earlier.

He dug out the safe water bottle and handed it over to Peter.

When Peter tried to take it, he almost dropped it instantly; his hands shook from even the effort of holding it up.

Aoife hadn't gone far, and she returned quickly. Dropping and kneeling to help him. Peter took slow sips from the bottle, a blissful look on his face.

Declan watched for a moment, feeling more and more thirsty.

He looked away. It was best he didn't think about it. He turned to look at Chuck.

"Okay, so I hear you understand what this is? Metaphysical, you said?"

"I think I understand, yeah," Chuck replied. "I've been here long enough."

"They only know about the hotel because of Aoife," Grace chimed in. "They've been here since Murder Sky."

Chuck frowned. "Still not used to that name. But, yeah, we were running from … something in the sky … and it took … Patrick … and then went into the forest. And, well, you know what's it like out there. Barely made it away from the slaughterhouse monster."

"Almost caved in my head," Cassie added.

"Almost cut me in half. But since then, we've been stealing from the fridge when we can. Taking little bits of food when it appears in the cabinets and surviving as best we can."

That made Declan think of a thousand questions. But one was way, way more important than anything else. He had to imagine Grace would've asked already—but even if so, he would ask again.

"But did you figure a way out?"

The silence was palpable. It rippled through the group.

"Well," Chuck started, then clicked his tongue. "Well, maybe."

Cassandra's voice went low and soft. "We've been trying to get another plan going—but it hasn't really had a lot of opportunities. We've been stuck."

Chuck ran his hands through his hair, and it stuck slightly from collected sweat. "The odds are a little better now. We didn't have the platform, the raft, for a while, so we couldn't even cross the water. We've been stuck on the shore for ten days, give or take? It's difficult to keep track around here. But we're nearly running out of everything we'd stockpiled."

Grace let out a sad sigh. "So, someone went across and didn't make it back?"

The silence flowed back in again. A blanketing quiet made Declan's pulse ratchet up again. Those looks on their faces—he *knew* those looks. Standing in a funeral hall for someone you knew. Trying to remember a voice you won't hear again. Finality. Awkwardness. He recognized that look all too fucking well.

Grief knows grief like an old friend.

"What happened to them?" Declan asked, filling that silence.

"We don't know," Cassandra said. "Well we don't know specifically how they died."

"They went to get water from one of the sinks," Chuck said. "Evelyn and Ike took one of our only refillable bottles with them. And then they never came back. We assume The Baron got them—or one of the others."

"'The Baron?'" Declan asked. "Was that … who we heard talking?"

"Probably one of them," Chuck said. "There are three monsters that live in this house. We … try to avoid them."

Peter let out a rattling cough again, but it sounded a little better. Aoife helped him take a few more sips.

Declan had even more questions about that—but they still hadn't told him the answer to the one that mattered.

"Okay, so what's your escape plan?"

"Well, we learned some stuff from the last try, enough that we might have a new option," Chuck said. He glanced at Cassandra. "Do you want to tell them? It's your story."

Cassandra stared into the fire, some memory taking her away. The firelight seemed to mold the shape of her jaw. Starvation was obvious then, in her cheekbones, in her jaw.

She didn't look up from the fire, but she started talking. The rhythm of her words had an almost tempo to it.

"We tried to sneak out. We made a ruckus to draw them away, but it didn't work long enough. I don't understand how monsters like that could sneak up on us, but one of them did. Then we got separated for a little while. I ran into one of the other two. The monster boxed me in. He was going to … well, I grabbed a chair and threw it at him. It broke against his…"

She shivered.

"His, uh, body … and the chair fell apart. He kept moving at me. I got the leg of the chair and stabbed him in one of his thighs…"

For a second, Cassandra stopped, losing her momentum, her pace. She took a steady, calming breath.

"You want to stop?" Chuck asked. "It's okay."

"No, I got it. I got it." Cassandra winced and shook her head. "So, he bled, okay. That's what's important. He bled stuff that seemed like actual blood. The monster let out this sound and started yelling at me, talking like he does. Then I stabbed him again. And again. And then I got away."

Cassandra's jaw quivered, and she sucked in another breath.

"I got *away*."

She said nothing more. She was crying a little.

Chuck waited a moment, then picked back up the conversation. "So, that's when we learned the pieces of this place can hurt the monsters. Maybe any weapon can, but we don't really have weapons."

"I stopped the … abattoir monster," Grace added. "For a little while, actually. I stuck a piece of one of the trees into it, and it really didn't like it."

"That's good news," Chuck said. "We think that's why the raft works too. It really shouldn't. It shouldn't be so easy to balance it, either. Even in normal circumstances, it should've broken down ages ago—and here, well, the water's … not better for any material."

"It burns like hell," Peter muttered. "The worst thing to ever go down your throat."

Grace winced. And Declan looked over at her. She looked haggard. They all looked haggard, but she was his fault. Still his fault.

"We lost someone in that escape attempt," Chuck continued. "We got pushed back down here. The monsters don't cross the water, so it was the only option."

"How many have died, exactly?" Grace asked.

Declan didn't want to know. Didn't want to hear the answer. But Chuck shifted and cleared his throat. His voice was rough and tired.

"I lost my best friend during Murder Sky…"

He trailed off, letting out a long breath.

Cassandra nudged him with her shoulder. "Are *you* okay?"

"Yeah, I'm okay, Cassie. Well, as much as I can be. Anyway. One thing at a time … one thing at a time. So, since we've been here … well, they weren't all with our group, but I've seen seven people die personally, one way or another. We lost Zoey during our escape attempt. And then we lost Ike and Evelyn recently. It's a lot."

Declan glanced around at all of them. Six people with minimal food and water, and only a bad fire to keep them warm. The air could be actively toxic. They could be taking in fumes right now.

"So … we'll need to *fight* our way out, then?"

CHAPTER 16

"We can't," Aoife interjected. "*He* can't."

"I think we might not have a choice," Peter said quietly, tiredly. "If we stay here…"

Those words sounded wrong.

A ping—an electric thought, racing up Declan's spine. Like the phrase unlocked something. It wasn't a pleasant feeling. It wasn't a pleasant thought.

"That's been this whole place," Declan said, a little louder than he intended. "This whole time. We don't have *choices*."

Chuck turned his attention away from Aoife and cocked his head. "What do you mean by that?"

"Oh no, not this," Aoife said. "Can we not talk about this? Or any of this right now? Can we not speculate on the nature of our fu—freaking doom?"

"I'm sorry, Aoife, but I think this is important," Chuck said. "Your name's Declan, right? Declan, what do you mean by that? What *exactly* do you mean by that?"

Declan almost didn't know how to explain it. But, as he looked in his mind for the right words, he found it had a shape, form, and rhythm. Like everything else in this horrible place, they had a fluid logic—a symbolic shape.

"There kept being only one thing to do," Declan explained, thinking hard as he did. "Grace and I just kept having to make only one choice. The forest was a hallway. The house is basically a hallway. Even going down the stairs was mandatory. How often, Grace, did we say we had no choice in just the last two hours?"

Grace talked quietly, mostly to herself. "A path we can *only* choose—something outside us … forces outside of us … *oh god*—"

Her hands went up to her face, feeling at her tear ducts. Running her fingers down her cheeks. She pulled them away, blinking a few times. Staring at the pads of her fingers.

"Are you okay?" Declan asked.

"It was … I could remember some of what I saw when I looked at the screens."

Cassandra fixed her with a hard stare. Chuck quirked up an eyebrow and leaned slightly forward.

"Oh, you looked at them for too long, didn't you."

It wasn't a question.

"Yeah," Grace said. "It wasn't like I could exactly see what they were—it wasn't like reading a book or something. But I know what it told me. Climate change. Environmental disaster. Ecological damage and how it will affect *everything* else. Take away everything else. It showed me the future, or lack thereof … if it's allowed to … continue."

She looked over at Declan and frowned.

Declan kept trying to form the right words. "Are we talking about philosophy or environmental science here?"

"Both, I guess." Grace ground her teeth in thought. "You know, all of that stuff upstairs? The penguins, the bears, all of that? How it had emotions attached? How we couldn't trust ourselves? All of those feelings were hopelessness, one way or another. The feeling that nothing can get better under all of this. That it will only pour on more and more, limiting us. Taking away our choices, dreams, regardless of what we want—of what we did… it's the end…"

Grace's eyes went wide, and her head dipped slightly. A tiny streak of colored slime leaked down the edges of her eyes. She seemed to stare at something no one else could see.

Then she slapped herself across the face.

She did it so hard that it made Declan's ears ring. A massive red mark bloomed across Grace's cheek. She didn't wince in pain; her shoulders shook, and she gritted her teeth. Then, her whole face relaxed, back to normal, and she took a ragged breath.

"Oh god, it's still in me."

"I've never seen that," Cassandra said. "Never seen someone pull out of a spiral."

"It's not the first time," Grace said, her voice strained. "Declan talked me out of it."

Chuck blinked in surprise. "He *what*? That worked?"

"I told her that there might be hope, I guess," Declan said. "It was all I could think to do."

"It was hard to hear him at first," Grace said. "But it got through to me, somehow."

Declan leaned a little closer to her. "Do you need … I don't know. Can I help you?"

"No," Grace said. "I just … let's just keep talking through this. I don't know if it matters if any of us are okay or not anymore."

Declan looked at her for another moment, seeing how much of what she was saying was just putting on a brave face. It seemed genuine, but he wasn't sure. After a moment, he tried to relax his shoulders and slow his pulse. He turned back to the others.

"Okay, so, does that add to whatever you've got, Chuck?"

Chuck sat back. "It does, but I don't know if that can help us. It makes sense. It fits with everything else we know. I've seen two people get … emptied out like that, and I don't think anyone tried to *talk* them out of it, but it seems to have to do with hopelessness or nihilism."

Grace cracked her jaw and winced. She talked while rubbing the bottom of her mouth. "So you understand what some of this is?"

"He's got theories, certainly," Aoife said.

"The theory makes sense," Cassandra shot back.

Declan's voice almost sounded excited. If they could figure out what was happening, surely that would help get them out of this place.

"So what is this place?" he asked.

Chuck ran his hands through his hair. "I've been here a while, and I've been making and thinking about many, yes, 'theories,' but they've held up so far."

"I still think it might be aliens," Peter said, "but your idea makes more sense."

"It could still be aliens, somehow," Chuck said. "I don't know the bigger stuff yet. I don't know about the sky or the clay that Aoife described covering the Kraken Hotel, but this field, this house, I think I get it. This place was built with or based on our understandings."

"What?" Declan asked, even as his mind worked on the implications of that statement.

"Whatever all of this is, it's themed on stuff. It feels too precise to not be based on what we think about topics. Climate change, environmental disaster, and pollution are complicated and scientific and have many more subtleties in their real-world manifestations, but this place is metaphorical *and* real. It's all the worst of it—the nightmares and worries and anxious thoughts. When I think of pollution, I think of disgusting water. I *think* of random garbage. And that's what's down here."

Declan was sure he'd given that speech before. And, for a moment, he didn't want to believe it. It sounded a little too complex, a little too philosophical—

—but he couldn't argue with what he had seen—

—what had happened.

Was it really so strange to imagine that one Earth-ruining thing could beget another?

"So, it's all symbolic?" he asked.

"Symbolic, but can kill us," Cassandra remarked.

Chuck nodded. "That's what I got; that's my understanding. It sounds weird even to say it. But look around us. This used to be a forest around a tiny Illinois town. I've been through here looking for cicadas when I was younger. Me and my cousin played here. And now it's made of things that feel like what would flash on a screen for a montage if you were trying to get across the horrors of human-based climate change."

"What about all the … bodies?" Grace asked. "Why are they being hung up like that?"

Declan's pulse rose as he remembered. "I can explain that one."

"You can?" Chuck asked.

"Yeah … I can. So, I'm a vegan…"

"Okay?" Chuck said.

"Now's a weird time to say that," Cassandra said.

Declan shook his head gently and pushed on. "I'm a vegan *because* of what I saw. I was online, looking at random funny animal videos when I was younger, and I came across … or I got curious and searched for, maybe … I don't recall—but I found out what a slaughterhouse is *like*. What they do to the animals that we eat."

Declan had to take a breath; it was almost *too* easy to bring those memories back. It was almost too easy to imagine what it must have smelled like, what it must have *sounded* like.

"And I couldn't … no animals … *never*. And then, even after making that decision, I found out what it is doing to the planet. The meat industry is adding so much to climate change, it's nauseating."

"Oh, god…" Grace said, putting her hand over her mouth. "So … the people were hung up like…?"

"Like cattle," Declan said.

"Dead people strung up like dead cattle, bleeding, in a field of scorched ground," Chuck said. "Fitting."

"Fuck…" Declan said.

Grace let out a shuddering breath. "That makes too much sense. I could see … the damage that it's all going to cause. What is going to happen in the next few decades."

"Is that why the boards work, you think?" Declan asked. "Why it hurt the monster? Because it's something *they* made?"

"That's as good a reason as any," Chuck replied.

"But it doesn't tell us if we can *escape* once we do something," Aoife interjected. "All we know is that the monsters in the house can be hurt. We don't even know if it can actually kill them!"

Chuck pursed his lips, but the glimmer in his eyes that had appeared while he told his theory hadn't gone away. He looked up for a second, pondering.

Declan looked away at the fire, trying to think. It was a lot to process. And he almost didn't want to go too many steps through the metaphysics of it. That made his head hurt.

"We could at least get the entire house," Chuck eventually said. "The slaughterhouse monster, presumably, wouldn't be able to get in. If we can kill the three monsters, we have food and water. And we *need* that."

Aoife made a noise in the back of her throat, maybe anger or disgust, but it was interrupted by a strong cough. When she cleared her throat, she glared.

"Chuck, you've been a good leader, but that'll get us killed," she said.

"So will staying here, in this place," Peter said quietly.

Aoife looked over at him, frustrated. "Dad—I mean, Pete, we aren't ready or even physically up for something like that. We'll be slaughtered."

"We have so many people now, Aoife. That could be enough."

"I... I..." Aoife stopped talking, looking away from everyone else.

"Maybe we can do something about that sickness if we do," Declan offered. "That alone could be worth it."

Aoife looked back at Peter. A shiver passed through her body, and she closed her eyes for a second.

Then she let out a weak sigh.

"I think ... I think we should sleep for now."

"I'd love to," Cassandra muttered. "This day has been exhausting."

"That might be a good idea," Chuck said. "We can talk about the plan after some rest. Declan, Grace, you're obviously free to sleep here. There's no real privacy, but we won't make much noise."

"Aoife snores, actually," Cassandra said, mainly to herself.

Aoife didn't seem to hear that remark. She and Peter quickly walked off a little way toward a collection of beach towels and two backpacks. They didn't look back—and seemed to be quietly talking.

Even *considering* sleeping made the exhaustion come back for Declan. His arms were lead. His body was balanced on the horrible knife edge of being extremely tired but so anxious it was hard to hold on to relaxation. There was a bone-deep thrum and shuddering rumble in him.

"That sounds like a good idea," Declan said. "Grace and I have been on our feet for a long time."

"I could fucking use sleep, yeah," Grace said. "You don't happen to have any sleeping pills, do you?"

Chuck frowned. "No, can't say we do."

"Yeah, that sounds about right."

Grace stood up slowly, then looked down at Declan. Declan reached up. She took his hand, and they both stood. Still alive. Still together.

CHAPTER 17

There wasn't a day or night to the place. Just a fixed light level. The horrible sludge water moved in and out, leaving more trinkets in its wake. A can of soda. Two colored strings, one off-white, one mint green of used dental floss. A straight razor, rusted to hell and back.

It was only as they got about thirty feet away from the fire, away from where the others were resting, that Declan felt comfortable speaking again. Felt like breaking the silence of what they knew, what they had learned, and what it all meant about the fucking state of the universe.

"This is messed up," he whispered. "But I think all of it is right, err, real, anyway. And I think we're going to have to get into a fight with a fucking monster tomorrow."

He paused for a moment and looked over at Grace.

"But what do you think?"

Grace took a long time to answer—so long that he wasn't sure she had heard him. She was staring into space, the skin around her eyes raw and her mouth a thin line.

She made a small sound in the back of her throat, like breaking a seal. Then let out a little whoosh of air.

"I guess so," she said.

"You don't want to?" Declan asked.

"Well, of course, I don't *want to*," she snapped, then blinked a few times. "Sorry—god, I'm so tired."

"I meant … it doesn't matter what I meant. Are you okay to fight?"

Grace looked at the coast and sighed again. It was like she was deflating. Each word she said, her presence, her gravity, all that signaled to the world that she was there, seemed to fold down into smaller and smaller shapes.

"I will be, have to be," she said. "Because you will … and because … ah, right … because we have no *choice*."

A shiver passed through Declan. Then the guilt. Sour and acidic. It was alarming how quickly it patterned itself when he noticed it. It quickly spread into each new thought, like color dye dropped into a glass of water.

"Thank you," he said. "And I'm so sorry. Again, I wish I hadn't gotten you into this."

"I know," she said, and her voice quavered. "I know … I know … I *know*. But … Declan, I can't keep hearing it. I don't know what I would need to say to you for you to forgive yourself. You're forgiven, *alright*? I need to—look, Declan, I *need* to sleep. But I can *never* sleep. I know you get worried. And I love you, Declan. Platonically, I love you. But right now, I can't keep … I can't keep assuring you it's not your fault. I can barely assure *myself* anymore. I watched my dreams *run* away from me."

Declan's jaw went tight. He wasn't sure he'd ever heard that before. A platonic love. A friend saying that to him. It almost brought him to tears. Everyone who'd said they loved him was dead or gone.

And he almost broke down—almost went even more emotional on her. But she'd said what she *didn't* need, and he wasn't so selfish as to force his feelings on her more.

So, he shoved them down.

"Okay. Then … uh, let me … how can I help you sleep? Is there something I can do?"

Grace sat down against the plain wall and more crashed to the ground than sat; she laughed, making the edges of her voice crack.

"I wish you could—but I've been dealing with this insomnia for *so* long, I've burned through everything my insurance offers, and my savings, and a good chunk of my parent's savings before they gave up. Nothing helps. *Nothing … helps.* God, I'm so tired, Declan."

Declan sat beside her—he didn't know what to say or ask. The desire to help burned without an outlet. *He'd* been the one falling apart, so often buried under emotions. *She'd* always been smiling, happy, ready to bring people food, give him a calming word, and be a pleasant presence.

But this person, sitting next to him, was like sitting next to a dying fire with nothing to feed it. And he wondered now how much of that happiness was something she'd had to force herself to do. How much of her kindness and calmness was an effort she either offered or was forced by the world to embody?

How much was a mask she never let slip?

Declan opened his mouth to speak again but *stopped*. The next words mattered, and the next words he wanted to say were the *wrong* words. So, he kept looking.

He wanted to offer her solutions. To throw ideas at her, even if he wasn't sure of them. Dredge up stuff he'd heard on the internet, stuff that he'd observed in people with different sleep issues. Or to ask about yesterday when they'd fallen asleep in the forest and how it compared.

But he stopped himself.

He didn't know her experiences. Didn't know those patterns. He hadn't lived them. Whatever he offered as commentary was more for him than anything. Declan needed to take a different approach.

"When did it start?" he asked.

Grace tilted her head back. And for a moment, anger flashed on her face. Genuine anger. And Declan had no idea where it was being directed. But even if it was at him, he would be there for it.

"College," she said. "I went to this college outside of town with so many loans. It had a simple name—I think it was named after some donor or some historical figure who had a lot of money and wanted there to be a school. And for the first year, it was great. I was studying so many interesting things."

She grabbed her own arm and squeezed hard like she was feeling if she was still real.

Declan sometimes wondered that himself. This place made it all seem like he couldn't be.

"But, well," Grace continued, "I was up all night for a project once. I was so stressed out—I had been putting it off and putting it off. I was dating this girl named Katrina, which made it hard to focus on other stuff."

She squeezed her arm even harder, and something like anger, but more complicated, flashed through her eyes.

"But I did the project on time—I made it. It took an all-nighter and some seriously unadvised energy pills, but I did it. I was so jittery; I nearly tripped and dropped the whole thing twice."

Declan wanted to chuckle at that, but the way she said it was like she was still mad at herself.

And as she kept talking, bitterness crept into her voice, arcing her syllables like she was halfway to spitting out the words.

"I turned it in, didn't nap, didn't sleep great the next day, and… to compensate and keep up, I had this week where I drank so much coffee and took those pills that I had heart palpitations practically hourly. When I finally got myself back into a rhythm that didn't feel like I was dying, I slept seventeen hours and missed two classes. And that was probably the last day I felt energized for a long time. When I got moved out of my dorm and back to my parent's place after a semester, I couldn't fall asleep. It was like the stress had stayed with me. Like I had morphed into something."

She glanced at Declan, and her eyes were getting bloodshot.

"You ever been on a rollercoaster right before it started? The anticipation, and maybe even a little fear?"

Declan didn't like rollercoasters. He'd feared heights most of his life—but he just nodded.

"Well, half the time when I go to sleep—or when I should be tired—I have that feeling flush over me. It's in my blood or something. Sometimes it wakes me up, and I can't imagine sleeping for hours more. But sometimes … like right now, I have it, and I'm so awake, and I'm *so* tired. I'm so fucking tired."

Declan slowly, doubting himself, reached out his hand. Like she had for him. He could do that much.

She stared at it and then took it but didn't squeeze back. It was so weak and uninterested. A thrum of guilt again, new, fresh, surging, painful, flared in Declan's chest.

After a second, Declan pulled his hand back.

"And then what happened?" he asked.

"I had to drop out after that. When I came back, I was missing every other class; teachers were always mad at me. One I think actively hated me, and I hated me too. I was always mad at myself. I'd keep trying something or other, looked stuff up online, and it would help for a little while—yoga, warm milk. I even tried getting massages every day for like a week. Nothing worked long-term. I hated it when my mom insisted I start taking sleeping pills after I dropped a mug of coffee and ruined some papers. But I took them—I took them and hated the side effects. But they work for me—even when it makes my stomach churn and… and other things."

Declan nodded. "That fucking sucks."

She looked at him and had several emotions flash across her face, but she cried at the end. It was like all the places her mind went eventually pushed toward one big drop. Tears poured down her face—human, normal tears.

Grace's face screwed up further in pain.

"It's so … I can't…" she said, choking on her own words. "I *hate* it. Those pills make me depressed; they screw with my mind. I can't focus. I keep forgetting things. It takes all I have not to mess up every tenth order, and the diner's the only place that would even *hire* me. I'm such a fucking burnout—a failure. A *waste*."

Declan didn't know what to say; he looked at her with as much care and empathy on his face as he could manage. Though he didn't actually believe it would help.

Grace gave out a little gasp when she ran out of air. "I'd just love a good night of sleep … before we all die."

"We're not going to die," Declan said quietly.

"You don't know *that* Declan…"

There was another flare of anger in Grace's eyes, in her expression, but it cooled so fast, and her voice came out defeated.

"Okay, fine."

"I mean," Declan said, "I'll do everything I can to protect you. You can just stay by me, and I'll do whatever I can. And we won't be alone. I know I shouldn't, but I trust these people—and they are survivors. They've been here for so long and are still alive."

Grace dipped her head to her chest and let out a small, steadying gasp. She said nothing else, and when Declan tried to muster any more of his own words, it all felt like ash on his tongue.

But selfishly now, he wanted to talk more—to say something. Because she was right to be worried about dying. He certainly was. And he wanted his own comfort.

But he kept it to himself and simply sat. Hoping, in whatever small way, his presence would help.

Grace closed her eyes and sat a little more still, but he couldn't tell if she was actually asleep. He wondered how many nights she'd spent doing something similar.

After a moment of watching her, Declan stared out at the pond. The lights above hit the murkiness in strange ways. For a second, a beer bottle surfaced like a dolphin coming up for air.

He pursed his lips. He understood why whatever made this horrible place had chosen what it did. If the goal was hopelessness, they'd found the representation that fit.

Pollution, garbage, and plastic. Poison for the whole world.

Declan tucked himself into a ball, not wanting to look anymore.

CHAPTER 18

DECLAN WOKE UP TO A HORRIBLE NOISE. A splashing, wet sound. Almost like someone hardcore vomiting into a toilet.

His eyes snapped open, and a soft scream escaped his mouth. Adrenaline splashing away tiredness, he kept looking around for where it was coming from. Only another splash made him look upward.

A section of the ceiling hadn't opened so much like a shaft or a pipe as it had a mouth. The surrounding material, somewhat visually blocked by the rushing down filthy water, was metallic and made of jutting wood planks and long girder-like constructions, but it *moved* like a mouth. It flexed like the inside of a throat. Contracting and shifting like it was spitting up a wad of phlegm or bile. A cat yacking up a hairball with aggressive, shuddering, painful wracks of expulsion.

But what came down were bodies, trash, and buckets of fetid water. Entire forms landed with bellyflop smacks. The bodies were long dead, rotting, and had distinct holes in their heads. They sank down. The water filled their gaping mouths and open wounds.

The opening in the ceiling closed with a soft gulping sound. The spot where it had opened wasn't easy to spot. It blended in well with the nondescript ceiling of that strange place. But now that Declan knew what to look for, he kept spotting them.

The ceiling was a hive of them. So many closed mouths.

A vomitorium for corpses.

Declan started shaking. He looked down at the water. Peter had said something about it burning. It was acidic, caustic, and digestive.

No, not mouths—wrong direction. Wrong way to think of it. Down, not up.

Esophagus.

This was a stomach, a pit for waste, fed by ... above.

Declan didn't want to know how the bodies found their way below.

And when some of the bloated corpses floated back up to the top, the process started. It progressed in the ways all food eventually progressed.

It wasn't fast at first, but Declan had seen science experiments where you melt a coin with acid—and this was the same, but with a meaty smell accompanying it. Fizzing carbonation at every point the liquid touched. The gradual wearing away of an entire body.

Declan couldn't look a second longer. Not when cheekbones poked out of a face. He couldn't stop whimpering.

Grace moved next to him, letting out a yawn. "Declan?"

Declan tried to say something, but the words didn't quite make it out of his mouth.

"Declan? What's happening—what is—"

He lurched forward and pulled her close. She was taller than him, but he did all he could to cover her eyes.

"You don't want to see," he hissed. "Just … *please* don't look. It's not something you want to know."

Grace had been slightly squirming, but she stopped almost immediately. Her breath caught. After a second, he could feel her nod.

"Okay—are we in danger?"

"I don't think so … it's just … horrible."

"Okay."

It took so long, but the sound faded. The carbonation hiss got quieter and quieter until it stopped altogether. In Declan's mind, he pictured dead people's faces sinking into the water, becoming one with the fetid juice.

"It's over," Chuck called out.

Declan pulled his head up and moved to let Grace unfurl.

"What the fuck was that?" he yelled.

"We call them The Drops," Chuck said. "Sorry, I didn't think to warn you—they don't happen that often."

"That was horrific," Declan shot back, unsure of who he could be angry with—but certainly angry. "What the actual fuck."

"This place is *literally* made of anxious nightmares," Cassandra chimed in.

"Yeah, and I think I'd like that to be the last one of these I ever see," Chuck said. "So, let's get ready."

"This is a fu-freaking … *fucking* bad idea," Aoife said, her voice shaking.

"Noted," Cassandra replied.

Aoife's shoulders dropped, and anger flared across her face, but she didn't say anything.

"Do I want to ask what that all was…?" Grace said. Her voice wasn't nearly as ragged as last night—if it could be called night in a place always a little illuminated—but it wasn't full of her nigh-iconic peppiness anymore.

"No, probably not," Declan said. "Just … you *don't* want that water to get on you."

Grace automatically glanced in that direction. Looking at that fetid, rotten pond. "I already didn't."

"Then don't worry about it," Declan said.

He stood, wincing, and looked over at the other four. They all seemed to have gotten better sleep than he had. Chuck and Cassandra moved around with purpose and energy. Aoife had many emotions on her face, but she seemed to be doing fine enough, given everything that happened to her. Even Peter was a little better, having not coughed since Declan got so horribly woken up.

Declan was sore. His back was sore, his legs were tender, and his neck hurt whenever he moved wrong. The wood wasn't made for sleeping on.

"Okay, I guess it's time," Grace mumbled, shifting to stand. She winced and touched her hip. "Wish I'd at least laid down and gotten one good sleep before … yeah."

"I will protect you. I promised," Declan said. "I meant it."

Grace glanced at him, giving a soft smile, but said nothing. The rings around her eyes looked even worse than they had before.

Declan had to fight the impulse to reassure her more.

"Okay, so, how are we doing this?" he asked to the air.

Chuck looked over at him. "So, when I first got here, we figured out how to pull up some of these boards. They're not connected to anything. There are no nails— just gravity and precise measurements, I guess."

Chuck leaned down and ran his fingers along the wooden coast briefly, then his hand stopped. His fingers were clearly straining, but he tugged hard at the boards with mostly his fingernails. It finally popped up. With his other hand, he grabbed the underside of the plank and picked it up. He held it above his head and waved it around for a moment.

"Careful about the holes you make. Ike almost … uh, yeah … he almost fell in one time," Chuck said, his face falling for a moment. He took a deep breath, then continued talking. "We each are going to want at least one big board, and if we can carry others—maybe we can sharpen some of them down to something at least a little like a knife."

"If we can get a sharp enough one, I can whittle," Peter offered. "I used to do it for fun as a kid."

Chuck nodded. "That could work. Otherwise, start tearing up planks. We can also use the oars. I don't know what time it is upstairs, but if it's still daytime, I'd rather do this during it."

Grace went to work straight away, leaning down. Her nails weren't long, but she got a plank up in short order.

Declan watched her do it a second time and then tried for his own board. The wood was slick, and the space between boards was narrow. His fingers were quickly shaking from the strain.

It took four tries, and when he finally got one up— nicking the pad of his finger in the process—it was much lighter than he would've hoped. It felt almost hollow.

He waved it around a little, feeling the air's resistance from such a wide object. It wasn't like a baseball bat or something; it wasn't made to be a weapon.

Declan lowered the plank to his side as his stomach sank.

This was a terrible idea.

He'd wanted to escape, obviously. Wanted Grace to escape, *absolutely*, but now that it was actually underway, he had no idea how this could possibly work. It was *so* dangerous, a deadly idea.

He didn't know what the three monsters upstairs were like, but if they were even close to the thing outside, a few boards would do *nothing*.

As he stood there, his heart in his shoes, it became clear that they all knew the same. Even Chuck had worry in his eyes. Concern. Doubt.

Peter instructed Aoife to snap some planks into sharper edges and had this crestfallen look whenever Aoife wasn't looking. He went to work carving the end of planks into makeshift spears and knives.

Cassandra walked around with her mouth tight and her motions clipped—like autopilot, trying to not think. She quickly picked up boards, moving across the narrow coast and getting some of the best ones.

As Declan made what preparations he could, he did the same: trying to force himself numb to all this. Not feel the pangs of hunger. Not think too hard about the stabbing, hollow feeling in his gut as he passed out the remaining food to the others and refused any for himself. He only took a single sip of water before passing the other bottles around—even if his tongue felt like ash.

Inevitable. Don't think—

—don't think about the outcome.

About death, his, hers, past, upcoming, them all. Screaming.

Try not to, at the very least.

Eventualities, inevitabilities, forgone conclusions.

That really was this place, wasn't it? Barely a metaphor. Climate change. His teacher had mentioned climate issues in passing; the internet had given him a much bigger look. Overfishing. Forest fires. Diseases that couldn't survive before now, but given the heat they needed, could spread further.

He'd gone to his dad crying about it. The memory practically overtook his mind, taking him away from this digestion basement. His dad had gotten this look on his face—this grave look. And he'd told him about it. Looking back, Declan wasn't sure his father had done the best job of presenting the information. It had scared him for months. But what was a father supposed to say to his child? What do you tell anyone when they're that young? Climate change was something bigger than any one person or community. It was bad decisions—greedy decisions—made before, during, and would be made more without Declan's chance to choose. And now the outcome felt set in stone, and hope a naivety afforded to lucky moments.

Be it the hospital burning, digestive juices melting flesh, or solar radiation cooking the streets and cracking the pavement: it all ends in fire.

As these memories assaulted Declan and allowed in almost formless impressions of memories tinged with emotions, Declan saw himself move, but barely felt the action of it. Like he'd stepped back and was piloting a puppet. Sadness sat in the past, and eviscerating fear taunted in the future. And he chose the past to stare at as much as he could.

His legs knew the motions; let them do the walking.

CHAPTER 19

ECLAN ONLY RETURNED TO HIMSELF AS they boarded the raft. As they made their decisions and set up their places. Grace was the best of the rowers on account of being the least starving or thirsty. Declan found himself with her and Cassandra on the first ride across.

And it was silent for the first few paddles, then Grace's head jerked with surprise.

"Uh, wait," Grace said, mid-paddle. "The door."

Declan looked over and blinked in surprise. He'd mostly forgotten about the door between the two underground sections. It had been probably the least weird of the weird things to occur in the last while.

But now it was closed.

Panic edged into Grace's voice. "But we opened it before."

Declan's pulse rose, his thoughts spiraling.

"It's fine. It closes every day," Cassandra said quickly. "It's a little like a valve."

Grace sighed. "Oh … of course it does."

"But what *causes* it?" Declan said.

"I don't know," Cassandra said. "Magic or something? I stopped asking questions about this place a long, long time ago. Chuck's the comic book nerd. I let him think about that stuff."

"No, I understand it's … magic. But is there maybe something underneath the water that moves it? Are we sure it moves on its own, and not with … help?" Declan asked. There were probably hundreds of skeletal corpses in the water *right beneath them*. What were the chances in a magic hell that they *didn't* move? That underwater zombies weren't constantly trying to seal them in? Probably extremely slim.

Cassandra pursed her lips for a second. "Not that I've seen. It's so slow—I think it's almost like how automatic doors close behind you. If there was something in the water, it would've killed us a long time ago."

"O-okay … that's a good point," Declan said. "Well, we'll need to get it open again, though."

"Yeah, it's a pain of a door," Cassandra said, shrugging. "It's easier if you push than pull. Seeing just two of you do it was impressive—we usually have three people for return trips. Well, except Ike—he could do it himself. But he was a bodybuilder."

Grace moved the oar in a clean arc, sending them shooting forward again. "I've had to hold a lot of heavy platters. You end up kind of strong. Still was really difficult—I don't think I could have done it without you, Declan."

"Uh, thanks."

"You were a waitress?" Cassandra asked absently.

Cassandra looked back at the coastline. Declan followed her eyeline. Chuck, Aoife, and Peter looked so small against that possibly infinite expanse of wooden coast.

"Uh … *yeah*, of course?" Grace said.

"What?" Cassandra said, glancing back. "I'm just asking."

Grace actually let out a small chuckle. "No, no, I'm sorry. I just assumed … most people from Quill Point know me on sight. They stop to talk to me all the time. I've been serving at that diner for *years* now."

"I never was much for going out," Cassandra replied. "I worked from home. Programmer."

Cassandra absentmindedly ran her thumb over a friendship bracelet. It was rather dirty and sweaty but stayed taut on her wrist.

"My brother kept talking about making games when we were growing up together. What he said was cool, and when I looked into it, I ended up really enjoying working with computers. They're easier to understand than people."

"Oh, okay," Grace said quietly. "That's cool."

The silence returned as they managed the last bit of distance to the closed door.

Declan flexed his fingers a few times, wondering how much help he would be opening that door. Every day of this was slowly wearing away at him. His stomach was rolling at the lack of calories. He felt a little dizzy. A little thrumming in his head, like the worst kind of energy.

But he wasn't going to not help.

They stopped alongside the wall, and he still slunk forward. Balancing on the wood and balancing the weight on the raft, he put both hands on the door and pushed.

Like Cassandra said it would, the door moved more easily—but the water also sloshed something fierce. Something floated to the surface of the water. A grinning skull with a soda can wedged in the bolt gun's impact hole. Little strands of flesh hung around the jaw, melting even then.

Below it, Declan could just make out the arching line of a spinal column.

The image fucking seared into Declan's mind.

He scrambled backward, upsetting the weight of the boat. It wobbled.

Grace screamed.

And Cassandra darted forward. She shifted to readjust the weight, wincing as a drop of the pond got on her arm, making the skin red and agitated. The raft kept bobbing, threatening to capsize.

Cassandra grabbed Declan's leg. He almost kicked at her on reflex, but her grip was strong. She dragged him to a new spot on the raft, the plank of wood in his backpack pressing into his spine. The raft slowly stabilized.

Declan stared at her, gasping.

Cassandra looked back at him with her eyes wide, and her nostril slightly flared.

"Dude, what the *fuck*?"

"…sorry." Fear still stewed in Declan. "I didn't … sorry."

"I need you to keep it together. I'm not dying because you freaked out."

Declan nodded.

"Good." Cassandra let out a long sigh. "I'll open the fucking door, and you just stay there and keep us level. Grace and I will row now."

"Uh … okay…" Grace said.

"Got it," Declan said, nodding.

"*Good,*" Cassandra said roughly.

Then she turned, ignoring the skull with a spinal tail, an old popcorn bucket, and a few pens, and pushed the door the rest of the way, grunting slightly as she did.

Declan listened to her instructions. He sat still as they continued along. He focused on breathing through his nose. Calming the panic. He eventually timed his breaths to Cassandra and Grace rowing.

Not knowing where they were going, it had felt so much longer of a trip last time. But now, in seemingly no time, they reached the platform at the bottom of the stairs.

The raft bounced slightly against the side. Cassandra—no doubt with tons of practice at this point—easily stepped off. She turned and looked at Declan. Then, after a long second, she held out her hand for him.

He almost didn't take it. Almost. He didn't deserve more help from her. But he also didn't want to capsize the raft after all that.

He took it. Cassandra's hand was bony, sharp, and strong. She practically yanked him onto the platform. Then she immediately let go and moved to sit on the closest of the staircase steps.

Declan turned back to look at Grace.

"Be careful," he said simply. He wasn't sure he should say anything more.

"I'll be right back," she said. "Keep an eye out."

Declan nodded.

Grace shifted so she could better row alone. Then spun the raft around slowly. She took an audible breath, then paddled out toward the door again.

Declan watched her for a few moments. She looked so lonely, going across a sea of rot and death. Maybe she'd always been lonely. Being friends with every person when they ate at the Ink Well Diner and friends with no one when they weren't.

"Are you two together?"

Declan spun around.

Cassandra hadn't moved from her spot on the third-to-last step; she hadn't even sat up. If it wasn't for a raised eyebrow, it almost looked like she hadn't spoken.

"What?" Declan said.

"Are you? You two? Together?"

"Uh, no," Declan said.

"Do you want to be?" Casandra asked, shifting forward a little. "You two seem close?"

Declan blinked a few times; such a mundane topic was exceedingly strange given all that had happened. Well, dating and crushes were mundane topics for most people. Declan had been isolating himself in small ways long before he'd been doing it as a lifestyle choice. After his dad died, he'd not been in much of a position, location, or mindset for anyone to ask him questions about his personal life.

"What? No, we're friends," Declan replied. "Why are you asking?"

Cassandra shrugged. "I'm curious. I've been living with the same three people for a long time. We've cycled through every conceivable conversation topic imaginable. It's something new to talk about."

Instead of thinking about what's about to happen, Declan added in his head.

"Aren't you mad at me?"

"A little," Cassandra admitted. "You almost got us killed."

"I really am sorry."

"Yeah, yeah. Honestly, the number of times any of us have almost gotten one of the others killed … I would be perpetually mad at everyone, all the time. Don't fuck up again."

"I won't … I won't."

"And you can make it up to me by answering my question," Cassandra said.

Declan blinked, then nodded. "Okay. No, I think of her as a good friend. Grace is probably my only friend anymore. But I'm also not into girls, and I don't like to date friends, anyway."

"Ah, okay," Cassandra said, sitting back. "And her?"

"That's not my business to say."

Cassandra shrugged her shoulders. "I respect that. Like I said, I'm just curious. It's sometimes hard to tell how people feel about each other. I wish they wore little tags or something. It could be different colors, even. Angry. Sad. Horny. In love. Out of love, but still fucking. It would be exceedingly helpful."

Declan pursed his lips and glanced back at Grace. She'd made it back through the door, and he could barely see her paddling off in the distance. The sound of her moving water gently echoed against the low ceilings. Faint ripples were still cascading outward from the path she took. A sheet of jagged plastic painted a now faded and splotchy blue moved across the surface for a moment before there was a faint hiss, and it collapsed back into the water.

Looking at the water for too long made him think of that melting corpse, of how many bones must sit far down.

"Are you and Chuck together?" Declan asked, turning away from it all.

Cassandra pursed her lips. "I was waiting for that question. No, we're not. He's been a lifesaver, literally, several times. And, honestly, one of the few people I don't mind—I *like* spending time with. But I don't feel that kind of stuff very often. And it's more often for girls than boys, anyhow. All of that genital and face-smashing stuff seems mostly pointless."

Declan nodded at that. "Um, yeah, I know people who think like that."

"Sometimes thought I was the only one."

Declan shrugged. "I don't think there's much that's truly unique to any one person."

His gaze drifted up that dark staircase, then to that door.

"Can you tell me more about what's up there? The *things* up there?" he asked.

Cassandra's expression went deadly still. It didn't feel like anger from before on the raft, but it instantly killed any comradery or casualness Declan was feeling.

She leaned her elbow on the step, mind going somewhere else.

"I don't think you want to know much about them. It'll be better for everyone if we hit them until they look like bloody paste. You'll want to be staring at their corpses."

Behind him, he could hear the rowing get closer. The others talking softly. Everything was closer. Death and pain and fighting were getting knife-to-the-neck close.

"I think I should have some idea," Declan said. "Do they have, like, weapons?"

Cassandra let out a little wincing noise. "Sort of, yeah. They're very dangerous. But they mostly will try to eat your head."

"*What...?*"

"You know zombie stories, the ones where they're always going for the brains? Similar. Chuck's been trying to figure that one out for a while. I think that, yeah, he's totally right. This place *is* a fucked-up metaphor … a lot of the time. But it's not all one-to-one. They're monsters. We're fighting monsters. Monsters sometimes eat people."

"Three monsters," Declan said.

"Lot more than three mouths to worry about, though," Cassandra said, then winced. "Shit, I really don't like talking about this, Declan. It makes me … anxious. Just hit them repeatedly until they stop moving and then some more. We'll be okay as long as we don't run into all three at the same time. They aren't as … powerful … if they're split up. We've been lucky about that. If one raises its hands, smack it down. If one tries to touch you—*don't* let it touch you."

"Please," Declan said. "I need some clarity."

"I haven't … seen them as well as you think. They don't exist the way you or I do. That's what Chuck says, anyway. I'm not sure they even look the same to everyone who sees them. But they look like people. One is a … slime person. Another is a … demon, I guess. And one is, like, a *lot* of people at once. That one you don't want to touch you."

"Okay … thank you…"

"Do you feel better?" Cassandra asked.

"No."

"See."

Declan nodded. He moved the wood plank from his backpack to his hands, feeling how light it was again. He hoped all Cassandra had said was true about it working better on them than it seems like it should.

"I really hope this works" was all he said to her.

"Don't hope—hit harder," Cassandra said. "Hope didn't save the people we saw die."

Declan nodded at that. Tried to think that way about it. It was a better mindset than he was having. Better than fear and worry and dread. Go forward with all he had and then more.

If not for himself, then for Grace.

He promised he'd protect her.

The paddling got a little louder behind him. Declan turned to see the others arrive. All had such grim faces. Aoife looked terrified but hid it poorly. Peter had this resolute look on his face—that kept breaking from winces of pain almost every thirty seconds. Chuck's hands were tensing and un-tensing at his sides.

Time for war.

CHAPTER 20

HE STAIRS WERE QUIET, THE SHADOWS
long. The world was silent as they rose back up into
the house, moving as a group. Ready for anything. Ready
for nothing. Ready, perhaps, to die.

Declan's hands tightened around his weapon as Chuck
opened the door to the hallway. He expected everything
to descend into violence. For the monsters to be standing
on the other side, ready to eat his brains.

But it opened quietly, and Chuck and Cassandra
stepped out and stood on either side of the entrance. A
faint breeze, like an air conditioner kicking up, flowed up
the stairs behind them, making Declan shiver.

They passed through, one at a time, staying in the
hallway—not even daring to go into the room with the
monitors yet. It was too exposed. It was too dangerous.

They'd only get one chance at a surprise.

As Declan moved into position for their next advance
at the back with Peter and Aoife, he glanced around at
all of them. All his fellow fighters. Survivors. Covered in

muck and sweat, with cracked lips from dehydration and tired eyes from nights of terrified, uncomfortable sleep. *They* were all survivors—he was lucky enough to have them. In another universe, the one where he had gone alone, he would have been long dead.

Another moment passed. Still and quiet. Then, with a gesture from Chuck, they walked forward into the computer room.

Everyone knew not to look at the screens—but Declan could almost feel the heat radiating off them. They were still there and showed what they showed.

Declan couldn't shake the feeling that the entire house was waking up and noticing them.

In front, the fish display moved.

The taxidermied fish shivered, abandoned their stands, and swam in the air in little circles. Their open wounds revealed flexing muscles and bones shifting from their aggressive dance.

"I don't like this," Aoife whispered.

"I'm not sure what this is," Chuck whispered back. "Maybe we should just go back—"

The fish all stopped. Momentum unnaturally skidded to a complete standstill.

The fish jerked into pointing arrows, all pointing at him. Their side-facing eyes focused on the group, on Declan, and their piranha jaws flashed open, widening. Too wide for a fish's jaw.

The teeth went all the way back.

And then the fish laughed, and all popped into a red mist.

"Shit," Cassandra yelled.

"They know we're here; get ready," Chuck said, shifting his weight to better hold an oar. "Remember our plan—"

His voice went out with a rush, a gasping choke, and Peter, Grace, and Aoife screamed at the same time. Declan tried, but the sound got caught in his throat.

His mind sputtered, his vision going sideways for a second. The air was shifting to allow something through. The distinct sound of a key going into a lock, a latch clicking, and hinges screaming from misuse.

There was no chance for a surprise. Never was. The monsters were already there, getting up from their kitchen table and leaving the eviscerated corpses of workers in uniforms. A factory worker. A service worker. An artist. The victims were covered in a sauce that was melting their flesh and filling the air with the pungent, nauseating smells of garbage islands and oil spills.

These monsters were a force of nature—more like wind or a wave than people. Declan could barely think or move.

Yet he knew what was happening.

The three walked toward them through the narrow kitchen, walking forward in a single line, grinning at the group. The three that lived in the house could fold reality itself. They were impossible forms of shifting miasma, of impressions and emotions rendered in physical space.

"I wasn't aware I ordered something for delivery."

Declan's arms locked at his sides. He gritted his teeth against the feeling. It was like a migraine, a splitting head-ache, a sharp blow to the head. They *were* what was on those screens. They *were* what took hope and sucked away dreams for a better tomorrow.

As Grace had described, he saw an oil painting of his hopes for a future. His own wants and desires.

But within the swirl of his own mind, Declan remembered the only thing that could stop this. The only thing that had worked. He reached for Grace. His fingers brushed her arm, and she let out a little gasp of pain before bracing her hand on his shoulder.

Declan reached with his other hand to touch Chuck's back.

Grace's fingers tapped Aoife on the temple.

Aoife grabbed Peter's arm. Chuck put his hand on Cassandra's shoulder.

They were, in whatever way, connected.

Gasps of pain, then relief, sounded around Declan. Those mental assaults, eroding attacks on dreams and hopes, even when there were three at once focusing their attack, were weaker against a group. They couldn't so easily be pushed into despair as they would've been alone.

The vice holding his arms to his sides crackled away.

The monsters walked closer.

"Go … attack!" Chuck yelled, his voice strained. "Get them!"

Cassandra moved forward, up toward the stairs, weapons held high. Chuck followed her after a second.

Declan forced his foot to move one step, then another. It was trudging through tar, overcoming inertia, but when he was running, he was *running*. Adrenaline and momentum in perfect tandem. He was racing at the monsters with all he *had*.

And, as he did, they crystallized into forms that made sense.

He could see the monsters.

Like Cassandra had said, the one in front was roughly shaped like a person.

But also a nightmare.

It was The Baron. The Oil Baron. The Profit-For-Any-Reason. Made of oozing liquids. Gasoline, diesel fuel, and crude oil swirled in a constantly shifting, layered lava lamp pattern, tinged with foul-smelling puffs of car exhaust that was his blood. His head was a face-shaped plume of gray industrial smoke. His lower body was a mound of oil with tiny lashing tentacles extending outward.

Cassandra swung at The Baron with one of the wooden oars. The Baron widened itself out to cover her, long stalactite and stalagmite configurations forming into a snapping oil jaw.

The wood connected, hitting harder than possible.

At that point of impact, the structure of The Oil Baron collapsed around the wood, clinging to it like cotton candy meeting a paper cone and then thrown backward off the wood as a formless lump. The Oil Baron paint-splattered across the curtain and into the kitchen sink. Instantly, the mass churned with rage, snapping jaws forming out of popping liquid pustules, and started to reform into a body.

But Cassandra wasn't paying attention to that, and neither was Chuck. Both kept barreling forward with Declan bringing up the rear. His feet still propelled him forward, almost without his input.

The second of the monsters squared up to meet them.

In a burst of speed accompanied by the sounds of rustling papers and scratching pens, Chuck and Cassandra were off their feet and flying over Declan's head. Swept aside by his attack.

Declan's mind had trouble catching up to what had happened. There was nothing between him and the second of the monsters.

Behind him, the sound of Chuck and Cassandra crashing into the wall.

In front of him smiled The Monopolist.

With so many smiles.

The Price Fixer. The Overwhelming Force. The Anti-Consumer.

It had perhaps once been a single monster, standing only slightly taller than Declan, but now it was an amalgam—a collection of power. Each figure was visible, each figure intertwined.

Its body was a crowd stuffed into an elevator, each carrying suitcases fused to their hands, flesh and faces sewn together with pen nibs and wide threads of rolled documentation. They were a cone, tall to the ceiling, and their bodies spiraled upward like a funhouse reflection.

The Monopolist reached out a hand made of hands—

Declan shrieked in abject pain. The skin of his cheek was pulling off the bone—sucked in by a gravitational force that couldn't be. It only pulled on that one spot, for now, but as the skin tore, the blood sprang forward, leaping across the air like a bridge of ants. *Eager* to join. *Delighted* to merge. The Monopolist was nothing if not accommodating to its acquisitions.

It was only because Declan had seen the power of Cassandra's single strike that he found the resolve to slice out with the plank, swinging it like the most awkward sword.

The "blade" connected with The Monopolist's hand and knocked it out of the way. The skin of Declan's cheek sloughed forward; the connecting strands of protein underneath had been severed.

"Be a part of the future," The Monopolist said, each of his mouths forming into charismatic, practiced grins. *"Record profits! Record sales! Who else are they going to buy from?"*

Declan screamed back at him. A formless yell with no thought. He stabbed forward with the plank of wood. It connected at one of the seams, lodged between two of

The Monopolist's people. Declan tugged sideways, prying at the gap like he had a crowbar.

Once again, the boards worked better than they should. Had more effect than they should have. The Monopolist's pieces were connected down to the organs, and severing them sent the combined blood volume of two adult bodies spraying out like a geyser.

"Bankruptcy! Scandal!" the other heads screamed in a whining pitch.

Multiple hands pointed out, each adorned with class rings and fancy watches.

Declan fell backward. His heart—the actual muscle in his body—was trying to move *forward*. The pain was worse than he could imagine. The skin of his stomach, chest, and his tongue's entire length was trying to leave his body behind. His fingers popped like he'd tugged at them. His neck gave a soft crack as the vertebrate strained.

Then Grace cleaved The Monopolist's side like a pro-baseball player swinging for the fences. The wood *cut* its way through the wall of bodies, exploding out blood and making the monster howl in pain.

The Monopolist's many mouths opened unearthly wide, and the sound of a fire alarm blared through them. Blood continued to pour from their wounds, spraying like a firehose, some of the blood aerosolizing, turning into a metallic-smelling smoke. The alarm noise grew frantic as a shudder stretched along its form. The curling, connected mass of businessmen pushed against each other in panic, shoving at their flesh. This time, they wanted out. It sent strange ripples in their flesh that spiraled into the air, shaking the surrounding oxygen.

"You signed—counter sue—this isn't the way forward—synergy—"

Aoife joined in, as did Peter. Arriving at the fight and tipping the balance more. They bashed The Monopolist repeatedly as he slunk back, waving his many hands, attempting to point but having each attempt knocked away. The spatial laws of the kitchen, already unstuck from what it should be, kept warping and expanding to allow The Monopolist places to slink back and reclaim ground.

Declan couldn't believe this was working. That they were hurting something like that—really hurting it. Even as blood ran down Declan's face like a runner's sweat and he lay on the ground, clutching his disconnected facial skin, he almost smiled.

Then the thought passed through his mind.

There were three.

Grace let out a ragged scream that started as a swear and went far beyond the intended sound. If her soul could make a noise, this arrived from there. She snapped the board in two, holding them like knives, and stabbed in a frenzy.

Declan stood, trying to spot where the third one was. Pain flared across his face; the sounds of violence and screaming made his head spin. He picked back up his weapon but stumbled as the air warped.

The pitch of The Monopolist's cry shifted upward dramatically, quickly going out of a range that humans could hear.

But before it got that high-pitched, it sounded like a call for help.

The third of the monsters walked up. He was confident and full of swagger.

He was The Lobbyist. The Legal Loophole. The Blameless. The most normal looking of the three. His white skin had the perfect tan, his eyes were blue-green, and he was almost exactly six feet tall. The only thing that even marked him as inhuman was the way he moved like he was underwater. The edges of his greased, slicked hair, both beard and upon his head, waved in some impossible current. But his tan suit wasn't wet; his stylish blue tie was crisp and starched. Pure gold cufflinks glimmered in the kitchen's light, devoid of watery rust. The same was true of his thin wire glasses that made his piercing gaze even more pronounced.

He flashed them all a smile and adjusted his tie. A toothy, charismatic grin pulled straight from the most generic business card.

Aoife took a swing at him, aiming for his head.

The Lobbyist's movement had the strange gravitational flow of an anemone waving in a current but was *remarkably* fast. The Lobbyist caught the edge of the plank and only winced slightly as it cut a huge gash into his hand. He shoved back on it, making Aoife stumble and almost drop her weapon.

"*How dare you hurt us,*" The Lobbyist said. "*We produce the largest amount of foodstuff in the Quill Point area. Without us, how will we feed the many mouths that require feeding? Are you an enemy of industry?*"

Declan's ears hurt so badly from those few words alone. But Aoife was getting it so much worse. She clutched at both her ears, blood aggressively leaking around her palms. A violent nosebleed gushed down her face.

"*I think you'll find that our paperwork is entirely in order,*" The Lobbyist said. "*We were well within our rights to use this power. I move that the only recourse is that you give us our deserved…*"

The Lobbyist glided forward, standing tall over Aoife.

Time literally slowed as the next words gathered their power.

Peter disengaged from attacking The Monopolist. Rushing to help. But moving a little slower, a little too slow.

Grace continued to wail on The Monopolist, but her blows did less and less damage. The skin of The Monopolist began to steadily regrow everywhere she wasn't actively hitting. He whipped composite hands at her, forcing her to back up and repeatedly duck.

Having reformed, The Oil Baron glided past as a living puddle, going down the steps. Going toward Chuck and Cassandra, who were slowly regaining consciousness.

Declan tried to yell out—to which person he wasn't even sure—when a single word from The Lobbyist slapped at his eardrums and sent him stumbling.

"*Profit.*"

Nearby ceramics cracked. The faucet exploded upward, spewing water. Declan clutched at his heart again, an arrhythmic thumb slamming his chest.

"*You are impeding profit. The shareholders are entitled to the profit of corpses. As many Quill Point citizens as we can supply is profit. The God of Greed gave us the seed capital to get him profit. My hands are tied—*"

Peter brought a swing so hard at the side of The Lobbyist's head that it snapped The Lobbyist's jaw. His words trailed off as his neatly trimmed beard grew increasingly soaked with runny, too-watery blood.

The Lobbyist's face turned to that of a demon in an instant. Horns. A red fire behind the eyes. His broken jaw grew full of yellow fangs.

"*I did not concede the floor,*" he said.

Then he backhanded Peter.

There was a loud crunch. Peter's nose no longer pointed in the direction it had, and he collapsed backward with red forming across his eyes as blood leaked in.

He fell next to where Declan was still trying to recover from the mental assault of those words. Declan fell to his knees almost entirely on instinct and felt Peter's wrist. There was still a normal heartbeat, if a heightened one, but that wasn't the main problem. Blood was pooling in Peter's mouth, and each time he breathed, it sent sputters of blood. He wasn't getting air.

Declan grunted as he flipped Peter on his side, letting the blood and saliva pool in the lines of the linoleum tile. After a gagging spat of chunky blood, Peter's breathing came out ragged but functional.

A buzz went through Declan, adrenaline trying to force him into action. Making his breathing happen at a faster and faster rhythm. He gritted his teeth, tightened his hand around his weapon, and stood back up.

Only for Aoife's screams to pick up again.

Declan's eyes widened, turning to see. He ran forward with his plank of wood like a lance.

Aoife was holding up the remains of her weapon, the rest jutting out from a deep cut in the side of The Lobbyist's face. She scrambled backward, hyperventilating.

Declan aimed for The Lobbyist's stomach, the spearpoint hopefully able to skewer him.

"Don't interrupt me," The Lobbyist said, ripping the plank out of his face and tossing it hard. Though it wasn't heavy, it knocked Declan backward like he'd been punched in the chest.

The Lobbyist swung a wide kick that knocked a fleeing Aoife to the ground. She clutched at her side, then moved to scramble away. In one step, The Lobbyist stood over her and pinned her neck with his foot.

It was just enough pressure to make her wheeze.

"*You are in breach of contract*," The Lobbyist said, fire still blazing behind his eyes. "*You are to allow us regular business operations at once.*"

The Lobbyist's leaned down and wrapped his fingers around the back of her neck, closing it like a vice.

She sputtered, unable to speak.

Declan recovered, moving forward for another charge. But he could already tell he wasn't going fast enough. Still—he charged.

The Lobbyist picked Aoife off the ground effortlessly. His demonic face flickered and sputtered like frying grease. Less and less of his form looked like a cohesive whole or even known reality. Through the buttons of his suit, through the gap between the tie and the collar, was only a fluid that didn't make sense.

A fluid that any soul knows as decay and rot with no other proof. That knows it like one knows they are being watched or that death is approaching on a deathbed.

The Lobbyist reformed into an all-too-solid state. His jaw re-hinged, healed with a crack, and he bit into the top of Aoife's head.

Her skull, skin, and hair parted like he'd taken a big first bite into a pear. A short resistance, the smallest resistance, before the teeth sliced through to soft, oozing meat.

Aoife went slack. The tension of her shoulders, the movement of her arms, and her flailing legs all stopped immediately. Her eyes lost something behind them.

The Lobbyist jerked his head away, trailing wet strands in his beard. He audibly swallowed, then turned and chucked her body behind him. Aoife landed on the table with the other humans they'd feasted upon.

When he turned back with a grin, looking pleased with himself, he found Declan's plank spear dug into his stomach. Watery blood oozed from the wound.

The Lobbyist coughed, spraying Declan with blood.

"I suppose that's the price of business, huh? On a more personal note, I do so love the taste of failed dreams. Care to try to bribe me?"

Declan didn't answer. He shoved his entire weight into pushing. And the plank sunk into The Lobbyist like he was made of already melting butter.

The watery red blood bubbled and fizzed around the wound. The Lobbyist looked down with what seemed genuine surprise. The skin around the wound kept trying to reform, heal like his jaw, only for the skin to grow more and more rotten in real-time.

"Maybe we should call a recess—I think the defendant, the client … the … the market could use a…"

Declan pounded both his arms on the thin line of wood still visible, driving it all the way into his stomach. Pushing it so the spear tip burst out The Lobbyist's back.

The Lobbyist's fiery eyes finally went out. He collapsed, the skin and muscle rapidly rotting off his bones and the blood evaporating with chemical hisses.

Declan didn't even have a moment of relief as he stood over the corpse. Sweat was pouring down his back from that attack alone, but there were still two other monsters. Still more chances for another one of them to die. Aoife's blood was still pooling where it had splattered. It was probably running down Declan's face.

Declan yanked free the weapon from the remains of The Lobbyist, every muscle in his body screaming from exertion. He still needed to help. He still needed to fight.

CHAPTER 21

HELP WAS NEEDED EVERYWHERE IN THAT war zone of a kitchen.

Grace was exhausted, stumbling, gasping, as she took swing after swing at The Monopolist. The skin on her arms was red and bloody from where they'd almost been yanked away.

The Monopolist was back to gleefully smiling. He closed in. Taking the blows and healing from them too fast. The wounds sealed like closing mouths.

Declan moved to help her, only for another sound to happen back in the computer area.

Chuck screaming.

"Fuck you!" Cassandra spat before her next words were swallowed up by the sound of rushing water. "Fu … all…"

The Oil Baron was looming over Cassandra and Chuck, having reformed into a towering oil column. From his palms poured forth a horrible smelling slick that attached to their mouths, poured down their noses, and attempted to seep through their tear ducts.

The Oil Baron cackled with glee.

"Running out of capital, are you?" The Monopolist said. *"We will always win. You can't afford to keep this up!"*

Now Grace was screaming too.

Declan looked back and forth.

Grace was clutching at her stomach, spasming in pain. The hair on her head twisted in the gravitational pull, follicles flying into The Monopolist's outstretched hands.

Chuck and Cassandra were swinging their weapons around weakly, unable to do more than slightly disperse The Oil Baron's long, suffocating oil. And everywhere they failed to hit, the slime grew more caked on, stiffer.

All of them were going to die.

All of them were fucked.

They had been from the beginning.

Declan would be alone in this place. Left to scream out his last as these things took all there was to take, and then they'd eat anything that remained of his corpse.

And for a second, Declan almost welcomed it.

Hadn't this been why he'd left in the first place? A way to leave Quill Point—leave all that had happened there and the memories of his father? A way to get away from everything?

A horrible end, but an end.

He froze up one more time, unable to help.

Unable to think.

He closed his eyes for a second, trying to block it all away. Trying not to see what was happening.

"Another successful acquisition is all but assured!" The Monopolist said.

Declan's eyes snapped open. And, in a rush that almost scared him, a new emotion flowed. Rather than the sadness of before, the apathy of before, the existential nightmare of before, there was only rage.

Rage at all of it. Every last fucking second of it. All the monsters and what they represented.

Rage at what the world was allowed to become.

No, *made* to become.

His jaw twitched. A slight shudder passed along his shoulders. His vision, for a moment, was very, very clear.

"Living things … are not … a fucking *business asset*!"

Declan picked up the smaller piece of wood lying on the ground, Aoife's lost weapon, and twisted his body like he was throwing a disk. He flung the wood as hard as he could. The piece soared through the air and smacked The Oil Baron in the back of his head.

Like before, the monster's oil frame collected around the piece of wood, forming a wad, moving with the arc of the wood—

Chuck and then Cassandra gasped as the airtight seal broke.

—and The Oil Baron smacked into the wall.

"And they are not for fucking profit!"

Declan let out another yell, full of that cold, clear, furious emotion. He ran at The Monopolist, his eyes blazing, the wooden plank once again leveled like a spear.

He hit The Monopolist dead on, skewering five parts of him in one move, cracking bones and shredding the monster's skin as he did. Momentum carried him almost a foot into the monster's hide before Declan's feet skidded from resistance.

"Die! Die! Die!"

The words kept repeating from his mouth, spewing forth, almost out of his control. He braced his shoulders and kept pushing. Declan was crying but didn't even notice.

His arms shook, but with a meaty squelch, more and more of The Monopolist split open like a ripe fruit. The monster let out a wail that didn't even pretend to be based on human speech.

Declan snarled. "Leave them all alone. Leave them all fucking alone!"

He went farther and farther. The center of the mass wasn't the same as the wall of bodies. The Monopolist had a core. Something sat there in the center, cocooned by the bodies.

It glowed a horrible light. A red, unearthly eminence that looked like nuclear blood, like pain in bad dreams.

"Stop it," Declan shouted, his voice hoarse, unrestrained. "Just stop all of it!"

His feet shuddered; his ankles flared with pain. The skin of The Monopolist was reforming. A pulling energy, a horrible gravity, tugged on Declan in multiple directions. This far into the creature's flesh, he wouldn't simply get an organ pulled out—Declan would be shredded into strips and streaks. Splattered, torn apart, thrown.

The bones in both his shoulders popped in opposite directions. The top of his jaw darted right, the bottom left. His hands were being forced apart, his knuckle bones growing increasingly stark as they tried to escape his hands.

Then another pair of hands wrapped over his own.

Grace was beside him. Her eyes blazed with anger he was sure mirrored his own. No mask anymore—for either of them.

Together, they pushed. And together, they caused massive damage. Blood gushed, marrow snapped, and muscle fibers whipped like angry electrical cables inside The Monopolist.

The sound was muffled and warped, but Declan could hear The Monopolist scream for The Lobbyist to save him. To stop his imminent death.

Grace and Declan cut deeper. Thrashing their way. Making a door to the center of a monster.

The core was the size of a bowling ball, pulsing erratically. A heart—but a rotting one—pumping blood along labyrinthian lines like hanging strings. It was the thing that most connected the gestalt creature to itself.

The plank of wood sunk into it easily with a crisp popping sound. The heart let out a tired whimper in a human voice before breaking apart.

The entire structure that was The Monopolist, in out-of-synch voices, cried out in pain and anger that swiftly turned to bubbling hisses.

The inside of a cone where Declan and Grace stood wobbled and stretched. The Monopolist's heads turned inward with a snap, staring at Declan and Grace even as blood pooled down their chins and their entire form ran like wet pain. Amalgam hands pushed inward, grabbing at them, waving at them.

"It's collapsing!" Declan yelled, looking around in a panic.

Grace nodded before a hand hit her on the side of the head. Her mouth opened in surprise, blood running down from the spot. She slumped against Declan—hopefully only unconscious.

Declan almost fell from the sudden weight but kept her balanced on his shoulder. The Monopolist was looking more and more like a melting candle. Wet chunks landed on Declan's arms and back and slid down his hair. He ducked around the snapping arms and walked out of the hole he and Grace had made.

As they stepped out, The Monopolist fell apart.

Two of the three monsters were dead.

And the house did *not* like it.

Chapter 22

THE WALLS BECAME TRANSPARENT. THE underlying fluid that made up much of the land-scape, the structure, and the monsters were slightly visible, wobbling and shifting in the air. The house groaned like a wounded animal; any space warped by the monsters before was snapping back into normal proportions.

Declan looked across the way. Cassandra and Chuck stood behind The Oil Baron. And, for a second, The Oil Baron was more a structure built around a globule of that strange fluid.

The monster was perhaps only ever a single drop of that fluid.

Cassandra and Chuck swung from both sides, simultaneously hitting that singular globule with the two oars.

It burst. And The Oil Baron sunk right through the ground.

"Is it dead?" Cassandra said.

"I think so," Chuck said. He looked over at Declan. "Did we just win?"

Declan stared back at them. Aoife was dead. Peter was unconscious and maybe actually dead. He hadn't checked. And Grace was, at the very least, concussed.

"The monsters are dead" is what he replied.

A howling sound, far away and close, childlike and inhuman, shook the world. Everyone froze. It got a little louder, then faded away.

Cassandra glanced around nervously. "Okay, what was that—"

The room, the space, and the walls blinked away to fluid, then back to normal. Then again—and then again. It reminded Declan of a computer glitch. It happened ten more times, making his eyes hurt.

Then it seemed to stabilize. Staying visible again.

But there was a faint sound basically everywhere. A humming. A creaking. Like the gears in a clock winding down, down, down. Or the last drops of a canister of water splashing on the parched earth. Or a bomb about to go off.

Chuck's eyes went wide.

"They were the metaphor! It was based on them! The house is just—"

Spiderweb cracks raced along every surface with bone-snap pops. Flakes of plaster danced down in an instant snowfall. A low earthquake shudder passed across the floor.

"Everybody out!" Cassandra yelled.

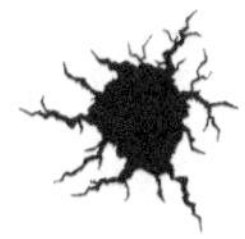

In the flickering, dissolving metaphor, they ran through the kitchen covered in so much sprayed blood. Weapons abandoned—no plan anymore but fleeing. Past the taxidermied polar bear that was there, and then it briefly wasn't. Declan banged his shoulder on a wall when he briefly couldn't see it. For half an instant at a time, layers of the floor would not exist, and the slight drop made his stomach lurch. Made him almost fall over twice.

Grace didn't stir as he carried her through the nightmare, her breathing only slightly increasing after the third unexpected drop.

The sound of an annoyed child was off in the distance, like the faintest of thunderclaps. A boyish, petulant cry.

Declan recognized it, somehow, as the sound the sky made when it took people. The countdown during Murder Sky. His mind flared with white-hot panic at the idea that another monster, the monster that was bigger than the town, might also want them dead.

He somehow found the strength to run faster.

Chuck was the first out the front door and into a shadowy night with Peter slung over his larger shoulders. He passed through during an instant where there wasn't even a door. Declan had to skid to a stop and pull it open when it reformed in front of him.

He heard a puffing breath behind him as he did. Cassandra was taking up the rear, pulling along Aoife's corpse.

"What are you doing!?" Declan yelled.

"I can't just leave her here!" Cassandra snapped back.

Declan didn't argue with her. He opened the door for her and Aoife. Then followed her out of the house. He didn't know how long exactly they'd been down in the basement, but the stars were once again gone, and night was as it had become in Quill Point. The field of bodies looked even more eerie now that they were cloaked in shadows.

He didn't pause to look, moving down the stairs as fast as he could with Grace over his shoulder.

Cassandra was already at the bottom step when the entire structure finally fizzled out of existence. Declan wasn't so lucky. He was still three steps off the ground.

His stomach flew right up into his throat as he dropped. The hard, charred earth slapped his chest, and Grace flew out of his arms.

She rolled three times before stopping with a painful-looking final flop. So painful that she let out a harsh groan. Her eyes snapped open, blurry and tired looking.

"Fuck," she swore, her voice deflated. She grasped one of her shoulders and shoved at it, wincing.

Declan could hear the soft pop from where he lay.

"Fuck, fuck that hurt," she hissed before rolling to sit and looking around. Her eyes went wide.

"We need to go," Declan said, pushing himself to stand.

Even more spots on Declan's body ached. He was sure he'd broken a rib or a toe or something.

"What's happening!" Grace said.

"We killed the monsters, and the world's falling apart—"

The rest of the field flickered. Only the human bodies, draining down their blood, were really there. They were suspended by metaphysical curving hooks being made to resemble trees.

But, more importantly, something else flickered in and out of existence. The tree line. The path they'd entered from. It all blinked away. And there was the faint glow of Quill Point streetlights.

"Fuck, never mind. There's no time," Declan said, pointing. "Just run for the edge! Just run for it."

He grabbed her hand as he ran past her. She winced, but got up and held on. They ran together. They'd walked into this hell together. They would leave together.

"There's so much…" Grace said, glancing back. "This is impossible…"

"It doesn't matter. Just run," Declan said.

Cassandra was ahead of them. Aoife draped over her back. Chuck was still further ahead, carrying Peter. Peter faintly groaned but still wasn't moving much.

They were closer to an escape from this place than anyone had ever been.

"Oh my god," Grace said, glancing back again. Her voice was at the edge of tears.

She stopped running.

Declan moved forward a few steps, then jerked to a stop, unwilling to let go of her hand. He spun to grab her shoulder, her other hand, whatever he could to keep them moving.

And then his eyes bulged, and he stopped in his tracks.

The sight was another impossible thing in an impossible place. And it was so much bigger than anything else.

Everyone speculated on what was happening to Quill Point. What was happening or had happened to the rest of the world. And now Declan knew just a bit more of its secrets.

There was another barrier between Quill Point and the rest of Illinois. The dark clouds of Murder Sky were still here, never left, and they touched the ground. Five thousand feet in front was a wall of pure shadows. A wall that went up to the clouds above.

And along that unbelievably large shadow wall were breaks in its surface. Sections instead were red and glossy. Sections with hundreds of moving … somethings.

Declan looked for a second too long.

Symbols. Flowing red symbols. So far away, he could barely see them. They weren't flat, like symbols. Not writing, exactly, but they held so much meaning. They curved and moved in ways that defied all sense of spatial reasoning. They were everything and everywhere, and Declan's mind started to—

Grace slapped him so hard that it made him bite his tongue. Blood ran down his chin. But it was enough: he looked away. But even the memory of the symbols grew in his head.

Something like slime was condensing around his tear ducts.

"No, not you, not now. Come on!" Grace yelled so loud it made Declan's ears ring.

"But we're trapped…"

"No, I can see the way out—and you can too."

"But it's so much. It's even more than the monsters. How are we supposed to—Grace … I think… I wanted to help… I think I wanted to volunteer. I wanted to be an activist… Grace, imagine traveling the world and helping people. But that's never going to happen, is it?"

A flood of dreams pushed up. A deluge of wants and hopes moved into his mind as fast as they could melt into a watercolor slurry. A whirlpool that was all he was, and it would leak from him and leave nothing left.

"Maybe it would be easier to not care—"

Grace stepped in front of the sight, filling his vision. She placed her hands on his cheeks and touched her forehead to his. He blinked, trying to hear her.

Grace was here… he was supposed to protect Grace…

He blinked, wobbled, then put his hands to his eyes and flicked away the sugary-smelling slime that had flowed there.

"We are getting out," Grace said. "You and me, okay?"

"Do you promise it'll be okay?"

"We'll make it okay."

Declan nodded at that. Believed it because he *wanted* to believe it.

"Okay. I'm with you."

"Good, then come on. I need you. I need you to make it through this."

Declan shuddered, then whispered back under his breath. "I love you too, Grace."

Declan closed his eyes very hard for a moment, then turned and stared unblinking at their destination. That line of freedom. They were so close now. Whatever was pushing, tugging, on his mind—the increasingly con-suming memory of those symbols—it could *wait*.

As he ran, the impossibly dense foliage flickered back into existence in batches before disappearing again.

"It's reforming," Chuck yelled from far in front. "We need to get out now!"

"I'm trying," Cassandra screamed back, dodging around a hanging hook as it briefly became a cedar.

Declan didn't know what wind he was on now. Second wind? Third wind? But a slight surge of adrenaline went through him again. Pushed him to run a little harder *one* more time.

He could feel Grace's hand in his.

A cackling whir. Behind them. A clockwork tick, tick, slotting into place.

"Oh no," he said in quiet horror. "No, no, fuck no…"

"The slaughterhouse!" Grace yelled.

"Fuck" was all Cassandra said in reply. She kept running.

Grace ran harder, pulling a little in front of Declan.

The forest wall stretched out in front of Declan. Closer now. Almost there. It flickered to an impassable prison. Then salvation once again.

God, so close.

The slaughterhouse monster mechanically screamed behind them, scuttling so fast it made a faint whistling noise.

Chuck took a forward jump and cleared the barrier. He and Peter collapsed into a heap on the other side.

Then he wasn't visible as the tree line flickered back to impassable.

The change lasted longer this time.

It took a full ten seconds before it changed back again.

Cassandra went through next. She put her head down and with one more burst of speed escaped. She skidded, then slumped, dropping Aoife as gently as possible. Before she could do much more, Chuck grabbed her into a spontaneous hug.

Then they disappeared again. Maybe fifteen seconds this time. Declan was too tired, too ragged to count. But it felt longer. It seemed longer.

The barrier disappeared again. And Chuck and Cassandra were looking at him. He could see in their eyes how afraid they were.

The metallic clicking got a hell of a lot louder.

The monster—the first, and now last monster in the burned forest—of industrial farming, slaughterhouses, and butchery, was almost upon them. Eager to take one or two more victims.

Declan's legs burned with an almost liquid agony. A curling, awful sensation that went down and up his bones.

His newest adrenaline rush was shorter, leaving his body with almost nothing to give. Declan felt more and more like he was throwing himself forward more than running.

Any second, he expected the adrenaline to run out and for his body to simply leave him, drop him, shatter him on the grass—to die.

But no matter what, his grip on Grace's hand was ironclad—a vice in another vice. He would only let go if it meant throwing her, somehow, someway, over that line.

The way out was visible less and less. Now, a static flicker, a glitchy change. Whatever they had broken by killing the three monsters was healing—and it was healing faster.

The thundering boom of Murder Sky's petulant yells was getting louder and more gleeful.

And then….

No more flicker. Quill Point sealed off. It lasted ten, then fifteen, going on twenty…

It's not going to open!

But Grace didn't stop. Didn't slow. Perhaps it was momentum or faith, but she ran *harder*. Declan had no choice but to keep pace or die. His legs were progressing beyond the sensation of being on fire to *being* acid. He was lagging, gasping, panting, failing, stretching the length of both their arms to uncomfortable limits when he couldn't keep pace with her.

The trees finally flickered again. Grace burst over the line.

Something felt like it snapped somewhere in Declan's body. A muscle or a bone was pushed completely out of where it should be. He screamed but didn't stop. It didn't matter if he was hurt, only if he stopped.

Inches now. An arm's length away.

He pushed off the tips of his toes. Flung himself—

—right into a face full of dense foliage.

It was a wall of jagged edges. It was the prison of trees.

His mind had to catch up to what had happened. And then a soul-shaking spasming shudder, a jagged heart palpitation, a scream that almost ejected his soul.

He was trapped.

God, no … he was dead.

The pathway out was gone. The metaphor healed around him. The metallic chomping of the metal monster gaining on him. Sounding so eager to finally bore a hole through his forehead. To drain his blood out and leave his body as wasted meat.

No! No! No!

Wait…

He could still feel Grace's hand. He was still *holding* Grace's hand!

She was tugging on the other side.

It was a clean hole, just enough for his arm to pass through. The only remnant of his escape. Grace was tugging *so hard*.

Maybe all the people on the other side were trying to pull him through.

As the passage tightened, thorns scrapped Declan's arm. Blood ran down to his elbow. His fingers ached. Grace kept tugging. His legs wobbled beneath him. Grace kept tugging. He could almost hear them yelling for him. Crying out for him.

The memories of the symbols pulsed in his head. They pushed at everything else. They wanted all he dreamed of *out*, removed, beaten, and stomped. This place, whatever it was that took over Quill Point, didn't want originality, hope, joy, community, friendships, stability, or, or, or…

It already took his father. It wanted to take even the happy memories of him.

It was so good at ruining beautiful things.

He half-turned to see the monster upon him. The creature of whirring blades and endless heat. Of taking. Of spoiling and rotting and reducing to only raw material.

The strain on his arm was immense. It hurt so much. But Declan almost didn't mind that pain. It was the pain of people—a worthwhile pain.

And he could feel more hands in his.

More than he'd ever known.

The monster leaped at him, excited. Like it was too eager.

And, at this moment, it *was*.

Declan ducked—the bones in his shoulder popping from all the strain.

The mass of blades and heat sliced into the wall of trees. A great crashing cacophony, almost more like the sound of breaking glass. Surging pops of destroyed twigs and acrid, fiery hisses as leaves burned instantly.

And it was a way out.

It left a massive hole. A doorway to the other side. Now broken apart into smaller forms, the monster scrambled to block the escape. Each slashing for Declan.

Declan half pushed himself and was half pulled through the opening. Several blades hit their mark, slashing at his face, shoulders, and arms. They were cut with such hot metal that it instantly cauterized the wounds.

It hurt like nothing else in existence.

But he made it.

Declan landed on a normal street in the perpetual cold air of Quill Point.

Declan flipped around, prepared to kick away the monsters that came through. But they didn't follow. The opening closed swiftly, with a great rustling sound as the tree's limbs bent and shifted to patch the wound.

And, for that last moment, Declan could see the whole of it.

Tiny halogen eyes staring with malice.

Hundreds of bodies bleeding. Hung like pigs before being carved.

The horrible house, the respite of monsters, rebuilding itself like a reforming mold.

The dark sky was full of red symbols and impossible sights.

And, among it all, made of the sky, the clouds, and the unearthly material that formed it all, was the angry face of a child screaming. Unhappy that it had lost fresh blood for its machinations.

And then, the wall of trees fully sealed itself away. Hiding the hell beyond.

And Declan, despite everything, was alive.

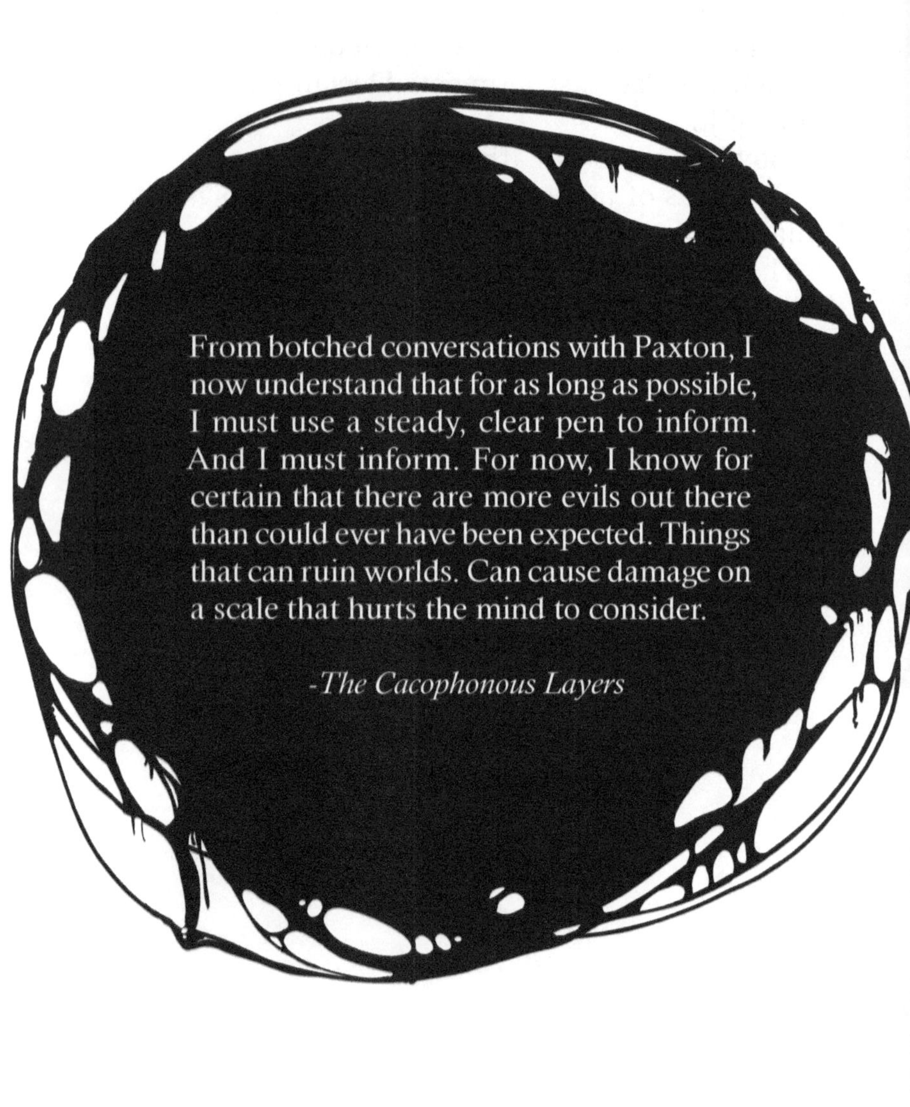
From botched conversations with Paxton, I now understand that for as long as possible, I must use a steady, clear pen to inform. And I must inform. For now, I know for certain that there are more evils out there than could ever have been expected. Things that can ruin worlds. Can cause damage on a scale that hurts the mind to consider.

-The Cacophonous Layers

Interlude 1

Rest Stop

SEVERAL WEEKS EARLIER

CHARLEY DIDN'T USUALLY ENJOY DRIVING. Apocalypses have a habit of making unpleasant things worse. That and rushing, pushing ninety, in the most chaotic I-80 he could imagine, blitzed on enough caffeine to make his stomach hurt, at an hour that Charley hadn't been awake for in what felt like an eternity, with his crush near him constantly, and the intermingling smell of piles of snack foods.

"Look out!" Dereck yelled.

Charley yanked the wheel as hard as he could, moving his foot off the accelerator. The two-lane backup whipped past. He glanced at them out of the corner of his eye. The top of one of the cars was smoking. No time to worry about that right now.

"Yep!" Charley replied.

"Fucking—"

"On it," Charley yelled, merging three lanes in quick succession.

The random honk behind them, screeching through the air, only made Charley more stressed. On reflex, he flipped them off.

"Why are there so many people trying to *drive* right now?" Charley said.

"How should I know?" Dereck replied, grabbing the handle above the car door. "People have places to be at the end of the world."

"Well, so do I!" Charley took a sloping turn almost too hard, getting them eerily close to an easily lethal drop. Then he made the curve and zipped forward.

"Maybe we should slow down," Dereck offered weakly.

Charley glanced at his review mirror. A sedan was coming up behind them. Behind the wheel was a woman. In the seat next to her was a little kid—a little boy with blond hair and pinkish-white skin that looked like his mother—in a booster seat. The kid was crying so hard that Charley could imagine what he sounded like. Charley almost crashed into a stalled car as the other car caught up behind them fast.

"One second," Charley said. "Please be quiet."

Charley sped up a little more and cleared a massive collection of cars. None of them had crashed—just clustered.

People who were affected sometimes stopped driving in the middle of the highway.

He went back down a ramp to street level, sped up a little more, and pulled off to the farthest side. He put the car in park right in front of a pileup, watching as the mom zoomed by, her kid still full-on crying.

Unless a car drove at them opposite the usual traffic—which wasn't *impossible*—they were safe for the moment.

Charley turned off the engine. No sense in wasting gas.

He stared at Dereck, who stared back. His light gray eyes were wide. Remnants of orange juice caught in his beard hair from the one time he'd tried to take a drink. He had a tomato sauce stain on his shirt from a disastrous personal pizza attempt.

That memory helped calm Charley down.

"I think maybe we should take a break," Dereck said. He reached out and touched Charley's shoulder. "We can't help anyone if we crash."

"Okay," Charley said. His breath was slowing gradually, the adrenaline in his veins calming inch by inch. "That's probably a good idea."

"Drive only when you're comfortable, okay?" Dereck said.

"Okay … okay."

Charley glanced at Dereck's hand. He hadn't moved it yet. He very much liked it being there. It was calming. It was stable. It was another person in a nightmare world.

Dereck's expression changed slightly, and he took his hand away. He let out a breath. "Seriously, are you sure you're okay?"

Charley's thoughts were foggy from stress, foggy from everything. But he nodded. He looked around. A few cars whipped by on the other side of the road divider, and one police car screamed past them. But, for the driving he'd been doing, it was almost calm.

"Yeah. Yeah, I'm okay. Let's find a rest stop."

"Okay. Okay. Good idea. I like that idea. Uh, question, where do you think we are?"

Charley pulled out his phone and quickly checked their location. His car was too old to have a built-in charger, and the one he'd stolen from the convenience store was shitty.

"Somewhere in Nevada."

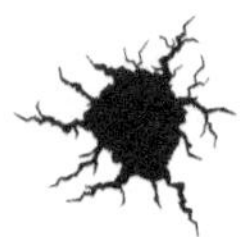

Driving slower was torture, but it proved safer somehow. Even going a hundred, panicked drivers would try to pass them. So, it worked best to cruise in as straight a line as possible and not even try to get out of their way.

Charley flinched basically every time it happened. But he and Dereck went along, looking for a way off I-80.

The first three offramps they tried had cars stalled on them. Charley did not expect honking to make anyone move, so he didn't even try. The fourth one was clear. It had intense tire marks and pieces of a bumper off to the side, but they could go down.

The area was extremely cookie-cutter. A place that could exist anywhere in the continental United States. Full of more chain restaurants than the average, dying mall. Three gas stations were all in competition with each other. It would've been almost comforting, a sight from Charley's one road trip with his family, his mom, dad, and his sister Cassandra if it wasn't for all the reminders of what was happening.

Like everywhere they'd seen recently, it had the sense of being vacated—like a stage after the show was over, full of abandoned props with no context left to them. All that architecture and commerce lay like a corpse.

It wasn't *totally* lifeless, though.

There were a few other active cars around. A person walked across a street hurriedly, clutching a greasy bag like they expected it to be snatched away. Three larger men stood alongside a massive shipping truck, sipping coffee and smoking.

Even the signage still worked. It declared its wares above them as they drove. Advertising flashed for products Charley wasn't sure would ever be purchased or produced again once the world ran out. He was surprised to feel some loss over soda brands he'd drank all his life and takeout restaurants he'd splurged on when he was too tired to cook.

Dereck's stomach growled. He grimaced. He said nothing.

Charley glanced over at him. They still had plenty of snacks from what they stole from the gas station. The car couldn't hold everything—but it held a lot. It also might have to last for a *long* time.

"Do you want food?" Charley offered. "If we can get some here, we should."

Dereck's stomach growled again. "I'm not going to lie—I would kill for a burger or something. But is it safe to get out?"

Charley looked around. The people didn't look like they cared much about what they did. But he also didn't know the full scope of what was happening to the world. All he knew was that people were going catatonic randomly.

"You can beat someone up if we need to, right?" he asked.

Dereck had the beginnings of a six-pack, wiry arms, and strong legs. And while Charley was happy to look at them, he didn't know if it translated to actual fighting.

The most violent thing Charley had ever seen Dereck do was crush a beer between his hands.

"Uh, sure. Sure."

"Cool … then yeah … let's see if they're serving food, I guess."

"Maybe they'll give us something for free," Dereck suggested. "Apocalypse discount."

"Maybe," Charley replied.

Charley turned into the parking lot for some chain sandwich joint. It was for a brand he'd never heard of. A faded blue and gold sign for a free large fry—if you got a drink—was stuck to the side of the glass. Going off the displayed cost, Nevada had significantly cheaper food prices than California, or it was woefully outdated.

They parked, and the stillness of the car felt like it leaped up Charley's legs. Staying still meant the apocalypse could catch them. Staying still meant things could happen to his sister and his father. Movement was safer—even on those hellish roads.

But he needed a break. He *needed* one. The anxious energy of before would make him unable to drive or function.

"Hey," Dereck said gently.

"Hey," Charley said. He half-turned his head. "Sorry, it got to me a little."

"Yeah, it gets to me sometimes too."

Charley looked over at him and faintly smiled. Then he looked off to the side again.

"Hey, Dereck, I've been wondering?"

"Yeah, what's up?"

"Now, I don't mean this as anything—I don't… why did you decide to come with me?"

Dereck sat back and let out a little whoosh of air. He let out a chuckle. "I mean, the world's ending, dude. I wasn't going to be alone with that."

"But what about your mom? Why are you with me and not her?"

Dereck pursed his lips, and his head dipped a little. "Right. I didn't tell you."

"What?"

"I guess I didn't want to tell anyone."

"Umm, are you saying—"

"Yeah. Cancer," Dereck said. "She lost to it like six months ago. She wasn't getting treatment for it—we didn't know about it. She wasn't going to see a doctor, and then it got bad. The credit card company she used has been tailing my ass, trying to get me to take on her medical debt. I never even bought a new car after I crashed one, but they wanted me to take on *thousands* of dollars. Or … they were, I guess."

He glanced out the window and gave the strangest little laugh. "I guess we don't have credit card debt anymore, huh?"

Charley sat there, stunned. What could he possibly say to that? He'd met Dereck's mother. She was funny, comforting, and lively. A seventy-year-old who seemed as carefree as her son. She'd winked at him when Dereck had taken off his shirt, and Charley had tried to hide his reaction.

And she was gone. Already gone, even. He'd been so busy with work, hobbies, and life—how had he let something like that *happen*?

"I'm so sorry," Charley said.

Dereck leaned his head into the headrest. "Yeah, me too."

"I..."

"So, that's why I went with," Dereck interrupted. "Grief is… it's no way to live. My mom told me that when my dad passed. 'It's not worth it. Be happy that they lived. Isn't that what you'd want for your loved ones when you go?' I try to live by that. And I've got no one else but you, Charley. And, like, you've been a good friend to me. I haven't had many of those. But even I know you need them during the apocalypse."

"Thanks," Charley said. "Thank you. I appreciate it. Uh. I appreciate … you."

"My pickers not been the best always," Dereck continued, smiling a little, maybe at a memory. "Lots of boyfriends, not a lot of successful boyfriends. Met a lot of fellow surfers, but none of them could talk with me about video games. I think I picked right this time."

Charley could feel a blush coming on. Could feel things happening in his body. His breath quickened.

"We should—uh, let's get you some food, yeah?"

Dereck put his hand on his shoulder again—*the same spot*. Charley wondered if it was on purpose… had some deeper meaning.

"Sure thing."

Dereck pushed open the car door and got out, leaving Charley sitting there momentarily, trying to catch his breath. Trying to stop his heart from bursting right out of his chest.

Dereck slapped his hand against the car trunk a few times. Charley opened it. Dereck pulled out a bat. The bat. The only weapon they had. Back at the convenience store, they hadn't been able to get into Brad's safe that might've held a gun. And the reminder of why he might need a baseball bat got Charley out of his head again. He stepped out of the car, hoping Dereck wouldn't spot anything different about him.

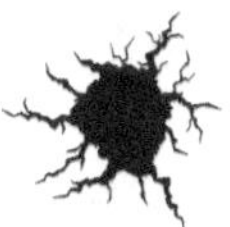

The heat outside wasn't terrible that day, but the inside of the restaurant's air conditioning was still cranked too cold. Charley shivered basically as soon as they stepped inside.

The seating was slick plastic with minimal vinyl, and the booths were tall and narrow. It smelled like grease. Oh, sure, burgers and fries and sugar, but mostly grease. Charley had worked at enough fast-food restaurants to know instantly that the employees hadn't taken care of the place.

Only one worker was there, and he didn't look up. He was probably a teenager, probably fifteen or sixteen. He wore a blue uniform, multiple shades between the shirt and pants and apron, and had a cheap snapback hat with the restaurant logo. His hair was light blond, his skin was a pale white, and he had a pair of askew glasses right above a suggestion of a mustache. A lit cigarette lay on the counter, dripping ash and worryingly still too hot to be next to the pile of tip money.

The worker didn't notice them. He kept thumbing through the bills he'd pulled out of the register. Lots of ones and fives. He was going through it in a loop, somehow both loosely and with quick furtive motions. It was efficient, in a way: he went through them all in the time Charley and Dereck stood there.

"Uh, hello?" Charley asked.

His loop slightly slowed, but that was the only acknowledgment he'd heard them.

"Hi!" Dereck said too loudly. "Hi there!"

Charley's pulse lurched. A warning bell was surging in his mind. This was bad; this was wrong. They should go back into the car.

"Uh, Dereck," he muttered. "I don't think we want to—"

"Are you okay?" Dereck asked, taking a step forward before stopping.

The kid's hands went slack in slow motion. The dollar bills dropped to the ground and onto the counter with a faint rustle. He tilted his head, then shook it with no emotion.

"Okay?" he said. "Ha-ha. Ha-ha. Okay? Ha. Ha."

A shiver went up Charley's spine. He hadn't laughed. He'd said it as words.

"Uh, dude…?" Dereck began.

The kid let out a long breath. "Why are you here? Nobody comes here. This is a failing business."

"What?" Charley asked.

"My dad owns this place," the kid said, waving an arm half-heartedly. "Wanted to make a business. But that restaurant over there…"

He pointed, then let his hand drop to his side.

"…they kept underselling us. They sell their food for way cheaper. No idea how—I bet they put plastic in their meat or something. They'd have to. My dad knows the butcher personally, and there's no way they could make a profit. But oh well."

He leaned forward against the counter. The lit cigarette was close to his arm in a way that couldn't be comfortable.

"That's just competition for you, I guess. What do you want?"

Charley frowned. There was something about how the kid talked overall that sounded off. Sometimes during the night shift at the convenience store, a trucker or nurse would show up desperate for coffee or a slice of pizza.

This kid sounded a little like that. Tired. Tired physically. Tired of the world. Tired of how it was going and would go.

"What's your name?" Charley asked.

The kid sighed like Charley had asked him to lift something heavy. "Kenneth. It's Kenneth. Not that it matters. And, seriously, what do you want?"

"Did something happen to you when Quill Point … happened?"

"Probably," Kenneth said. "I don't know. I know we have two-for-one specials. Maybe order some."

Dereck tapped Charley on the shoulder. When he looked, Dereck shrugged and then gestured for Charley to order.

He supposed he was right. As far as Charley knew, there wasn't a lot they could do for someone affected. At least Kenneth wasn't lying on the floor, catatonic like some people.

"What are the specials?"

"Does it matter?" Kenneth asked, tilting his head. "I'm not actually going to charge you anything."

"Cheeseburger with bacon," Dereck said.

Charley frowned but then shrugged. "Uh, gyro, no onions."

"Sounds great," Kenneth said, although he clearly had no opinion. "I'll be right back with that."

A moment later, the sound of a patty hitting the grill sang out. Charley couldn't say he relaxed, but felt a little better not having Kenneth stare at them like they weren't there.

"What the fuck?" Dereck said quietly. "That was … weird."

Charley looked around for anyone else in the restaurant. Ghost town. No one was sitting at the booths. No one was coming around to the drive-through—the place was empty and dead.

"I think this is what's happening to people," Charley said. "The people in the cars. The people in the videos."

"What do you think did this?" Dereck asked.

"I wish I knew" was all Charley could think to reply. "Demons, maybe?"

"Weird type of apocalypse for demons," Dereck commented. "I would expect more … damage, I guess, if it were demons."

"Yeah … fair," Charley said. "I don't get why … whatever this is … wants people like this. And why it's only some people?"

"I don't know. I wonder if it's random."

"Yeah, that's a good question," Charley said.

And it was. But he didn't have an answer. So, they stood there quietly as Kenneth made their food.

They didn't have to wait all that long. Despite acting like a puppet dragged through the process, Kenneth made their food at the usual pace of a fast-food joint. A few moments later, he returned and placed two generic brown bags on the counter.

"Here. Enjoy. Or not. I'm going on my break now," Kenneth said.

He picked the cigarette off the counter, sucked it down hard, and then walked to one of the booths. He sat down roughly, then hummed a jingle that Charley didn't recognize.

Charley looked at him and then back at the food. He felt like he should do *something* for Kenneth. Help in *some* way. But what was there to do? This was impossibly widespread, and they didn't have a cure or anything.

At least Kenneth had shelter and some level of food storage. He'd mentioned having a father—and maybe he would come back around.

"Are you okay?" he called out.

"Ha-ha. Is anyone?" Kenneth said. "Is anyone that's alive okay?"

Charley frowned. "Is your father coming back?"

"Yeah. He went to go talk to his friends. I stole this cigarette from him." He held it up, letting the trail of smoke drift upward. "I don't really care if he gets mad about it."

Charley glanced at the group of people he'd assumed were all truckers. One actually looked a lot like Kenneth.

"Okay—uh, sorry whatever happened, happened," Charley said.

"It's just how the world is now," Kenneth said. "Not like I can do anything to change things."

Charley nodded, unsure of what part of that he agreed with.

He turned to look at Dereck. "Let's get out of here."

Dereck nodded and grabbed the bags of food off the counter. "Yeah, sounds good to me."

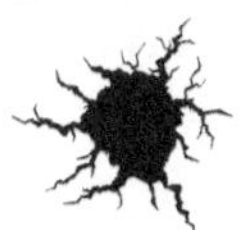

After backing out and merging onto the main road, they went underneath the interstate bridge and drove farther.

Charley glanced in his rearview mirror one last time at the restaurant and the people still around.

He wondered how many places were like this. There wasn't *much* infrastructure here—nothing too dire to fall apart. Airports or hospitals must be nightmares.

He shook his head gently. He could only do so much. Panic was so easy—but it wouldn't help.

They followed the main road a little farther, then took the first turn they could off into a suburban area.

The stalled cars were less common on the back roads, but much more annoying. One had been parked sideways, gumming up a whole road. The next few streets were a maze. It looked like someone had a massive house party, and then no one left. Charley eventually resorted to driving through people's yards.

He immediately felt guilty about long lines in the grass, but no one ran out to yell at them. No one was going to run out and yell at them. They stayed on the grass until they made it to the next turn.

"I used to live in a place like this," Dereck said.

"Yeah? Back in California?"

"No," Dereck said. "We used to live in Illinois, actually."

"Was it by…?"

"No, the other side of the state. You see this one?"

He pointed at a two-story house, mostly painted white, with a brown-red roof. It looked very much like a lot of other houses around them. The mailbox was painted sky blue with a little yellow sun on one of its sides.

"The mailbox looks, like, identical. I used to love going to get the mail. I never *got* any mail, but I used to love bringing it back inside."

"That's cute," Charley said.

"Thanks. It's funny what brings up memories."

"Yeah, it is."

Charley kept driving. Looking for somewhere to stop. His mind wandered a little. Wandering, wondering, thinking.

"I wish I understood what was happening to Kenneth," he said.

"He sounded … empty," Dereck said. "Like he'd been worn out. It didn't sound all that different from some people I've talked to on the beach. You meet people there sometimes who aren't… they aren't always doing so well. And people just write them off. But if you talk to them, they always have these stories about things hitting them so hard. I don't think many people hit rock bottom who weren't pushed halfway there."

"Yeah … but I guess that's the world we're in. Or were living in."

Dereck made a slight sound in the back of his throat. "Yeah, it fucking is, isn't it?"

Charley glanced at him. "I'm sorry."

"For what?"

"You shared something wholesome, and … I derailed it. And now we're talking about how many people are suffering. It's… it's not… I don't know."

"It's the apocalypse, Charley. Of course, you're worried. There's no need to beat yourself up for having normal emotions. Frankly, I think you're really strong for not freaking out more. I could never keep my cool … if things like … your dad … happened to me."

"You say really nice things to me," Charley said.

"You have a lot of things I can say nice things about."

Charley looked forward. It was a lot these past few days. It was a lot these past few hours. It was a lot for a long, long time.

"Do you think the whole world is going to end?" Charley asked.

"I don't know," Dereck said. "I think… I think we need to try to save who we can. And do what we need to. But I think, beyond that, all we can do is hang on. It's like a bad wave—a bad start—sometimes the best thing you can do is not fall over."

"That's a bit cliché," Charley said.

"Fine, you caught me," Dereck replied, actually chuckling.

It was good to hear him laugh. Charley liked his laugh.

"Let me try this, then. You heard Kenneth—that's what this is doing to us. It's taking away hope. I think we need to not … how do I put this…"

Charley glanced over at him. There was something different in his voice. He thought he saw a hint of a blush on Dereck's face.

"What?"

"I think that—hmm … I think that the things that make us happy and feel alive… they're more important now than ever. It might be silly to say so, but it feels a little like fighting for those things."

Charley's face was full-on burning now. There was no way that Dereck couldn't see that.

Charley kept thinking of his own dreams. Things he'd imagine happening.

"Hey, that looks like a good place," Dereck said.

Charley managed to pay enough attention to see the empty stretch of green. A tiny public space in the suburban sprawl. It was flat waves of grass and only a few trees, but it seemed better than a random yard.

"Uh, sure—I guess it's a picnic then," Charley said, then instantly realized what he'd said. "I mean … we can sit on the grass and stuff."

"Yep! Sure! Picnic it is!"

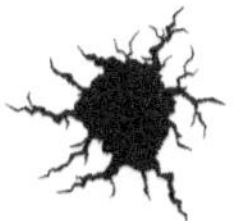

Charley had his pick of parking spots. The most activity he could see was a wrapper for a burger store rolling across the grass like a tumbleweed, caught by the faint, warm breeze.

He turned to look at Dereck. "Pick a spot for us, I guess."

"Sure," Dereck said a little too quickly. The paper bags rustled as his grip on them tightened.

Dereck got out of the car and walked into the field. He seemed to pick a spot arbitrarily and dropped to the ground.

Charley once again found himself sitting in his car, feeling like his pulse would go through his chest. But this time, Dereck's words rang in his ears. He exited the car as quickly as he could and walked over. He didn't know what Dereck meant by what he'd said. He didn't know if he meant it like he wanted Dereck to mean it.

I just… I just… I just … am going to go on a picnic. With my crush.

"Burger's pretty good," Dereck said, gesturing with his food. He'd already gotten a big bite out of it. "I should've asked for ketchup, though."

"Oh, well, sorry."

"It's okay. Here, uh, sit down."

Charley did, feeling somehow conscious of his entire body.

Dereck handed him his gyro, and Charley opened it slowly. He'd ordered it automatically. Most chain restaurants made it the same. He couldn't speak to if it was close to the real Greek food. It probably wasn't. But at least it was familiar.

The lettuce was a little more bitter than he would've liked, and they'd skimped on the tzatziki, but otherwise, it was a welcome break from mostly beef jerky and coffee all day.

"So, how was the game going?" Dereck asked. "You talked about it over chat a few times, but I think this has been the first time we've talked without yelling where a sniper is hiding or something."

"Some designs, some code. I'm not sure I'll finish it now."

"Dude, unless the world actually blows up, I'm sure you will. And I'll be the first to play it."

"How do you know?"

"Dude," Dereck said, talking around another bite, "because of how you *talk* about it. Even if we have to break into some computer lab after we save your sister to make it, you'll make it."

It was suddenly hard for Charley to imagine eating any more of his food.

"Do I talk about it a lot?"

"Oh, it's all you *ever* talk about," Dereck said, his voice warm. "But I like it. I like it a lot. I like knowing people passionate about something—who really care about something or other."

"Oh … okay … so, then … uh … I know you really like surfing."

Dereck took another big bite of his burger, chewing in thought.

Charley couldn't help but notice that when Dereck was lost in thought, his nose twitched. And he'd have the softest sway to his shoulders.

"It's not quite that I like surfing specifically," Dereck eventually said. "I like the freedom of it. I think I'd like to go boating if I had the money for a boat. When I'm out there, when I'm doing it, I forget. There's all this stuff piling up in my mind, and I like not having to do anything but surf."

Charley's blush hadn't even gone away fully—and now it was returning full fucking force.

"I always thought that it was super cool about the… about the surfing thing. I bet you're really good at controlling the water."

Dereck gave out this quiet laugh that trailed off. Every iota of Charley's mind latched onto it.

"You make it sound like a superpower," Dereck said.

"I mean, I can't do it."

"I could teach you a little sometime if you want." Dereck leaned over and bumped him with his shoulder. "Not like the water is going to go anywhere."

Charley was sure his heart would pop out of his chest. "That sounds… that sounds like fun. Sure."

Dereck shifted beside him.

When Charley turned his head, Dereck was sitting closer to him. So close.

"Would you really want to?" Dereck asked, sounding almost shy.

"Uh, yeah, it sounds fun."

"I… okay. Um. So, you *would* like to go to the beach with me sometime?"

"Yeah...?" Charley was failing to understand something and increasingly worried about what it could be. His head felt a little like it was spinning. "I … sure … I would…"

Dereck took a deep, deep breath. "Charley, you know I just asked you out, right?"

"What!" Charley could feel himself closing in on hyperventilating. He scooted back a little, unsure what to do with his hands. Unsure of what to say. Okay, *now* his heart would burst out of his chest.

Dereck's face filled with panic. "I'm sorry! I … uh … I thought you were—maybe I'm just bad at reading signals? Sometimes I think it's flirting, and I—forget I—"

"You're not!" Charley interrupted, his voice louder than he intended. "You're not bad at it. No, it's okay. I… I've had a massive… I mean, a big, I mean … I've had a crush on you for a long time. I just… I didn't think you liked me—"

"Dude! You're fucking cute, nerdy, *and* passionate, and you talk to me like … you get me! I didn't think about it at first, but it's been in the back of my mind for a long time. So, yeah, I like you. I like you a lot."

Charley opened and closed his mouth a few times. He didn't have words for that. His mind had fled for a moment. It was up in space, or in his shoes, or somewhere. He wasn't even sure when he'd responded. He wasn't sure when he'd started to tear up a little.

"I felt so alone when I moved here. I didn't think I would—I wanted to strike out on my own. But my schedule … it's not great for meeting people. And then you were there. A friend who I got to see all the time. And then I couldn't help but—"

Charley scooted so they were so close again.

"I'm so happy you're here. I'm so happy you're with me. Going alone, I can't imagine. Thank you."

"Of course." Dereck held his gaze. "Of course."

The remaining food had long since been abandoned. It lay on the ground. They were sitting right next to each other, facing one another. Charley felt like the words in him wouldn't stop now.

"Things are so complicated, and I don't know what will happen. And I don't know how long anyone on this planet is going to be alive. And maybe that's not a good basis for a relationship, and maybe it's selfish to even want something when everything is going wrong. When I'm worried about my family. About myself. But I think you're right. I think being as happy as we can and holding onto things is *important*. And I would be so happy to go surfing with you. I would love to show you the game I made. To—to—"

Charley stopped and gave an awkward chuckle.

"So, I guess yes, I would like to go on a date."

Dereck sat there. His eyes were wide. His breath elevated. When he spoke, his voice slightly quavered.

"Can we count this picnic as our first date?"

Charley couldn't help but smile. "Sure, why not?"

"Can we kiss on our first date?"

Thought sputtered out. The floor dropped out. He was made of fire, electricity, and all sorts of energy while frozen in stone and iron. To talk was to be rendered breathless. To interact with the possibility of *actually kissing Dereck* was almost unbelievable. That Dereck, hot surfer, kind soul, an amazing friend, had asked him that was beyond...

And if he answered—

"Yes, we can."

Charley knew Dereck was strong, but didn't know he could effortlessly pull him onto his lap. He also didn't know that, up close, he still smelled of salt water, of the beach.

He didn't know that his beard was softer, his body warmer, and his lips electric.

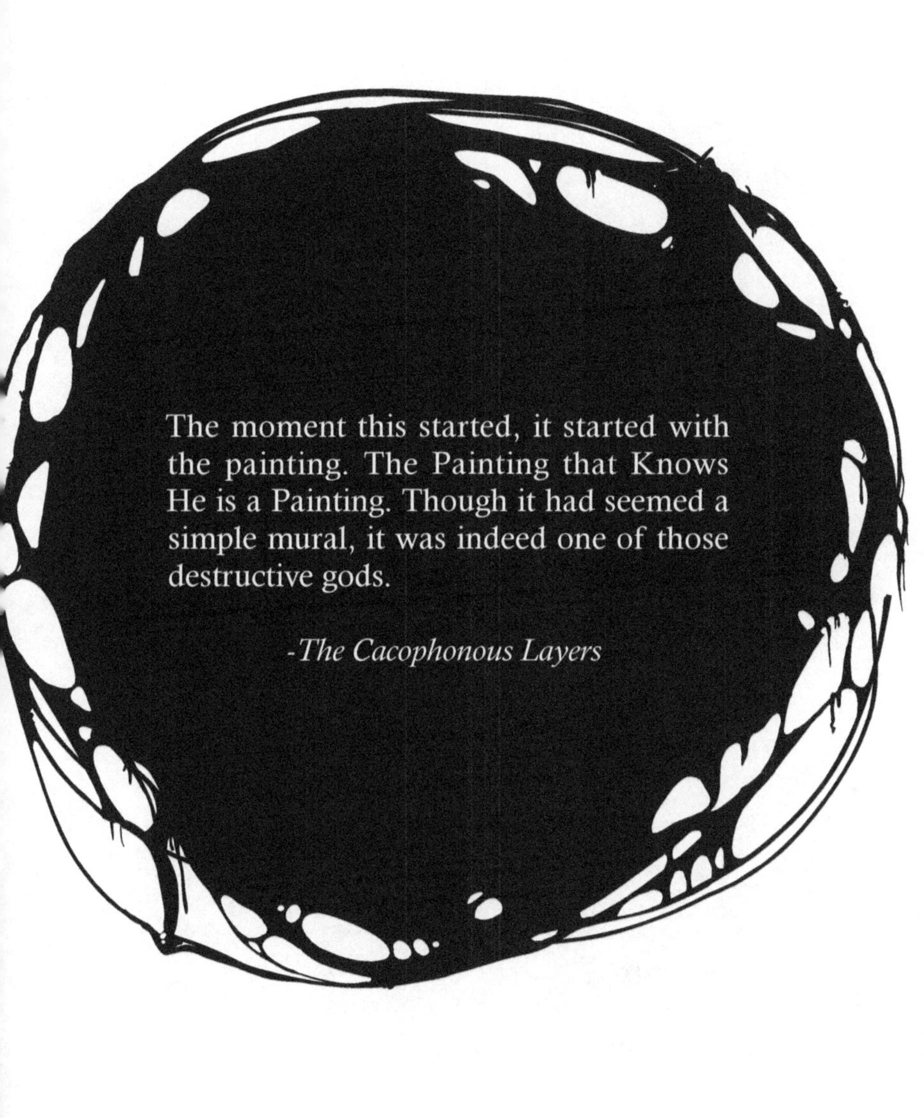

The moment this started, it started with the painting. The Painting that Knows He is a Painting. Though it had seemed a simple mural, it was indeed one of those destructive gods.

-The Cacophonous Layers

Interlude 2

Witness

Bree lost track of time. Then herself. Then all of it. A formless mass of existence. A moment that could be any moment. A lock with no key with a clock that didn't tell time. A level of peace that was anything but. The fake hotel room—her prison—was *pleasant*. She didn't dare open the door and see … whatever was out there… but the hotel room was comfortable. The bed was comfortable. The temperature never got too hot or cold. If she wanted it, the table in front of her would have food. It was even vegan friendly. And, if she desired it, if she got bored enough, a phonograph would appear in the corner of the room and play strange songs. Some she'd even liked.

Bree knew it could be worse for her—but it was also *such* a false metric to think that way. A selfish metric, really. Bree's body could be used for any number of murders and destruction as she sat in gilded boredom. Though she could barely hold the memory, she knew what she'd already been used to accomplish.

The "surgeries" she'd been present for.

Constructing body parts.

What she'd been used to summon.

Calling it a god felt uncomfortable. Even if she had no other context for such a thing. Doing so acknowledged a greater cosmology and span of existence than she knew what to do with. It didn't mean there wasn't a heaven or hell, but it meant there were more layers than she imagined.

Because it was inarguably a god. *The* God of Greed. A being of wealth hoarding and exploitation and currency valued over human life.

And, if she was being honest with herself, she wasn't surprised that the first and perhaps only deity she was sure of existing represented that concept, given what she'd seen so far in her life. Her father, The Mayor of Quill Point, treated the acquisition of wealth with a reverence that could be called worship. And though she'd been shielded from its effects all her life, she knew that human suffering, either directly or indirectly, was what greed demanded.

She'd spent a lot of time thinking about that.

Thinking was the main thing she *could* do. Even if it gave a slight time signature to this eternity. Even if it made it worse to think, she spent lots of time thinking.

Or crying. Or curled up into a ball.

But mostly thinking.

She was pretty sure, if she got the chance, she was morally obligated to murder her father.

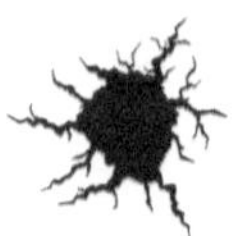

Perhaps it had been a week. Perhaps it had been a billion years. But something changed finally, and Bree's mind was *jolted*. It was a simple but *distinct* change in the air current.

Bree lowered her hands from her eyes, wiping away the tears.

And she found herself looking at the little girl.

The little girl, who was not a little girl, still kept up some pretense of her appearance. She looked almost human, instead of that horrible clay monster that had helped kill over fifty people in the Kraken Hotel. Her skin, irises, hair, simple tee shirt, and jeans were all the same gray as Bree's sculpting clay.

The little girl folded her hands and leaned her chin on them, smirking with a smirk that barely hid malice.

"Hi, Bree," she said simply.

"Fuck you," Bree spat. "Get the *fuck* away from me."

Bree knew yelling at a monster was like banging her hands against the side of an undetonated explosive, but she still enjoyed the little girl's faint frown.

"Well, that's not the welcome I was expecting," she said. "I wanted to have a chat like we used to."

"Slink off and die." Bree stood off the bed, looking down at the little girl. Her hands formed fists—though she knew well that violence was impossible in the dream hotel room. "I want you to get out of my head *now*."

The little girl rolled her eyes. "Can you imagine the cognitive dissonance of a piece of lint yelling at someone who just noticed it on their shirt? It's *funny*... but absurd in a way that's almost not worth it."

The room rippled with *those* symbols. Bree instantly covered her eyes, then shut them as tightly as possible. Those horrible symbols could break reality—could break *her*.

But the mental pressure from before only built a little before stopping short. A knife held up to her throat, but not cutting. Bree still didn't lower her hands.

"Please, go away," she muttered. "Or let me out."

"Well, I can't do the latter, so ... I guess..."

Another little rush of air. The sensation of the symbols faded gradually. Bree opened her eyes when it had been gone for a long time.

The little girl had left the room, and it was as it had been. Letting out a sigh, Bree sat on the bed.

The bed had become significantly less comfortable.

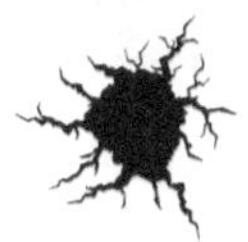

Waiting, anticipating, and worrying was a harsh timer in an endless existence. Bree *knew* that the little girl would eventually return. That it could happen at any time, and then anything could happen.

Hoping it would help with the anxiety, she willed the phonograph on. Instead of music, it produced the same sound as the timer during standardized tests at her old private school.

She turned it back off pretty quickly.

When she ate some of the food, for variety's sake, it got gradually less pleasant with each individual bite. Soon enough, most of it wasn't even edible. The fruits showed signs of rot. The bread got a white, creeping mold.

The smell wouldn't go away.

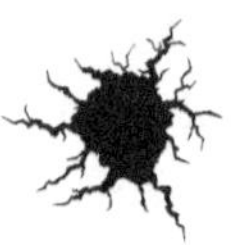

A little rush of air happened some infinity later.

Bree sat up in bed. The little girl was standing on the other side of the room.

"I'm … sorry," Bree said.

"Oh, it's fine. You can't hurt my feelings," the little girl said. "Imagine you being able to hurt my feelings? Imagine I cared enough about you to consider your words hurtful!"

She let out a childish laugh like a ten-year-old delighted by a cartoon character's antics.

"No, no. You couldn't ever. I am here because I am interested in visiting. You won, you know, Bree. Last person standing inside the Kraken Hotel. Even if you got it on a technicality. You are, in some small part, a part of all of this. Sadly, humans, or any sapient, self-aware beings born of the hosting Layer, are required for this process."

"…what process?"

The little girl stuck out her tongue. "Wouldn't you like to know?"

A part of Bree wanted to surreptitiously guide this conversation and gather information about what was happening; another part of her knew that knowing too much about what was happening was potentially dangerous.

"You know I can hear you thinking, right? You're not going to trick a boot, ant." She giggled again. "Oh, look at me. I guess I'm spending too much time with my brother."

"Can I at least get to choose how I say things?" Bree asked.

"Why would I grant you any care at all?"

"I don't know. Why would you?"

"Now there's a good point," the little girl said. "Perhaps I'm bored—or perhaps there is an element to this that requires some mental resources, and you were picked to supply them."

"Is … that what's happening? Are you taking my mind?"

The little girl smiled and, for a second, in the cracks at the edge of that smile, was pulsing energy—something dangerous and inhuman.

"Bree, I've taken plenty of human brains right out of the skulls of your little town. The meat architecture is plentiful; we've got enough to build a monument to it. We've literally got enough to end the world."

A shiver passed up Bree's spine. "So, then … what do you need me for?"

"Surprisingly, a lot," the little girl said. "We're more reliant on humans than I like."

Knowing a possibly omnipotent being was killing people was bad enough—she didn't want to know the nature of The God of Greed's offspring. But it's hard not to think about that question loudly.

The little girl nodded along.

"What I am, Bree, is born knowing what I am—and the minutia of being more than that. I know the nature and purpose of my existence. Tabula rasa is not our nature. We are too conceptual to be bound by ignorance."

"I have no idea what that means."

The little girl chuckled again. "I know you don't, Bree—you can't conceive of it yet. But it works much better if you agree with the core conceit for all involved."

Bree scooted forward to the edge of the bed. She tried to keep her mind quiet.

Eventually, the little girl sighed. "I came here to explain, yet I'm at a loss. Why did we have to be born here, with English as the primary language? It's a mess of a linguistic tongue."

She clapped her hands together.

"It's like this, Bree: my father was born. And then, by his existence, so were we, but only eventually. It should've been fifty years for my father's maturation, but it ended up being a lot longer. Once he matured, though, my brother and I spawned as our father waited in the wings. Though I only use blood relation terms because it is the cleanest terminology. Technically, all the others running around your town are of the same kin as me, but they aren't worth granting such terms. *They* are more like … spontaneous generation. Like flies manifesting from a rotting corpse."

"But what *are* you? Gods as well?" Bree asked.

"My father is a god. I'm a demigod, a more specified, but less … all-encompassing version of what he is."

"…okay," Bree said.

"I suppose the metaphysics of the Layers isn't exactly important to you, is it?" the little girl said, her slightly squeaky voice more and more out of place with how she was talking. "The point is this, Bree: we need your conceptualization; it's why we're willing to work with you a little here. It is as real a resource as gold. Magic—if you want to call it that—always needs a sacrifice."

"Are you just going to kill me, then?"

"Actually, no!" the little girl said. "Didn't I *tell* you that you'd get to be immortal? I really meant it, Bree. I really hope you'll be a part of all of this forever. All those other people, all of them we ripped apart, stole their bones, blood, dreams, thoughts, and their…"

She trailed off into a delighted laugh. A laugh that kept getting louder and more warped. A shadow, a hazy image, of something taller, with skin that shifted like bugs crawled underneath it, sporting an impossible grin, was there for a second, then gone again.

Bree shrank back. Even if she'd seen that form before—knew it was what the little girl was—it was still a nightmare she could barely believe was real. Was here. Was something actively in front of her.

Her body, her survival instinct, told her that being near this demigod was the worst thing she could do.

The little girl smirked at her and continued talking, her voice gathering speed and excitement.

"Those little lint balls, bugs, amoebas, what have you, were necessary in the same way crude oil is for an engine. Calories. Kilowatts. Charcoal. Once a god is born, it takes a lot of death. And we've killed plenty—and will kill plenty more—to fully ascend. But raw power is one thing, and concentrated, tethered to a Layer is another. We need a live, experiencing mind to springboard and process and form our ideological manifestations and go more, more, *more* places born *of* thought. That'll be you, Bree. Our navigator, architect, or propellent. Thinking and knowing, forever."

"*No,*" Bree said so suddenly, and with such force, she surprised herself. "No … I would never fucking agree to that. Whatever that means, I would never—"

The little girl waved her hand dismissively.

Bree was in a white void.

Only not a void, exactly. There were walls, but it was hard to place exactly how far away they were from anything else. She reached out her arm and touched nothing.

Then a shift. The walls thrummed to a beat. A brief pulse of pink.

Bree's heart stopped.

The muscle that pushed blood through her veins, that got oxygen everywhere it needed to be, stopped working.

Death, as sure as anything, flooded out from her chest, fading and yet burning her, scorching nerves to ash in its wake. Each failing cell was a withering vine.

Everything except for Bree's mind died.

That part of her could perceive what was happening now that no air was flowing, no sensation was happening, and no blood was pumping. Rigor mortis was already starting in her face.

Another pulse of pink.

Her heart restarted. Her body shuddered with a gasp that forced air into deflated, empty lungs. The passage of blood moving back through each vein and capillary was individually felt and syrupy.

Somehow, coming back alive hurt even more than dying.

The wall was pink.

Again.

Twice more.

And now she was back in the dream room, the fake hotel, staring with wide eyes as the little girl hummed and examined her pure-gray nails.

"You see, Bree, I was asking and *not* asking. The thing about greed, especially greed on a systemic scale, is that it asks, sometimes so sweetly, that you think you may give your own answer. You *could* do *this*. You *could* do *that*. Ha-ha. But the often unsaid and comfortably, conveniently, unacknowledged reality is that if you're not choosing what's expected by a system you didn't pick, you are also choosing to die of starvation."

She stared at Bree, and her face was a mask.

"So you have a choice. And I own the consequences. And I have not a single iota of empathy."

Bree was shaking and couldn't speak.

"So I give you the option to say no again. I really, truly mean that. But if it's all the same to you, you're now a part of this process. A step that's coming down the pipeline soon enough. And, in the meantime, I need you to form as many opinions, perspectives, and visceral memories as possible. But, Bree, I really think you'll like this part—you'll like it a lot—I'm letting you out of my control to do this. I'm taking my hands off the wheels and trusting you'll drive *carefully*. The Lords of Greed won't touch you—but that's about all I can promise for safety rails. Oh, and before you get any ideas, there *are* other options if you crash and die. It won't stop things if you off yourself; it won't stop our ascendancy. You let your body end up all bloody and unmoving, that's your problem, that's a shame—I would *love* it if you were the one at our helm."

Bree got her mouth to move.

"Wait … but…"

"Bye," the little girl said. "Have some fun."

The little girl was in her monstrous form. She reached up with her clay hands and slashed them through the ceiling. A crack spread quickly, running a line across the ceiling and to the floor. The space beyond the cracks grew visible as it widened—

Bree woke up. There was no gradual awakening, no gentle twist out of the dream. Instant ejection into utter alertness. Adrenaline surged through her, and her flailing arms only stopped because of the ropes binding them.

She was in a large and tall room. Somewhere she'd never been before. It wasn't well lit, but Bree could still see well enough what was in front of her.

What was happening in this room.

The boys with their skin ripped open.

An impossible sphere.

Her father. The Mayor of Quill Point. Glowing with golden energy.

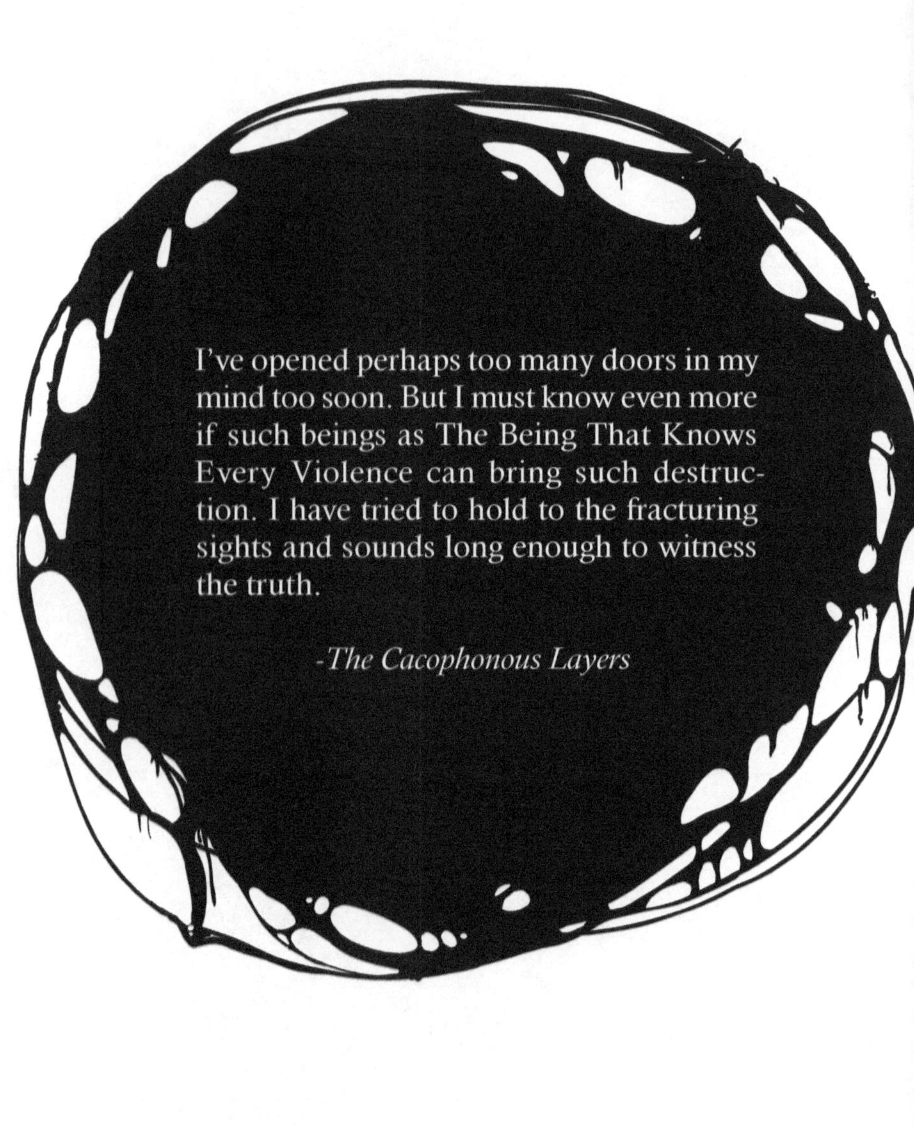

I've opened perhaps too many doors in my mind too soon. But I must know even more if such beings as The Being That Knows Every Violence can bring such destruction. I have tried to hold to the fracturing sights and sounds long enough to witness the truth.

-The Cacophonous Layers

Part 2

The Deepest Secrets

CHAPTER 23

SINCE PIPER WAS LITTLE, SHE'D ALWAYS seemed to notice things about those around her that others didn't. When her friend, Rebecca, got upset with her over her ruining a surprise present, her preschool teacher, Ms. Daffodil, took her aside.

"Piper," she said, "you need to not tell people everything you know."

"But why?" Little Piper asked. "She asked me her secret, and I told the truth."

"Yes, but you didn't need to tell her that way. You could've said something else."

Little Piper frowned. "Are you telling me to lie?"

Ms. Daffodil smiled then. "No, lying is wrong."

"Then what did I do wrong?"

"Nothing, Piper, absolutely nothing. It's a good thing that you can tell what other people are doing. When you get older, it'll be very good that you can tell that sort of thing. But people will get upset sometimes. Some people don't like it when you *know stuff about them. People can get very mad if you tell them their secrets."*

"So … what should I do?"

"Don't lie," Ms. Daffodil said. "Just … let them tell you what you already know. It might make them happy to tell you. And if they don't tell you, don't rush them or push them. Maybe they'll tell you later."

"Okay! That sounds good."

Ms. Daffodil then looked around secretively. "And I'll tell you something cool, Piper. Sometimes, if you listen closely, the world will tell you all sorts of secrets about itself. Listen to the wind at the field when we're on our next field trip. Maybe you'll hear another group playing. Maybe some crickets. Maybe cars driving by. You never know what you'll hear. Curiosity is powerful."

Little Piper nodded furiously. Because not even her parents had figured out yet that she could always tell when adults meant what they said. And Ms. Daffodil meant every word.

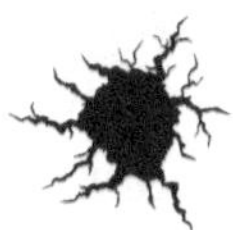

And those skills, for they were skills she could work out like any muscle, had only grown with age. Piper liked to imagine a massive stack of papers, and she was the only one who could sort through all the stimuli printed on them to see the real notes.

But it often felt like people couldn't help but tell her things.

Sometimes it was with words. She'd strike up a mild but friendly conversation with a customer at the grocery store she'd worked at, with a neighbor in the morning before their commute, with someone at a bar on weekends, or even at the dentist's office waiting room—that last one was quite the strange day. Usually, within ten minutes, she would know more about these people than she knew about her own cousins. She wasn't even sure what she did to prompt it. People spilled their guts. Their traumas, their breakups, their financial woes. It was like a planned monologue, and she'd said the cue. Piper had developed a theory that most people carried a lot of mental weight on their backs and were waiting for the right time to divulge it.

But it was when secrets were told without words that Piper got excited. That was the skill she could keep improving. She wanted to make the impressionistic, her intuition, into an activated, reliably usable thing.

And on that day, she was sitting on a log by one of the bonfires and trying to read the script directions of a play happening right in front of her.

The question she was wondering was if she was the only audience.

Zaahir clearly had a crush on Hope. That much was obvious. Piper had no doubts about his motivation. As Zaahir bustled around the impromptu campsite, moving furniture around the circles and circles of tents, he kept looking at her.

Piper could understand why. Hope was *gorgeous*. Her unique academic look wasn't so much "preppy" but still captured the aesthetic people loved online. Since Murder Sky's cold took over, Piper had only seen her wearing a gray long-sleeved sweater with a college logo on the back. Hope had paired them with loose brown pants and boots. She had almost assuredly planned for them to match the color of her large-framed glasses. Her skin was dark brown, and she had hazel eyes.

But while Piper *knew* she was people watching, knew she was surreptitiously looking, Zaahir kept catching himself staring. His shoulders would lift and then drop. The thought process of *She's so pretty* followed by a *Don't stare!*

Piper easily spotted the other half of the equation. Hope was also into it. She was barely reading the book she had. And not because it was a macroeconomics textbook. Zaahir would glance at her for slightly too long, and she would look up right as he looked away, then the tip of her nose would twitch, and then she would read again.

Piper couldn't blame her either. If she wasn't rooting for this relationship to happen, she'd happily try dating either of them. Zaahir was *handsome.*

Zaahir's style had a dash of that college aesthetic but more skewed business casual. A blue t-shirt and black blazer draped his tall, slightly wiry frame, and his sleeves were rolled up, revealing lean muscles. His dress shoes had gotten messy at some point. A similar fate had befallen his usually trimmed beard and wavy black hair—both of them getting a little shaggy since the apocalypse. His skin was medium brown, and when he smiled to himself without realizing it—which he did again after looking at Hope *again*—the corners of his brown eyes noticeably crinkled.

That pattern—Zaahir looks, then Hope looks, but no one says anything—happened *twice* in five minutes.

Piper was mostly watching it out of the corner of her eye. She kept her head pointing toward the fire. She also didn't want them to see her smile.

Piper's ears pricked up. Hope had just let out the tiniest sigh. Oh! Her feet were planted a little more firmly on the ground. Her hand tightened on the book cover.

That looked like … yep, Piper was almost sure: Hope was psyching herself up.

Shy, but overcoming it.

Piper was so tempted to intervene somehow. Nudge this along. But she'd been wrong about this sort of thing before. She didn't want to cause an awkward scenario instead of an adorable one.

Was there a way to open up a possibility without locking anyone into a social scenario?

Piper's thoughts were interrupted by her brother Sean sitting down beside her.

Piper glanced at him. Sean and Piper always looked a lot alike. Sometimes people assumed they were twins, but Piper was three years older than him. They both had light brown hair, medium brown skin, and brown eyes.

"Here," Sean said simply, offering a lump of tinfoil. "Saanvi made it."

Piper frowned. Maybe the meet-cute would happen organically. It seemed to have every chance of that as is. If one of them would just get up the nerve.

Besides, the smell was quickly demanding her attention. She hadn't realized how hungry she was.

The tinfoil was warm, and a thin trail of steam escaped from within. She ripped off a chunk of naan and placed it in her mouth, even if it burned her a little. Saanvi always made the best naan.

"God, I haven't eaten all day," she muttered around a bite.

"Same. At least it feels like it," Sean said.

"I think it literally has been twenty-four hours," Piper said. "At *least* twenty hours."

"That sounds right."

"Do we know what happened to Grace? It doesn't seem like food gets organized without her."

"Went into the forest," Sean said.

Piper's mouth went dry. *The* forest. No one ever came back. One of the big, horrible, worrying mysteries of Quill Point and the broader apocalypse.

"Well, that's not great. Do you think they'll sort something out?"

"Don't know," Sean said, then took another bite of naan.

"Do you think we'll get the next scheduled meal?" Piper asked.

"I hope so."

"Yeah, me too."

Piper quickly finished eating. There wasn't a lot to go around for each person. The Mayor's Men were less likely to notice unapproved food in smaller portions.

But now that her body had gotten some food, it called for more. Piper ran her hands over her stomach.

"Uh, this sucks."

"Yes, it does," Sean said, shrugging.

Piper looked at the fire for a few more moments. It wasn't all that distracting, but it crackled and moved nicely.

"What were you about to do?" Sean asked quietly.

Piper was taken aback for a moment but then chuckled. "Intervene, maybe. Probably cause a little trouble."

"They'll figure it out."

Piper glanced over at him.

"You think?" she asked.

"Not a lot else to do but eventually talk," Sean said.

"That's true," Piper muttered, "that is very true."

The bonfire continued to crackle in front of them. Its sparks casting up toward that night sky. She followed them with her eyes on instinct, but then quickly glanced back down. The sky was dark at night—but those strange red and orange tendrils were probably still up there. Anything could be, really. Monstrous hands made of shadows. Whatever had been above the Kraken Hotel before … well…

Her gaze instead drifted to the pile of logs blazing in the bonfire. Seeing the mesmerizing passage of heat as it molded them orange and wore them away.

Her stomach grumbled again, but that food helped more than she'd realized. Something in her stomach plus the heat of the bonfire was a potent cocktail. Her eyes kept fluttering closed.

Sean yawned next to her.

"I think I might tuck in," Piper said.

"I've got a watch," Sean replied. "Second day."

Piper was probably the only person in the world who could detect the annoyance in his voice.

"Sorry," she said.

"Don't know why the Mayor's Men can't do it," Sean said.

"Yeah…" Piper said, biting her lip.

That was another mystery on top of all the others. The Mayor of Quill Point and some of the Mayor's Men were hiding something. The police chief hadn't been seen in a long time, and most officers were "spread too thin across Quill Point."

Or, in other words, the Mayor's Men were in charge now.

"Well, if there are rations tomorrow," Piper offered, "I can handle breakfast. You sleep in."

"Thank you," Sean said. "Good night. Love you."

"Love you too," Piper said.

She gave him a side hug and then stood. Her legs were a little sore—she'd been sitting, people-watching, for probably the last few hours. Not a lot to do today. She needed to rest for her turn taking care of the older people, the little kids, and the people who weren't doing so well without access to a hospital.

As she walked toward her tent, she glanced at Hope again. She was blatantly not reading her book, not even a little. Just watching and waiting for a signal.

Zaahir wasn't paying attention, though. So, Hope's perfect, random, targeted glances wouldn't reach anything but the side of a tent.

Okay. That'll work.

"Goodnight, Hope," Piper called louder than necessary.

Hope jolted in her seat, glancing her way in confusion. Her gaze eventually landed on Piper, and she smiled.

"Goodnight!"

And … there we go.

Zaahir looked over. His gaze naturally fell on Piper, but she met it only briefly before glancing at Hope. Zaahir's eyeline automatically followed hers. Then Piper quickly turned her back on the whole thing, hurrying away. The less they paid attention to her, the further away she got, the more likely it would feel like an opportunity, like almost serendipity—

"Hey, Zaahir, can you … uh, help me with something?"

Piper smirked. She could imagine Sean rolling his eyes behind her, but she didn't care. That was a perfect maneuver.

CHAPTER 24

Piper walked up to her tent. It was a small army surplus tent scrounged up once she'd been *informed* that her house had a gas leak after Murder Sky by some Mayor's Men. She'd heard a few people say similarly.

She'd still got some of her stuff out to the tent. Her mattress sat on the floor. She'd grabbed a little lantern that she put next to it, and they'd gotten a good amount of her books.

She plucked one of the mystery novels off the pile and fell into her bed. It wasn't on quite even ground, but it was comfy enough. She cracked the book open, read the opening page, remembered how it ended, and then let it fall onto her chest.

She debated getting something else from the pile—even if she *had* read them all—but stared at the tent ceiling instead. The biggest mystery was this town. Quill Point was the biggest piece of information she'd never been able to find.

Did Murder Sky happen everywhere? Or just here? What was it? Why had it happened? Why was *only* the Kraken Hotel attacked by clay monsters? Why *did* the Irena Ink Memorial Hospital burn, and how did it burn that fast? Was it supernatural, accidental, or arson? She'd heard all the theories people threw around. Aliens. The government. Magic. Some biblical or otherwise supernatural apocalypse.

It didn't help that people, even outside of the mass events, had been experiencing various strange things. Reports and rumors of ghostly figures. Mostly sightings of Irena Ink. Her picture would shimmer or move somehow. Sculptures of her seemed to blink. Piper didn't know what to make of them—she believed those things had happened but didn't know what that even suggested.

She didn't know the rules of all this.

She didn't know the ways to *learn* the rules.

But The Mayor of Quill Point knew something. He was planning something. Last week, he'd rounded up tons of dollar bills from people around the bonfire. No one was charging for anything anyway—what did money matter in an apocalypse? It didn't make *any* sense. And things that didn't fit together always bothered Piper. Grated like sand in a shoe.

And nothing made sense to her.

What was hidden from her in those whispers, furtive glances, and dodging questions?

Maybe they were responsible for all of it?

She didn't know how, but maybe The Mayor did this purposefully? Or at least knew it was happening soon?

Piper sat up for a moment, looking around the piles. Didn't she have a horror book lying around her, somewhere? Haven had recommended it to Piper the last time

Piper was at Stylus Books. Haven told her that Milda had liked it.

Didn't that have a plotline about someone summoning something? A demon? Piper didn't enjoy thinking that sort of thing could be real—but it had been proven possible. There was no sense in demarcating what could and couldn't be real anymore.

She was still glancing over the pile when she heard something.

Piper blinked a few times in confusion. She tilted her ear toward the sound. Was that … *screaming*?

Yes, it was.

Yelling and crying for help.

Screaming was bad everywhere. Obviously. But screaming in Quill Point *could* mean—

Piper was out of her tent in a second, eyes wide and her pulse thrumming. Her heartbeat was not even a beat, but a continuous hum that felt like it would burst out of her.

Shit. Shit. Shit.

She darted in the last direction she'd seen Sean. The screaming was getting closer, but not coming toward her.

Other people were noticing too. People were peeking out of their tents. Peeking out with fear in their eyes. Murmurs ran like an electrical current. Some people were already asleep this late into the night—though not for much longer.

A pounding run was nearby. Running right at Piper. It wasn't in the same direction as the screaming. It was coming from over *there*—

Sean practically crashed into her as he rounded a corner and skidded to a stop.

"Are you okay?" he asked.

"Yeah—you heard that too?"

"It sounded like a girl, I thought…" Sean cut himself off. Then looked around.

Piper almost said something, but snapped her mouth shut when she noticed it.

The noise had stopped.

Piper's heart rate made it harder to probe for a new noise. Sean was breathing a little hard but trying not to. The stillness was electric. Then another bout of running closed in. Piper tensed up but didn't move yet.

Zaahir arrived from a different direction.

His eyes were wide.

"I heard screaming," he said.

The other people were moving now, some grabbing their bags, looking like they would break for it. If this was anything like what had happened at the Kraken Hotel, Piper didn't blame them. But she didn't want to get caught up in some rush.

"What's happening?" Zaahir asked.

"We don't know yet," Sean answered.

"Shush," Piper said, putting her finger to her lips. She tilted her head in a few different directions. "I'm trying to figure out where that came from."

A roar of anger sounded out. Human sounding. It wasn't a long enough sound to get any more information. Whatever was making it was moving alongside the camp—not into it.

"Fuck," Zaahir swore under his breath.

Sean's voice was quiet. "Maybe we should—"

This time, the scream was loud enough. It was obvious the direction. Off to the west of the encampment. Probably near the tree line.

And then there was jeering. And then there was laughter.

"Mayor's Men," Piper whispered.

"Fuck," Sean said. "Fucking … if they…"

Determination passed across Sean's face. He looked right at Zaahir.

"There's no time to get people," Sean said. "We need to go."

Zaahir nodded. Piper noticed them exchange some fraction of some communication. Then they sprinted toward the sound.

Piper paused for maybe a second. Watching them run. Her mind whirring. She glanced around her. But the people closest were parents with children. Hope wasn't nearby—Piper assumed she was the direction Zaahir had come from. There wasn't a quick backup.

Two. Zaahir and Sean. *Only* two.

The Mayor's Men usually worked in groups of three, if not entire hordes of them. The two could be walking into, at the very least, a fight they couldn't win.

Piper thought for another moment. Then followed them.

CHAPTER 25

Piper recognized the screaming woman's voice. It was Grace's voice. Beloved waitress of the Ink Well Diner. And should-be missing person. The fact she'd returned from the forest somehow was a mystery for another time, though.

As she ran, the cold snapped in as she got away from the bonfire. Quill Point's darkness flowed in like liquid night as she slipped outside the tent's rings. Unlike the cars and phones, the streetlights still worked, but they weren't nearly enough to dispel those hazy patches. Dead cars blocked long fields of view and interrupted light rays, adding shadows to everything. Piper shivered. She already knew it was the apocalypse, but it felt so much more like it at that moment. Obscured and cloaked, the forest seemed like a horde of approaching monsters sweeping through an empty world.

Silence wasn't the sound of that night though. Piper's breath and heart were loud enough to dull it slightly, but the crickets and frogs sang a surging chorus. The long drone swelled around her as she ran. Piper was sure she'd had lonely dreams like this.

Then another angry yell pierced the illusion. And the animals stopped.

"Let me fucking go!" Grace screamed.

"Aren't customers supposed to be listened to?" one of the Mayor's Men replied.

"This isn't a fucking joke! Do you know what's even happening?! Do you know what's out there? We're all going to *fucking die!*"

Up ahead, Zaahir and Sean were standing behind a parked car. They almost yelled in alarm when Piper stepped next to them, ducking down behind the car.

Sean glanced at her and frowned.

"No," he whispered.

"Already here," Piper replied quietly.

Sean grimaced but said nothing else.

Piper peeked around the car. This couldn't go well. Four Mayor's Men stood in the light of a bent and flickering streetlight.

She'd learned their names far before they'd been Mayor's Men. Some she'd even gone to school with before everything.

Two had Grace by her arms. Those would be Liam and Tristan.

Liam was the shortest of them. He had a bad sunburn on the tip of his nose but was otherwise pale white. He was wearing an army jacket too big for him and some fingerless gloves.

Tristan was of medium height and build with white skin, and he had close-cropped black hair. He wore a horror movie tee shirt and jeans with several rips around his kneecaps.

Grace struggled against them weakly but clearly couldn't lift her body up without help. She looked *wrecked*. Grace's clothing was covered in blood. Her pants had bramble stabbed into them, and a black eye steadily formed on her left eye.

Then she noticed Wyatt. Wyatt was a big guy with very tanned white skin and many visible muscles in his arms. He liked to wear big, loose shirts with logos for random products.

He also had a body slung over his shoulder.

Piper's stomach dropped. She ducked back and covered her mouth to stop a scream from getting out. Had they *killed* someone?

"Let us fucking go!" Grace demanded again.

Hunter stood over her, stoic. The streetlight cast his pinkish complexion in shadow, and his dark blue shirt and tan pants faded into the dim lighting. Of all the people that Piper had grown up knowing in Quill Point, Hunter had always been the hardest to read. His big brown eyes only revealed what he was paying attention to—nothing more. She'd never got him to spill anything about his life during conversations.

Hunter reached to his hip and pulled out something that glimmered underneath the light of the streetlight. A fold-out baton. Piper was sure those weren't legal.

"You two are requested by The Mayor of Quill Point," Hunter said coldly. "You were reported stealing food from the rations, then you injured multiple people. Billy's nose is *still* bleeding."

"*Bullshit*," Grace spat. "They tried to murder—"

"Will you shut up," Liam said. "Don't try to blame us!"

"Arthur shot a *gun* at me!"

"Maybe you wouldn't get shot at if you stopped talking and listened!"

Grace shook her head slowly. "Do you not hear me? This isn't important. The forest is full of *fucking monsters*. The Mayor has been sending people into a meat grinder—"

The flash of the baton was a silver blur against the meager light.

Grace let out a shriek, and her head dropped. She squirmed to grasp at her face. Tristan and Liam dropped her with a painful thud. Grace leaned over the pavement, and the steady drip of blood was horribly audible. The baton's length was now flecked with crimson.

Hunter cleared his throat. "You two are requested by The Mayor at the courthouse, and you *will* listen to me."

Zaahir made a noise in the back of his throat and moved to step around the car. Piper caught his arm at the last second, pulling him backward. He practically fell over but managed not to yell out.

"What the hell," Zaahir whispered.

"Look at their belts," Piper said.

Sean glanced around the car, his shoulders raised, and then he shifted back out of sight. "Dammit. They all have them."

"Yeah," Piper said. "I think The Mayor's arming them now."

"We need to do *something*," Zaahir said.

"We can't fight four people with weapons," Piper shot back.

Zaahir gritted his teeth. "Then what are we *supposed* to do?"

"I don't know," Piper said.

She kept trying to think of anything they could do. Hunter had said "you two," meaning Declan was at least likely alive, and if The Mayor of Quill Point wanted them, they weren't likely to do anything lethal *yet*. A quick glance showed the faint motion of Declan's breath. Yep, alive, at least somewhat. There was remaining travel time to do something, then, but very little ability to intercede.

"We need a different plan than fighting," Piper whispered.

"Do you have one," Sean asked.

"Not yet."

Grace let out a low, pained, but angry groan.

"Hit her again," Wyatt said. "She'll be less rowdy."

"No," Hunter said, his voice unyielding. "There's no need for that."

"Fine. But why did we let those other three go?" Liam complained.

"Forget about that. He asked for Grace and Declan. So, we're bringing him Grace, and we are bringing him Declan. Come on, The Mayor doesn't like it when we're late."

Grace barely resisted when Tristan and Liam yanked her arms again and dragged her. The tips of her shoes made little divots in the dirt as they moved her. Declan shifted on Wyatt's shoulder as he walked, his loose legs swinging.

Piper bit back her own angry yell. She wanted some way to leap out and crack noses or something. Super strength or telekinesis would be useful.

"We need to ... keep following them ... but..." Piper chewed at her thumbnail. "But we need..."

She glanced between the two.

"Which one of you is faster?"

"Zaahir," Sean said immediately.

Piper couldn't help noticing Sean's frown as he wondered why she might ask such a question.

Zaahir looked taken aback for a moment. But then nodded.

Piper looked back out around the car. They were getting farther away. Disappearing, then reappearing, between the working streetlights. She looked between Zaahir and Sean for a long moment.

"Okay, Zaahir, you go get reinforcements. Sean and I will keep tailing them."

"No," Sean hissed. "*You* go back."

There's no way I'm not finding out what's happening.

Piper shook her head. "We don't have time to argue about this. Zaahir is the fastest—and we don't know what they'll do to Grace. We need to at least be able to distract them if they do something."

"You shouldn't even be here," Sean said.

"Do you think I'm leaving you alone?" Piper asked.

"You're going back," Sean said.

"We don't have time. I'm following you. I'm not staying here. And Zaahir is the fastest. Come on."

Zaahir looked between the two.

Sean worked his jaw. Piper was counting on years of her stubbornness to convince him this was not a battle worth having.

"Fine."

Piper turned to Zaahir. "Get as many people as you can. Hurry."

Zaahir nodded and then sprinted off in the other direction.

When she turned back to Sean, he looked more worried than angry. She understood. She appreciated that he wanted to be a protective big brother in this scenario. Now was not the fucking time for it.

CHAPTER 26

QUILL POINT WAS A SMALL TOWN, GEO-graphically speaking. But it felt huge without cars and phones. Roads went on forever. Five minutes in a vehicle—an hour on foot. Tracking the group was like following a spaceship gliding through space, fixating on the movement among the darkness.

As they ran, the wind seemed to push at them. Piper's eyes watered slightly as icy, almost winter air hit her face. The crickets and frogs started back up their surging chorus, sounding to Piper like a warning.

But they still caught up quickly.

The four Mayor's Men were slower. They had to carry two bodies. If it wasn't for Sean and Piper already knowing what would happen if they rushed at them unprepared, they could've easily overtaken them.

Instead, they ensured they were always out of their sightline, keeping a ways back.

Someone had apparently knocked Grace unconscious. She didn't even keep her head up anymore. As the courthouse lights crept over them, she looked so small.

They were running out of time.

When the group stopped and stood there, Sean and Piper stopped and went behind another car. As worrying as it was having the vehicles randomly dead around town—never once working since Murder Sky—they made a convenient hiding place.

Staying low, Piper looked around the ground. Maybe she could chuck a rock at one of their heads and snatch Grace and Declan quickly. She grimaced after a moment of looking. How were they supposed to carry two people while outrunning four?

Sean nudged her side, and she broke from her reverie.

He pointed out into the dark.

Two more people were walking up slowly. Piper grimaced. The Mayor's Men were bad enough, but knowing that Arthur and Brook were involved made this worse. Arthur beat up a child last week for taking an extra piece of bread.

Six to two, now. Bad, *bad* odds.

"We can't do anything," Piper said bitterly, ducking back down.

Some faint conversation wafted over to them, but it was impossible to discern what the individual members were saying. A rapid-fire beat of words and probably instructions.

"What is this?" Piper asked.

"Nothing good."

More talking rattled back and forth between the two groups. Then Liam, Tristan, and Wyatt split off from the group and ran into the night. As they rushed past, Piper grabbed Sean's arm and pulled him farther into the dark.

The three of them looked determined—which was never good.

Once they'd left, Piper slunk back over to see what was happening.

Brook and Arthur didn't need Hunter's help carrying Grace and Declan. He trailed behind them as they all walked up to the front of the courthouse. The front door opened as they did, letting out even more light.

Piper frowned. She had expected the tall, muscular stature of The Mayor of Quill Point, but the two people opening the door were shorter, much shorter.

Two children. They looked vaguely familiar, like someone's kids she'd seen in a group setting. She shivered but couldn't quite tell why.

The group of them stepped inside, and the door shut. And the slam of that door was so loud that Piper flinched.

CHAPTER 27

ASILENCE THAT ONLY HAPPENED IN THE deepest parts of nature washed over everything. The distance between them and the door to the courthouse was now an open darkness without even other people to follow.

Their reinforcements hadn't come yet.

But whatever was happening, it was happening now.

Piper knew Sean wouldn't agree with them sneaking into the building, or with following them even further.

So, she didn't bother asking.

"Come on," she said.

She darted forward quickly and felt the wind of Sean trying and failing to grab her arm.

"No. Piper."

Piper didn't even turn around. She walked as silently as she could between cars and up toward the door. She could hear Sean scrambling after her, swearing under his breath.

Once this was over, she owed him one.

After all the walking she'd done that night, this final distance felt so impossibly small it was almost a shock when she reached the door. It was a normal door, maybe a little more ornate than usual—but it felt huge and imposing.

But it wasn't locked.

Sean's hand grabbed hers before she could push open the door. She looked over at him with annoyance.

"What are you doing?"

"I'm going after Grace."

Sean stared into her eyes. "You're trying to find out something."

Leave it to Sean to notice that.

"I can do both things. I think we *need* to know both things."

"We need backup," he said.

"By the time Zaahir and everyone get here, we don't know what'll have happened. Maybe they'll have fucking ritualistically sacrificed them or something."

"Piper!"

"Sean! The Mayor is up to *something*. It's all I can see sometimes. Maybe this is connected to all of it. The Prayer Spire, the hotel, him taking all that money, the houses. Fuck, maybe even Murder Sky. And if he is, then we need to know. I don't know how much longer anything in this town will hold together. So *many* people are already dead. I want to save Grace and Declan and anyone else they've taken. And I want to *know* whatever we can that might save this town."

"I don't want you to get hurt," Sean said. "I don't want to see your body around that Spire."

Piper pursed her lips and tried to make her next words count. "If we don't do something—I won't be safe anyway.

This town is running out of food and medicine. We just saw the Mayor's Men beat the shit out of someone. I don't want to sit around a bonfire and wait for whatever heavy blow comes next."

"Piper—"

"Mom and Dad are on the other side," Piper snapped back. She looked at him hard, trying to make her words have enough force to overcome *whatever* he said. "If I wasn't sure that the forest is too dangerous, I would already be going."

Sean banged his hand onto the side of his leg in frustration. Then he let out a long, long breath. "Fine."

Piper nodded. "Thank you. We'll keep each other safe. I promise."

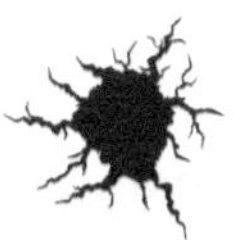

All of what she'd said, and the mysteries attached, raced through Piper's head as they went down the corridor. She felt certain that if they could find and save them, it would also reveal everything else.

Besides the strange door slam though, the actual place was mundane. The courthouse was a building of big rooms and hallways with very tall roofs and not a lot else. Up above them hung mostly off lightbulbs encased in intricate glass. It made the expensive floral wallpaper and the dull brown runner carpet into slightly shadowy forms.

Their passage through felt aimless after a few moments. They hadn't heard any noise, talking or otherwise. There might have been soundproofing going on. Each door didn't even have a little window to look inside.

The signs also didn't help. Discolored marks on the walls showed the plates had likely been moved around.

B-1. E-2. Q-3.

"Why would they do that? Is it a code?"

"Not that I can tell." Sean moved his fingers around, muttering numbers. "Yeah, no idea."

"I guess we have to try them at random."

"Quietly," Sean warned.

"Of course," Piper responded. Then looked around, glancing at each door like they might reveal a secret. A feeling of dread kept building in her. It was almost like carbon monoxide or radon. A heady, pushing sense of wrongness. Of death lingering.

She picked door C-3 to start.

It was a judge's room. Empty and with lots of seating. Normal, mostly—but—

Piper blinked in confusion.

In roughly the spot where she'd seen so many lawyers on television pace and deliver biting speeches was a bed. King-sized. The bed had been made meticulously; the nice-looking cotton sheets were tucked in at the sides. Next to it was a small dresser with a few books on top and an unlit lamp.

"What … the…"

"I guess the Mayor's Men get to sleep here," Sean said.

"He said that we had to be outside, in the cold, because this place was … fuck, what did he say, 'too chaotic and damaged to bring upon our fair citizens.'"

"He lies," Sean said quietly.

"I know he does. And I knew it was a lie when he said it, but I didn't really think about how much … just … god, he's an *asshole*. He *wants* us to be suffering."

Piper closed the door. She felt a thrum of anger that helped dispel that still lingering dread—but there wasn't time to dwell on it.

Sean pulled open another door. Another courtroom. No bed this time. But it was still a big enough room to fit another ten people, maybe more. Even if they slept on the floors, it would be better than what they were getting.

They turned a corner and found yet more doors misnumbered.

A closet full of mops.

Meeting room.

Filing room.

Finally, Piper opened a door and paused. Despite it being normal, something seemed off. Her nose twitched. In front of her was a nice, enormous desk with a chair behind it. The desk was over seven feet wide and had only a small cup full of nice pens on top of it.

She stepped in and then sniffed the air. There was a faint lingering smell. Something awful. A coppery, pungent odor.

"I think I found something," she said.

Sean walked over to her and immediately covered his nose. "Ugh—what is that?"

Piper took another step into the room, pushing the door wider open. Her shoe stuck to something. Something tacky. A surge of panic went through her. Piper didn't want it to be what she assumed it was.

She counted in her head, then looked down.

The blood was dry. A thin sheen of reddish remains caught the light in the wrong way. Piper slowly pulled her foot back. When she stepped somewhere else, it left a faint outline of her shoe.

"Uh, gross…" she said. Slowly, then more quickly, she scraped the bottom of her shoe against the floor. It kept leaving little red streaks.

Sean moved past her, his face grave. He stepped over the puddle into the room proper.

Piper finally got her shoes clean enough. Her stomach was rolling, and it felt a tad hard to breathe. She tried to contain the nausea and followed Sean.

Sean stood all the way by the desk and was staring at something.

With every warning bell chiming in her head, Piper turned to look.

There was another room within the room. A normal door. And underneath was a huge puddle of now-dried blood. It looked like a creature, an octopus, of spreading blood tendrils. A piece of morbid artwork.

Piper stared at it. She'd said, "Ritually sacrificed." Knowing that *was* a possibility. This looked very much like that sort of thing.

"Oh, I have to, don't I?" she said aloud to herself.

She looked down at her feet and swore that once she got the chance, she would burn these shoes in the nearest bonfire.

Sean didn't stop her. He followed right behind as she stepped across that sticky pool. At least the door handle had nothing on it.

"I hope she's still alive," Piper said. "Please, don't be— please be—"

She opened the door quickly and couldn't help but close her eyes. Behind her, Sean gasped and then almost instantly started to hyperventilate. She could hear him scramble backward, screams failing to escape him.

She opened one eye.
Just one.

CHAPTER 28

S HE NEEDED TO GET OUT. SHE NEEDED TO get out. *She needed to get out.*

Reinforcements, *now*. As many people as they could. They needed to arrest him, stop him…

What had he done to those people?

How can a human do that to other people?

She couldn't stop her screaming. It was so loud it echoed and hurt her own ears. Closing her eyes as tightly as she could, she slammed the door closed again.

"We need to leave," she cried.

"Yes," Sean managed to say. "Yes … get out…"

They ran out of the room, going back around the corner, back toward the exit. They needed to be out of this building. Never come back. Piper could never step into a place where … not stained with—

"What the fuck was *that*?" Wyatt said.

Piper skidded to a halt. Mayor's Men. They'd come back from wherever they'd gone. She didn't know any other direction to get out of the courthouse.

"Someone's here," Liam hissed. "Someone who shouldn't be."

Piper looked at Sean in a panic. He froze for a moment, then gestured at one of the storage closets and pulled open the door. They both piled in. Piper shut the door and made herself small.

"Fuck, do you think they followed Brook in?"

Their voices were so close. Piper held her breath as best she could.

"I don't know," Liam said. "We don't have time for this. He needed the gold now."

"He's not going to want an interruption," Wyatt shot back.

"Fine, check the rooms."

Piper's heart sank. Looking around, there wasn't anything that could be considered a weapon. The mop was a tiny thing made of plastic—not even a hefty piece of wood.

One door opened with a bang.

"Nope."

Another, somehow even louder. Closer.

"Nothing."

Piper was sure her heart was about to burst. It thudded in her chest like it wanted to escape her ribcage. Next to her, Sean's hands were in fists. There was no way they would *win* a fight—not like this.

Piper tried to keep her voice as quiet as possible while still being audible.

"We should run when he opens another door."

Sean looked at her. It was hard to see in the dark, but he nodded.

Piper gently spun the handle and pushed it open a single crack. She leaned forward, putting her head right up to the doorjamb.

Wyatt was wandering from door to door slowly, a heavily laden backpack tugging at his shoulders. He threw each door open with one hand and brandished his baton with the other. His knuckles jutting out from how hard he was holding the hilt.

Liam stood in front of a painting of Irena Ink, tapping his foot impatiently. The painting was swung back on a hinge, showing a staircase.

Piper's eyes went wide.

It was like something out of one of her mystery novels. An honest-to-god secret passage. The staircase was rough-hewn and stretched down into the dark. It was made of a dark stone, like granite or cobalt. But it had a slight shine, like it might be slippery. It curved off after a moment, feeding into a spiral.

"Come on," Liam said. "We need to go."

Wyatt flung open another door and peered in. Piper was sure he'd see her looking out if he turned around.

"You got to be thorough about these things," Wyatt said. "It's always the last one you check."

"Then *go* faster," Liam said.

Wyatt rolled his eyes and walked almost directly toward Piper and Sean. Piper's heart dropped, and she couldn't help but close her eyes again. When a different door, very close, opened, she snapped her eyes open.

"Fuck—go!" she said.

Sean and Piper burst out of the door.

"Jesus Christ," Liam yelled, flinching backward.

Piper ran as hard as she could, clearing the corner before Wyatt let out his surprised swear. Adrenaline coursed through her, telling her only one mission statement: get out.

But even as she bolted, something nagged at her. Brook, Arthur, and Hunter had gone inside earlier. Wyatt and Liam were right behind her. That was five—where was—?

"Hey guys, wait up, would you?" Tristan called out. "Unlike some of you, I've been walking *all fucking day*, can't you—"

Piper nearly bowled into Tristan but froze in panic.

Tristan stared back at her. His eyes were wide. He dropped the metallic water bottle he was carrying, and it clattered to the floor.

Sean apparently had a better reaction time than her.

He threw his entire body weight at Tristan, smacking him into the wall. Then, before he could do anything, Sean punched him in the cheek. The force knocked Tristan's head into the wall with a harsh thud.

Tristan let out a grunt of pain and slid to the ground, feet sprawled out in front of him.

"Guys, intruder," he muttered, dazed.

Piper glanced at him once then ran again. The two others were so close.

"Tristan, I swear to god," Liam said. "You're supposed to—oh, whatever—*we require assistance*."

Piper was still running, but she somehow felt slower. A chill wrapped its way around her spine. The air took on a staticky quality. Sounds dulled like they were underwater.

A part of her mind screamed warnings.

She pushed forward—she *needed* to get out.

Until the hallway plunged into impossibly deep darkness. Not just the lights went out—the concept of light disappeared in front of them. It was a wall—a solid thing. Floor to ceiling.

The sensation. The same sensation. When the world had become something different and horrible.

Murder Sky.

She scrambled backward on instinct. She bumped into Sean. He was standing stock-still, trying to breathe but only getting wracking, panicky gasps.

In that darkness, there was a faint giggle. Like a child happily playing in another room. Then, twin eyes blinked open in the darkness. Glowing yellow eyes, about a child's height off the ground.

A little boy stepped into sight, smirking.

"Hello, little bugs. Scrambling over the surface of a picnic table, I see."

The little boy raised a single hand and flicked out his index finger. Piper's hair shifted backward. She didn't dare move. It felt like a thumb suddenly hovered above her head.

"Normally, I'd see how many I could stomp on," the little boy added, "but I think we could use the company."

Piper's mind screamed again, and she had to force it back down. It wanted her to hide. Hide in a corner. In a vent. Under the bed. Anywhere the monsters couldn't get her.

"Handle them," the little boy said.

Piper let out a single sharp scream when Liam grabbed her arm and pinned it behind her. It *hurt*. She didn't resist, though—her gaze was caught on the childish and yet impossibly cruel look that little boy had.

"Trust me, you're going to want a few insects on hand," the little boy said. "It's best to practice."

Sean let out a faint noise from the back of his throat as Wyatt grabbed him and pulled him along. He didn't resist either.

And, what made it worse was the little boy seemed to know on some level how afraid she was. Though maybe that was how he always looked at anyone.

"Now, news to you, 'Mayor's Men,'" the little boy said. "That was your first and last calling on me. Don't need me again. Don't ask for my assistance again. Or my sister's assistance, either. I will make you understand what it feels like to be tossed into this planet's sun. I have many more important things to do than deal with you."

He tilted his head like he was listening to something, and slowly, a wicked smile passed over his lips.

"For one thing," he continued. "I have to deal with a new infestation on this Layer."

"Yes, of course, uh, sir," Liam said.

"Thank you so much for your help, sir," Wyatt said.

Tristan nodded his appreciation as he stood back up, rubbing his head and glaring at Sean.

The little boy chuckled again then stepped back into the shadow wall. Instantly, he wasn't visible. It whisked him out of sight like plunging into a dark cave. Then those yellow eyes stared out for a long moment. When he blinked, they disappeared.

The hallway slowly, like a sunrise across a field, regained its light and returned to normal. The little boy was no longer there.

Piper couldn't stop staring at that spot. She kept looking even as they pulled her backward. She only turned when they shoved her toward the stairs, toward a walk down that she could only think of as a descent into death. The reaper's skeletal arms were happily outstretched for her.

CHAPTER 29

⸺⸺⸺⸺

THEY TRAVELED DOWN THAT DARK SPIRAL staircase. It looped four times, going well into the dirt. If this building had a basement, they would have been past it. Deep into the core of Quill Point.

Piper's mind latched onto thoughts of what could be down there. Human sacrifices laid across a stone dais. Stone monuments to unknowable creatures. A pit of blood and guts.

Instead, a solid gold orb was floating in the middle of a simple, sparse room. The room had no other way in. No other way out. The walls didn't have symbols or prophecies scrawled on them in jagged lines. It was a cone of a room, cavernous and stretching, tall and wide. Covered in shadows and illuminated by wax candles burning in rusted sconces.

The orb was silent except for the faintest humming and a chilly breeze that washed off it.

Piper could barely feel her own body as she stared at it.

Her fear popped and sputtered like grease, burning, flaring, threatening to become the strongest surge of panic she'd ever experienced, but never fully forming.

Only after she'd been looking at it for a full minute did she notice some people in the room. Flanking her on both sides were Mayor's Men. Arthur on her left. Brook on her right.

Both look irritated and bored. Arthur had rolled up his dress-shirt sleeves, scratching at a mosquito bite. Brook was tapping his foot.

"What took you so long?" Brook asked.

"Yeah," Arthur said. "This is already dragging."

"Sorry, we found some people snooping around," Liam said.

"Yeah, they almost got away—but I caught them," Tristan added.

"Yeah, sure you did," Wyatt said.

Arthur glanced at Piper and smiled.

Piper looked away.

"Well, we could always use some more people," Arthur said.

"Let us go," Sean said weakly, his voice full of the same fear Piper was feeling.

"Yeah, sure, we'll do that. Let them go, boys," Brook said.

Nobody moved. Arthur broke into a laugh. The others followed, their voices echoing in that strange place.

Someone cleared their throat behind them.

Everyone stopped instantly.

"Good job, boys. The world will forever recall your contributions to all of this. You might find yourself filling the pages of local legends hundreds of years from now. People may even sing songs about you."

The Mayor of Quill Point stepped around the orb. He looked out of place among the shadows and dancing fire-lights. To see him anywhere but behind a desk or podium was out of place. His suit was immaculately blue, tight against his lean muscles. His clean-shaven chin and neatly trimmed auburn hair were the picture of professionalism. His pale white skin reflected the harsh gold light, and it held in his brown eyes.

Muscular, tall, savvy, charismatic, good-looking, unethical, and ruthless.

Was it any wonder he'd won the election so many times?

The Mayor seemed to detect Piper's examining, rage-filled gaze, and he gave her back a look that didn't hide a smug, posturing superiority. Perhaps a thousand times, she'd seen him folded into the knots of a liar, even when almost no one else could. She'd seen the stiffness of someone waiting for the wrong question to unravel it all.

None of that was here. None of that was left.

This was, she understood with a queasiness, another flare of her almost panic, the real man who'd been in charge for so long.

"Ah, Piper! Sean! So nice to see siblings spending time together. I see you two have decided to be a part of something so *grand*. What an excellent and fortuitous happenstance. When I got this going, I was so surprised to learn so many of your generation were willing to participate in matters. Grace and Declan here have also agreed to be a part of things. I have a personal assignment for them in mind once a few more preparations have been made."

He gestured behind him like he was opening a new shop on the corner. Piper could almost hear the slice of metal scissors.

She looked over by a quiet Hunter where there were three people.

The Mayor's daughter, Brianna, was unconscious and tied to a chair in the shadows. Her purple, pink, and red streaked auburn hair fell like a curtain around her face. Her pale white skin was sickly, and her lips were cracked.

Next to her, on her left, was Grace, semi-conscious, a slash across her face, and clearly not going anywhere soon.

And, on the other side was Declan. Son of the now-dead owner of Quill Point Pets and Supplies. He had some kind of injury on one side of his face, the skin there looking bloody and loose.

"They all have agreed that this is good. I like that you have as well. Now, make sure they understand the severity of trying to leave."

Arthur took out a pistol from his waistband and held it loosely. Liam pushed Piper's shoulder until she got the message and sat on the ground.

Arthur lazily muzzle-swept Sean.

Sean sat down quickly. Wyatt stepped away from him.

"What are you doing?" Piper asked desperately. "What is … *this*?"

The Mayor of Quill Point raised an eyebrow. Then chuckled and gently shook his head.

"Have you not worked it out yet, Piper? Have you not put the pieces together? I heard you were speaking with your peers about all the theories. Heard of you badgering my Mayor's Men. You were on my list of problems not yet solved, in fact. You too, Sean. And sundry others. It takes a long time to handle a list that long, and some were faster to gather. But, make no mistake, and make no assumptions, I don't *underestimate* the youth."

He glanced at the orb and smiled like it was a painting he'd acquired. It hummed a little louder.

"As to what this all is? Well, it's no benefit for you. I'm not a big fan of benefits and do not consider intruders part of my constituency. But my dear Mayor's Men deserve the world. And I'm giving it to you."

With each name, The Mayor of Quill Point said, he looked at them and warmly smiled—and Piper's stomach turned because they were genuine smiles.

"Tristan. Arthur. Brook. Wyatt. Liam. Hunter. I have called you here—my favorite of your ranks—for the most special day. One of the last of an old world, in fact."

Then The Mayor's gaze dropped sharply on Piper.

"And we may need a few unfortunate losses in that lurch toward greatness. The pursuit of immortality is a resource-hungry one."

Piper's eyes widened. *"Immortality?"*

The look on his face, as focused as a knife's edge and as full of energy as a match meeting gasoline, made her heart skip a beat. That unbridled, unfiltered, unhidden pride made her blood run cold.

"Of a sort. Of … a sort. But don't ask any more questions, Piper. The masses aren't going to get much of a say over anything ever again. Not that you have in a long time."

He looked back at his Mayor's Men.

"Now, now, now, I shall keep the preamble and the runaround for the masses; let's cut through the noise. What you are looking at here—"

He gestured to the massive golden orb.

"Is an aspect, but only an aspect, boys, of a *god*."

Piper's eyes went wide. That was the answer then. Of all the conspiracies. Of all the theories. The hidden ideas demanding to be unraveled. Every sleepless night was definitively answered. How was it done? How was the world changed? Well—

It was divine. Or damned.

"A god," Tristan said, voice full of wonder. "Not just something powerful. We are serving an honest-to … we are serving a god."

"Yes," The Mayor said. "A piece of one, not yet fully powerful—not yet what it will be."

"Is this an egg?" Brook asked tentatively, fearfully.

"That's a fair assumption and not far off." The Mayor gave him a smile. "You could call it an egg. You could call it a core. But it is a small aspect of him. He's in his adulthood, so the best way to think of it is a beating heart. But comparing such things to patterns of animals is to think of it as something on our terms. I prefer to simply think of it as an opportunity for everyone who knows how to capitalize on it."

So many new questions popped into Piper's head. But she couldn't voice them. She couldn't ask them. All she could do was imagine what this might mean—or already meant. She'd hoped that this was limited to Quill Point. That her parents were safe, at the very least.

But what level of destruction *could* a god do?

"Now listen closely, my friends, my Mayor's Men," The Mayor of Quill Point continued. "I have to tell you this tale. Many years ago, a being known as a Fly found our world. Like the flies we are familiar with, they are attracted to rot, decay, and toxic things. Only they are attracted to the metaphysical, to things that we cannot necessarily see but that can be felt and *known* to be falling apart. And when they lay eggs, sometimes, just sometimes, they birth into gods."

Piper couldn't help but stare at the golden orb as he spoke. It hummed louder and louder—like it was enjoying hearing about itself. She tore her gaze away, looking around. Even her brother was enraptured. She debated getting up and running, but there was no way she could get more than a few steps before something awful happened.

The Mayor didn't seem to even notice her. His face was ecstatic, his words moving faster and faster, his gestures more and more expressive.

"And this particular egg was formed, laid, and born in the center of a town rife with financial and political corruption before it was even made. You know it as Quill Point. Irena Ink may have founded this town, but her brother funded it—and funded it on the backs of labor practices bordering on inhumane. Or perhaps not 'bordering.' Illegal overtime and what you would call 'wage theft' now were common and practically affected every contractor and employee who helped develop the land. Over a hundred deaths spilled blood here because of lax safety measures. There certainly are many other places in this country and beyond where it could've been laid, but the Fly chose here, and the Fly's progeny soaked up the pain and evils of unchecked greed and moved toward … Emergence."

Arthur was now so enraptured that he wasn't paying much attention to his gun. Piper zoned in on it. That might get them out of here. Maybe even stop what was happening—assuming bullets could hurt that orb.

She sat up slightly, preparing.

"Are there other gods?" Tristan asked, his voice almost breathless.

"I have only the writings of our dear founder to go off of, but she spoke of others. Spoke of gods that transcended our understanding of the world. But only two others did she mention by any sort of name. Irena spoke of a sharp-edged, thrashing thing. A god she would only refer to as 'The Being that Knows Every Violence.' The other is more abstract—her description strange. During her youth, at some local art show, she saw what she called 'The Painting that Knows He is a Painting.' I believe it allowed her to know these things at all."

"Whoa…" Tristan said.

The other Mayor's Men chimed in with their own appreciation.

"Yes, it is very impressive. I don't know why Irena tried so hard to stop it. She could've been what we are going to be. She could've found power in propping up a god and allowing him to be all he can be. Like I wanted for Quill Point when I was elected, and so do I want for you. And now, she—"

He glared at the orb with a different, *hostile* look.

"—won't even slow us down."

Piper stopped inching forward when a horrible hissing sound came from the orb. She looked over in alarm. Steam and electrical sparks formed at the top of the orb. The sound turned more human. A faint scream of anger, anguish, and fear. The steam coalesced, concentrated, above the orb. Piper could swear she saw a face in it.

Irena Ink's face.

Then, with a whoosh, the steam floated up into the ceiling and went through it.

The Mayor of Quill Point let out the faintest chuckle. His shoulders relaxed with a sigh. He held his hands up to the sky in a grim mirror of those corpses around the Prayer Spire.

"And that marks it to the hour, my Mayor's Men. That marks the last barrier, the last thing that stood in the way slipping off. The barriers of reality have been loosening. And now is the time upon us of victory and our own form of ascension. Twenty years of feeding this god of greed by any means available to me. It is ready for its next stage."

CHAPTER 30

THE AIR GOT STATICKY AND SYRUPY. THE walls squirmed when Piper looked at them. The noise from the orb had started low, an almost imperceptible sound, but the orb was singing now. A song that wasn't in sounds a human mouth could make, but the meaning was clear. It was a thrumming orchestra of happiness. Malevolent, horrific, *happiness*, full of the deepest bass notes and the shrillest mewling tones.

"You have brought gold and currency," The Mayor intoned.

His voice wasn't human anymore. It was layered with an undercurrent of that strange song.

"You have brought the things that bind those to power and damn those without. *Give them to me.*"

Liam rushed past her, stumbling over himself to hand over wads and wads of crinkled cash from his army jacket's pockets. Wyatt pulled off his backpack and took out a handful of golden jewelry.

Instead of taking any of it, The Mayor of Quill Point gestured to the base of the orb. The Mayor's Men laid them there like the human sacrifices Piper had expected.

Piper couldn't move much. A force was pinning down the air itself. Her heart might stop if she fought hard enough against it.

The orb whispered forceful phrases and commands among its cacophonous music. Those words made the already shimmering air thrum like a waveform, move like strings pulled into tightened knots.

The Mayor of Quill Point's head snapped back, and he whisper-sang in a hushed, pained, taut voice.

"No one will own; they will bleed to try. No mercy will come; condemnation will thrive. It is a cycle—it is a cycle—it is a cycle; by loss, only more loss is begotten, and no one will catch as all but the highest will fail. And power will grow without extending a single respite.

"By humans' greed, I am—"

The Mayor of Quill Point held out his hands, and the gold orb liquefied from a flash of surging, horrific heat. A loosely spinning, surging, roiling collection of molten gold rose into the air. A section of it extended like stalactites, like The Mayor was a magnet pulling on it. Jagged and sharp, they found The Mayor's veins as darting lances. The gold glowed as it moved through his veins, up his arm, and into the rest of his body. His heart and brain both shone through his skin.

The dollar bills surged into his hands, flowing there from impossible wind, and became perfect, crisp. They glowed slightly, like radioactive material.

"—by my will, I am a part of Greed."

The Mayor's body shook, spasmed, golden lines moving outward from his veins.

Piper gasped in pain. The pressing sensation stopped—or was rather pulled away from her. The orb was condensing in on itself, less liquid again. Hovering higher now, it sang a taunting, gloating song.

Piper forced herself to stand. If she would get any moment to do anything, now was it. Her legs were wobbly. Her heart was pounding so hard it gave her a headache.

The Mayor's Men and The Mayor of Quill Point didn't even notice.

They were focused on serving this horrible thing.

"Come here, Tristan," The Mayor said, "and receive payment for all you have done."

Piper crept over to Sean. She glanced at the others, and her heart dropped. Grace, Declan, and Brianna were on the other side of the room. There wasn't a chance to get across without being spotted. She fought back tears. All of *this,* and she couldn't even save them. The guilt churned in her gut. But she kept moving. At least she could save her brother. At least she could save someone. She put a hand on Sean's shoulder. His entire body was shaking with fear; she had never seen his pupils so wide.

"Come on," she whispered, taking him by the hand. Cold sweat covered his skin, but he squeezed back.

"Brook, my leader," The Mayor said. "I'd like to think of you as a friend. Please take this money and continue to look over my Mayor's Men, or … no, I should call you something better. You are a ruler now. You are a Lord of Greed."

Sean got to his feet. Piper started slowly going toward the way out. The staircase up.

"Liam, please, you have been such a help—allow me to pay you your dues. Be a true Lord with the others.

Be a Lord who prevents people from doing anything I *wouldn't like*."

Piper froze, and on instinct, looked back.

The Mayor was smirking. A golden light shined from behind his teeth. He picked up the next dollar and held it out to an eager Arthur.

And The Mayor said the next part while looking straight into her eyes.

"Arthur, may you continue to use violence to achieve the goals of The God of Greed. May you be the first to invoke its power. May you find that with enough, you can do anything you want."

The Mayor snapped his fingers as soon as Arthur took all the money in one of his hands. An explosion of golden light sparked in both his hands.

The syrupy energy came back. It ballooned through the room. Piper's blood seemed to freeze in its veins. A great pressure, like being underwater, filled the room. She struggled, unable to even breathe properly.

But when the screaming started, it was not from either Piper or Sean.

The Lords of Greed were becoming monstrous.

Arthur's teeth exploded in size. They shoved open his jaw and his mouth stretched and grew to accommodate. The tips of his teeth grew next, making long marble columns with crowns of knives. He clutched at his face, moaning with pain between tortured gasps and shudders. Paper-ripping sounds filled the room. Arthur's skin opened like gasping mouths. A line from the outside of his forearm up past his sleeve, across his forehead from temple to temple, bared the muscles underneath with a smack. He didn't bleed so much as the blood vacated him all at once. Copious amounts—buckets of it—were vomited, shed, and ejected from him in a resounding waterfall of a wet slap. Where it couldn't immediately escape, it soaked through his clothes. Spurts of blood flowed out from his pant legs and spilled over his shoes. The room instantly filled with the overpowering smell of copper.

Now Piper and Sean screamed.

Brianna woke up suddenly in the corner of the room. She screamed so loud.

Grace cried out. Declan woke up from the noise, then thrashed to push himself away, only to bump into the wall. A whimper escaped him even as he breathed erratically.

Arthur wavered where he stood, not even falling over. He seemed confused, his body language one of tiredness and aimless movement. Then a faint rustling sound from within him. Something white and fuzzy pushed its way out at the edge of the ripped skin.

Arthur opened his mouth, showing off multiple rows of short teeth going down to his uvula, and the rustling sound increased. He cocked his head. In an impossibly fast rush, the mold grew more.

It pushed itself out from each open wound, stained pink at the tips with the remaining dregs of blood. A heat shimmer wafted off the mold, making the Lord of Greed, Arthur, slightly hazy.

In a rush of wind again, the rest of the money flew into the air, forming a tornado. The other Mayor's Men didn't even yell before the bills slapped against their chests—and the same changes started immediately.

The other boys mutated quicker, dropping copious blood as their teeth grew to impossible sizes. They shook and staggered.

The orb pulsed harder and harder, almost like laughter.

Piper's eyes hurt. Her body ached. But she moved her foot backward a step. She gritted her teeth so hard it made her jaw pop, but she took another step after that.

Once again, the weird essence in the room was stopping. Retracted. Pulled back toward the orb.

The Mayor laughed right along with the orb.

"My Lords of Greed, here is your first assignment: round them up! Kill who you wish, kill when it strikes your fancy, but funnel the rest of them into the businesses, stores, and the Spire itself. They might still give something of their lives before this is done. Force the sick and stab the injured until they comply. Retirement and empathy are both *over*. The world may be ending, but everyone needs to work or spend, *no matter fucking what!*"

The orb shot straight up.

The ceiling of the building didn't stand a chance. Dozens of feet of concrete, wood, dirt, pipes, and insulation all melted, burst apart, or were shoved aside with extreme force.

It rained down on the Lords of Greed. A block of concrete hit the side of Brook's head, and it shattered into dust. He didn't seem to notice.

They were all looking at Piper and Sean. The eyes above their horrific mouths hadn't changed into something monstrous *physically*.

Piper didn't know that much adrenaline and panic could surge into her body and not kill her. She didn't think that her pulse could even rise that high. It choked her until it made her able to run faster than she'd ever run.

The Lords of Greed followed so fast they didn't quite obey the laws of physics. They jolted forward like they'd been sped up on a tape. Tristan, Brook, and Liam had overshot completely, ending up on the other side of the conical room. Hunter had smashed into some part of the wall that Piper couldn't see. Wyatt was looking at his hands, not yet charging at them. But Arthur crashed into the wall nearby, snarling with a mouth full of the wall. He reached for her, and the side of his hand shattered some of the stone bricks on contact.

Piper scrambled backward then went up the steps with Sean. They made the first of the spiral tower's turns. She didn't look back. Sean and Piper held hands, pulling each other forward.

Behind them came more crashing, more violent impacts. The structure of the tower itself shook. More crashes blasted out as the ceiling kept falling. Piper ducked as a lump of dirt with flecks of metal fell past her on the steps.

Piper stumbled as a step shifted. Sean moved ahead, stopping when she tugged on his arm.

"Piper!"

Long cracking noises and stony groans sped underneath her like cracks forming in a frozen pond. Piper jumped up to the next step. She glanced down. A section of the step she'd just been on collapsed into itself, falling below.

A Lord of Greed—no way to know which one from that awful sound—roared beneath them.

"Keep going, keep going," Piper yelled, the words spilling out.

Another massive rumble passed through.

"Come back here!" Brook called out behind them. His voice sounded human.

"See what a god can do!" Arthur added.

But when they laughed, it didn't sound even remotely human. They laughed dry and crackling, like raging fires and snapping bone.

Piper and Sean didn't stop running for a second.

Up ahead was the back of the picture frame that hid the staircase. Neither Piper nor Sean bothered to slow down to open it. They burst through the fabric, stumbling out into the hallway.

Piper's lungs screamed. She didn't want to run anymore. She didn't want every atom of her body to be electrical and charged with panic. But they didn't have that luxury.

While the courthouse had seemed like such a big building before, now they cleared the hallways in moments. Carpet flying by. A turn. More running. The front door was right there.

Sean reached it first and flung it open.

Piper barreled behind him. It was all momentum now. She didn't think that anything could stop her except death. Nothing would overcome the panic and fear of what was following down the way, laughing as they did.

But there was one thing.

She'd forgotten something in all this. Among the panic and revelations and near-death, it had left her mind. She'd made the plan. It seemed like the most sensible thing to do a lifetime ago.

Piper had forgotten that Zaahir had gone for reinforcements.

And they'd arrived at precisely the worst time.

CHAPTER 31

PIPER SKIDDED TO A STOP AS SHE LOOKED over the crowd. Zaahir had gotten at least forty people to help. All looking ready for a fight. She recognized so many. Fathers and mothers. People around town. People she'd known her whole life. In another time, another situation, it would've been heartwarming. Quill Point citizens—barring the obvious outliers—were united. They were taking care of their neighbors.

"Run," Piper gasped, moving into the crowd and getting as far away as possible from the building. "Fucking run."

"Monsters … behind … us…" Sean sputtered out next to her. "You all need to—"

An explosion of wood and sound.

For one crystal clear moment, there was stillness before everyone's mind processed what was happening.

Piper's heart beat out one.

Two.

Three.

Sped-up movement. A blur of white fungus and flying flecks of blood. Piper didn't know that person's name, only their face. He had a kid, maybe a teenager. Got broccoli a lot at the grocery store. Was in a bowling league the one time Piper went to a bowling alley with some friends. He might have been good at it.

The monster that was once Liam had a jaw that could go so wide.

It could wrap around a person's neck like a scarf.

Sit with needle-point edges, only slightly breaking the skin.

And then pressure beyond. Even a mechanical device couldn't match the efficiency, the swiftness of it. Maybe there was a moment when the airways collapsed, the bones snapped inward, and blood vessels popped like juice in a cooking steak. Maybe. But from an outside perspective, the head was attached, and then it wasn't.

There was already blood dripping to the ground from the monsters. Already falling off them as a residue of their transformation.

But then there was *blood fucking everywhere.*

Piper didn't know medieval war zones, eras of only swords, knives, and arrows, but it must've been like this. Fleeing people, shrieks, screams, and it was so … so … so … loud…

The crowd scattered. Piper got swept along by it, buffeted by it. Hands and feet and hips and sides slamming into her, swirling around her. Sean's hand was yanked out of hers.

Someone shoulder-checked her. Another screamed so loudly it made her ears hurt.

And then a gurgling sputter.

A wet slap of blood tangled down her hair and sprayed across her forehead. It dripped down, and she instinctually wiped some away on her arm, then stared in horror at the runny lines coating, weighing down, her arm hair. It was still so warm.

Piper hyperventilated. Her mind spun and seemed to almost stretch. She couldn't remember the last time she'd prayed, but hymns were flowing out of her without even a thought of what they meant.

She almost found it hard to understand what was happening around her. It wasn't the panic, but the sheer conceptualization of these events. What she had seen. What she was a witness to.

How was it someone to the side of her, someone with a name and face, was there, and then there was a strong breeze, a blur of motion, and blood splashed down the front of her shirt? Why did she now understand that the snapping of human bone is so loud? How in any world could the horrific destruction of a person happen twice more before she could process the shock of the first?

Piper stumbled when Arthur blitzed past her. Her skin crawled from a white mold patch touching her arm. She scratched at that part of her arm even as her fingers shook. Strips of skin instantly gathered underneath her nails.

Sean screamed.

That sound sliced through all other thoughts. Her gaze locked onto it, unwavering even as another person bumped into her.

Arthur had her brother's chin in his hand.

Piper glanced around for something, *anything*, she could do. The gun at Arthur's hip caught her eye. Even after transforming, he still had it. She hadn't gotten it before—but now—

Would shooting him even work?

"You are going to go into the nearest building and make yourself useful," Arthur yelled at Sean.

"Okay…" Sean choked out, tears flowing down his cheeks. "Okay … I will… I … will…"

Blood pooled around Arthur's hand as his nails dug half-moon slices into Sean's chin.

"I know you will. You are going to do whatever we ask. My god has given me a gift. A gift to demand. Now go!"

He shoved him away, and Sean fell to the ground, hands over his head, guarding from another attack. He disappeared from Piper's view as a mass of people were forced to move. Two Lords of Greed blitzed at the crowd, killing anyone who ran in the wrong direction or fell behind.

Piper took a wavering step toward where Sean had disappeared.

Then Arthur spun around and grinned like he'd always known she was there.

"Do you know how powerful this all feels, Piper?" he asked, his voice still impossibly normal, his mouth massive. "It's like everything is changing for me."

Piper froze.

"It's like everything is changing for everything. I can feel—god, my God of Greed, I can feel his essence—"

Piper could feel something too, not inside her, but around her. The air was changing. It was flowing differently. It was—

Oh, Jesus Christ, no.

Arthur tilted up his head at the same time Piper looked.

The warped sky that had started it all was waking up. Despite it being nighttime. Despite it being the starless, moonless void, those same orange and red streaks of day glowed nuclear and neon and spiraled out. They'd always looked like you could reach up and touch them—but now they were actually lower.

Piper ducked as a stream of it looped down above her head. She scrambled back a step as another noiselessly struck the ground. Each was about six feet wide and almost translucent.

Arthur reached out and touched the side of one, electricity crackling at the contact, dancing down the length of his forearm. There were little pops and hisses as residual blood burned.

"The god is emerging," he said reverently. "It has been such an amazing day."

Another stream flowed into a curling spiral above him, and Arthur gave a little delighted laugh.

Piper tore her eyes away.

She'd spotted a chance.

She ran forward, trying not to gag from the rotting smell of decay coming from those shimmering mold spots. Trying not to whimper at the sheer fear that burned in her.

Piper grabbed the handle of the pistol.

She'd never held one before. Didn't know if she could just pull the trigger and fire. There was something called a "safety" that she'd never looked into.

She hoped Arthur hadn't bothered with that.

She pulled the pistol out of his holster and pushed it into his abdomen.

Arthur's blissful look instantly disappeared. He snarled. Swung for her.

She fired.

The kickback of the firearm tore it from her hand.

Arthur staggered, clutching at the spot with one hand. But even a weak backhand with the other knocked Piper off her feet.

CHAPTER 32

For a few seconds, Piper only saw white. She lay on the ground, dazed and in pain. Her ears were ringing louder than she thought possible. A burning sensation was shooting out from her jaw. When she put her hand there, the bone popped back into place with such agony she wept instantly. Blood quickly filled her mouth, and she swallowed a little before spitting the rest on the ground.

Piper rolled to her side. Pushed herself up, then fell back down. Her body couldn't take any more running—any more fighting. She kept blinking as her vision finished returning.

Arthur was still standing there, clutching his stomach. Blood was coming from the angry new rip there, but much less than expected.

He wobbled. His expression was as blank as a corpse's. Arthur moved his hands away from the wound. It was *shifting*. With a familiar rustling sound, a mass of putrid white mold pushed itself out, filling up the hole. Long stalks moved out and twisted with strands of skin, running lines like stitches, tugging the skin toward the mold until they were pressed against each other.

Arthur lurched, leaned over, and gagged, and what could only be his intestines and deflated stomach fell out of his open mouth. A thick plug of mold was briefly visible in his mouth, like a long probing tongue, before it sucked back inside.

Arthur stood up again, his posture ramrod straight.

He laughed with his whole body. That crackling, twig-snapping laughter. He sounded euphoric when he spoke.

"Oh. Thank you. I could see him for a second there. I could see my god in all his glory. He's such a massive power, stuck in such a small place. He yearns to spread over … everything."

Arthur studied Piper for a moment.

"He won't let you stop this. He won't let you hurt us. You're nothing compared to the scope. But—"

He tilted his head, nodding along to something. His shoulders stiffened. He was standing somewhat away. Another impossible blitz of motion. He was standing over Piper. Above him, the sky was developing more layers of tendrils, lacing through all of Quill Point.

"Oh, you are lucky in ways you can't understand. Come along, Piper. I can hear The God of Greed's grand plan in my head—he's saying things to me. We need a journalist; we need a reporter. He *needs* one. We need a *mouthpiece* to speak for the end of the world."

Piper looked around in a panic. Her eyes fell on the pistol. It was a few feet away. Maybe if she shot him somewhere else, he'd die. Maybe if she shot him until the gun ran out.

Maybe—*maybe*—

Arthur scooped Piper up with ease. He didn't force her to her feet. He carried her draped over his arms. The pistol got farther and farther away. She struggled weakly and reached out for it, but Arthur's fingers dug into her arm so hard she gasped in pain.

"I wouldn't struggle," Arthur said. "I only can't kill you."

Piper stopped. She collapsed slightly. Her jaw still hurt like fire. Her body was beaten up. The rotting stench of mold coated her tongue, mixing with the blood already in her mouth.

And her mind surged with questions.

Where's Sean? Where's my brother? What happened to Grace and Declan? Are they even still alive? Who is alive? Will I be…?

"Look, Piper," Arthur said. "Your new office."

On a different day, Piper might've assumed she was seeing a hallucination. A dream, even. But there was a god in Quill Point. There was horrible magic.

She didn't know its rules.

The building that Arthur was walking her to had never been in Quill Point. That squat building with its huge antenna was new. The hill it sat on, with a long winding path and beds of roses, was not a part of this town. Quill Point didn't have a local news station. It was too small a town for that.

It was, however, real.

The flowers shouldn't have been bleeding, but they were. The top of the radio tower shouldn't have squirming tendrils of red and orange around it. But it did.

Because reality was being warped by a god that didn't care about humanity except for what it could wring out from them. And it had a special place all planned for her.

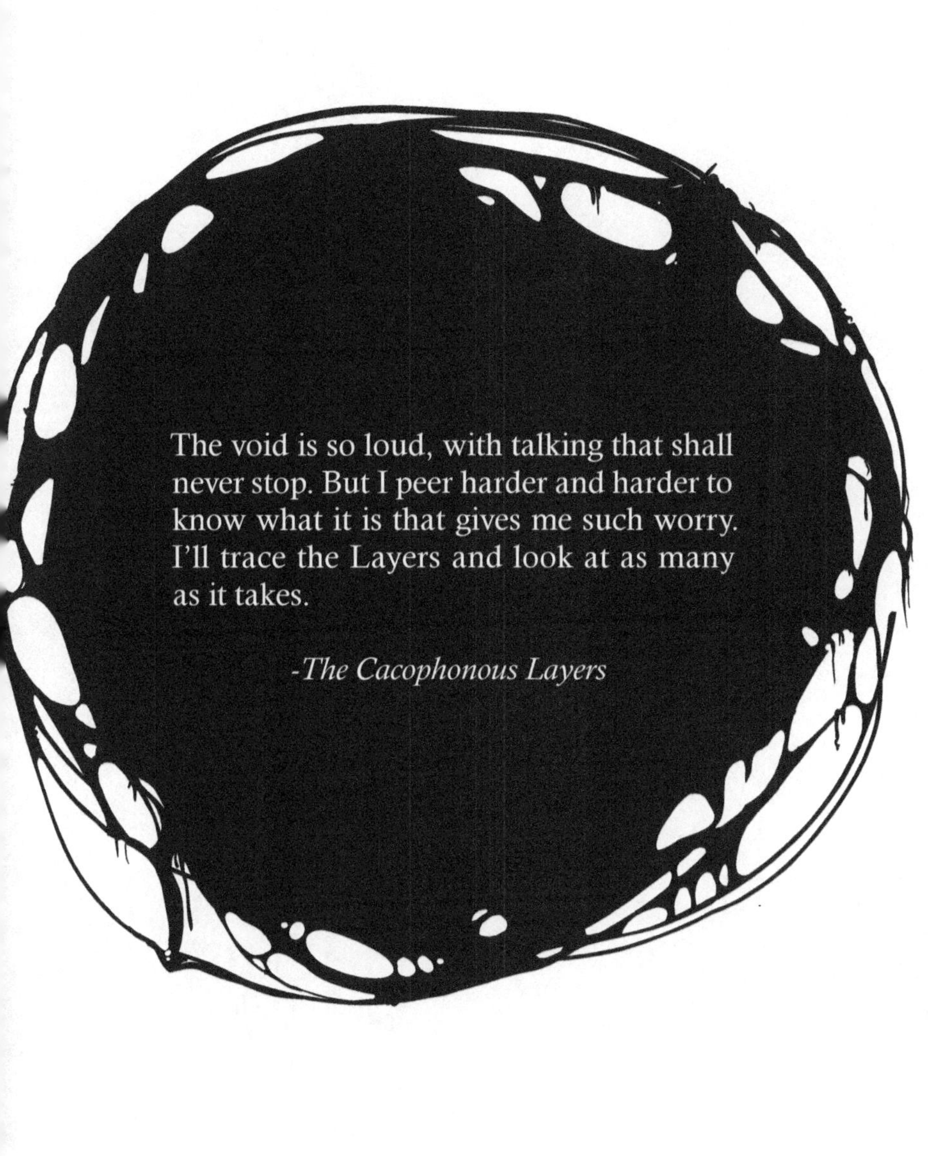
The void is so loud, with talking that shall never stop. But I peer harder and harder to know what it is that gives me such worry. I'll trace the Layers and look at as many as it takes.

-The Cacophonous Layers

Interlude 3

The Incursion

FIVE THOUSAND FEET OF OPEN GRASS SAT between the military observation stations and Quill Point's exterior shadow walls. No one had stepped foot on that grass for over a month. It had grown wild and gone to seed with thin stalks and spikey clusters. A mass of dandelions took over one section, their snow-white tops awaiting a breeze to spread their influence.

It was here, in the late evening, after the sun had already gone down, that reality ripped open a few inches off the ground. Not metaphorically. The strong and dense membrane rippled and parted, and there was the sound of a perfect, clean paper rip. From it emanated impossible sounds.

From a seam only a few feet wide, spilled forth more words than any person or machine could hope to parse. It was narration and oration layered over and over and over itself with trillions of different speakers in billions of different languages. It wasn't so much "loud" as it was unceasing. It was old, new, and endless on a scale that any Layer's universes and galaxies could not hope to emulate.

After a moment, a woman named Juniper dropped through the opening and landed on the ground with a grunt. The rip in reality closed behind her instantly, leaving a faint echo of those constantly spoken words.

Juniper was tall and muscular. She wore a pair of combat boots, high-rise jeans, and a blue turtleneck sweater. Her hair was a light russet—pulled into a tight ponytail—and her skin was tanned white with heavy sun-burning except on the bridge of her nose and ringing her eyes. Strapped to Juniper's back was a chainsaw with each tooth made of a different metal, some much longer than others.

Even when she was still, it seemed like she was a special effect added in postproduction. Like she was new footage laid over a familiar movie. Her smallest movements, even her breathing, were *different* from the world around her.

She glanced around on high alert. Her hand hovering toward her back, toward the handle of the chainsaw. When nothing seemed to happen, she focused on the wall of shadows in front of her.

She looked it up and down with practiced appraisal.

Then grimaced. Pursed her lips. Shook her head.

"Just great."

A stalk of grass twitched off to the side of her. A rustle as something moved.

She didn't *quite* teleport to that spot. Juniper *had* taken footfalls to get there, but it wasn't as many steps as should've been required. And the speed of it was hard for the brain to parse. Even tinier movements, like her grabbing down into the grass, were unearthly fast.

She held up a scared bunny, its tiny chest heaving and the rest of it frozen in fear. Juniper held it for a second.

"Huh, don't have these. Cute."

She placed the bunny back on the ground. It quickly hopped away from her, disappearing down into its burrow.

Again, the field was silent.

"Don't like this."

Juniper pulled the chainsaw off her back and held it one-handed, like a sword. Her finger danced over a switch, but it remained inert as she walked too fast back to the shadow wall.

She pulled something from her pocket that looked like an older cellphone. It was roughly the same shape and had a little screen and number keys. But it also had something on its back, vibrating the air with a heat haze.

Juniper placed her thumb in the center of the black screen. It scanned with a green light, then immediately called someone with a shrill but quiet ring.

The other line picked up on the second ring.

"How it's looking?" Klein asked.

"I'm at the source. It's not looking good."

The signal sputtered several times, crackling with snippets of the same endless talking that came through the rift in reality. Juniper rolled her eyes, waiting for it to finish.

"What does 'looking bad' mean in this context?" Klein asked. "How far along is it?"

"I'm saying we fucked up. We might have a seventh on our hands here. It's already Isolated a town, and from the looks of it, we're close to a full Emergence."

"What?!"

"I'm unsure of what kind of god it is, but I'm almost sure we can't derail this without serious losses."

"How the fuck did this happen?"

"How should I know? That's your fucking job!"

On the other end of the line was a heavy crash and the sound of breaking glass. "Dammit, dammit, dammit. How is it *that* far along? We just picked it up! It shouldn't even be able to Isolate, let alone Manifest on a Layer! Fucking *dammit*! We need to send *everyone* we can on this. I am not letting a fucking seventh divine shit storm fuck up even more fucking Layers. I'm sending twelve, no, twenty to deal with this. We are going to seal this thing before it gets out."

"Do we even have that many?!" Juniper replied.

"I don't fucking know. But I'm sending whoever I can. Get a way in so we can start busting heads as soon as they arrive. Get it done ASAP. That's a direct order, June."

Juniper frowned and almost said something, but closed her eyes hard for a moment, then relaxed. "I'm on it."

"Good." And then Klein's voice softened a little. "But … uh, June, do be careful."

"Of course," she said.

A faint whining click, and the connection severed.

Juniper put the phone back into her jeans pocket and flicked on the chainsaw. There was a minor sonic boom. All the grass nearby went flat against the ground. Electricity crackled and danced across the chainsaw's guide bar, turning it faintly blue.

Then the chain spun.

To say it spun fast would be a massive understatement. The teeth of it were imperceptible. Molecules and atoms parted in its path, and the resulting fission energy barely stayed within a small, contained field around the machine.

Juniper whipped the chainsaw over her hand and cut down into the side of the shadow wall like she was wielding a broadsword. For a moment, there was a horrific grinding sound, and then it cut into the side of the wall. Her entire frame shook from the vibration. She cut a thin line, then yanked the chainsaw back out. The cut didn't seal itself shut.

Grinning wide, Juniper started cutting a circle. She stabbed into it at one point, then dragged it along a smooth path.

Juniper had made it about one-fourth of the way when the air nearby her head shifted.

Training saved her life.

In a barely controlled skid, Juniper moved a hundred feet to the side, narrowly avoiding a massive shadowy hand that slammed into the dirt forcefully enough to leave a crater.

The shadow claw dusted itself off and lifted back off the ground. It connected like a marionette string to the shadow wall. With a slight ripple, ten more appeared in quick succession. Some hands were so big that they could easily crush tanks.

One of them darted forward like a striking cobra.

Juniper slid around the side of it, then sliced. The entire structure of it burst apart into fine particles instantly.

Hundreds of feet above the ground, one of the massive hands turned its palm upward and curled its fingers. When it uncurled, a little boy that was not a little boy stood on the palm. He cracked his knuckles as the hand lowered him to the ground.

"I was wondering when someone like you would show up. It's so loud when someone from another Home Layer shows up. You've got to stop the infestation *quick*. Some bugs actually can do some damage."

He stepped off the hand, fell almost ten feet, and landed in the grass.

"But I think you already know that you aren't able to do anything now."

Juniper's body went very still for a moment, and then a grin spread across her lips. She held the chainsaw's handle with both hands out in front of her and lowered her center of gravity.

"You're a demigod, yes?"

"I am." The little boy held out his hands, and the shadow claws all moved in tandem. "Why do you ask?"

"Because I've never gotten to kill one before."

The little boy smiled wide with a delighted laugh, bouncing slightly on his feet. Then, instantly, he was a tall, humanoid creature of stormy clouds covered in rows of undulating, sharp-nailed hands.

His voice was still that of a young boy.

"Do you think you can do anything like that, you tiny, impossibly unimportant speck? Do you think you will have any effect on this or any universe at all when I kill you?"

Juniper crossed the distance in a blink. She swung the chainsaw right for the demigod's head. He ducked, and a tiny piece of his cloud form seared right off him, exploding into a bloody mist.

An inhuman howl of anger erupted from his mouth, and the shadow claws descended like rainfall on Juniper's head. She glanced up once before launching herself backward. With quick hops, her feet barely touching the ground, she narrowly avoided each hand as they descended like a bombing run.

Two flew at her from either side. She leaped straight up—easily ten stories. While up there, six shot at her. She evaporated them before she even hit the ground.

But when she landed, she stumbled slightly and let out a faint gasp. The chainsaw sagged in her hands.

"Leave," the little boy yelled. "Leave now."

He snapped his fingers, and several claws nearby him dove into the earth.

"Leave, and I have no reason to kill you."

"Somebody sounds scared," Juniper said.

She straightened up, took another calming breath, and then moved forward in another blitz of motion. Halfway through it, she stopped her momentum, kicking at the ground so hard she made her own crater. Dirt shot up into the air, clods of it flung about. She took an angled jump, reversing her direction with a flip.

A millisecond later, claws burst out of the ground like elongated tire spikes where she would've been.

Rows of them in all directions popped up out of the ground, moving in on her, sending clumps and rocks and plant matter flying.

The spikes moved so fast, got in so close. Panic flashed across Juniper's eyes. She prepared to jump again, looking up, before having to whip the chainsaw above her head in time to stop a descending flock of hundreds of hands. Each evaporated on contact, but their bevy pushed her down, making her knees almost buckle. A scream of defiance rushed out of her as she pushed up against it, her arms straining, the electrical crackle of her chainsaw growing all the louder—

A clawed finger pierced her left lung.

The second shattered part of her hip as it plunged into her lower intestine.

A third, almost surgically, went right underneath her sternum and then up toward her windpipe.

Blood exploded out of her mouth. The chainsaw dropped to the ground, whirring for a few more seconds, then stopping. The strange beyond-reality look to Juniper faded for a second, then sputtered back into sharp focus.

"You know what? That was kind of fun," the little boy said, now looking like a child again. "I expected that to take less time. But you are a fast little bug, like a cockroach dodging a boot."

Juniper gasped out another gush of blood before hanging her head, her breaths getting shallower and shallower.

"I really can see a silver lining to this. I have been wondering what happens to the corpse of someone from another Layer. How does the fabric of it all react? And does it hurt more or less?"

He raised his hands, and twin claws hovered on either side of Juniper.

"You tell me."

With a clap, the claws crushed Juniper's body with a wet smack. When the shadow claws pulled back apart, all that was left was strange, staticky, glimmering in the air and a lot of blood. The static popped a few times, then faded away.

The little boy shook out his shadow hands, splattering blood across the grass. He chuckled to himself, then hummed a faint song.

He walked over to the shadow wall. The massive hands slunk back into it, disappearing as fast as they had appeared.

The little boy glanced back once.

In the distance, amidst blaring sirens and flashing lights, multiple tanks and snipers aimed at him. Satellites were zooming in on him, looking at him. Calls were being made, describing what had occurred down a chain of command.

The little boy gave a derisive snort. A doorway opened in the side of the shadow wall, and he stepped back into Quill Point.

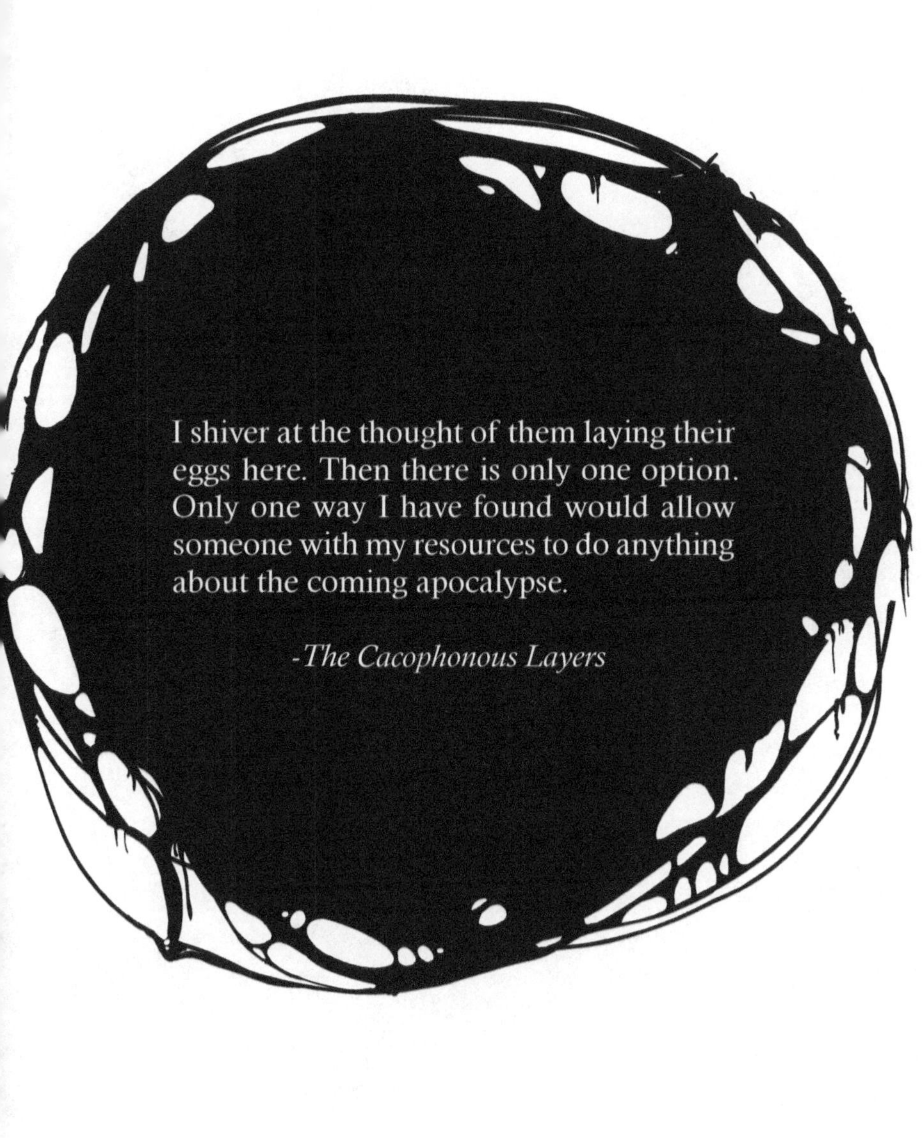

I shiver at the thought of them laying their
eggs here. Then there is only one option.
Only one way I have found would allow
someone with my resources to do anything
about the coming apocalypse.

-The Cacophonous Layers

Interlude 4

Tomorrow

Before the Emergence

Zaahir was sure that Hope didn't *actually* need help with anything—but Zaahir couldn't turn down a request for help. If someone needed it, and he could provide it, then he did it. And this was an especially happy instance of that rule. As far as Zaahir was concerned, he'd gotten an absolute stroke of good luck. He'd been looking for a reason to walk over and talk to her for *days* now. The moment had never been right; the universe hadn't given him a sign yet. Maybe this was that sign.

And at least he felt *mildly* prepared. He knew a lot about her from friends he'd admitted his longstanding crush to. She liked math, economics, and sociology. She got dual degrees in college for those last two. In short, incredible. In short, Hope was amazing.

Also, kind of intimidating.

He struggled to come up with some way to approach those topics in a flirty way as he followed her. Something fun, a little casual, not too heavy, but also showed that he cared about something she cared about.

She was walking ahead, going through the rings of tents, not yet noticing his dilemma.

They passed Saanvi putting out the fire she'd used to make naan and stashing away the pan so the Mayor's Men didn't see them making unapproved food. Zaahir waved to her. She waved back and then winked at him as soon as Hope passed her.

Well, as long as Hope can't tell.

But I want her to know I like her, don't I?

Zaahir shook his head, dispelling the thoughts. Maybe it wasn't so complicated. Ultimately, people were people, and they liked similar things. Hope would probably enjoy a compliment as much as anyone else.

He could call her cute. Right? Zaahir could scarcely ever stop thinking about how cute Hope was when he was around her. Her glasses were always sliding down her nose, and he—more than once a day—imagined reaching over and propping them back up. And then kissing her nose, then her forehead—

No, that line of thinking was unhelpful. Girls get compliments on their looks all the time. Hope surely got complimented on it *all the time*. If he was going to come up with a good compliment that made her feel good, it should be something more personal, more *special*.

Okay. Let's do this.

"That must be a tough book…"

Hope paused and turned around. Her hazel eyes made something in Zaahir's chest do a shuffle step.

"What was that?" she asked.

"Your book … there … it must be challenging?"

She frowned. Zaahir awkwardly pointed. Hope looked down at the book.

"Oh! Oh, this. No, I've read this a hundred times. I mean, not a hundred. That would be silly."

"Yeah—yeah, it would be," Zaahir said.

"But, um, I've read it … I think five times? I found it at my uncle's house. I mean, not this copy. The old one fell apart. The spine was all … crinkly. Yeah."

Zaahir was having a hard time not looking at her lips. Just the *most* difficult time.

Hope chewed on her bottom lip for a second, then seemed to notice that she'd done that, then let out an awkward chuckle with too much air.

"My grandpa was a … was a mathematician. He said I could keep it when I kept reading it whenever I visited."

"That's cool," Zaahir said. "I guess you were always really good with numbers."

"I guess I was … thank you. That's nice of you."

"You're welcome." Zaahir tried not to notice how dry his throat had gotten. He looked around for a second. Anywhere but in her eyes. "So, what did you need my help with?"

She looked around, glancing one way and then the other. Her voice lowered to a whisper. "Can you keep a secret?"

"Uh, yeah. I can do that," Zaahir said.

"Cool," she said.

Hope took a few slow steps in the same direction they'd been heading.

"Then follow me for a little longer," she whispered. "It's right over here."

Zaahir followed, occasionally glancing behind him. If it was a secret, it was a secret from the Mayor's Men.

Hope walked to the back of one of the tents. She reached underneath, pulled out one of the stakes, and shifted the tent to the side. Underneath it were rows of long green stalks.

"Plants?" Zaahir asked.

Hope nodded. "Can you help me take some of these out?"

Zaahir kneeled down. "Are these carrots?"

"Yeah. There are also some potatoes in another patch nearby," Hope said. "We leave them uncovered when we can—but the Mayor's Men take any food we try to grow. And I haven't seen much of it come back to us."

"I didn't know they stopped us from even *growing* food. What the hell are they thinking? We're going to run out."

Hope shrugged. "I wish I knew. Things really feel like they're getting bad."

Zaahir nodded. He'd been rushing around trying to help where he could. Stuff to carry; stuff to move. People who needed what medicine they had. But he wasn't sure how long things could hold together in Quill Point.

"Well, we'll do what we can," Zaahir said.

Hope nodded at that but didn't respond. Instead, she leaned down and felt around in the dirt for a few moments. Then pulled up. A flash of orange among residual dirt, and she was holding a carrot. It wasn't as big or as vibrant as Zaahir had seen at the grocery store, but there was still something almost life-affirming about seeing a food item in the wild.

"Here, take this and put it in that bin over there," Hope said, handing over the carrot.

Zaahir glanced around until he noticed a small plastic bin. It was more suited for someone moving between apartments, but it looked recently cleaned. He put the carrot at the bottom.

Hope pulled up another carrot and held it out to him. "Thank you, by the way."

Zaahir looked at her hand. Thought about holding it. Running his fingers over her palm—

"Sure," he said. "But I think you could've done this on your own."

"It's easier with help," Hope said simply.

Zaahir asked no further questions. Even with the massive amount of overthinking he was engaged in, he knew well enough to not ask more questions. He was hanging out with Hope, alone, by themselves, with no one listening. Why it was happening didn't matter.

He pushed the bin forward with his foot so it was right next to her and then kneeled. Hope effortlessly removed another carrot from the ground. After dropping it into the pile, she slid her hand under the tent. She pulled out a pair of yellow rubber gloves.

"Do you want to get one?" she asked.

Zaahir shrugged. "Uh, sure, why not."

"You're right-handed, yeah?" she asked.

"Yeah—are you left-handed?"

Hope smiled. "Yep. Statistically rare as it is, I was born left-handed. My Catholic aunt was always a little weird about it."

Zaahir put on the glove slowly; the traditional thick rubber always felt weird. He flexed his fingers a few times.

"Do I just pull?" he asked.

"It would be easier if we had a garden fork for this, but that would make it too obvious. But, yeah, the ground here is pretty loose. You should be able to get it out of the ground."

"Do it again. Let me watch," Zaahir said.

Hope looked at him for a long moment and gently smiled, before returning to the little garden. She reached down and got another carrot almost effortlessly.

"See, like magic."

"Okay, yeah, seems possible," Zaahir said.

He reached down, and after a little shifting, a little feeling around, and then some pressure, another carrot popped out of the ground. He held up above his head, smiling at the little orange vegetable.

"Hey, I did it!"

"Good job," Hope said with a small laugh. "Be quieter, though."

"Right, sorry, sorry," Zaahir said.

Now he couldn't help but smile. He had done it. Someone hungry would eat this specific carrot—and he was, in a small way, responsible for that. The fact the Mayor's Men didn't want them doing this only made it more fun.

The two worked silently for a few moments, easily moving through the bed of carrots. A few broke in different ways—some were stuck too firmly in the ground—but it was a good crop. The bin filled halfway quickly.

"I didn't know you liked gardening," Zaahir said. "Or do you not, and this is just for the food?"

"I mean, it's nice to help," Hope said, wiping away sweat with the back of her wrist. "But I like plants a lot. I think nature is really special."

"I wouldn't have expected someone who likes math so much to like nature," Zaahir said. "Or, I'm sorry ... was that the wrong thing to say?"

Hope chuckled. "I got what you meant. The thing is though, math is just the language *of* nature. It's one way we can make sense of it. If I add one carrot to ten carrots, it's now eleven carrots."

"Oh, yeah, I suppose that's true," Zaahir said.

"It's really nerdy, I know."

"No, I think it's really cool. That's a really cool way to look at the world. All connected like that. I know that's a common idea, but I know that when you say it, you know so much about it. You really mean stuff. You put your whole heart into stuff, I can tell. I think that's special."

"Thank you," Hope said, turning her face away. "That's a sweet thing to say."

Zaahir could practically hear a smile in those words. And his mind latched onto it. His stomach flipped.

That was a sign. Do something.

Zaahir was already mildly sweating from some tougher carrot pulls, but now he felt horribly warm. His heart rate was rising, and his palms damp.

If you're going to ask her out. You should do it now.

While Zaahir desperately tried to think through what to do, Hope pulled off the glove, moved the bin, and then covered the whole thing with the tent again.

"Well, that was quick," she said, standing back up. "I thought that … that might take more time. I guess…"

Zaahir stood up a little too fast. He was kind of dizzy. "Hey, uh, Hope?"

"Oh, uh, yes, Zaahir?"

"Oh, I'm sorry. Did I interrupt you?"

"No, it's okay," Hope said. "I just wanted to thank you for helping me. It was nice to have someone else. Uh, yeah … it takes a little longer to garden by myself. That was all."

Now, now, now. Do it now!

"You're amazing."

Hope blinked a few times in confusion. "…thank you?"

Now that Zaahir had let words out, more were flying too fast for him to stop them.

"I think you're amazing. We're, like, the same age, and I can't believe what you've accomplished already. You have *two* degrees. I know it's a really weird time for me to ask—and I don't know where we could have the date, or have a date, or be in a date, err, ah … would you like to go out sometime?"

Hope's hand went to her mouth as a massive smile formed. "Yes. That would be … that would be great, Zaahir. I would really like that."

"Oh, oh good, I'm so glad to hear that," Zaahir said, his smile in every word. "I was running out of ways to say date."

Hope burst into a giggle. And to Zaahir, it was wind chimes and twinkling stars.

"How about tomorrow?" Zaahir asked.

"That would be great," Hope said. "Let's do something tomorrow. We can have dinner or something."

"Fried carrots, maybe?" Zaahir said.

"Sure!" Hope replied. "It's a date."

Zaahir's hand felt drawn to hers. He wanted to reach out, wrap her fingers in his. Hope seemed to move closer to him too. He couldn't believe so many idle thoughts might actually happen—

Off in the distance, a scream sounded out. Hope's smile fell. Zaahir turned toward it.

"What was that?" Hope asked.

"Oh no," Zaahir said. "No. Fuck. No. I think something's happening."

He spun back to Hope. Her eyes were wide.

"Do you think it's another … is it happening again?"

"I don't know. Maybe."

"Fuck." Hope clutched the side of her head, her voice on the verge of tears. "No, not another thing. Not another—"

She shook her head violently, then let out a sharp breath.

"Okay, we got to do something. We need to not let it—we need to get moving."

"I'll go tell the watch," Zaahir said. "We can start getting people away from whatever's happening. You stay safe—I'll do what I can."

"Okay," Hope said. She nodded to him, then to herself.

Then she moved from tent to tent, trying to wake the sleeping people inside.

Zaahir watched her for a moment before running toward the sound of screaming.

After the Emergence

The Mayor's Men were monsters. Boys and men that Zaahir knew—but was not particularly fond of—were now ripped-up creatures with impossible fangs and a shimmering heat haze rolling off them.

And they were killing people around him. So fast and so effectively that Zaahir could barely process the change. Friends were alive, and then they weren't, and the severity of that shift didn't match the physical reality. There should've been final words, explosions of light, or tearful goodbyes, like in the movies. Not a thud and vacant stares and no hope of recovery.

When a person near him died, he couldn't help it. He dropped to Robin's side and performed compressions on his chest. It didn't matter that there was a hole in the side of Robin's throat where sticky blood clung to severed strands: He was a person, dammit. He was a *person*. Zaahir hadn't been able to help during Murder Sky. The things that took people then were too fast, too powerful, but this was another chance, right? *Right?*

He was still trying to wake Robin up when a kick hit him in the side. It was an immense hit, like a car clipping him, and it sent him rolling across the dirt.

"Go, now!" Tristan yelled.

Zaahir let out a groan and clutched at the impact spot. He was sure a rib was broken. Every time he wheezed, and he couldn't stop wheezing, it hurt right there. He sat up and looked as Tristan's new monster form stalked forward.

"Get going," Tristan said. "Now."

As two people screamed and ran past Zaahir, he realized Tristan wasn't specifically talking to him. A crowd of people were running in that direction.

They were being *forced* in that direction.

Tristan locked eyes on Zaahir, and there was utter stillness for a second. The screams dropped out, and Zaahir could only hear the rapidly rising thrum of his pulse.

Tristan raised his leg, his shoes covered in blood. And brought it down on Robin's head. Some level of skull structure remained around the massive hole. Tristan pulled his foot back out, and the sneakers he was wearing were shredded and dotted with new fluids.

Something shot up Zaahir's spine. A surge of emotion, adrenaline, or some other hormone. The pain in his sides seemed to numb somehow. He sprang so nimbly to his feet it almost surprised him, and he ran. Ran after the people already running.

"Go, go, go, now," Tristan screamed. "We are your *lords,* and you will treat us as such. We are your Lords of

Greed! And you will *go*. Our god needs everyone ready for this!"

Zaahir had been on his feet a lot. He'd done an awful lot of running that day. Between chasing after Grace, gathering people back at the bonfire, and then marching to the courthouse. He could feel blisters forming. His calves had gone past burning into a numbed, awful ache. Even his lower back and arms were sore from the running.

It mattered little. The running overtook. His heart thudded out a simple message:

If you stop, he will kill you.

Tristan laughed. A crackling thing that sounded more like fire. And when the other Lords of Greed joined in, delighted, chorusing, celebrating, it had the distinct sensation of being chased by a wildfire. A blazing, scorching inferno that would rip apart everything and anything it could.

Zaahir almost didn't notice when the sky's streamers appeared, suddenly diving from the night sky and touching the Earth. He almost ran into the semi-opaque column that formed in front of him. But some part of him caught himself in time, flinging him out of its way.

The column sang a song of electric wires, toxic sewage, and deadly third rails.

Zaahir narrowly avoided more as they flowed down, making spirals, cages, and intricate lattice patterns. It was like looking at the inner workings of a building, all wires and piping.

"Keep going!" screamed Tristan, though he sounded further away.

Every sound did, actually. The world around was dropping off, overcome, and overridden by an ambient hum.

Zaahir looked over his shoulder and saw the smokey forms of the Lords of Greed glitching across the landscape. A flash of lightning ripped across the sky, and for a split second, he could almost see, standing above everything—

His foot painfully smacked into the side of a rock. He swore as he fell forward. Trying to avoid landing on his damaged rib cage, he rotated mid-fall as best he could. It still hurt when he crashed into the ground.

His breathing now a thrum almost matching his heart, he tried to see what that had been—what was standing out there. Instead, in mere seconds, he saw more death.

A woman tripped, couldn't get up fast enough, and died.

A man turned around in a panic and fired a single shot from a pistol, missed, then died.

And the tendrils dropped like vultures over the bodies. Covering their forms. The bodies evaporated into a red mist, and the bones cracked and shattered into a powder. The mixture shot up the tendrils, flowing over Zaahir's head. He watched it sucked down the line, his eyes widening in horror.

"Hey! You!"

Zaahir forced himself to his feet and pushed his body forward once again. His arms chopped at the air. The corners of his vision seemed to narrow like an aperture.

In front of him, growing taller by the second, the focal point, the ending point of those bloody shoots, was a spire.

The Spire. The Prayer Spire.

It was much taller, stretching *past* the night sky into a hole that made Zaahir's eyes hurt to look at for too long. It was a space of air that wobbled. That was fuzzy and static, with the faintest whispers of people speaking, lost in the breeze.

And from around that center point, stretched more columns of tendrils. They were filling up the sky and making everything he saw parted, sliced, and divided into lines of red and orange.

The Prayer Spire's tendrils moved after so long remaining dormant. Those tendrils lifted the thirteen corpses off the ground, dangling them like marionettes. The bodies' mouths flapped and jerked, forming words that grew more in synch until they became chants.

Zaahir almost stopped running. Despite the death behind him, his instincts wanted him no closer. This unfathomable, unearthly, unreality that Quill Point had so swiftly become.

The blood and bone traveling the channels met its end-point and sprayed at the hole in the air. The whispering voices got a little louder.

"Oh my god, Zaahir!"

He tore his gaze away, gasping, and his eyes landed on Hope. She sprinted toward him. Her eyes were wide, her hair stuck to her face by blood, but she was alive, and she was there, and Zaahir looked away, looked away, looked away from the nightmare that was real.

She crashed into him with a hug and then pulled back to grab the sides of his arms.

"What's happening!?" she said. "What's going on?"

Zaahir's mouth moved, but he couldn't form words. Nothing he could say would adequately sum up the things happening right now. He didn't understand them—didn't want to understand them.

"I... I ... monster..." He shook his head. "The Mayor, the Mayor's Men, all of this—I think it's related... I don't—"

Above them screamed a sound like a plane flying overhead, a firecracker soaring to its explosion. They both looked up.

A golden orb was moving through the sky with electrical crackles sparking off its metallic skin. It sped up, moving lower and lower, and flew right above Zaahir's and Hope's heads, sending their hair rippling.

They both turned on instinct to follow its trajectory and watched as it crashed into the side of the Prayer Spire and exploded. It exploded into golden fire. A massive, hissing, angry conflagration of golden flames and golden sparks.

A wave of heat rolled off it, making them gasp in sudden pain. Their skin and clothes would've been lit on fire any second, but the sensation sharply stopped. The golden fire stretched higher up the spire, though, almost but not touching the spot where reality seemed to unravel.

The Mayor's Men, now apparently the Lords of Greed, screamed out into the night behind them.

"It's almost time!"

"It's almost here!"

A few survivors ran past them.

Zaahir's stomach dropped as he realized they were being pushed specifically to that golden fire, to that horrible rip in reality.

Hope must've made the same calculation. She tugged on his arm, her voice cracking. "Come on. I don't … we don't have a choice here."

He followed her.

From all around Quill Point, people ran to the Prayer Spire. They streamed in, fear coating their every expression. People that Zaahir met at local concerts, from shopping around town, from the gym, dates, and all manner of his time in Quill Point.

It was, in a very real way, almost his entire world in one place. His whole life as it had been, condensed and lined up and crowded around a burning, golden fire, which promised nothing good, nothing hopeful.

They ran to the group. They ran for whatever safety in numbers there was against something like this.

And buildings were rising to cover the skyline of Quill Point, forming with no construction but golden light, red and orange tentacles, and hissing static. Each was an ugly, blocky structure, massive and imposing. Or were strange, abstract structures with details that didn't fit. The virus from the sky spread through everything Zaahir could see, taking over existing buildings as quickly as making new ones.

Zaahir felt like cowering, like crying, but all he could do was hold hands with Hope, and stand by the surviving neighbors, friends, and fellow members of Quill Point, as the Lords of Greed closed in on them, smirking with monstrous smirks.

But instead of attacking, they all stopped outside the glow of the golden fire, among the shadows.

A foghorn blast rang out, making people shriek and cower. Someone pointed; everyone looked up to see him. The Mayor of Quill Point, standing upon a shadow hand, spread his arms wide.

His eyes glimmered gold.

"Welcome," he said, his voice unnaturally loud, "welcome to the final part of a grand plan older than anyone here. I know you are afraid. But I assure you that everything is going exactly to plan. I assure you, my constituents, that I know what I am doing and that everything will go as it should to achieve the loftiest goals."

Purple lightning cracked across the sky, and Zaahir could swear he could see that thing again. A figure, giant, towering, hundreds of feet tall in jagged, bone-white armor. But when the light faded, he couldn't even see the silhouette.

"Consider this my inauguration," The Mayor said. "Consider me now under a vast and powerful authority. The God of Greed grants untold riches. You may call me The Duke of Quill Point. The King Regent of Quill Point. The Ascended Mayor."

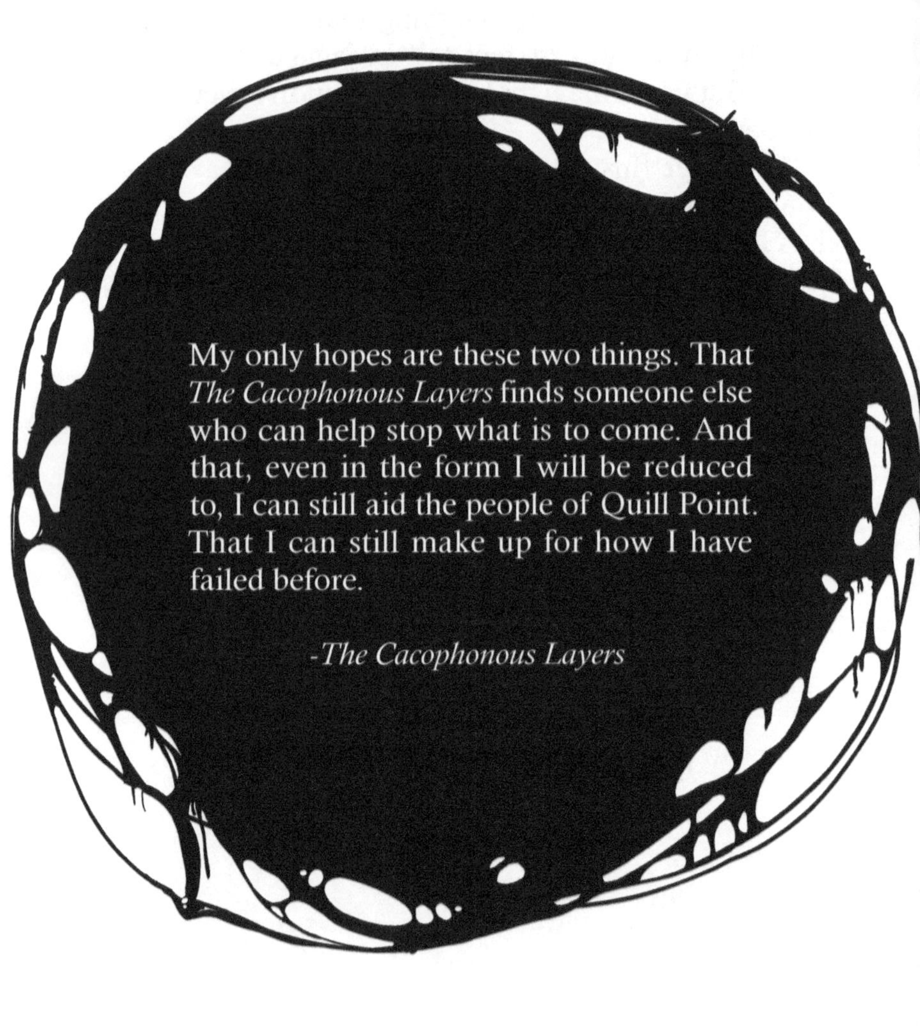
My only hopes are these two things. That
The Cacophonous Layers finds someone else
who can help stop what is to come. And
that, even in the form I will be reduced
to, I can still aid the people of Quill Point.
That I can still make up for how I have
failed before.

-The Cacophonous Layers

PART 3

KNOWING TOO MUCH

CHAPTER 33

Thea's life revolved around books when it came to memories, relationships, and even finances. Every significant memory had a book tied to it. If asked, she could recall the look of each book she was reading when something happened in her life.

The motivational self-help book she read before giving her valedictorian speech was mostly yellow, with an otherwise bland cover design. She'd been muttering a passage from it the entire walk up to the stage.

The novel she'd been reading right before she had to deal with her first overflowing toilet at her first apartment on her own had been mostly blue with stylized people on the cover. It had been a romance novel focusing on a professional baseball player falling in love with a merchandise seller who was at each of his games.

When she first met her now-wife Cynthia at Quill Point's roller-rink after she and her twenty-something friends had gotten rather drunk, she'd spent the last week reading cookbook after cookbook to find foods that wouldn't break her budget. She'd eventually found a recipe for a decent hamburger and squash casserole.

The day leading to Thea's first date with Cynthia, after weeks of hoping, wondering if Cynthia would ask her out—or if Thea should go out on a limb and do it—she'd been reading a horror book. Reasoning that, no matter what could go wrong, it couldn't be as bad as what happened in the gore-soaked supernatural horror book with a pale blue cover of smiling monsters looking out the windows of a haunted house.

She'd been too nervous to read much of anything the night before she proposed, but she'd tried the same trick the week leading up to it—but horror literature proved too intense. Instead, she read a memoir that talked a lot about marriage and—using little tabs that wouldn't hurt the pages—marked the sections that made her so happy she almost cried.

On their sixth anniversary, Thea had only just finished reading the book she planned to give Cynthia. It was a compendium of stories about successful business owners throughout history. Thea hoped it would give Cynthia the confidence to start that coffee shop she'd always been talking about. She knew it would work. Cynthia was too driven, too savvy, not to be a success. She just had to convince Cynthia of that.

And when Thea signed the final papers to inherit Quill Point's only book shop, Stylus Books, from her late grandmother, she'd been reading a mystery novel about a detective who focused on unsolved missing person reports. The cover of that one had been all shadowy and noir-like, but the story was more heartwarming than she'd expected.

When she couldn't fall asleep, she remembered those books.

When she was stressed, she would reread one.

Each was a friend in their own way.

Companions, confidants, and ready and willing to cheer her on for whatever she faced. Anyone who knew her, even a little, knew that books were a part of Thea's soul.

So, it only made sense that when Thea moved into her new business and set up her desk at Stylus Books, she had a copy of each book on a shelf behind her. First editions if she could get them, and at least hardcovers if she couldn't. And she left openings on that shelf for whatever would come next.

Had Thea known what was to happen, she might not have left more space. Had she known that not only would Quill Point fall to an evil god but also that she would face things beyond anything she'd ever expected, perhaps she would've been careful to never associate any books with what was to come.

But she didn't know the story of her own life.

CHAPTER 34

THEA'S FIRST FEW YEARS OF OWNING HER own business were beyond hectic. Even on calm days, there was *so much* paperwork, stocking, logistic, and other sundry aspects of the job she had to learn fast to stay afloat.

She would spend so long at her desk her legs were often sore.

Thus, leading her to a walking habit.

Whenever she closed shop or found those moments of free time that amazed her every time they existed, Thea would walk around Quill Point. These trips had no particular destination in mind but often drifted toward whatever was happening downtown.

Back in those days, when the town was a more lively place and not the sleepy town it would become, it wasn't uncommon for some other local shops to set up little booths and have teenagers look over them, hoping to entice more customers.

But Thea already knew the local businesses. She was friends with the owners of most of them. It was the art stands that interested her. Local creatives would put out whatever they had. They were rejuvenating.

And Thea had quickly learned that people enjoyed local art hanging around her small bookstore—and so did she. So, the walks became in her busy mind justified, and she took them more and more.

On one such excursion, on one stressful day, when a hiccup with her latest shipment had caused her a literal headache, she went looking for something to fill up one of the last prime blank spaces on her wall.

And, quickly enough, she happened upon a stand with an extensive selection of paintings. The stand was improperly built, looking like it had every chance of falling, but the paintings were *fantastic*. Thea couldn't help but walk up close to a freestanding easel and look over the sublime abstract representation of a boat bobbing at sea, with a storm hanging off in the distance. The seagulls swooping past the boat, skimming the water, looked so realistic that she could faintly hear their calls.

"Do you like it?"

Thea blinked in surprise. She'd lost herself in that picture more than she realized. She leaned around the painting and tried to find the source of the voice.

And it took a second. The man sitting in a fold-out chair was wearing the same palate of colors as the paintings on either side of him: a bold split of the left being oceanic blues and the right luscious greens. Even his pant legs were the same shades. It made it look a little like his head was simply floating there. He had suntanned white skin and wore a tan beanie covering his hair.

"Oh, sorry, didn't see you," Thea said. "I … love it. They're great! Are these yours?"

"Thank you!" the man said brightly and sat up in his chair.

He gestured around at the myriad pieces. They stood on easels, leaned against the table he sat behind, or were propped up by pieces of wood jammed into the dirt.

"Most of them are mine," he said, "but I am showing off a few for some of my friends."

"That's nice of you," Thea said.

"Yeah, some of them are busy with classes right now. I graduated last year and have been trying to do this full-time."

He stood up and took off his beanie, revealing black hair that dropped almost to his eyes.

"But that's me oversharing. What's your name?"

"I'm Thea," she said.

"Julian," the man said, giving a half-bow. He smiled when he stood back up. "What do you do?"

"Oh, I run the local bookstore. It's called Stylus Books."

Julian chuckled. "This town is really funny. Everything is named after something to do with writing utensils or ink. Or you just name it after the town. You even named the hotel after a giant sea monster, of all things."

A strong laugh bubbled its way out of Thea. "Yeah, I know. It's a quirk around here. Between you and me, I honestly thought about changing my store's name to something else, but I just couldn't break the tradition."

Julian smiled, and it went to his eyes. "It's because of the town's founder, right? I saw a picture of her in one of the shops."

"Yeah, Irena Ink. With a last name like that, it's hard not to want to give the whole town a theme."

Julian nodded and then walked over. "So, are you looking for some art?"

"Yeah," Thea said. "I have this one corner in my shop. I put a chair there—this one older gentleman likes to stop and read—and I thought it would be nice to hang something up there."

"Oh, well, then you're in luck. As you can see, landscapes are *my* specialty. Any of these could be good to set a tranquil mood."

Thea gave him a smirk. "Good marketing there."

Julian smiled and shrugged. "I did say I wanted to go full-time."

Thea looked around at the paintings. A lot were similar—boats or ships with storms on the horizon. But one caught her eye. Unlike some less detailed depictions of the boats, this one was rendered absurdly lifelike. It was painted red, bobbing among whitecaps, and on the deck of it were tiny but impressively detailed people. Some had life jackets, and some were visibly yelling at the sky.

Thea was having trouble looking away from it. She walked closer, eyes locking onto one of the tiny figures. One of them was a man with a distinct shirt design.

"Is this … you?" she asked, holding out her finger, being careful not to touch the canvas.

"Yeah, I'm in a lot of the paintings," Julian said flatly.

"That's … fun," Thea said, though she suddenly felt a little more on edge than before. "It's an incredible piece."

"Thank you," he said, his voice perking back up. "Before you make your decision, I would be remiss if I didn't also show you some of the stuff my friends have made."

"Uh, sure," Thea said, having to physically tear her gaze away from the image. It was like her neck didn't want to move.

Julian guided her to a small cluster of paintings off to the side of the tent. They were leaning against a small wooden fence recently planted into the ground. Most paintings were on smaller frames and had different styles to them.

Thea nodded in appreciation at an eclectic still life depicting an untitled book, an apple, a milled hammer with a broken handle, and a sleeping cat, all on a large wooden tabletop. The painting looked like a snapshot.

"That one's called *Life on a Table* by a new up-and-coming artist. This one—"

Julian leaned down to wave his hand in front of a painting of a man with outstretched arms sprouting thistles. He was screaming, but his mouth was full of dark green, five-pointed leaves.

"—is *The Wrath of Her.* She told me she saw it in a dream. It's not the strangest dream she's told me about. Not by a long, long shot."

Thea walked along, nodding but feeling increasingly uneasy. There wasn't any specific reason for the feeling, at least not that Thea noticed, but more and more, it became clear: no one else was coming near the tent. The market was full of people—or had been. They'd been milling around, talking, getting food from the two trucks that stopped by, but no one was near this art. Somehow or another, Thea had entered a private showing.

And, as they continued it, Julian's voice had a quality that made it more like she was listening to nonsense in a dream than speech. She retroactively knew what he'd said, but felt confused during the telling of it.

And she couldn't quite recall what the last few paintings had actually looked like.

Thea cleared her throat.

"Thanks. Thank you for the show. I really liked it. But if I'm being honest, I'll just have the first one."

Julian stopped abruptly. He half-turned and put his hand on a painting in a golden frame. He traced it with the tip of his finger and chuckled.

Thea noticed his hand left a faint streak of color. It was the same as his skin. But before Thea could get a second look, he whipped it away with his palm.

"Oh, that's a shame," Julian said, picking it up. "I really like this last one. It's a special painting of him. It's very, very special."

Thea's mind whined in warning; she tried not to glance at the painting. But her eyes twitched and spasmed and hurt. *Dragged* to the frame until she gave in and looked.

This painting appeared initially very abstract. An exploration of colors and lines. But there *was* a picture there. It just wasn't immediately obvious. It depicted *something*. Only when she noticed a person's side profile did it slot into place. Only then did her eyes decode it.

It was a little like falling. The painting was so three-dimensional. There were several sections to it: boxes placed within larger boxes.

Thea's head swam a little, trying to parse each layer. The artist had clearly been skilled—putting so many details into one frame must have been difficult.

The deepest layer, the smallest box, depicted a crudely drawn person. A blue stick figure but one given as many details as possible without losing the simplistic nature of the design. He was leaning against the edge of his box. His knees were bent so the tips touched the other side, and his legs were long enough that his single-line feet lay flat against the wall he leaned on. His head was tilted back against the wall, and his stick arms with stick fingers were in a vaguely haughty gesture. It was a side profile with only a line for a smile and a dot for the eye, but it told Thea everything about his personality.

The next layer up was the same figure, but he was more detailed and painting the deepest layer. His hands and fingers looked more like real ones, although still made of visible blue brushstrokes. In his hands was a huge brush and palette streaked with blood and bile. His posture was like someone finishing a painting with a final, inspired flourish. He mostly faced away from the viewer; only the barest hint of one of his dot eyes was visible.

The third layer up was the same figure, now rendered almost lifelike, with blue, shiny skin, and was wearing a dark blue suit with bright red buttons. He gestured to a plaque right below the second layer box with squiggles on it instead of writing. A pair of museum stanchions stood on either side of him, with a red rope hanging low behind him. He was turned away only slightly; his eyes were white ovals with a dot for a pupil.

The fourth and final layer was someone sitting in a chair, looking up at the smaller layers hung up as a painting on a wall above an austere fireplace. His now perfectly realized blue hands were spread out over either side of the chair's arms. In one hand, he loosely held a cup of acid-green liquid. In the other, a knife that dripped with fresh crimson blood. The back of his head had distinct rivulets of denim blue hair, long enough to touch the back of the chair. A faint line of cigar smoke drifted up above his head.

"He doesn't just show up to anyone, you know," Julian said, sounding far away. "Only when it would be the most interesting does he allow someone to interact with the original artwork."

Thea's pulse was so forceful it felt like someone was hitting her chest each time her heart pumped. And simultaneously, her heartbeat had slowed so dramatically that she feared passing out on the spot.

Her mouth was suddenly so dry that rather than responding, she swallowed hard, trying, and failing, to breathe properly. Instead, a faint rasp flowed out of her mouth.

The smallest image, the crudest layer, turned his simplistic head. His mouth-line was the shape of an orange slice, with lines crossing between the top and the bottom that suggested gigantic teeth.

The painter's layer, the second furthest down, moved his brush and swirled together bile and blood. He tilted his head and shifted so he was looking directly at Thea. His mouth had the faintest suggestion of lips and teeth.

The third layer, the museum curator layer, dropped his arms to his sides in a huff, like he was no longer excited to show off the painting to whoever was in the room with him. He leaned forward toward Thea, quirking his mouth in amusement.

The fourth layer moved the wine glass to where its mouth presumably was and then deposited an empty glass on the chair arm a second later. The other hand dropped the knife to the ground, where it dug deep into the wood, almost down to the hilt. A small pool of blood formed there.

He stood up from the seat. His suit was coated in blood. Stained, soaked, dripping down on the seat.

Thea tried to let out a scream.

To beg for him not to turn around.

It was a migraine while looking at the sun. It was garish colors when nursing nausea. A refusal letter in the mail for a dream college. Seeing the corpse of a best friend and knowing that all history with them was over, backward, limited, stuck in the past and only the past.

Please. I don't want to know.

He turned around, and his face was the whole canvas. Lines of paint swirling in the shape of a mouth, blotches of color were his eyes. He gazed at Thea and said something that would change the course of her entire life.

"This world," he said, "is only a story being told."

Thea staggered backward, falling to the ground as she shrieked and gasped. Her hands came up to defend herself, but nothing hit her. The damage was inside.

Inside her skull but audible to the air were the sounds of keys unlocking padlocks. The *click*, *turn*, and *clunk*. Everything she looked at ceased to exist, blinking away and then coming back. When she glanced down at the ground, she could see the void of space, then the planet's molten core. Then collections of diamonds, so far down she couldn't fathom the miles of drop.

Dirt, rock, grass. Normal, but not.

Familiar, but so forever different.

Julian slowly lowered the painting to the ground, the canvas now blank, and studied her for a moment. When he smiled, little flecks of his skin and teeth ran as liquid down his chin. His hands dripped, hissing when it touched the grass.

He drunkenly giggled, slapping his knee. "I never tire of that."

"What … did you do to me?"

When she propped herself up to look at Julian, even as he was rapidly falling apart into splotches of primary colors and half-formed constructions, she could see the thing behind all of what she was seeing. The festering, rotting anti-matter that was Julian's true existence.

"I can see you," Thea said, her voice harsh. "I can see you there, you rotting thing. Get off this…"

A severe twinge of pure pain in her left temple. She clutched the side of her head with an agonized moan.

"…off this Layer. Or…"

Another stabbing sensation, this time from the front of her head to the top of her neck, in one fiery, almost liquid-like rush. She gritted her teeth against it, sucking in harsh breaths.

"…I'll make you."

Julian winked and chuckled. "Good luck with that. You'll not even remember this. It's too many doors at one time. Your mind will shut most of them until it can open them comfortably. Or you'll die. Sometimes humans just die."

Julian titled his head, looking at her closely. His eyebrow slid down the side of his face and dripped to the ground. He clicked his tongue exactly fifteen times. Then he smirked.

"No, I guess you'll survive. In that case, he'll be enormously pleased to see whatever you do next."

To anyone without Thea's new abilities, it looked like Julian collapsed into a splash of paint on the ground, dropping like whatever had been holding his form up had been yanked away.

But to her, she could see the bubble that was the core of him, the floating center of his existence, disappear through a rapidly closing hole in reality.

And, as soon as he did, the tent and all the other paintings went blurry, like a heat haze, and then faded away from sight and existence, no longer supported by a demigod or god to keep them constructed.

Thea's head felt like it was being put in a stand mixer. Each point where a skull bone connected to another was being yanked apart like cracking open a crab's leg.

Her head *jolted* backward to the sound of an immense door slamming closed. The force of it made her fall back, and she lay staring at the sky. Faint clicks of latches sealing sent relaxing pulses down her arms and legs.

Thea made noises like she'd woken up slightly sore, rolled herself to sit, stood up, and dusted herself off. An expression of shock and confusion lingered on her face for a moment before fading.

She took off walking back to Stylus Books, disappointed that she'd not found a good painting to hang up.

CHAPTER 35

Thea said she'd invented the Mug of Ink because she wasn't much of a morning person and still needed to open the shop. But that wasn't strictly true. She was *not* a morning person, having developed her sleep patterns from being up late reading, but the combination of very dark chocolate, ristretto, cinnamon, slight amounts of vanilla extract, and eventually, for promotional reasons, a tiny amount of black color dye wasn't invented *that* strong for just bouts of insomnia.

It had been because of the dreams haunting her lately.

And they weren't her normal nightmares, either. These were things she'd *never* imagined before.

These were things she didn't have words for.

The process was not gradual, either. It happened every night.

She and Cynthia would lie down, talk a little about their day, and then Cynthia would turn over exactly twice, adjust the pillow once, and then be out *cold*.

Thea always smiled when she heard her breathing make the switch.

Once that happened, Thea had to face her *own* sleep. The exhaustion would crawl into her head and push down her eyes. Thea tried to think of sleep like closing her bookstore for the day. Switches thrown one at a time, books put away where they belonged, letting the place rest for another day. Dark, comfortable, familiar sounds removed the world until the sun and the alarm started it all again. A pleasant, gradual process, full of stress-free bliss.

But lately, if she let herself drift even a little and closed her eyes, she would plummet into a dream for the entire night. And she would wake up each day not feeling well. Sometimes, she'd find her body cramped into a protective ball, clutching her stomach or head. Her doctor had suggested sleeping pills. Her dentist suggested a guard to prevent her from grinding her teeth.

But the dreams couldn't be escaped.

They happened no matter what she tried, and they were vivid. So vivid that she could often remember large snippets of them going into the following day.

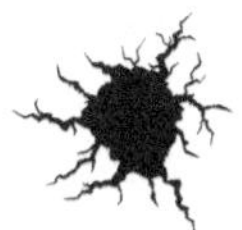

Thea stood in front of a blank wall in a room without doors. She was only there a short while before, in front of her, the air would wobble and then part. Showing something else beyond.

It was a place that made little sense, for it had no structure. There were no walls, floor, or ground, only constant strings of letters and symbols. They formed a lattice-work, a hallway, a pit, or a slope. She couldn't touch the lines, though. Thea passed right through them. But she could hear them—those words were narrated by a billion unceasing voices. If she wasn't in a dream, she wasn't sure how long she could stand the noise.

Sometimes she would spend a long time looking into that opening, listening to the cacophony of words, hoping she would wake up before stepping inside. But that never worked. The time differences between dreams and reality could outwait her.

Eventually, Thea would step into the chasm and fall.

It didn't work like Earth's gravity. It was more a general drifting. If she used the portal as a baseline, she went downward if she did not set her body in any general direction. After a few days of this, it was easy to influence the trajectory.

The portal would always close behind her.

The word strings had a logic to their configurations. They had points of creation where they burst forth from, streaming out in every direction like disgorged confetti. She'd seen hundreds of such spots already, focal points, and had no reason to believe there were not trillions more.

She only had to follow a line. And when she got to a focal point and focused on it, it would open into another portal.

And, through those portals, Thea saw ... things. Things that made her strong vocabulary falter for adjectives. In one, an impossible amount of fire and blood spun in a tight spiral, a wheel orbited by silver moons populated by monsters that sang to each other as they passed. In another, she saw a planet that appeared to function entirely under the rules of fluid dynamics, with the only solid part of it strange bones submerged in the liquid.

But sometimes, most times actually, Thea saw populated places with lots of bipeds. Sometimes they were humans, sometimes not, but they would live in buildings that looked almost like buildings she would see in any city in her world. Sometimes the architecture didn't make sense, but they felt more like home than she expected.

One night, though, was the worst night yet. She saw something that horrified her to her core.

CHAPTER 36

ONE NIGHT, IN ONE DREAM, SHE OPENED a portal and saw nothing much. It was very dark and cold, and even in a dream, being there felt a little unsafe. When nothing happened, she peered closer, ducking her head into the portal.

Thea could make out, so far away, floating objects: shiny, metallic, and silver. They blinked with little computer-style lights. Blue, then green, then off. Then repeat.

Thea stood outside the portal for a long time, debating. The dreams only ended after she visited somewhere. One place a night.

She stepped through and floated—but with no control this time. Willing herself to move did nothing. There was nothing to push off of. Thea imagined this must be what spacewalking was like.

She was aware she shouldn't be able to breathe and that she should be impossibly cold, but the environments of the dreams never seemed to affect her. Thea let herself gently float in the void, waiting for whatever she was here to see.

A few of the little dots of metal got closer. There were quite a few out there. Each drifted independently, silently blinking their lights.

Finally, one of them drifted close enough for Thea to grab onto a handle sticking out the side of it and pull herself to the hull. She bumped into it gently.

The surface of it appeared made for climbing. Along it were handles and divots. She climbed, looking for anything else about it besides metal and lights. She eventually found a thick glass window.

Thea's blood ran cold, and she screamed without air.

It was holding a person. A man was stuck inside it. Metal tentacles held him in place, pulled him back, yanked on his shoulders, forced back the top of his head, and strained his joints.

The man was grimacing in pain, fighting against it, but unable to do more than squirm. Various readouts pulsed around him, showing his high heart rate and low oxygen levels.

In a panic, Thea looked for a way to open the ball. Tried to find a latch. She found a small, red handle and was about to open it. She braced to pull—

And then stopped.

She might survive without air in this dream, but who knew the rules for this man? She might send him flying into the void of space without a suit.

Thea looked around at the other space pods floating nearby. All of them could have people inside. All of them could have people stuck floating in the void.

She looked back into the pod and screamed again. A long metal tentacle reached, extended a long needle from its tip, and plunged it into the man's neck. He passed out almost instantly, and the tentacle and needle retreated.

The heart monitor showed a slowing pulse.

Thea shook her head, not understanding. Not understanding why this was here, what was happening to these people.

Above her flooded a ton of sudden light. Artificial and glaring.

Thea glanced up to see something massive, metallic, and covered in sickly green lights float by. It was so big she couldn't tell its shape. Or how many pieces it had. It was made of many parts and connections, yet a whole creation.

It continued past her, guided by massive engines, moving so fast.

But by its glaring light, she could see where it was going. A planet, unlit by any sun, floated far, far off in the distance. Thea's mind tried and failed to parse the size of the planet.

A burst of light on the surface of the planet. Then more. Sleek missiles, hundreds of them, flew at the ship. They took only a few seconds to hit their targets.

The explosions were too bright to look at. Thea looked away, covering her eyes. A few seconds later, a massive shockwave smacked into her, sending her flipping, spinning, and tumbling through the void of space. Soaring over the clusters of trapped people screaming inside their pods.

She woke up, clutching herself.

And then had an even worse dream the following night.

CHAPTER 37

"**D**EAR, YOU'RE OVERWORKED,"
Cynthia said. "And this is coming from me."

"I know, I know," Thea said.

Thea's eyes burned so much that she could barely look at the paper in front of her. She shifted the form around, revealing the lines and lines of things she needed to read on the form beneath it.

"But what am I going to do?"

Cynthia approached her desk and picked up the little white bottle. Thea had been carrying it around in her purse but had taken it out and forgotten to put it back.

"Well, I don't think you should take any more of these," Cynthia said. "You can overdose on caffeine pills."

"You're right," Thea said, smoothing back her hair. "I'm getting a little numb to caffeine lately. It's not really working for me."

"Well, that's a little concerning, dear. Can you hire someone?"

Thea tilted her head. "What?"

"The shop has been doing really well, right?"

"Yeah," Thea said. "The regulars keep buying me out of stuff. I guess I shouldn't be surprised. Nana somehow kept this place going. It seems like Kurt buys a new romance novel every other day."

"Yeah, I know. He reads them at the café. It's like watching an engine getting gas. He'll read half a book by the end of his first espresso."

Thea chuckled while rubbing her eyes. They were a little foggy. She gathered up the papers, shifting them until they were in a neat pile. "Well, would you look at that, you and me keeping Quill Point citizens happy."

Cynthia smiled. "Yeah, but you need to keep yourself happy too."

"I'm happy," Thea said, taking her wife's hand. "So happy. I get to sell books."

"I know you are, love, but imagine how many more you could sell with another pair of hands."

"Who, though?" Thea asked.

"The only thing this town seems to have more of than older folks are young adults. Put up a sign. They'll rush right on in, I promise. I've got that one girl working part-time now at the café, Erin, and I found her so fast I was left blinking."

"Okay. I think you're right. I'll start looking tomorrow." Thea put away the papers into the desk and locked it with a small key. Tomorrow was a good time for several things. "Do you want to get some kind of dinner? I don't want to cook."

"I could cook," Cynthia said.

"No offense, my everything, but I'm not sure I'm willing to trust any more dishes from you that aren't pasta."

Cynthia pouted, but smiled almost instantly. "Okay, fair. I'll admit. I'll stick to making the best dang coffee in the world."

Thea walked around the desk and offered her arm. Cynthia intertwined hers with Thea's.

"The best in the whole universe, my love. Are you ready to go?" Thea said, looking at her with a faux-serious expression. "Ready for a night on the town after so much drudgery?"

Cynthia burst out laughing, tilting her head back as she did. She moved to wrap her arms around Thea's shoulders and pulled her in close. "Sure. Where do you want to eat?"

"Let's go the Ink Well. I want to check up on Caleb."

"I heard he and Sarah broke up," Thea commented.

"Yeah, that's why I want to check on him."

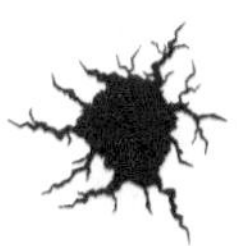

The help wanted sign lasted four days before Thea hired someone. The first applicant, in fact.

They wandered in after stopping and looking at the sign outside for a moment. They had stylish golden glasses with square frames and little earrings resembling beads. Their skin was white, a little sunburned, and they wore a suit jacket over a button-up and had on maroon dress shoes.

"Hi, I hear there's an opening?" they asked.

Thea smiled at them. "Yes! I'm looking for someone to help me out around here. Are you interested?"

"Very," they said and walked up, offering their hand.

Thea took it. They had a firm grip.

"Good handshake," Thea said.

"Thank you. My name's Haven. I'm local."

"Hello, Haven. Nice to meet you. My name is Thea. I think I've seen you around town. Mind if we have the interview right here? This shop isn't much bigger than it looks. I don't really have a back office."

"That's fine," Haven said, glancing around. "Um, I'm sorry, there doesn't appear to be a chair."

"Oops," Thea said. "Sorry—let me grab you one of the reading chairs."

Thea got up and wandered toward one of the little nooks she'd set up for customers. The closest one had a small pile of romance novels stacked next to the seat. She smirked to herself. Looks like Kurt had been trying to find something new. Hopefully, she'd have time to order fresh ones for him.

Thea picked up the chair, bracing it against her knee for a moment to get a grip on it. It wasn't light. She walked across the small store, making sure not to bump any shelves.

She placed it down in front of Haven.

"So, I figure we can start a little informal." Thea moved to her side of the desk. "I think the most important question is how you feel about books?"

Haven sat down and pondered for a moment. They pursed their lips, slightly humming. "How do I put this? I adore books, Thea. This was the first place I picked to ask about a job because I think it would be amazing to be around books all day."

Thea nodded. "Why do you like books so much?"

"I like how they have breathing worlds," Haven said. "Movies and video games have that too, and I love a good movie or fantasy game, but you get so much detail in

326

a book. Sometimes they feel like the characters are real people you could meet someday."

"But why do you want to help *sell* them? This isn't a library; we'll mostly work *with* books, not be reading them. But … you *can* get a discount once you've worked here for a month."

Haven looked around at the bookshelves and then back at Thea. Thea knew that look in their eye. The rest of the interview would likely be a formality, depending on the next answer. They were already hired in Thea's mind.

"…there have been books that mean a lot to me. And I don't remember how I found them. If it was my parents who first showed me, my cousins, or I saw them at a bookstore. But if I can be why someone *finds* a book they love, that would be incredible. And the discount does sound nice."

Thea smiled.

Good answer.

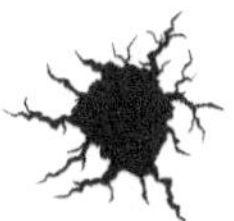

The day had been uneventful. Saturday evenings before dinner were often the slowest part of the week. People were usually handling errands or chores or driving out of Quill Point to somewhere with more to do. There was usually a brief rush after dinner when people would wander around on the sidewalk, but that was still a few hours away.

Another perk of hiring someone was that instead of long stretches of silence during that time of day, Thea sometimes got to talk about books.

"Just hold them up," Thea said. "I know basically every book in this place now."

"Can do," Haven said.

Thea watched as Haven moved around the horror shelf, ducking down and rising on their tiptoes to get a better look at the selection. They pulled one out and held it up.

"What do you think of this one?" Haven asked. "Is it any good?"

"Okay, maybe I need you to bring it a little closer. I just see … knife stuff. What's it called?"

Haven lowered the book to look. "Uh … *Sliced Bones* by Xander Carter."

"Oh," Thea said. "He's a local. Yeah, I liked that one. It's a little gory for my taste, though."

"There's a horror writer in Quill Point?" Haven asked.

"Yeah, we stock his books here. We sold out of one of them—I can't remember the title. He's pretty prolific."

"Huh," Haven said. "Maybe I'll take a look."

"Yeah, feel free. I'm sure Xander would love to have another fan."

"Cool," Haven said, putting it to the side. They reached slightly up and pulled another book off the shelf.

"*Alien at the Window* by Y.G. Clark?"

"Not really scary. It's more a coming-of-age story with some spooky sections."

"Oh, that won't work," Haven said, putting it back on the shelf.

After a few moments of Haven browsing with no more questions, Thea returned to what she was looking over. Finance sheets were all over her desk, but she'd barely made a dent. She wrote out a little equation, then let her pen drop out of her hand. She was drifting. The sleep deprivation was always getting to her. She found herself thinking of the previous night's dreams.

She'd seen a burning skyscraper covered in something she had regretted investigating. It was on fire because of the swarming, climbing, spinal columns covered in strange red anemones that sprayed flames from their too-big, circular, gasping mouths.

Thea shook her head, trying not to remember anymore.

"How about this one?" Haven asked.

Thea jolted. Looking up, Haven had snuck up on her and was now standing on the other side of the desk. They held up a book with shadowy figures with glowing green eyes sitting in the front seats of rows and rows of cars.

"*The Nightmares on The Road 2: Final Commute*?" Thea muttered. "I liked the first one more. I think it was scarier when there was only one of the driving monsters."

"Oh, do we have the first one?"

"Not currently," Thea replied, rubbing her eyes. "I can order one or two, but it's an older horror book. Why are you asking about so many horror books, anyway? I thought you liked fantasy more. Or is this for a customer?"

"It's for a … customer. A potential … customer. She said she likes horror books, and I thought I could convince her to come by and get one or two sometime."

"Oh, is that so?" Thea said. It was hard not to notice the faint blush on Haven's face. "Well, thank you for the marketing. Feel free to invite her sometime."

"Okay," Haven said, unable to meet Thea's eyes. "Thanks."

"Do you know what kind of horror she likes?"

"Uh … she said she likes really scary stuff."

"Scary stuff, huh," Thea said, barely holding back a smirk. "Go find me *Miasma Days and Blood Nights* by

Winona Connolly. She's absolutely the scariest writer I know of."

"Thank you," Haven said.

"Well, it's always good to find someone, right?"

"Yeah … the more customers, the better," Haven said.

"Right," Thea said. "Sure."

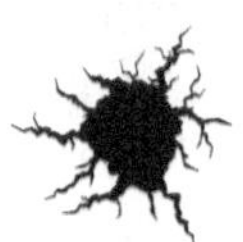

Haven brought by a girl named Milda a few days later. She was blond, a little shorter than Haven, and had a pinkish complexion. She wore a business casual-style white blouse, a black business jacket, and a tan skirt. Thea tried her absolute best to not eavesdrop on their conversation. A real, concerted effort.

She lasted maybe ten minutes.

"It was like about this house—no, I'm not selling it right," Haven said. "It's about this *massive* house that's burned down so often that the architecture is a mismatch."

"Yeah?" Milda replied a little quietly.

Thea glanced at the front of the store. No new customers.

"Uh, yeah, and it was—it was really spooky. I mean, scary. You told me you liked the really scary books."

"Sometimes I do," Milda said. "It sounds like I would like this one."

Thea stood up and silently walked over to the other side of the shelf. It was only a few steps, but the mounting silence in the bookstore made her wonder if the two of them knew she was right there.

"Cool … yeah. You should get it…" Haven said a little quietly. "Or, you know what, I can get it for you. Do you want me to buy you the book?"

"Oh, no, you don't have to—"

"Well, if they do, then they'll get an employee discount," Thea said, stepping around the bookshelf.

Haven jolted and backed up, bumping into Milda.

They spun around. "Sorry, sorry."

Milda laughed. "It's okay. She spooked me too."

"So, who is this?" Thea asked, unable to keep a small grin off her face. It was too cute. "Is this the Milda I keep hearing about?"

Haven's face was swiftly growing more and more red. It crept up their nose. Their pupils couldn't be wider.

"You talked about me?" Milda asked, her voice neutral, but a little redness was creeping into her cheeks now.

"Only a *little*," Thea said. "I was hoping to meet one of Haven's friends one of these days. They have so many, but I only see them when they come by to pick Haven up."

"Oh … okay," Milda said with a soft smile.

Haven temporarily could not look at either of them, adjusting a book on the nearby shelf that didn't need to be adjusted. Brushing away dust with the back of their hand. Humming quietly underneath their breath.

Thea cleared her throat. "Well, I am so sorry for startling you. But, Haven, you should absolutely cash in your employee privileges for this lovely young lady. In fact, what book were you telling her about?"

"Uh … *Miasma Days and Blood Nights*…"

"Oh, I need to offload that one, anyway. Have it for free!"

"Thank you so much," Milda said. "I didn't catch your name."

"Oh, it's Thea. Please browse and see if there's anything else you might like here."

Haven opened their mouth like they were about to say something, but Thea gave them the smallest wink and turned away quickly.

"I'll be at the front when you're ready to check out," Thea added. "I love seeing people reading."

"S-sorry … about that. She's … she's eccentric," Haven said, voice hitching. "I guess this book's free if you want me to get you it, and maybe another one too… if you want."

"That's so nice of you, Haven. How about I pick a book for you too?" Milda said. "And then we can…"

Thea stopped walking about halfway to her desk.

"…we could read it at the coffee shop or something?"

Thea couldn't help herself.

"If you do, say hi to my wife!" she said over her shoulder. "She owns the Quill Point Café."

"H-how about we just go to the park?" Haven interjected. "That sounds fun. We can read there … after my shift."

"Take the rest of the day off," Thea said, sitting down at her desk. "After you pick out the books, you can have the rest of the day off, Haven. Full pay vacation day."

Haven spun and looked at her, blinking. They gave out a little sigh, then smiled. "Okay. Thank you so much!"

"Have fun," Thea said. "It's probably going to be a slow day."

"Thank you so much," Milda said.

"If you ever need a place to hang out, please feel free to come by anytime. I'm sure Haven would love the company."

"Thanks, I will," Milda said, then looked back at Haven. "So, I'm going to get you a book too. Do you want a horror book or some other genre?"

"Um, well, I-I really like fantasy…" Haven said quietly.

The two trailed off into the shelves, out of earshot, and Thea sat back in her chair.

CHAPTER 38

THE STRANGE CLUSTERS OF WORDS AND symbols didn't just output. As some things flowed out, others flowed in. They were not a chain but a hub. It reminded Thea a little of how neurons worked. Everything connected to everything else if you traced it far enough.

She wondered if there was a way to find an end. Any edge. If she went up or down or left or right—as far as those directions had any meaning in that place—she would find a beginning. The first nexus from which other clusters sprung.

Not that she liked most ones she had visited so far. Not that she had a strong desire to search out more. These places were often horrible, warped, and messy. Full of creatures, monsters, or things she could barely count as living, but were certainly destructive.

One place had been beautiful, though. It had been so beautiful.

It had translucent streets and wires visible beneath, making way for the lush topside. Trees and bushes dotted everywhere. People moved in clusters, chatting among themselves. There were plenty of buildings, but they were always unobstructive. Part of the landscape. The buildings were made of something with the wonderful shimmering qualities of precious stone and glass's clean, crisp clarity. Musicians played every few blocks around the entrances and on small, raised platforms seemingly made for them.

Thea hovered lower to look around. A pair of teenage girls played some game on a small table. The board was tiered with three levels to it, arranged like increasingly large mesas stacked atop one another, and had pieces on every level. The pieces looked like little lightbulbs. Some orange and some green. One girl reached out and tapped the piece. It flickered and changed to a pulsing blue. She tapped a different spot on the board, and it reappeared there, then turned back to green. The other girl frowned, scratching the back of her head. She put her hand over the board and spun her finger. The board rotated with her gesture.

"Have you been practicing without me?" she asked.

"Just been watching some videos online."

She frowned. "Well, you got a lot better. I don't know if I can win."

"Round two?"

"Sure."

Thea watched as the pieces disappeared, and the three tiers collapsed back to one, then she floated away. This place was so full of interesting things.

A slow-moving air vehicle drifted in the distance, followed by people riding advanced-looking hang gliders.

The musicians below them played an airy, flute-like tune, and some fliers did little flips and dives in synch.

Thea wished they could hear her clap for them. She watched, smiling. After nightmare after nightmare, she was so happy to see one place had people simply happy.

She sat on one of the ample chairs and benches and watched the world go by for as long as the dream was planning to have her stay.

CHAPTER 39

Cynthia and Thea were reading in their very comfy queen-sized bed together. Thea was reading a book on various card and board games, and Cynthia was going through the still-surviving Quill Point weekly newspaper.

Cynthia scoffed and lowered the paper. "He got reelected mayor again."

"No one was really running against him," Thea muttered, still reading her book.

"Yeah, well, I don't like him."

Thea looked up. "Yeah, I don't think he's a good person either."

"But somehow, someway, he keeps getting reelected. That woman running against him, what was her name?"

"I—wow, I don't remember. That was like ten years ago, right?"

"Yeah, *exactly*. I smell corruption. That man will screw over everyone somehow, just for a little more power. Mark my words."

"Marked," Thea said, reaching for a notepad. "How would you like that written?"

Cynthia looked over at her and chuckled. "You know what I meant."

"I do," Thea said and leaned against her. "But at least he's not done anything yet—at least, that we know about. Maybe he's content power tripping as a minor politician."

"Maybe…" Cynthia said. "But if he tries to jack up rent on my building—"

"—you'll make him such a potent, priority shifting cup of coffee that he'll be forced to reconsider?"

Cynthia lowered the paper. "You really think it'll all be okay?"

"I really hope so," Thea said.

"Hmm, I like your optimism," Cynthia said.

"Thanks. I try."

Cynthia smiled at her and then opened the newspaper again. She scanned over the pages for a few more minutes, then stuck out her tongue at The Mayor of Quill Point's picture and closed it again.

"You going to be up very late, honey? I could sleep through a tornado right now."

Thea grabbed one of her many bookmarks and placed it in the section on ancient dice games. "No, I can sleep, I guess. Or try too."

"Still having bad dreams?"

"Yeah, they keep happening."

Cynthia scooted over to her and kissed her cheek. "Well, maybe me being nearby will keep all those dreams away."

"If you can fight off nightmares, then maybe that mayor *doesn't* stand a chance."

"Never mess with the person who controls the caffeine."

"More importantly…" Thea said before a yawn cut her off, "…uh, never mess with Cynthia Reed."

"Damn right," Cynthia said.

Cynthia stretched her arms and shifted underneath the covers. Her gray hair spilled out on either side of the pillow. Thea smiled down at her, playing with a strand of her hair.

"Goodnight, my love," Thea said.

"Sleep well, my love," Cynthia replied.

Thea reached over to turn off the light. The room plunged into a comfortable darkness. Cynthia shifted onto her side, facing away from her. Thea, the taller one, and thus usually the big spoon, curled around Cynthia, hoping that despite every other night proving otherwise, the dreams wouldn't find her. That she could have a night where nothing happened but a nice, pleasant sleep.

CHAPTER 40

Thea was always alone out in those interlocking lines. Never once had she seen anything to even suggest a presence. She didn't consider that particularly odd. It wasn't too weird a concept for dreams. Being alone in a big place was a common enough scenario for both idle whimsy and sharp nightmares. It was a rule of the place, a constant she never much questioned until the dream night she saw something flying out there.

It was so far away.

Thea didn't want whatever it was to *ever* be closer than that.

It buzzed. Buzzed in such a way she could hear it distinctly and clearly through the mass of sounds, yelling, and talking that usually filled the place of clusters. It was like the words, the talking, went quieter in deference. Or, perhaps, absolute fear.

It was miles away.

Thankfully, miles and miles.

Miles and miles and miles.

Yet so huge, so massive, that she could see it as clearly as it was flying at her face.

The only thing she could compare it to was a fly. A massive horsefly but paler. It moved, darted, and buzzed like it was searching for something.

Thea hoped with all that she had that it was not looking for her.

And then it turned in her general direction, and Thea clutched her chest. Her heart had skipped a beat. An attempt to scream felt like her own throat was choking her.

The fly had a smile. A long smile of pale gray lips. Stretching from one end of its body to another. Curving up. Gleeful. Knowingly gleeful.

Right above that horrific expression were eyes shaped like triangles, bulging outward from squirming sockets, the veins crisscrossing it a deep sickly purple formation over multiple vast, pit-like black dot irises. Its hundreds of thin legs moved in rows beneath it, waving like plants in a breeze. They ended in three-fingered claws dripping with white-green slime.

Thea had never attempted to run in that dream place before, but she did then. She floated backward as fast as she could, legs flailing like a desperate swimming maneuver, seeing the fly, the housefly, the hell-fly, float in her direction. The lines rerouted around it, wavered, snapped, and reconnected, forming a pathway for it to fly more efficiently.

The sound of buzzing got so loud.

That fly could swallow planets.

That fly could swallow galaxies.

It filled her sight, and a smell of rot wafted off it, unlike anything Thea had ever experienced. It wasn't the rot of garbage or corpses sitting out in the sun. This went deeper and permeated into the mind and the soul. During the worst upsets of life… during the most horrible crying, screaming, and grief… that feeling that passes briefly through, that should never linger for more than moments, too terrible to face… was *its* rot.

Thea could not escape it. It was so much more than she could ever imagine.

She clutched her dream hands over her dream head and prepared for obliteration. For her to be shredded into a million pieces. For her to experience something that her mind only knew as the worst possible outcome.

But then Thea woke up.

In her bed, at home, next to Cynthia, screaming.

And though Cynthia did all she could to help her calm down, Thea didn't even attempt to sleep for the next twenty hours. She only said she had the worst nightmare yet and would rather not talk about it.

CHAPTER 41

THE FLY DREAM WAS THE TURNING POINT for Thea.

No more traveling between places along the lines, no more elongated visits. Every night was a kaleidoscope. She'd only have time to witness a few moments of each place before she was kicked into the next one. It never became less disorientating. It was a dizzying display, like dropping through the layers of the Earth; only, each aspect of the Earth's crust was a whole other place, time, and reality.

And it all felt so real.

The wind of a beach was across her face. The beat of speakers pulsed into her bones. She had stood on planet surfaces that couldn't be and navigated spaces that didn't follow any of the rules of physics she knew.

Thea easily saw twenty new worlds a night. Sometimes many, many more.

And they stayed with her more than ever before. Unlike normal dreams, she stopped having the ability and privilege to let them fade into nonsense and unimportance in her mind.

Thea didn't understand how her mind could even catalog, hold on to, that level of input, and allow her to easily access them. But it could.

It could.

And it was bleeding into normal life.

It could find her mind's eye and slideshow innumerable, often contextless, horrors in the time of a thought. They interrupted, they slapped, and they intruded. They crept in.

Thea could barely shake the feeling of them being much more than dreams.

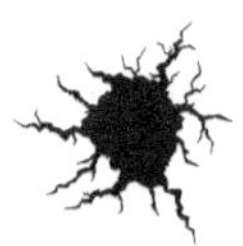

"I'm sorry," Dr. Edgar said. "But I'm not seeing anything wrong. The scan isn't showing anything."

Thea wanted to cry. She gritted her teeth and let out a long, long breath. "Okay. I get that—but there *has* to be something wrong. The dreams aren't stopping. I haven't gotten a good night of sleep in… I don't even know."

"Have you checked with—"

"I've checked with *everyone*!"

Dr. Edgar frowned but said nothing more.

"I'm sorry," Thea said. "I'm so sorry."

"It's alright. I understand that this is upsetting for you. I think it would be upsetting for anyone. Poor quality of sleep can cause many other problems. That's not my specialty, but there's been a lot written on the subject. May I ask how stress is for you—besides the dreams?"

Thea counted to ten in her own head and let out a breath. "Well, my wife and I are both business owners. Different businesses, if you're wondering. And, yeah, it's stressful. There's been, uh, a lot of financial pressure. The municipality has raised … uh, rent. It's a bit more complicated than that. And my insurance covers some of these appointments, but not all of them. We're definitely postponing any vacations."

"That certainly sounds stressful."

"Yeah. I don't know how I can keep my employee on. They've been wonderful, but I don't know how much longer I can afford it. I barely pay myself some weeks."

Dr. Edgar nodded. "It sounds to me like you're just stressed. If everyone you talked to hasn't found anything wrong, then I say it's stress. Not any medical emergency, just very intense stress. Stress can give you bad dreams. It can mess with your sleep. A piece of friendly advice: I'd see what you can do about your finances and… do you have friends you can spend time with? Hobbies that you really enjoy?"

"Yeah, I have some."

"Get away from work a little more if you can, then. Hang out with some of those friends. It's hard to hang out with people during adult life, but it's important. Do what you can to get sleep, as well. Just friendly advice, but I think it would help a lot. Certainly, it cost less."

"Thanks, Dr. Edgar."

"You're welcome. I hope things get better."

"I hope so too."

CHAPTER 42

THEA WAS HAVING A HARD TIME CONCEN-trating on the card game. Usually, she swept games like these. Henry was a little cautious and missed chances to get enough points, and Saanvi had an obvious tell where she'd tap her finger against the table. Sometimes, Thea would hold back a little to make the night more fun. However, dream memories kept seeping in.

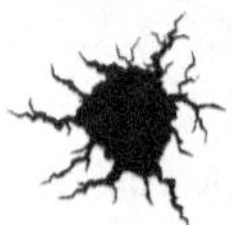

An ocean of crude faces, gasping like fish at the sky. An entire continent of those mask faces demanded in a language she could somehow understand for them to be freed from the spider silk wrapped around their ankles.

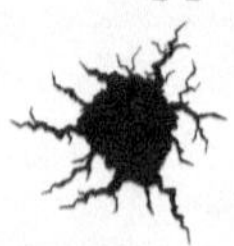

Thea marked the points for the last round. She'd got dead last.

"Are you okay?" Cynthia asked, smiling. "You should've destroyed us there."

"Just … um … thinking about other stuff," Thea said, forcing a smile.

Cynthia stopped smiling and leaned a little closer. "*Are* you okay?"

"Tired," Thea said.

"Oh, okay," Cynthia said. "Do you want to go home? I can make you some tea, and you can go to bed early."

Thea glanced at Henry and Saanvi across the table. Henry was frowning, and Saanvi quirked up an eyebrow.

"No, it's okay," Thea whispered to Cynthia. Then, louder, she announced: "I'm sorry if I'm acting a little strange. I've just been dealing with a nasty bout of insomnia. It'll pass—"

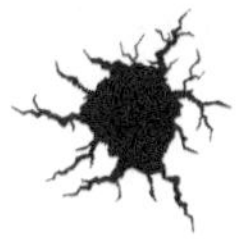

The man was covered in smaller men, and they all stabbed at him with ornate obsidian knives, setting free geysers of blood.

But that giant was on another giant and didn't notice his own injuries because he was too busy hurting the person on which he climbed.

And up and up it went. Stabbing, hurting: a fury aimed and screamed out so forcefully it droned out their own dying. Some would fall as they lost all their blood, killing most of their smaller attackers. But some survived, and some didn't notice. The chain continued unabated.

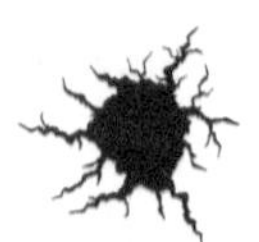

"—eventually," Thea finished saying.

No one had noticed. It had been in a blink, if not faster.

"I was having some trouble with that a while back," Henry said. "It turned out Buddy was just snoring a little too loud, and it woke me up."

"Maybe you should just adopt Buddy," Cynthia said. "How often is Xander having you watch him? I feel like he's with you more often than with his owner."

"It's more like joint custody," Saanvi commented. "Xander likes to do book signings at local bookstores. I think he's down south right now. He'll be back in a week or two and then will probably ask again in … four months?"

"Yeah, about four months," Henry agreed.

Saanvi chuckled. "I love that dog, but he is a handful sometimes."

"Only about *one* handful," Cynthia said. "It's always the little dogs who make the loudest noises."

"I think I read something about that," Thea added halfheartedly. "Can't recall why now, though."

"I'm sure it'll come to you," Saanvi offered.

"Yeah, *I'm* sure it will," Cynthia added, nudging Thea's shoulder with her own. "She's got a mind like a steel trap. I don't write stuff down; I just tell my better half."

Thea smiled and then gathered up the cards to deal them. "It's a blessing and curse. I never forget birthdays—"

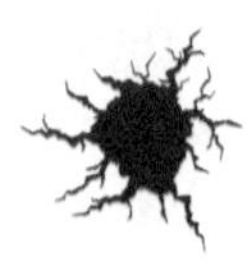

A woman, skin so pale, brown hair stuck together with sweat, starved, crying, sat in a vast room. The wallpaper was falling off in places, and the beige carpet was stained with long-ago spills. There was no furniture except the chairs that made a circle around her. And only skeletons sat in those chairs. Long-dried bones, with not even the dust of skin left to hold them in place.

The bones didn't move, but the air shifted, and far-off voices talked and argued.

"I'm sorry," the woman said to them. "I'm sorry. I didn't mean to break the rules."

The skeletons leaned forward as one, lurching to stare down at her. The room got so cold that ice crept up the walls. The woman let out a cry and hugged herself. Frostbite spread out from her neck, going to her face, and down to her arms.

"Please," she choked out, fog curling from her mouth like a chimney.

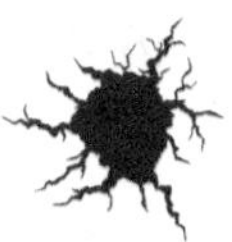

"—but also, I can never forget those times when I told the waiter that they should *also* enjoy their meal."

Saanvi laughed and held up her hand. "Oh, guilty of that too."

"I mean, maybe they were going to eat on a break soon," Henry supplied, smiling. "You don't know."

"That's true, that's true," Thea said, forcing a laugh.

After taking a second to quell the panic in her, Thea dealt a new hand of cards. She looked them over and made plans. It was equally not fun to simply lose on the spot.

"So, I hear that bastard got reelected *again*, somehow," Cynthia said. "He's gonna force out small businesses."

"Yeah, not happy about that," Henry said. "I'm not sure who voted him in, but it wasn't me. I guess we're stuck with this mayor for the next four years."

Thea sighed. "Well, next election, we should help boot him out. Then the next person can undo some of this."

"One can hope," Saanvi added.

"God, I really don't trust him," Cynthia said, frowning harder. "I just feel like something is going to happen."

"Do you trust this opening play?" Thea asked, throwing out two cards onto the table. "Or are you going to challenge me?"

The slight cloud forming around Cynthia's face faded. She smirked at her wife. "Oh no, the fangs are out. You're *not* going to win every game, babe. Not on my watch."

"We stand with you," Henry joked. "Well, at least for the first turn."

"Oh, so I'm the enemy, huh?" Thea said with a chuckle. "Well, let's just see about—"

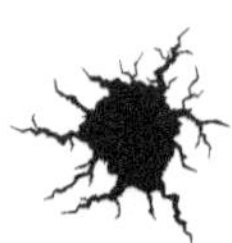

Julian

A large indoor mall with multiple floors. Bustling with people. In the middle of it all, there was a small kiosk. A man sat there. His shirt was a swirl of red and blue, and he wore a large beanie that almost went down to his eyes. His skin was suntanned and white. He was sitting on a tall stool and smiling as people walked by. He appeared to only sell pieces of generic white printer paper.

A teenage boy wearing a thin blue jacket and gray jeans with dark brown skin walked up to the kiosk. He was flanked by his two friends. A taller boy with a pinkish complexion and a series of pins up his vest, and a medium-height boy with white skin, a sports polo, and acid-washed jeans. They all look a little bored.

"Are you selling paper?" the first boy asked.

Julian spun around on his stool. "No, I'm selling caricatures. I'll draw them for you. Would you like one? It doesn't cost a lot."

"Sure…?" he said. "Do you guys want one?"

The taller boy frowned. "Uh, I guess so. Don't like, make it weird, though."

Julian laughed, more to himself than anyone else. "Don't worry—it'll be the best caricature you've ever seen."

He spun back, picked up a red pen, and made a single slashing motion. Then he let out another laugh. "See, perfect."

He held it up for the boys to see, and on the piece of paper the taller boy was rendered, in alarming detail, with a massive slash through his neck and his hands clutching at the wound as blood cascaded down.

"I think I captured your essence perfectly."

The taller boy stepped back in alarm, fear flashing across his face. "What the fuck?"

"Oh, you don't like it? Well, I offer a redraw at no extra fee."

He angled the paper toward the other two, who both shouted. The paper had shifted to show both with the same injury, clutching at their necks, screaming wordlessly.

"Now, I wouldn't call myself a fortune teller, but I would call myself a keeper of promises. Do you want to pay for it now—"

His body dribbled down over the stool, his legs, hips, and stomach all turning to mush, and his voice sounded deep underwater.

"—or how about you die a little later?"

The three boys screamed so loud, but no one in the mall noticed. They ran even as the carpet and walls stretched and warped, the paint cracking as the canvas of reality was stretched.

Julian picked up the red pen and then a second, holding both with the nips pointing downward. They glimmered. Sharp. As he sprinted at them, paint flew off Julian, staining the walls.

But even as he melted, he was so fast.

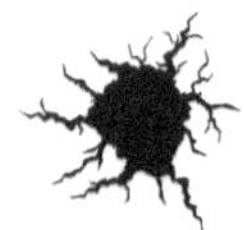

"—that," Thea finished saying.

She rubbed the back of her head.

"You know what, everyone? I think this might need to be my last game of the night. I'm exhausted. You guys keep playing, though. Don't let me ruin all your fun. You have a guest room, right, Saanvi?"

"Yeah, the second door down. Are you sure you're alright?"

Cynthia turned to her; those loving eyes were now tinged with fear. "Yeah, are you sure you're okay, Thea? We *can* go home if you want."

"No, it's really okay. Wake me up when you guys are done."

"…okay," Cynthia said.

"Love you," Thea said.

"Love you too."

CHAPTER 43

WHILE HAVEN TOOK A TRIP WITH MILDA, Thea pulled out a notebook and admitted that she had learned new words overnight. Or, at least, new definitions of existing words. Her dreams had shown her specific events, and then the words, and their meanings, had slipped into her mind unbidden. The process had been so seamless that it almost seemed like she must have simply forgotten learning them long ago.

The first was *Layers*.

She wrote it down and capitalized it. That word referred to the places she'd been going to. The places where the word lines emanated from appeared to be structured in layered segments, so the name made sense. She'd been visiting *Layers*.

The second word was *demigod*.

That word was an old word. Something like a god, but not quite on the same scale. The new definition in her head was specifically something made by a god that acted like a god.

Considering how many horrible things she'd seen on Layers she'd visited that could alter reality or cause mass destruction, she was sure she'd seen examples of demigods.

But there was a clarification to be made.

Below that word, she wrote another: *monsters.*

Thea knew plenty about monsters. They were in fantasy stories, horror stories, science fiction stories, all over literature. They also appeared in folklore, mythology, and urban legends.

But that word, in this context, delineated a being that was more limited than a demigod. It was like a worker ant, fulfilling a specific purpose.

And her stomach rolled as she recalled things that could be a monster's purpose across the Layers.

Finally, she looked down at the notebook and dreaded even writing the word. But the image of it arrived heavily. Thea almost felt like these words, or at least some of them, demanded that she write them down.

So, she scrawled across the paper, big and in scratchy letters: *Flies.*

Capitalized again.

She dropped the pen and looked at it. That innocuous word. Arguably, the most innocuous of the words—yet the worst. The thing that made every nightmarish Layer seem like nothing in comparison.

Flies. A Fly. That *Fly.*

A massive, hulking, enormous insectile thing between the Layers. She'd heard its buzzing a few times but gratefully hadn't seen it since the first instance.

Thea breathed hard, dispelling the memory as best she could. Thea shook her head. She went to close the notebook, only to find she'd picked back up the pen. Turning it over in her hand, she blinked in confusion.

In her handwriting, written at the bottom, was one more sentence.

The Gods of Rot must never find this Layer.

She slapped the notebook shut and shoved it so hard it went off the desk, clattering to the ground. Thea felt herself approaching hyperventilating, on the cusp of a panic attack. The dreams had been strange, horrible, and unrelenting for so long, but they were *dreams*. Not actual places. Not real. Nothing about them was real. These definitions of words were her mind making something up. She'd read hundreds of stories, all genres. These meanings, this hierarchy, were from something she'd read or her imagination invented wholesale.

They had to be. Had, *absolutely*, to be something fake.

Even if there were a multiverse of places out there, she couldn't peek into it, and there certainly weren't things traversing them. Not her—and not some dire, horrific, destructive gods.

Chapter 44

Thea was outside any Layer again.
After nights and nights of the most existential slideshow, it was almost nice to have a change of pace. Though Thea knew by now that her odds of having a pleasant experience were slim to none.

It didn't take long for her to notice the new stream of words. Instead of the usual, they were sickly green and flowed in a more jagged procession. Stopping and starting, like they were pushing against some resistance.

The Layer that they went to was visible and pulsing green. It reminded Thea of toxic waste.

She floated a little closer and saw that, in a nearly straight line with only a few deviations, a series of green word lines went back and back. Each Layer affected was that same green and appeared slightly collapsing inward on itself.

Even being close to it made Thea worried. She tried to listen to what spewed forth but couldn't place it among all the other sounds. She stared at the Layer, pursing her lips. She could go see what was happening. Could.

After pausing for a few long moments, she willed herself into the Layer.

It was … empty. Or almost. Thea had seen worlds destroyed, messed up, and full of death, but this one was almost nothing. The ground was gone in places, not replaced with anything but a blue void. Bones, broken at strange angles, lay among the wreckage, but nothing was alive. There wasn't any sound except for a hollow thrumming.

The sky was … colorful. Thea watched as clouds flowed across too fast for the wind. It had a background of neon pink, beige, and brushed silver sky. The faintest smell of acrylic paint hung in the air.

She walked among it all, into what seemed once a city—although only a few walls still stood. One such wall had many bones fused into it, permanently in dancer poses. Another was painted with an elaborate mural in now very dry blood.

In front of her was a stadium with a staircase that went to the top. She climbed the first few steps, then floated up the rest.

She didn't know what sport the stadium was for. She saw a field of fake grass with white paint across it, mostly formed into oddly placed triangles and a root-like series of branching lines. In the center were five metallic statues surrounded by at least forty rotting corpses or full-on skeletons. The corpses were covered in little red and blue streamers and a not-insignificant amount of glitter. Each statue was holding two enormous swords. Four surrounded a fifth.

A clock chime went off, so loud it made Thea jolt. The four statues all moved through a series of brutal slashes. But they never hit the center statue or clashed blades with the others.

The center one then stabbed out with both blades at a spot between two other statues. Then repeated the pattern for the other three directions.

The clock chimed again, and the statues all stopped and returned to their original positions. Then they tilted back their heads, opened their metallic mouths, and sprayed a weak stream of streamers and confetti.

CHAPTER 45

THEA FELT ENORMOUSLY ANXIOUS—HER skin crawling like several mosquitoes had bitten her. The air in Stylus Books had a cloying, almost humid energy. The back of her mind tingled.

She got up from her desk, not understanding yet what could evoke such feelings—but worrying more and more. This strange procession of sensations belonged in her dreams, not out here. She kept assuring herself that—as scary as it was—she was just having some aspect of a dream bleed into the waking world.

She walked outside to get a breath of fresh air.

And then stopped and looked up.

Globules of rotting reality spread across the sky, forming like suspended moisture; forming angry storm clouds; spreading outward as tentacles of red and orange.

A noise exited her mouth somewhere between a gasp and a pained sob. She stepped back until she bumped into the side of her bookstore. On instinct, she pinched up and down her arm as hard as she could.

"Oh god … oh no … no, no, no—"

A small boy ran across the sky. He was both invisible and visible to Thea. Sometimes he looked like a little kid, then would look like something monstrous, and then would be a being that *could be the entire sky.*

"Demigod," Thea whispered, then covered her mouth.

She hadn't said that.

Those words could not be *allowed.*

Because if she *had* said that, it would mean—

Reality tilted on its axis. The ground hadn't moved for anyone else. Thea looked down at her feet and couldn't stop panting. Her chest felt constricted.

A cold wind swept across Quill Point.

Thea needed to get to her wife *now.*

Thea wasn't used to running; she worked behind a desk. But she needed to get to the Quill Point Café before … whatever happened. Each apocalypse was different—but death was assured. The red and orange tentacles spread across the sky, stretching and reaching, so opaque that it was like they were made of floating oil.

Thea pulled out her phone as she ran, fingers flying to dial Cynthia's number. It didn't even ring. She looked down at it in a panic and shrieked. She threw the phone as far away from her as possible; it clattered on the street with several bounces of spraying glass.

She didn't understand *how* she could see it, but there had been a glob of rotting reality in the center of her phone. It had been spreading its way through the circuitry.

She shook her hand like the residue might still be clinging to her nails or digging into her palm and kept moving. The wind was getting worse. Tentacles were overtaking the sky—

The earthquake knocked Thea over immediately, the ground shifting beneath her. She hit the pavement hard, jarring her senses. Even as she lay there, she could see a shadow wall rise far off in the distance, stretching up above the tree line, and then farther and farther. And simultaneously, it dug down deep, curving to meet itself below.

They were in a bowl. One encasing, encircling, entrapping.

Above her, thunderclaps got louder and louder, and their lightning strikes were so bright she didn't dare look at them. Thea didn't want to know if they, too, were monstrous.

She tried to get up, only for another rumble to slam her stomach into the pavement and almost wind her. She gritted her teeth and crawled.

Houses, street signs, and fire hydrants collapsed and broke under the battering. Water shot up in a frothy plume and sprayed down on Thea, covering her glasses and making it harder to see.

The next lightning crackle had more to its sound than thunder could contain. It was also the sound of shattering glass and a taut snapping sound. What part of Thea's body perceived the change, she didn't know, but the sensation swept through her. It wasn't just that the *air* was changing, although it was, but the stuff that defined air, made up air conceptually, was being altered.

"Isolation," Thea said. "This is an Isolation…"

The doors in her mind, slowly opening, slowly acclimatizing her to what they had behind, crashed open now. The sound of padlocks falling to the ground and the opening—

and displaying—

and shifting of sights and sounds—

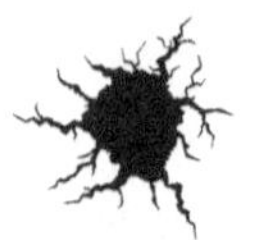

Blood spilled out of his chest, and the television, computer, cellphone, smart speaker, and smart home panel drank from him. A laugh crackling like broken audio spilled out of him even as every muscle spasmed and his heart failed.

This will happen again and again without end—

This is the meager side. This is what happens when a god lightly brushes against a Layer—

A god being born on one is so much worse—

A woman cast bones from a pile into a pit with many more bones. A graveyard was dug up. Every single plot. When she ran out, she reached up and scraped her fingers at her collarbone, leaving streaks of skin ribbons, red on one side, pale white on the other, beneath her once stylish and manicured nails. There was such a big bone in her collar. And it was so readily available.

It will demand suffering on a scale unfathomable to those on one Layer, who only know their Layer—

A monster with human mouths layered like shark teeth and happy eyes was whispering with slow-motion lips. The man listened closely. He took the kitchen knife and stabbed the monster repeatedly, even as the same wounds appeared on his skin. He didn't notice the knife fuse to his hand, nor the slivers of sharp silver that sprouted from each fresh wound.

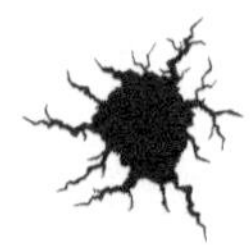

Thea writhed now, flipping over onto her back and then stomach and then lurching, kicking, spraying spittle, and her screams flooding out of her. But she could still feel *herself* as the images, knowledge, and broad scope went through her, absorbing into her muscles, brain tissue, and soul. The doors were open. Reality was open to her. Her mind could hold it now.

Well, maybe.

It's so easy to get lost in everything if you don't find—

"My … name is Thea…"

That helped. A little less pain.

"I run a bookstore in … Quill Point, Illinois," she continued.

She was in an expanding geometric sphere of realities, each slanted surface a compressed representation of an entire reality, and whatever one she held onto tried to rush away, gulfing her by distance and time. With a desperate grab, she claimed hers. Metaphorically, physically, and mentally, she held onto her Layer. It was a car driving away with everything you care about in the backseat, and you must run faster and faster, gripping the bumper even as it goes so fast that your feet aren't even touching the ground anymore and the wind is shearing at your face—

"I am married to Cynthia. I love her. I have loved her for such a long time."

She held that spot. Held her mind to one Layer. And it stayed. Her physical body stopped thrashing, and she sat up in the middle of the storm, in the middle of the earthquake, the water from the hydrant still pouring down on her. She held her head, her eyes closed.

The voice of The Painting that Knows He is a Painting whispered.

"*You're not real.*"

"Nobody is," Thea replied to the whisper and to herself. "Or everyone is. On all Layers. No matter the maker or the method. I am here. I am me. I am here. I love, and I feel, and I affect those who I meet. And they affect me. We are not alone. We are among others that really will be there."

It felt like dropping through the ground.

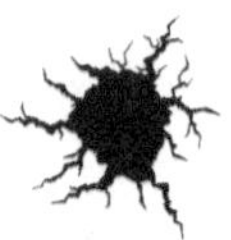

Thea found herself back in the empty room from so many dreams. And unlike every other time, it didn't feel strange. It felt like home. In front of her was a portal, but it didn't lead to the Cacophonous Layers; it led to the Layer where she was born.

"Where am I?" she asked. "What is this place, really? It's not a dream. None of this was ever really a dream."

She touched one of the other walls, and it rippled. She smiled to herself.

"Tell me what this place is?"

A gentle, peaceful sensation, like the concept of refreshing water, flowed through her head and across her scalp.

"Oh! A Sub-Layer. My own sort of Layer. But how does that work? What does that make me?"

No new information came to her, only that definition.

She shrugged and walked toward the portal, stepping through back to her own——

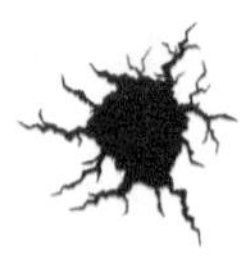

Thea opened her eyes and lowered her hands. Then she stood up so fast she blinked in confusion. It was like she'd snapped between poses.

She looked around at the damage. The rumbling had stopped at some point. So had the lightning. The fire hydrant still sprayed water, and its falling droplets reflected orange and red. Thea looked up at the sky. Not a bit of blue was left up there. She frowned and shook her head.

Whatever else there was to this, it could come later.

She needed to find Cynthia.

She'd never run faster in her entire life.

CHAPTER 46

THEA BOILED WITH ANGER, BUT DIDN'T make a sound. Didn't react—even though she knew what was happening. The Mayor of Quill Point had a faint haze around him, golden and rancid. He was already on the Rot Gods' side. Already someone who had given in to the rising god on their Layer. And she *could say nothing.* The people he was rounding up, asking to go, would never leave this town. The whole place had a shadow wall around it, and who knew what else was stopping people from fleeing? And she could do nothing to save those sent into it all. There was no way to reroute them.

Georgina and Terry's kid Albert was going. Thea had seen him when he was a toddler, stumbling, cooing. A man now—and possibly one about to die.

And Chuck offered to go. He and Thea had been friendly business rivals for a while now. He gave her some of his comics to sell, and he sold some of her fantasy and science fiction books at his shop, and every year they compared to see who could sell more. And possibly, he was about to die.

And Ms. Daffodil was going. The woman who'd helped teach practically the entire younger generation of Quill Point. She'd waved to Thea so many times, in so many contexts. She was as much a part of the town as its buildings. And she was possibly going to die.

And Patrick was going. A regular enough at her store. He talked fast; he read fast. Thea put aside business books for him semi-regularly, trying to gauge what he would like. And he was possibly going to die.

And Cassandra was going too. Thea didn't know her well, but she'd helped Thea immensely. When she'd inherited Stylus Books, the digital catalog had been woefully out-of-date, and Cassandra had helped program the new one and given her a discount on the whole thing. And she was possibly about to die.

But she couldn't help. Couldn't save anyone. Couldn't do a damn fucking thing. Even with the changes she'd noticed in her body since the sky changed earlier that day, the new way she could move, she was stuck.

Because there was a demigod *in the room.*

And it was a miracle already that he hadn't noticed her. He was still pretending to be a little boy, playing board games with some kids. Demigods were capable of mass murders in minutes, capable of detecting anything she did to manipulate the Layer, and he was right *there.*

It took everything Thea had to keep her movements human. To keep the speed she stepped at a normal human pace. She'd already allowed someone to bump into her like it was an accident when her reflexes were so fast she could catch a falling paperclip from across the room with the tips of her fingers.

"You okay?" Cynthia asked quietly.

"Just worried about them."

Cynthia glanced at The Mayor of Quill Point. "Something about this feels weird, right? I mean … well…"

"I know what you mean," Thea said. "Hopefully, everything is going to turn out alright."

"Do you think so?"

"I don't know."

The little boy was smiling mischievously at the group of people about to wander into the night. Thea shivered but managed to not even move her face.

CHAPTER 47

THEA HUDDLED NEXT TO CYNTHIA IN A dark Stylus Books, staying as far away from the front door as possible. Near them were Milda and Haven, trying not to make any sounds. Milda's mastiff Lola faintly whined from the crate that Milda had put in the back corner.

Thea had turned off the lights after the first inhuman voice shouted. Outside, the sky was very dark, and Thea could see, even from far away, that monstrous demigod shifting up in the clouds.

He was waiting for something.

"Ten!"

Milda barely held back a shriek, her voice coming out as a muffled whine. Haven breathed so hard. Lola growled quietly, no doubt able to hear what was happening out there even better than they could.

Thea had been through her share of tornados in Illinois. Had seen her share of extreme weather besides.

But never had she felt so close to disaster. The ceiling above her was flimsy compared to what was out there.

Her heart rate seemed to pulse in double time and a cold sweat washed over her. The demigod's influence spread so far across Quill Point that the odds of him noticing Thea were even better than at the town center.

"Nine!"

The ground shook. It was like bombs going off. The light fixtures swung worryingly above them. Thea shifted to better block Cynthia from any that might fall.

Lola barked louder and louder. Thea glanced back in panic. Forget the demigod detecting her, that sound might be enough to draw an attack.

"Eight!"

"Seven!"

With each number, Thea could feel tears building on her face. If those numbers were counting deaths, then who of Quill Point was already lost? Who of her neighbors were being pulled into the sky to die?

"Six!"

Off in the distance were bursts of light and the sharp cracks of gunshots. And people screaming. Lola let out barks that took on almost the sounds of a human yell. Thea closed her eyes and gritted her teeth with frustration. Guns would only make him target them.

"Five!"

A cold wind swept by outside. Stylus Books creaked and groaned in several worrying places.

"Four!"

"Three!"

"Two!"

More impossible bomb blast-like sounds. Somehow, the building was still standing, but out in the distance, massive shadow moved and destroyed. One slammed down so close that Thea couldn't help but let out a little whimper. Lola went quiet.

A keening sound, already so powerful, turned into a laugh.

Some of Thea's fear turned to anger. They were hurting her friends and scaring her family. Killing people she cared about.

She glanced around at her wife and friends' huddled, quivering forms. She didn't know how yet, not exactly, but she would get them out of this. Thea would save them.

"One!"

Impossibly large hands moved in the sky. The wind shook the trees into thrashing shapes. The hands lowered into view—and they slammed down, crushing something, and pulled it away.

"None!"

Thea stopped looking outside.

She'd seen endless horrors enough already.

CHAPTER 48

THEA STOOD IN THE CENTER OF STYLUS Books with her left hand up, fingers splayed, and palm facing away from her. She concentrated. She would succeed this time.

The air right in front of her palm shivered.

She relaxed her arm a little. It had nothing to do with physical force. The hand gesture was the only way she'd found it worked. It closed if she closed her hand too much, but she didn't need to strain.

She needed this to work soon.

Milda and Haven had barely survived what had happened with that second demigod at the Kraken Hotel. Only one other had been so lucky. Brianna had also survived, but she was The Mayor's daughter, and Thea had a feeling that *wasn't* a coincidence. She never outwardly told Haven and Milda to stop visiting her. Any warning she could give might tip off a watchful demigod, but she'd deterred them often.

And thank god she did—

No, no. Concentrate. There are only so many safe times to do this. The demigods aren't that close right now.

Thea imagined herself back in that room that was her own Sub-Layer. The room was colorful, the exact shades of blue she liked. It was the perfect temperature—it was literally made for her. And if she could go there so easily, then she could—

If she hadn't deterred Milda and Haven with the lie that Lola had been making worrying sounds, they could've been there when the horrific ritual had happened at the Irena Ink Memorial Hospital. Thea *felt* it when the god Manifested on the Layer, forming a physical form tied to a location. It had felt like she'd been lit on fire. The air, the floor, and her skin had been so blisteringly painful that she'd fallen to the ground. A second more, and she was sure that her organs, all of them, would've failed.

You need to fucking concentrate.

As she focused more and more, images trickled into her mind. After all that had happened before, she tensed against them reflexively. Letting them in had almost killed her, but they were necessary to this process.

The air in front of her wobbled, opening a pinprick of space. The whispering of a trillion voices hummed out from that tiny hole.

The images of Layers were slippery. Holding on to just one was an effort. She grabbed onto a memory and Layer in one mental motion. She needed a Layer untouched by Rot Gods and their monsters.

The place of songs and glass-like streets. The most beautiful of the Layers she'd seen. More importantly, a safe location.

The images of it flowed to her, wrapped around her like an embrace.

She concentrated harder. From the pinprick in reality, those wonderful songs spewed out. She gritted her teeth, but the portal only opened a little more.

Please. Please. I need to save—

Thea's legs buckled underneath her. She fell to the ground and could barely move. Her breath came out like a faint whisper, and her chest hurt so badly she clutched at it.

The opening in reality lingered for a moment and then disappeared.

Thea held up her hand, but it shuddered, and she had to drop it back down to her side. She was so hungry it made her dizzy, yet she was horribly nauseous. After another attempt to move, she gave up and lay there, staring at the ceiling. The mattress Cynthia and she had been sleeping on in Stylus since Mayor's Men took their place—Cynthia had *not* been happy about that—was too far away. The floor was not comfortable.

"Dammit," she whispered.

She needed to transport multiple people before the next phase of the god's birth happened. She couldn't be worn out by the smallest opening in reality. It had gone better than her previous attempts, but it was still not nearly enough.

And if she couldn't manage it in time… well, she didn't want to think about what would happen.

As she pulled in lungful after lungful of air and tried not to move, her eyes fell on the books around her.

And an idea occurred to her.

Chapter 49

Between the head librarian Felicity going missing and everyone's general preoccupation with the end of the world, the library fell into disuse. Unlike Stylus Books, it was at the edge of the town, so since Murder Sky, anyone who wanted books simply went to Thea for them.

The fact the front door to the library was even locked surprised Thea. What also surprised her was how easy it was for her to break it. She reached out, turned the handle, the lock caught, and then she kept turning it. The metal gave a little pop, and she pushed the door open.

Inside, it was exceedingly dusty, but not that dark. The big floor-to-ceiling windows let in a fair amount of light. It was a two-story building, but one floor was only a half story. At the back of the library, an overhanging area housed the children's section. Tiny, colorful tables stood abandoned at the top, and the shorter shelves seemed like people standing still. Several fans spun slowly up on the ceiling, doing just enough to disturb the dust directly beneath them.

Thea walked past a book drop-off slot and checkout area, peeking over to see if anything was hiding behind the desk. She didn't expect any monsters or demigods in the library, but it never hurt to make sure. The area behind the desk had a small swivel chair and more dust.

Taking a long breath, she walked to the stacks, out of sight of anyone. She'd never dug into any occult or arcane books, nor had her shop ever been stocked with many, but she knew a few authors' names that might help. And, if she had to, the library had a physical catalog somewhere.

The main person she was looking for was anything written by Paxton Ink. Irena Ink's brother. It wasn't exactly something most people discussed, but history books mentioned it. Even two very subtle nods in his biography. In chapter seven, he mentioned something about his sister having had experiences with the supernatural. In chapter fifteen, he mentioned something about her physicality that sounded awfully like what Thea was experiencing.

Absently, she took out a notebook from the backpack she'd brought with her. Paxton had written exactly three books. All around a hundred pages. One about birds. A collection of poetry. And a diary posthumously found.

She scanned the side of the shelves until she found the *I* section. With no one around, she let her body move how it wanted to—and it was like zooming in on an image. The world around her almost narrowed to let her pass through it.

She stumbled a little, then planted her feet with a pop that hopefully didn't break anything in the floor below. Holding back again, she walked slowly along, looking at the spines of each book. There had been one official, collated edition of that diary—but it was rare enough it might not be stored on the shelves.

Thea traced her finger along, one book at a time. Then— "Ha! Found it!"

Gingerly, she pulled it out and flipped it over in her hands. The cover had one of the few available images of Paxton Ink. It was black and white, but she could still see he had the same heterochromia as his sister and about the same complexion. He had blond hair poking out from under a bowler hat and a modest beard and mustache. He was standing next to the bones of what would become the courthouse. His hands were pushed into his gray suit's pockets, and his posture was carefree.

Thea flipped it open, scanning the words for anything that might help.

"*My love for the avian song began…* no, no, not that. Ugh, come on. Let's see. *The head of the team talked to me today about…* Oh, Christ all mighty. I knew he was an asshole, but this is pushing it. Come on. Uh, no, not that. Birds again. Poetry again. Something about whiskey. Come on."

A sound from the front of the library made Thea jolt out of her reading. She grabbed Paxton's other two books off the shelf and shoved them into her backpack. Making sure not to accidentally super-speed her way out into the open, she peeked around a bookshelf.

Three Mayor's Men were at the front of the library. Thea frowned: they were already dusted with Rot God influence. She didn't want to guess what a critical mass of that would do to them.

She kept watching. There was no way they could see her from the front. They might just move on.

She recognized them.

Frank. Bryson. Trevor.

Teenagers. None were over twenty. All were on the local high school's track team.

Trevor was the tallest with a pinkish complexion, and he wore a white muscle shirt. He was carrying what looked like a police baton.

Bryson was actually *in* his track team uniform, but with *Mayor's Men* spray-painted across it. Around both his wrists were blue bands. He had pinkish-white skin, and his black hair was cut short.

Finally, Frank, who Thea was pretty sure recently graduated from high school, was always a big kid. Easily around six-foot, broad, with very suntanned white skin and bright blond hair. He wore a large sports jersey for some basketball team Thea had never heard of.

The Mayor using kids, convincing kids to hurt people for him—it was hard not to think of him as evil as the demigods. As strange a thought as it was to her, at least the little boy that wasn't really a human was born destructive, created to be what he was. The Mayor, to whatever degree, *chose* The God of Greed.

The three hovered outside. Bryson said something, and Frank shoved him. Trevor laughed. Bryson spun around and punched him in the arm—it looked like he'd hit him hard—but Frank just laughed. Then they talked back and forth for a moment, too far away to hear, and moved to leave.

Bryson, however, looked down at the library's door.

Thea winced.

Should've fixed that handle somehow.

The change in their demeanor was lightning-quick. A slight glimmer in their eyes. A difference in their posture. What had been relaxed smiles became cruel. That dust around them flared with nuclear green light.

Frank kicked in the door with such force it sent a crack up the glass.

"Who the fuck is in here!?" Frank yelled. "You're supposed to be back at the bonfire."

Thea shirked back, out of sight. Through the thin line between the top of a shelf and the books, she kept her gaze on them.

The click of a baton expanding sounded so loud.

Thea looked down at her hands and flexed her fingers. She sighed.

"Fan out," Frank commanded. "You're not getting away with breaking the rules, whoever you are!"

"Yeah!" Trevor chimed in. "Not getting away!"

"We won't hurt you if you come out right now," Bryson said.

"Speak for yourself," Frank muttered. "They broke the fucking rules."

Thea adjusted the backpack on her shoulders so it wouldn't fall off. She grabbed one of the bigger books off a shelf and threw it over the top. It sailed through the air and crashed into the front wall.

It made a rather loud thud.

Thea winced. She hoped she hadn't hurt the book too badly.

"What the fuck!" Bryson said.

Trevor laughed. "What was that supposed to do? Was that a fucking threat? They're over there!"

Thea glanced around her. There was a small step stool right next to one of the shelves. It looked like it was made of metal. She zipped over to it, picked it up easier than she was used to, and then zipped back over to the edge of the shelves.

As she lifted it to toss it, time almost seemed to slow. She knew exactly where it would land. Exactly how hard it would hit the ground. She didn't even need to look.

Instead of looking, she took what felt like two steps and was at the other side of the row of bookshelves, nearly crashing into the window.

The stool hit the ground, cracking the wooden floor and producing strings of swears from the three Mayor's Men. Their shock alone was enough to slow them down.

In five steps, she was at the front wall. Her shoes squeaked slightly from the skid, but she didn't wobble this time. The boys were now investigating where she'd thrown from. They weren't even looking back when she opened the door, turned the corner, and then moved so quickly that she was three blocks away before they could even possibly have turned around.

CHAPTER 50

PAXTON'S DIARY TURNED OUT TO BE *mostly* useless. Thea quickly read it back at Stylus Books. It never directly said anything that could help. But several references to Irena's behavior confirmed her suspicions she was experiencing the same changes as Thea.

She'd never seen any official documents Irena wrote, but Paxton mentioned her prolific writing speeds multiple times. How she could hand-write faster than a modern printer. Her physical speed, too, had been extraordinary. She seemed able to go from one end of the house to the other faster than a person should be able to.

He even made one especially oblique reference to her conversing with him about "other places," but he brushed it off in the next sentence.

But then, when Thea was thinking about chucking the book across the room, she found a single passage.

Irena talked today about tracing the other places like a line. I don't understand what it means, but I worry about her obsessions.

Her eyes went wide then. The book spilled out of her hands, and she stood up from her desk. Each breath that filled her lungs felt like it was buoying her, filling her with energy.

Nervously, she reached out her hand again and closed her eyes.

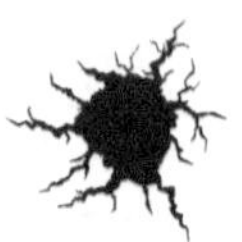

Her Sub-Layer was around her. She opened the portal to her Home Layer. Looked out at it. Then moved her focus broader. The Cacophonous Layers around her Home Layer let out its now almost familiar chatter.

The lines went in many directions, but one chained cleanly to the back of her Home Layer. She went to that line's Layer and peered into it.

It looked almost identical to her Home Layer. But it was too close. The newest Rot God could easily follow. So, she traced up the line. Another. Another. She didn't bother looking into each one beyond confirming that it was a connection.

Finally, one hundred away from her Home Layer, she peered inside.

The sky was a greenish-blue color, but otherwise was mostly the same. A few different aspects of technology; some societal differences. But the people were human, and the world had breathable air and the same gravity. It was a safe Layer, not yet corrupted.

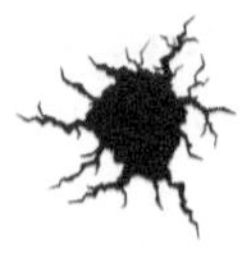

Thea opened her eyes and nearly shouted with joy.

She'd gotten open a portal about the size of a bowling ball. For almost five seconds, she could see the blue-green sky, and then it flickered. The image slide like a projector, displaying a different Layer, then another.

"Dammit," Thea said and focused again. The correct Layer slowly returned through the portal, but it was still so slippery. Unstable. It started to shift against her will. It wasn't long enough for anyone to step through.

Find the Layer. Try again.

It opened. Thea reached out to touch another reality, at least for a moment. As soon as her hand got close enough to feel the wind through the portal, it shrunk rapidly. Thea pulled her hand back as it snapped shut. She tried it again with her other hand, but the same thing happened. Anytime she got close to physically passing through her own portal, it collapsed.

"It's just me, huh? I can't travel *and* produce at the same time. Fuck."

Thea's back was slick with sweat. The sun had gone down. A quick clock check showed that she had lost about thirty minutes.

"Okay. If I can just keep to one Layer, at least I can get people out. I can get Cynthia out. I can get Milda and Haven out. I'm a later problem. This is still massive progress, Thea. Okay. Try again."

She ran her hands through her hair, her palms slick with sweat, and then shut her eyes. She traced a line from her Home Layer to somewhere safe.

CHAPTER 51

THEA ONLY GOT THE PORTAL OPEN A little wider. Still not enough for a person to go through. And only twenty seconds of the same reality. Still not good enough—and it wiped her out again.

People showed up during her subsequent break. Haven arrived as it was getting dark, waved to Thea, and sat down to read. A little while later, Milda showed up with Lola. She pulled a chair beside Haven and let Lola wander the store, happily sniffing at books.

Cynthia opened the door seemingly five minutes later, holding a thermos in one hand and finishing biting into a piece of naan wrapped in tinfoil.

Thea waved to her, trying to ignore how tired she was.

Cynthia folded back up the naan and went over, smiling. A similar smile grew on Thea's face instantly.

"Managed to sneak some coffee over to the bonfire camp," Cynthia said. "No Mayor's Men around. Guess they're too busy with The Mayor's evil schemes to pay attention to us."

Thea outwardly chuckled. Inwardly worried.

A thousand times a day, she debated telling Cynthia what was happening. But each time, she stopped herself, focused instead on solving the problem. She'd tell her when she could get them out—any sooner risked everyone. Even creating a portal nearby could draw something that could easily kill them.

"Well, tomorrow morning, some people are going to be very grateful," Thea said.

"I hope so!" Cynthia said. "I made them a strong, strong batch."

"Good," Thea said.

Cynthia nodded and reached into her pocket, pulling out another thing of tinfoil. "Did you want some? Saanvi was just making the last one when I got there."

"Sure, thanks," Thea said, standing up and taking it. Calories seemed like a lovely idea.

Cynthia nodded, then looked back at Haven and Milda and lowered her voice. "Hey, honey?"

Thea didn't look up from her food. She stared down at the naan, steadying her mind. Maybe now was when it was worth the risk. They would need to prepare for extra-dimensional travel.

"Are you okay?" Cynthia whispered. "I've been seeing something different in you lately. I know things are weird and strange … but are you okay? If you need help—?"

Thea leaned forward across the desk and kissed her wife on the forehead.

"I've been doing what I can too. Trying to help."

Cynthia frowned. "Are you trying to find something in those books?"

Thea glanced at the desktop. Paxton's diary and even his book on birds and poetry were lying there. Next to them were a few vague diagrams sketched on yellow notepad pages, each detailing things only she could understand.

"Yeah…" she said. "I'm doing research."

Cynthia pursed her lips. "Into what?"

Thea sighed. "Into all of this. This has … happened before."

Cynthia blinked, confusion overtaking worry in an instant. "This? I think I would remember if aliens invaded a town."

"No, not that … umm…"

Thea flexed her fingers. If she started making a portal, it would help explain it all. It would be easy to prove if she moved super-fast or bent metal.

"My love, I *have* been different lately. It's not just what's going on out there."

"Is it your dreams again?"

"Sort of," Thea said. "But they're not dreams."

"What do you mean they're not *dreams*?"

"I mean—" She pulled in a long breath. "Haven? Milda? Can you come over here? And bring Lola?"

Cynthia's eyebrows shot up. "What's going on?"

"I think it's easier if I tell everyone."

"…okay," Cynthia said.

Milda made a small sound, drawing Lola over. Haven seemed concerned as they walked over, still holding their place in the book with their thumb.

"Hi, everyone," Thea said awkwardly. "This is going to be hard to explain—"

Thea shivered and let out a nauseous groan. She gripped her stomach, then pressed a fist to her mouth. A cold sensation tingled through her shoulders and arms.

"Oh, that's not good," she said.

Thea fell into sitting in her chair.

"Honey? Thea?" Cynthia asked, rushing around the desk to stand next to her. "Are you okay?"

"Do we need, umm, can we get you something?" Milda asked, her voice quavering.

Thea's eyes blurred, but she could see something flowing through the air of Stylus Books. A wispy presence, like thin smoke. It flowed around the tops of the shelves and trailed between individual books.

Thea assumed she was the only one who could see it.

"No, I don't think you can help with this…"

Thea felt her mind yanked backward into her Sub-Layer, away from everyone around her. Even as she tried to stay, the pull got stronger and stronger. The strange smoke flowed to the desk between Milda, Haven, and Lola, curling around Paxton's diary, gently floating above it.

"…I'll tell you as soon as I wake up, okay?"

"Thea, *what* is happening?"

Thea's eyes were forcing themselves closed. "I promise, my dear, I will tell you everything as soon as possible."

The strange smoke flowed around her head. Another pulse of that horrible nausea hit Thea, but it wasn't from the smoke. It was out there, outside, from something nearby.

The smoke was calming. Almost familiar, in a way.

And then she slipped into her Sub-Layer.

Chapter 52

THEA HAD NEVER HAD A GUEST BEFORE in her Sub-Layer. The walls of the place widened to give the new person somewhere to stand.

Thea was less surprised to see her than she would've expected. Standing there, looking at her guest, it was like this meeting should've happened sooner. Even though Irena Ink had been dead for a rather long time now.

She looked like all the pictures and statues of her. A woman with pale white skin, silvery hair, and heterochromia. One eye was blue, the other brown. Except, she had an almost electrical aura around her. A spark that flared and glowed and occasionally made the tips of her silver hair move like an upward wind caught it, only for it to fall back down again.

Her voice sounded like it was over a bad radio.

"I've been trying to warn someone," she said, "but they couldn't hear me."

"I'm sorry, I didn't know how to look," Thea said.

"I thought that my death would be enough to stop it permanently. That burning up my soul would be enough. But The Mayor of Quill Point has been feeding it. Giving it more of what it wants. It wants greed, it wants people to take and ignore the consequences, and it doesn't even care about him."

"I'll do everything I can," Thea said. "Everything I can to stop this or at least get people out."

"This is my damn brother's fault," Irena said, shaking her head. "He attracted the Fly. I didn't realize it in time. I was too distracted by the Cacophonous Layers, by the sights and sounds of other worlds—even the terrible ones—to see what was happening before it was too late."

"What's going to happen to you now, Irena?"

Irena smirked. "Whatever the true afterlife is, it's not in the Layers. I don't know what happens next. I suppose I'll find out."

"Thank you for keeping us safe for so long," Thea said.

Irena's smile turned to a pensive frown. She shrugged. "It's only one form of safety I gave Quill Point. These rotting things are born of *our* actions. The gods don't cause themselves to be what they are. It'll never be safe when things that attract the Flies can happen so easily and when men like The Mayor can be in power."

"Whatever Layer we go to next will be better. I'll make sure."

"Just make sure you don't *keep* saying that."

Irena sparked again, brighter this time. Her hair flared out around her, and her form grew less and less stable.

"Let's see if Heaven exists."

The portal to the Cacophonous Layers opened. Irena Ink's soul flew out into it. She went somewhere else.

And Thea stood there for a moment in her Sub-Layer, before it felt like her entire body was burning. And she woke back up.

CHAPTER 53

THEA WOKE UP CLAWING AT HER ARMS, trying to stop the feeling of every nerve ending being scorched, reduced to ash, full of blistering oil. Cynthia jumped backward in alarm. Lola barked.

Thea blitzed to standing, accidentally knocking the desk over and sending it skidding across the floor in a dance of papers and books. She clutched at her hair, almost about to tear out a handful—when the sensation stopped.

"Oh shit," she said.

Milda and Haven stared at her from across the room. Haven was in the middle of pulling a water bottle out of their bag.

"How the fuck did you do that!?" Cynthia asked.

Thea turned to look at her so fast that Cynthia jumped again.

"I'm sorry, but I don't think I have time to explain."

Thea glanced outside.

They definitely had no time.

The sky was changing again. Despite it being night, long, slightly translucent tentacles flowed across the sky and hit the ground in various places. And where they touched, reality was breaking.

And the horrible sounds of monsters and death arrived alongside it.

"Yeah, no time at all. Haven. Milda. Cynthia. I need you to be as calm as you can. I'm going to get you somewhere safe. Somewhere where this isn't happening."

"What?" Cynthia said. "I don't understand. Please tell me what's happening? What's happening to you?"

Thea looked at her wife. At the terror on her face. And she wished that she could not only take that fear away, but that she also had the time to tell her everything. Without demigods around. Without the apocalypse happening. That she could lay her head against her shoulder and tell her all she knew about the universe and beyond it.

But there really wasn't time.

So, instead of answering, Thea closed her eyes.

Each Layer is born of another Layer. And each Layer makes new ones from it. It's a line going all the way back to the first. Thea followed a single line of creation, focusing on how each piece connected, tracing a path to where she wanted to go.

And reality, weakened and breaking, as malleable as it ever could be, parted in front of her palm.

Thea opened her eyes and saw that she'd made a portal big enough for people to step through. A stable portal. On the other side was that beautiful and strange sky.

She turned to look at Haven and Milda.

"I need you to trust me and go through."

Lola barked harder and harder in Milda's arms, squirming as forcefully as she could, but Milda and

Haven kept her from running and stood there, looking at the portal with fear and awe.

"This is a safe world. You need to go *right now*."

Outside the store, a laugh that sounded like burning started. Milda looked back and screamed.

Thea glanced over. A Mayor's Man had transformed. One was running outside, moving almost like she could move, so fast and unreal. His mouth was full of impossibly long teeth and his arms ripped open, full of rotting fungi.

"Please, go. They'll kill you."

"Are you going to be okay?" Milda asked.

"I'll be fine—you go fucking *now*."

"Is it safe?" Haven asked.

"Safer than fucking here! Safer than anything here! Go. *Go*. Go *now*. I can't keep this going."

Milda and Haven looked at one another. Haven nodded, and they both ran through the portal. Lola gave out one more loud bark before they passed through and disappeared.

And then Thea looked at her wife.

"I need you to escape."

So many emotions passed across Cynthia's face. She opened her mouth to speak, then stopped.

She then asked only one question.

"Can you follow us?"

Thea looked at the portal. It was shrinking. She didn't know how to pass through it herself yet. Didn't know if she could. But if there was a way, she would find it.

"I can. I will. I *will* find you out there in all of it. I always will. I *always* will. Please."

Cynthia pursed her lips. "You're lying to me, aren't you? You can't go through. I… I won't go without you. I'm not going to *leave* you here."

Thea gritted her teeth. The portal closed an inch only, but the edges of it were wavering, fluctuating. It wanted to switch. It wanted to shut.

"I'm so sorry about this."

Thea pushed her through the portal in a motion too fast for Cynthia to process. Cynthia let out one yell before her voice disappeared to the other side.

Thea closed her hand, and the portal snapped shut.

The citizens of Quill Point will return.
But not all of them are going to survive.

Book Club Questions

1. At various points in the book, we see the corrupt and harmful ways the Mayor's Men run Quill Point. If someone was honestly and earnestly trying to run an isolated town like Quill Point so its citizens were happy and safe for as long as possible, what steps should they take?

2. The strange house Declan and Grace find when they go into the forest has a lot of climate change symbolism, including multiple displays of dead animals. Does this house and its monstrous occupants do a good job of symbolizing/representing aspects of climate change? Why or why not? Where and how do they fail to capture aspects of the topic?

3. Charley and Dereck travel across an apocalyptic America and almost have multiple car crashes. How might you make the trip if you needed to get from California to Indiana/Illinois in a similar situation?

4. In Bree's conversation with the little girl demigod, they talk about how often things presented like choices are only a choice between compliance and suffering. Do you find this to be true? What are examples of choices that aren't really choices?

5. Have you, like Piper, ever had an experience where you could perceive what people were thinking, feeling, or going to do without them

telling you? What clues did that person give off that you noticed?

6. Going off The Mayor of Quill Point's description of how gods are created, what other metaphysical topics might be candidates for a Fly's egg?

7. Klein mentions six other gods existing. What do you think they are, and what do you think they represent?

8. Why do you think the Mayor's Men effectively banned gardening by stealing all the crops? What reason might they have for controlling the food in Quill Point?

9. Thea decides that whether or not she's real doesn't matter. Do you agree with that perspective?

10. Throughout Thea's story, we see many worlds, many of them horrific, but one world seems to have been fully through an apocalypse. What do you think happened in that world based on what's shown?

11. *Everything Will Burn* covers a lot of themes, including climate change, economic injustices, political corruption, and poverty. How do you think the book handled those themes? How did various characters reflect those themes? Were there any themes that weren't represented as well as they could be?

12. Who do you think will survive to the end of the series? Why?

Author Bio

OCTOBER KANE IS A HORROR WRITER and an avid horror fan, primarily found wandering in Florida. Since a ridiculously young age, he's enjoyed trying to come up with creative monsters, and after discovering that drawing them would never be his strong suit, he found a deep love for writing. Since then, he's focused on describing those monsters as vividly and gruesomely as possible. His love of cosmic horror happened much later, but it quickly became his favorite of the subgenres for its creative freedom and focus on existential themes.

When October Kane isn't working on his novels or other creative projects, he enjoys horror movies, terrifying podcasts, and all kinds of scary books, which surely has nothing to do with him being practically nocturnal. You can find out more about him online at www.octoberkane.com.